Big John Hill was already a monster

He heard the plane taxi toward the barn and outbuildings he had rented along with the field. The barn had once been a huge milking stall when his Daddy was alive and, with the equipment and pens removed, it was big enough inside to play professional basketball.

Or hide a small plane.

But they couldn't see from the barn, or hear over the roar of the engine. He wasn't sure how they would react to the sight of Big John Hill walking up to his front door with a little girl slung over his shoulder like a sack of feed for the pigs, but he remembered the time he was picked up on suspicion in Somerset. And how the other inmates had looked at him when they found out he had been arrested for molesting a little girl. Even some fag on trial for murder - probably seething with AIDS - had spit in his face and the guards just stood by, their faces hard and unsympathetic while he wiped his face with his shirttail.

No, better not let them see or hear, he thought, unlocking his door. He walked to the fireplace and pulled open a door that appeared to be a sheet of paneling, and shifted Jeannie on his shoulder. She moaned "Daddy!" and struggled weakly. John started down the steps into the cellar no one knew was there and patted her on the back.

"It's okay, honey." He said as he closed the door behind him. "Everything is going to be okay."

But he knew he lied. The Urge made him lie. He knew Jeannie would be bloody and hurt and screaming before too long, and probably dead shortly after. He patted her back again.

"I'm sorry, honey," he murmured. But he knew that was a lie, too.

Silver Tears

Ron Rogers

May 2012

R. E. Publishing

ISBN: 978-0-9855752-1-2

Dedication

For Anna, Kara, and Kristen for tolerating my hours and hours at the keyboard.

Acknowledgements

A special above and beyond award for Paul, who took his valuable time to read the book and offer his help and encouragement at the beginning. An extra thanks for Kara's help in proofreading and critiquing the text. Any errors are my fault, not hers or Paul's.

Prelude In Darkness

The world was past dying. Past dead. Death would have been easier than the dark, clinging hell that the planet had become. Death was quiet. The earth screamed with the pain of being. It moaned with the despair of existence.

The human that Karick once was might have felt the land oppressive. The thing it had become only found the black desolation amusing. It looked at the pools of seeping lava that oozed from the inexhaustible supply in the depths and smiled a dark, toothy smile.

Science still ruled the universe. The earth still spun in its orbit around the sun, the third of eight major planets. The moon still circled, albeit a bit more scarred than in previous days. But there were forces on that third world that might have defied the science of earlier ages, and the power was no more magic than the energies that once drove mankind to the stars. Karick yanked mankind back to the home planet with a savage satisfaction, using power that defied analysis, yet still as much a part of the cosmos as the more mundane force of gravity. How could Karick rule and feed without subjects?

Scientists from the time of nuclear energy and space stations would have called it a monster as ardently as those middle age serfs who knew that witches soured milk. They would have considered the twisted forms that served Karick demons. The slightly sulphurous breeze that drifted through the stone walls and carried with it the screams of souls in bondage would have convinced them that hell existed. They would have been correct.

It surveyed the land, and the land was not good. But it was as desired.

Infrequently, Karick left the palace and walked among the tortured, dying remnants of humanity that somehow survived on the fringes of its empire. The creature sometimes waited beneath the surface of a glowing lava pool for a human searching for some scrap of nourishment to venture close enough. Then it would explode out of the white hot liquid to embrace the man, woman, or child and pull the victim back into the depths. Often too quickly for even a cry of pain. Karick could feel the only human flesh boil and crumble beneath fingers like steel.

How they struggled. Wriggling, twisting as they cooked. As they drew molten rock into their lungs. As the lava burned through flesh, consuming it as a voracious carnivore would a meaty tidbit.

The squirming embrace was always all too short but the terror was oh so delicious. Humans were such frail beasts that Karick wondered that they lived at all. Bones splintered into powder. Blood boiled at the slightest provocations. Flesh wrinkled and tore at a touch. Inconceivable that Karick once was such a fleeting and delicate being those many millenia ago, but it was a truth undeniable by any living thing, even Karick.

Pleasant memories of past tortures, but it was time to deal with other visions of times gone.

Somewhere in the distant past, the inevitable surge of time and destiny was pushing the universe to its dark future. Karick knew that the exquisite earth torn by death and destruction was only a probability. And it inhabited a nightmare that may or may not be, no matter how real it felt. Karick knew, and examined plans made over years uncounted. The power it commanded was peaking. Time to move. Time to nudge reality and the universe to the proper course.

Time to Become.

Prelude In Science

The book might have been the next bestseller and all time literary classic rolled into one neat electronic pad, but she couldn't stay interested. She tried to convince herself it was because she was tired or because it really wasn't that good or because the display on the reader was fading, but she knew the real reason. She couldn't concentrate on anything as long as the deed was left undone.

In the background, some ancient rock group screamed about the darkest power.

She jabbed the power button on the tablet, raised her arm, then thought twice before throwing it against the wall. She held a pillow across her head, but even that couldn't shut out the tiny whispering voice in her head. The lab. She had to go to the lab. She *had* to.

Even though she knew she could not - or should not - do it.

Doc was on her case. Even knowing him all her life she couldn't understand how that weird, supercharged brain worked. He was a kinetic intellect on steroids. His mind bounced higher and farther than a compressed rubber ball. She could only begin to touch the fringes of his intelligence.

So, of course, she surprised them all - including herself - when she developed the resonance theory that made the projector work. Sure, they had tested "the" knife, and found some sort of residual energy that kept the metal vibrating ever so slightly on a frequency that defied analysis, but it wasn't until she actually held the handle in her hand that the theory bloomed in her barely adequate brain.

Now Doc insisted that the projector was as potentially dangerous as a hydrogen bomb with no safety. They needed more tests to ensure that the energies the theories predicted were safely contained. He even complained that the technology was so wildly contrary to conventional laws of physics that they would need a sorcerer to help control the device. In a totally unsurprising moment of predictability, her parents and Al agreed with him. Their problem was that they threw a major freak fit about the knife that had killed her sister. It wasn't as if she had used it to hurt anyone. She just analyzed the damn thing.

They were scared.

They were idiots.

No, that wasn't fair. They were just worried about her. But did they actually believe there was as much magic as science in the equipment? Why did they ignore her vibrational resonance theory? Too weird.

Bananaville, USA.

They meant well. But they couldn't stop science with well-meaning platitudes or good intentions. Everyone knew where that path led.

The band spoke of ruling you all.

She was accustomed to getting her own way, and well aware that some thought of her as a spoiled brat. Knowing something was true didn't make it any easier to accept, though. Sometimes she wondered if things would have been different - especially with Mom and Dad - if her sister hadn't died, but that was less than useless speculation. The past was past. A lot of people dead back there and her sister was only one of them.

That brought her back to the present, and the projector.

She paced around the room for a while, thought about accessing the project files from her computer, then realized that wouldn't satisfy her. She didn't want to read a book or watch TV or play any virtual reality games. There was only one thing she wanted to do.

She knew she should not do it, but she knew she would.

Without even thinking, she turned and walked to the door, grabbing her coat as she passed the closet.

The band commanded her to reach for the stars.

She stepped outside, into the future.

The Doc once said the future should be different, but it was just like the past, only more so. She would have thought that in thirty years, science and technology would have made the world unrecognizable to someone born in the previous century. However, her mom and dad seemed to have no problems adapting. They told her the only major differences they could see were that the computers were smaller and faster and the televids were bigger and louder. More cars used alternate power sources, but even those would have been familiar to a late twentieth century man. Fuel cells, exotic metal batteries, and pseudo-cold fusion extraction. (Or was that last one invented in the twenty-first? It was hard to keep track.) From what she had seen in books, the vehicles looked about the same, except a little sleeker and with a bigger variety of bright colors. GM/Ford still competed with Honda and Daimler. Planes still flew, behind schedule as always. Less pollution, of course, but that was a direct result of the declining use of petroleum products as fuel. Oil was too valuable to burn. Might as well throw dollar bills into the furnace.

No, a twentieth century man or woman may have been confused about a few things, though he or she wouldn't have been as lost as a nineteenth century inhabitant taken into the 1990's. That could change over the next few years, of course, but the 2040's would have been generally familiar to people of those same 1990's. Much as - so her mom and dad had said - that the 1990's would have generally familiar to people living in the 1950's. On the other hand, let's go grab a guy from the nineteenth century, and see how long it takes him to go nuts in the present.

Okay, so time travel was impossible. But still, it was interesting to think about, and what else did she have to do while the MaxSteer system ferried her to the lab? The trip was too short to take a nap, and she couldn't have slept in any case. She felt ready to explode out the top of the car. Road rage was an obsolete disease and she was probably as close to it as anyone gets these days. Those automated systems took all the fun out of driving. At one time she might have wondered why drivers were required to actually learn to drive, but she'd had too many system failures and manual control situations to wonder about that. Things happen, and the more complicated the system, the more things happen.

For just a microsecond, she considered and discarded the idea that the ridiculous notion might apply to the projector. She hadn't designed the autodriver, but she sure as hell had designed the projector, and that was the difference.

Nothing was going to go wrong because nothing *could* go wrong.

Nothing at all.

Ye gods! annihilate but space and time
And make two lovers happy.
         Alexander Pope: The Art of Sinking in Poetry

Part One

REALITIES

Chapter 1

When her daughter, Ricky, disappeared, Maria Quinones was in the bedroom, studying herself in a full-length mirror.

She heard the distant moan of traffic: horns, engines revving, the muted scream of a siren far away. And inside, Maria heard silence and the remote buzz of an internal alarm that would become a raucous clanging if Erica didn't appear soon. Maria packed their suitcases, only partly listening as her daughter played in the next room, or talked to Green Frog or vroomed cars on the carpet. She didn't notice at first when the sounds of an active little girl stopped.

She would soon, though. Erica "Ricky" Rose Quinones was never far from her sight or her thoughts. Not after what had happened. But for a while, the alarm was a vague unease just below the threshold of awareness. Ricky hadn't been gone long.

The white skirt might be nice, she thought, examining it at arm's length before she held it to her waist. Of course, it was too short, but the color contrasted nicely with her legs, dark and too long for the old, decrepit working mother she was. Perhaps with a white satin blouse, or would that make her look like a tall glass of milk? She had to choose something. Just the bra and panties she wore now would attract more attention than she wanted.

Brian would have loved this.

But it was a fleeting thought, no longer accompanied by a rage that had once scared her more than the prospect of spending the rest of her life alone. When he died, Maria had to cope with anger more than grief. She was mad at Brian for leaving her. Mad at the airline for killing him. Mad at God for taking him away. And furious with herself for not being with him in those final, fiery moments.

Sometimes, she wished she could have cried for him.

Her mom, a widow and a member of the elite group who had lost sons in one of the many Middle East wars, at least understood what Maria fought, if not how she fought it. Her mother had spent many nights holding Maria, rocking her, muttering in Spanish too soft and rapid for Maria to understand. But the rhythmic, musical sound must have been soothing, Maria knew, because of the hours she spent as a child wrapped in her mother's embrace, listening to that same Spanish litany. Then it had been accompanied by her mother's "silver tears" for her father. *Lagrimas de plata.*

Maria frowned as she straightened some of Ricky's things in the suitcase. The past crowded in, but she felt she had forgotten something now, in the present.

What her mother couldn't understand was Maria's apparent lack of grief when she lost Brian. She thought her daughter should perform according to a legend she brought with her from Mexico when she and her husband moved to Washington, D. C. Shining tears, *lagrimas lucientes*, given for the dead were a precious gift. Grieving was an ancient and honorable custom in the old village, and the tears of the mourners were collected by the soul of the dead. According to the legend, ringing bells represented the jingling of silver tears as the soul walked through the gates of heaven.

Brian must have walked quietly.

Maria loved her mom, but often wondered if she had been so changed by the tragedies that she was no longer recognizable to people who knew her when she was young. Some people let the world change them and some people change the world, and she suspected her mom was one of the former.

Maria wouldn't let her own adversity change her.

Sometimes Maria's unyielding anger seemed directed at herself more than Brian, the airline or God. She could have gone with him on the research trip. He had asked her to come; it would have been a great vacation. Maria had refused. She had to stay and study and work. At the time, she had been almost eight months pregnant and the doctors advised her not to travel. But she knew that the main reason was to finish her last quarter in college, to get that business degree before the little one came along and dumped a nursery load of complications into their lives.

Then there was the restaurant.

At the time, Brian wondered how she could attend college, cope with the pregnancy, and hold down the job as assistant manager for a large restaurant. Before he left that final time for Ireland, he had bought her an oversize tee shirt with a big red "S" emblazoned across the front, and "Super Mom" in smaller letters.

It was one of those rare occasions when Brian had been wrong. After the crash, Maria wouldn't have made it without her Mom. And Ricky.

She glanced around the room. The tinkling became a ringing with the continued silence.

When Erica was born, Maria's anger died away as suddenly as the burning wreckage had kindled it. When she held the little girl and she watched her squirm and the tiny fingers open and close, and the small, perfect mouth seek and find the milk at her breast, she thought she would explode with love. She wanted to inhale the baby smell and feel the soft skin against her cheek forever.

She never cried for Brian because that would have made the nightmare true, but wasn't surprised when the tears came for her new daughter. Somewhere deep inside her she must have expected them. Ricky looked so much like a tiny replica of Brian. And she knew Ricky wouldn't be that small, exquisite infant for very long. She tried to hold that moment, stop time and experience the pure pleasure of her baby girl sucking at her breast, wrinkled fingers clutching instinctively at her skin, Ricky's bright eyes studying her own with the most profound concentration.

Maria focused on such moments while her daughter grew, "memory snapshots" to file away for future reference. She always thought she could keep the images for the years ahead, when Ricky grew too old to hold on her lap like a tiny doll. When her little girl finally left.

She shied away from that subject. She didn't want to think about that.

Maria stared at the mirror for a few seconds and wondered again about the skirt. Yes, it was too short and showed too much below the hemline. So what? She was proud of her legs, as Brian had been, and he always told her to wear what made her look good.

The skirt definitely made her look good.

So she nodded, then cocked her head, listening. Too quiet. That internal alarm clanged and she knew it had been too quiet for too long.

"Ricky?" she called, spreading the skirt flat on the bed. "Where are you, baby?" Still silence.

She sighed and shook her head. Recently, Ricky had discovered hide and seek. At odd times during the day, she would find a tiny niche and hide herself until Maria could locate her. Usually it wasn't too hard. Most of the time she forgot to pull her foot in behind the curtain, or thought, if she was covered with a blanket and couldn't see Mommy, then Mommy couldn't see her.

Maria wished she would outgrow this game. Okay, so she was overprotective, but when Ricky was out of sight, she felt as though something sharp twisted inside her gut. Lately, even leaving her at the sitter's during work tied her stomach in knots. Good time for a vacation. Maybe a few days in Florida would relax her and take Ricky's mind off the game.

"Ricky?" she called again. "Come on. We have to get ready to ride on the bus to Grandmom's house."

Nothing, as expected. Her little girl might not be too good at hiding, but she was very good at staying quiet until found. Then Maria would tickle the tiny tummy and giggles like tin bells would fill the apartment, making her smile and laugh, too. She took a deep breath. Nothing to do but start the search. The curtains in the rest of the apartment were open, so she threw a robe over her bra and panties. No sense giving Mr. Ginsberg across the street a show - or maybe a heart attack.

The apartment was large, even by northern Virginia standards, and there were plenty of places for a three-year-old girl to hide. She was getting better, too. Maria saw no stray foot or arm when she walked into the living room.

"Erica Rose Quinones," she said. "Come on. You still have to take a bath." Nothing. As stubborn as her father had been.

The house had an empty feel to it. Sometimes Maria could enter a room and know someone was there. This time it felt as though the entire house were deserted. A lonely place at the edge of eternity, forgotten by all. An empty, dark place as deep as the ocean's depths.

An irrational unease that had bothered her lately returned and her brow furrowed briefly. We don't have time for these games, she told herself and the thought had a sharp edge that surprised her. An incident that occurred a few days ago flashed through her mind. She wondered why, then knew it was because the same feelings had tied a queasy knot in her stomach. Ricky had been napping when she suddenly sat up in the bed and pointed out the window. "Spotty barking," she said. "Spotty barking at cat." Maria had patted her on the back and told her Spotty, a neighbor's mongrel pup, wasn't barking. She must have been dreaming. Ricky had yawned, nodded and closed her eyes again. Less than thirty seconds later, a furious yapping drew Maria to the window. Spotty had a cat treed in the pine outside Ricky's window. The little girl continued to sleep. Then, as now, Maria had shivered. Where is that little rascal?

Maria searched the obvious places: behind the curtains, between the sofa and wall, in the corner under the desk. Still no Ricky. She walked into the kitchen and checked the cabinets within reach. The doors were secured with child- proof latches, but her little girl genius might have deciphered their secret. Not this time, though. Maria bit her bottom lip. Where now?

Back in the living room, she opened the doors to the end tables, also secured with the safety latches, but they were crammed so full of papers and gadgets she should have thrown away years ago that a mouse couldn't have hidden in there. She was running out of places.

The door: latched, with the safety chain in place.

All the windows were fastened.

She couldn't fit through the mail slot.

No doggy door, laundry chute, or vent to the outside.

Ricky's room was its usual pit of chaos, but with nothing big enough to conceal her. She glanced in the closet, but the winter clothes she had begun packing filled the bottom and no crack or crevice remained for a small body to slip into. Nothing under the bed, or behind the door. Maria checked everything twice to be sure, but no Ricky.

"Erica!" She had meant the word to be forceful and angry enough to scare her out of hiding, but her voice cracked and even to her own ears bordered on hysteria. Maria closed her eyes for a second and held her hands by her sides, slowing her breathing, calming herself.

Maria had checked everywhere but her own room. She had been preoccupied with packing, but surely she would have noticed Ricky sneaking in there. Or would she? Maria thought of the hundreds, thousands of times she dodged Ricky or stepped over her or her toys, or absently patted her on the head as she walked by, all without thinking about it or remembering a few seconds later. Ricky could have strolled by with Green Frog and an armload of tiny toys and she might not have noticed. That's it, she thought. Ricky had to be there. She didn't run into the bedroom. That would have acknowledged the panic she felt.

Squatting, she studied the area under her bed, and even though it was against the wall and too dark for her to see clearly, she thought she heard something moving underneath. She pulled the robe around her neck, over tight skin and sudden goosebumps, at the same time fumbling for the flashlight next to the bed. The beam probed underneath. Yucch! she thought. Nothing a good cleaning wouldn't take care of. The movement must have been her imagination. She put the light back on the nightstand. Maria sat back on her heels and her eyes were drawn to the only place left: the closet. Please, God, let her be there.

The closet was a deep walk-in with two rods for hangers stretching from end to end, and enough room for ten Ricky's to hide. She pushed open the bifold doors, flipped the lightswitch, and stumbled back at the pop and sudden burst of light. Darkness closed around her.

Damn cheap light bulbs.

She had started back for the flashlight when she heard a scratching from the corner. A very dark corner.

"Ricky?" No answer, not that she expected one. Erica Rose was as rigged for silent running as those old movie submarines on television. She pushed past the twin rows of coats and dresses and blouses, stumbling over a pair of shoes she'd thrown in earlier.

The closet seemed bigger than she remembered.

It reminded her of a fantasy series she had loved as a child, The Chronicles of Narnia by C. S. Lewis. Some of the children in that series had traveled to the fantasy land of Narnia through a closet, pushing past rows of coats and hats until the clothing turned to pine trees and the hard wood under their feet turned to soft earth cushioned with pine needles.

For a wild moment, she wondered if she had gone beyond the

closet walls into some fantasy place less hospitable and more sinister than Narnia. Steady, girl, she told herself. Worry, but don't get crazy.

She thought she saw something glowing, distant and remote, as though miles away. The darkness was complete around her, the clothing had closed in, enfolding her in a soft murky blanket except for a vague glow that she wasn't even sure was there. Then she heard the scratching sound, and she knew that was real.

But what was it?

For a few seconds she stopped, listening, trying to hear the sound of a little girl breathing, or suppressing a giggle, or maybe even snoring. She might have gone to sleep waiting for Maria to find her.

Nothing but a rasping scratch. Something hard against the wall. It could be Ricky's fingernails on the wallboard.

Or it could be something else, she thought. Ridiculous, she told herself. Get a grip.

She could wait no longer. Maria lunged into the darkness, toward the glow and the scratching sound, and felt something small and soft and smooth under her fingers.

Reality flickered, a fragile flame in a sudden gust.

Her body went rigid, and she wanted to scream but her lungs refused to move and her voice froze somewhere in the back of her throat, choking her, stealing her breath.

Maria saw a place too dark, filled with an encompassing sinister fog. A nightmare. Something like lightning flashed, but somehow only made the place darker. In the blackness she saw a shadowy being, visible only because it was a void, an absence of light or darkness, a contrast to the lesser blackness around it. Somehow, she perceived it clearly as it turned and looked at her, smiling with needle teeth, ebony daggers against the night. If she hadn't felt, with an irrational certainty that made her again wonder about her sanity, that the being was incapable of any sort of human emotion, she might have thought it examined her with the slightest hint of tenderness. Whatever it was, the thing scared her, touched something ancient deeply buried in memories no one should ever know.

And when it turned to her and smiled, it wore her face.

She told herself she was dreaming or hallucinating, but it was as though she stared into a dim, twisted mirror. The thing was like her and not like her, ebony dots like dark tears spotting its cheeks. Maria didn't think her face could ever be wrenched into that kind of evil, distorted sneer. For a few seconds, she couldn't move. Couldn't look away from the obscenely familiar features.

It mouthed a single, short word past pointed teeth.

She wanted to turn and run, put that warped face behind her, but she couldn't. Ricky was there somewhere. Whatever monsters she faced, she wouldn't leave without Ricky.

Maria unfroze and lunged again, groping before she felt a tiny arm under her hand and grabbed. For just a second, it felt as though something pulled back, then Maria held Ricky, hugging, clutching her tightly as she stumbled into the bedroom. She found the flashlight and cautiously probed each corner of the closet.

Nothing. Completely normal.

Maria sat on the bed, breathing hard and holding Ricky, who giggled and laughed. Maria made herself stop trembling. Her little girl would pick that up all too quickly.

"Ricky hide good," she said.

"Good," Maria managed to agree, ruffling hair like fine silk under her fingers. "And if you ever hide that good again, I will spank your little bottom until it looks like a bright red apple." But the girl only grinned. She'd heard that threat before.

What was that word the apparition whispered? Maria had the feeling that if she probed a little deeper, tried to remember a little harder, she would know the word. The prospect threatened to shake her body with uncontrollable shivering and she focused on the reality in her arms. There was no dark creature.

Maria needed the vacation. When she began seeing things that weren't there, it was definitely time for a little rest and relaxation.

She sat on the bed for a few minutes, rocking with her arms around Ricky, her little girl's warm weight reassuring her. She glanced at the full-length mirror where she had earlier admired the short skirt and a chill swept down her spine and formed a frigid pool in her stomach. She told herself again that she hadn't heard the word the thing said.

Ricky hugged her neck, but she looked over her shoulder into the closet. Into the blackness. Her eyes widened, as if she had seen something wondrous and magical.

Something familiar.

Then her little girl smiled, and the cold settled somewhere around Maria's heart.

Chapter 2

The nightmares were killing him.

David Lee Richards stood in the warm sunshine, hating it for the promise of life it brought to the morning. Hating the fresh, new smell of the light wind, and the way it tickled his nose and mussed his hair. Hating the almost perfect day because it would be the last thing he saw before he died.

A cool spring breeze caressed his face, and he closed his eyes, imagining for a moment that it was Suzy gently stroking his cheek. He swayed slightly in the wind, fifteen stories from the concrete below, ready to tip into oblivion at any moment.

Dave knew why he had stopped in that town. The sign on the interstate had drawn him off concrete strip's unending monotony. "SOMERSET REGIONAL AIRPORT - EXIT 160." The first thing he did was to go to the airport and sit for an hour or two, avoiding the dust from construction and watching the airplanes takeoff and land, not knowing what he looked for. Knowing he would never find it. No black silk clouds rolled in the sky. No dark hands threatening the air traffic.

The second thing he did was to find a building tall enough.

It turned out that the only viable candidate was an older hotel in the middle of a major renovation, part of a revitalization project in downtown Somerset, Virginia. Only sixteen or so stories, but adequate for the task. He had no idea why he had driven three hundred miles to kill himself. Baltimore had taller buildings. The apex of the Key Bridge would have been perfect. Just stop the car and heave himself over the short concrete barrier. Maybe it took six hours of driving to build up his nerve.

If Dave looked to the left, he could see the top of his car, parked just half a block away. He wondered if the Maryland tags had attracted any attention. The vehicle looked so small.

Dave just wished he'd picked a gloomy day to do this. A man shouldn't kill himself on a spring morning with new flowers blooming and birds singing nearby.

Maybe if he closed his eyes he wouldn't have to think about what he did. Just relax and let the wind swing him back and forth until he leaned so far over he couldn't recover. Enjoy the rush of air as he fell, eyes still closed, no sound from him as the ground waited quietly for his arrival.

Dave's eyes opened and he grabbed for the window frame. If he ever did let go, he knew he would scream all the way to the concrete.

Which is it, Dave? he asked himself. The nightmares or the sidewalk? One is quick, and, if there is any pain, it will be over in seconds. The other is slow - oh, so slow - and the pain lasts forever and ever.

Only three years of pain. He didn't think he could endure an infinity of the torment.

Just a few years ago, he couldn't have understood his despair, or why someone would want to kill himself. Things change, he always said. Kill yourself and you deprive a future self of the opportunity to build a new life. To live. To hell with my future self. The thought sent a violent shudder through him.

But a few years ago, he had a life. Dave had a wife and a baby son toddling around the house. He had a syndicated column called "Far Out" in over two hundred newspapers and two books on the nonfiction best sellers list and a dog and two cats, and a bowl of goldfish that he hated. Now, all he had were the goldfish, and he still hated them.

Suzy and Christopher died coming to meet him for lunch at the airport. A trash truck ran over the dog. The cats, sensing a change in the home they had known for so long, left without even a good-bye. The stupid goldfish just kept swimming.

"Suzy and Chris," Dave said aloud, and sighed. As he had a million times before, Dave thought, It's not fair. Suzy was too beautiful to die.

Before she consented to marry him in a fit of temporary insanity, Suzy had won a dozen beauty pageants and finished second in the Miss U.S.A. contest. Almost seven years before, Dave had been gathering background for an article on the endless pageants in America when he and Suzy glanced at each other and their eyes locked. Silent, subliminal signals and promises were exchanged, and Suzy smiled the smile Dave was to know so well. Despite chaperones and security and the press and full schedules and a set of watchful parents, Dave and Suzy were in a hotel room before midnight, gently rocking each other into ecstatic oblivion.

The next day, as the contest proceeded, Dave thought that he may have made love to the new Miss U.S.A. for most of the previous night, and - for a while - was apprehensive that the evening's vigorous physical activity might have left Suzy tired, or not at her best. When he saw her on the stage for the first time that day, though, he knew there was no problem. She looked even more beautiful, even more self-confident, even more like a winner than when he'd first seen her.

Impossibly, he loved her even more.

And when she looked directly at him and smiled, he didn't care if anyone saw him smile back.

While the outcome was still in doubt, he wondered what the judges would have thought if they had known one of the best of Suzy's talents was one she couldn't demonstrate on the brightly-lit stage.

She lost the pageant, no doubt due to the judges' poor eyesight and lack of taste, and no one remembers the second place finisher unless the winner does something stupid like expose more of her body than is shown during the swimsuit competition. A difficult though not impossible task.

They were married one blurry summer day and Dave later learned that the "odd" events that led to his fame and fortune started that same day. He once told Suzy, with a smile, that the two most important events in his life had occurred that day. The "Far Out" stuff started, and he got an extra tax deduction.

"Of course," he said, "it's a hell of a coincidence."

Just when Dave thought he couldn't be any happier, Chris showed up.

He was a pleasant surprise. Suzy was busy building a growing, profitable cosmetics business. Her semi-fame as a Miss U.S.A. contestant had led to a few commercials for perfume and beauty products, and one day she decided she could do better than whoever designed the stinkweed extract they wanted her to wear. So she started her own company, with products the average woman would want and could afford.

After a year or so, Essar Cosmetics was the fastest growing new business in the state of Maryland.

Dave was involved with his investigative reporting. Until then, he had managed to resist the lure of TV money and fame, but he didn't know how much longer he could hold out. Especially since everyone from the paperboy to the IRS wanted a growing chunk of his earnings. He was just becoming interested in the Fortean type events that seemed to be increasing in number, and those were the days before the column and books. Before Dave was rich and famous.

Suzy was too busy. Dave was too busy. They didn't have time for children.

So Christopher Robert Richards was born.

Dave took a month off after the baby arrived. He stayed home and cooked and cleaned and helped Suzy take care of Chris. He got dirty and sweaty and pee splattered and baby-poop stained. He never seemed to get any sleep, and the days were an endless sequence of feeding, burping, changing diapers, and cleaning regurgitated milk off everything in sight.

He loved every minute of it.

When Chris finally slept, Dave used to stand at his crib, staring at the wondrous being who had no existence only ten or so months before. Now, after nine months of growing inside Suzy and another month outside, he was a small, squirming miracle.

His second book had just come out when Chris turned two. Dave bought him a baseball and glove, a basketball, a football, a hockey stick and puck, and a set of golf clubs.

"This kid's going to get rich playing some kind of sport and support us when we get old," Dave had told Suzy. "I'm just covering all the possibilities."

Chris never made it to his third birthday.

That day at the airport, where he planned to interview a damn bunch of stubborn machinists, Suzy had news about a new line of men's cosmetics endorsed by a famous television personality that she couldn't wait to tell him, and she wanted to show Dave what Chris had learned in day-care.

He remembered walking into the parking lot to wait for them, and seeing a dark cloud formation that churned and roiled until it looked like a left hand, minus the index finger.

Dave saw the black hand slap the plane, and send it screaming above his head.

He could close his eyes and feel the pressure of the explosion, see the yellow-white ball of flame mushroom into the air and how the hand cloud seemed to hover above the carnage for a while before it broke apart. The sound was like a violent storm gone mad, like a thousand crashes of thunder at once. Sometimes, at night just before the scene woke him from the nightmare, Dave thought he heard laughing from somewhere.

The crash killed 97 people. Ninety-five on the plane and two on the ground.

Other reporters said it was lucky the death toll wasn't higher. There had been only one car on the road leading to the airport. If the crash had occurred during rush hour, dozens more would have died.

Those two were enough for Dave.

Now, Suzy and Chris were gone.

Now, three years later, a once slim Dave Richards stood fifteen stories above a very hard sidewalk, his fat butt pressed against the concrete, swaying slightly, his stomach hiding his feet, and his legs not too steady with the extra fifty or sixty pounds he had picked up since they died.

He refused to return home after the funerals until his sister had cleaned out any trace of Suzy and Chris: clothes, toys, everything. For a while, he thought he'd gotten over the hump. He couldn't write about the airport, but did eventually return to the "Far Out" column again, using file material until he could find the initiative to do the legwork again. A few weeks after the funerals, he thought that he had settled back into the single routine from his bachelor days.

Then, late one night when the house was quiet and he sat, reading a book, he absently looked up and said, "Suzy?"

No one answered.

He realized what he had done and put the book down, then held his head in his hands. Until that moment, he didn't know. Did not truly realize in his heart that Suzy and Chris were gone and would never be back.

He cried. When he stopped crying, he stuffed his mouth with whatever was handy. When he couldn't eat any longer, he cried again.

Between crying and eating, he had no time to write or research. The columns were delivered later and later. They re-edited and reprinted old articles, but eventually fired him and hired someone just as famous to do the job. His reputation as one of the most meticulous researchers and writers in the nonfiction market deteriorated rapidly.

What he did have was plenty of time to get fat, and plenty of royalty checks from the books on the "Far Out" incidents to buy the appropriate quantities of food.

The last time Dave bothered to check, he was about two thirty-five or so. He suspected he was now pushing two fifty, or more. Before the accident, his weight never fluctuated more than five pounds from one hundred eighty.

Now, standing on a narrow ledge above a very distant, very hard sidewalk, he had an ominous feeling the weight would do the job his resolve couldn't.

Dave looked down at the sidewalk and swallowed. It looked miles away. So far, none of the early risers on the street below had seen him, and the tops of their heads resembled specks of pepper swirling around in bowl of soup.

He held the edge of the window and closed his eyes for a few seconds. When he opened them, he had decided to get off this ledge, and back inside. If he wanted to kill himself, he would do it the slow way. Another thirty pounds or so and odds were he would die of a massive coronary.

For a brief moment, he wondered if death by severe overeating could be considered suicide. It was probably in the same class with smoking, alcoholism, and drug use.

In other words, yes.

Tiny beads of sweat popped out on his forehead as he inched toward the window. His foot hit a large white pigeon feather and Dave watched it drift slowly toward the street below. When he crawled out, he had stood and slid away from the window with uncaring nonchalance. Now, terrified, he pressed his body against the building as though it were a new lover.

He was almost inside when his foot slipped in the mottled, slick pigeon droppings.

Dave clutched the windowsill with his left hand, and even managed to get his right hand up far enough to grasp the edge of the frame. He hung there for a few seconds, straining, grunting, not even able to call for help.

He knew he couldn't hold on.

When he was one hundred eighty pounds, he could have pulled himself up and practically vaulted into the room. At two-fifty, all he could do was sweat and hold on for a few seconds.

Then let go and bounce. Or splatter.

"I really don't want to die," he said aloud, just before his fingers slipped and he began his windy rush to a sidewalk rendezvous. He closed his eyes and didn't scream.

He wondered why.

A looming sense of inevitability overwhelmed him, like the dread he'd felt at the top of a roller coaster ride, but a hundred, a thousand, times more intense. Die, he thought. I'm going to die. I'm going to splatter like a fat, overripe tomato when I hit. An almost inaudible whimper escaped between his lips, and he opened his eyes just a fraction of an inch. Three windows whipped by in quick succession and he closed them again. A woman had been standing at the second window, and he remembered the shock and horror that flickered across her face as he passed. The scene, glanced in just a split second, burned into his memory, and he could still see her raising her hand to cover the "O" formed by her mouth.

He didn't, though, see her complete the motion.

Oh, Jesus, he thought. How long is this going on? Why haven't I hit yet? He opened his eyes again, and through a screen of terror, knew he was only halfway to the hard, silent sidewalk. His mind must be in overdrive, thinking and looking for a way out, frantically seeking survival.

Deja vu, he thought.

Once a mobster, somewhat perturbed by an article Dave had written about the gentlemen's nocturnal activities, had cornered him in downtown Baltimore. In that dark, smelly alley, the handsome, blond killer had smiled and walked closer, holding his silenced automatic like a crucifix before a vampire, while Dave crouched in a corner.

His mind had seemed to race and accelerate and consider a hundred then a thousand then ten thousand possibilities for escape and survival. Even while he tried to make himself a smaller target, his hands were feeling and searching for something he could use to fight back. Something he could use to survive.

He was living in slow time.

His fingers had closed on a plastic handle, and he looked over and saw that it was a half-full jug of Clorox bleach.

The kind addicts afraid of AIDS used to rinse their needles. The kind that had a warning that said "Avoid contact with skin and eyes."

Dave didn't know why it was there. Probably some heroin user kept the bleach in that dirty alley, ready in case he found drugs.

He didn't care. He tightened his grip around the handle and waited for the mobster to walk closer, even as his eyes scanned the rest of the alley. He had to look scared so the mobster wouldn't suspect. No problem. His mouth was dry and tasteless, his hands shook, and an uncontrollable twitch tortured his jaw.

The punk only smiled broadly as he approached, raising the gun to center it on Dave's forehead.

Dave had screamed and swung the bottle.

He swung it so hard that the next day he couldn't raise his arm above his beltline. He swung it so hard that the plastic bottle didn't bend or collapse, it exploded and showered both of them with corrosive liquid. But Dave was ready, and his eyes were closed.

The blond man got a face and both eyes full of the bleach, then screamed himself, but held onto his gun, waving it around and firing at random. Dave found something else to pick up - a three-foot length of steel pipe - and swung it as though he were hitting for the center field fence. There was a hollow pop as he connected, and a shock that ran up his arms and made his teeth ache. The gunman stopped screaming and dropped without another sound.

Dave had stood above him, breathing hard for a few minutes before he walked into a corner of the alley and threw up.

The police didn't even arrest him. They questioned him for a couple of hours and, satisfied that he acted in justifiable self-defense, let him go home.

Again, his mind raced and his thoughts were streaks of bright lighting as the incident replayed behind his closed eyes.

This is what people mean when they say their life flashes before their eyes just before death, he thought.

He had to peek again, and saw the large white pigeon feather dart and swirl as he passed it.

The sidewalk was closer.

He screamed.

Then he looked down. There was a single, solitary figure below him. A man in a tee-shirt and shorts, expanding rapidly from ant to human proportions. His thin, scarecrow face turned upward, his expression shocked and, oddly, angry.

Dave looked away and screamed louder.

And, though the concrete was still a few seconds away, Dave Richards suddenly plunged into a cold, dim fog that could only be death.

Chapter 3

In a small, pleasant country town called Clarion in the county of Clarion in the land of Virginia - the kind of serene village that incipient yuppies and chronic Manhattanites would spill a Coke on their lap to avoid - an event decidedly unpleasant and unserene shook the normally unshakable residents to the soles of their flat-bottom sandals and hob-nailed work boots.

Clarion was a rural county in a rural part of a rural state. The area's biggest claim to fame was the Blue Ridge Parkway, which divided the county like a vein of concrete gold and transported tourists from all over the country to that little piece of heaven. Tiny arts and crafts stores and antique shops were scattered over the county like celery seeds flung atop a batch of country style potato salad. Each and every one had a bathroom, a soft drink machine, a rack of Country Good snack products, and a pile of T-shirts and sweatshirts with "CLARION? WHERE THE HELL IS THAT?" and the picture of a befuddled city slicker printed on the front. The locals often remarked there was more truth than not in that slogan. It was hard to find a native who hadn't pointed a lost and confused Yankee back to the Parkway, after first selling him a bag of chips or a soft drink or a souvenir shirt. Of course the Yankee had to visit the bathroom, too, or else he wouldn't have had a real reason for stopping. Easier to admit his bladder was full than to say he was lost.

Most of the populace understood, though, mainly because half of them had been city slickers themselves at one time or another.

The most avid pro-Clarion residents were those who had, in the sixties, been anti-war demonstrators, commune members, and free love advocates who had lived far to the north or far to the west. They had been called flower children and hippies and scum and communists, among other things. Having been filtered through the turbulent seventies and the Reagan eighties, they retained most of their ideals, though tempered with a little insight into how the rest of the world looked at reality. In Clarion, they ran little restaurants, herb shops, rare book stores, sewing and fabric centers, and organic health food stores. They advocated gasohol and oat bran and clean air and clean water, most of which they found in Clarion. Meditation and "centering" were still important to them.

The old timers, whose great-grandfathers' grandfathers had lived in Clarion, looked at the newcomers, took off their caps and scratched their heads, then said, "What the hell!" and made them welcome. They had seen far stranger things in their days. The natives, sometimes affectionately and sometimes not, called the new people those "back to earthers," as though that was something new in the county.

Clarion, being a place of plentiful water and largely uninhabited forest land, had a reputation of being a refuge for makers of the "juice." The high-powered, 110 proof kind of juice. The "guvmint" people had found stills in barns, outhouses, tunnels dug in basements, caves, valleys, hills, lowlands and highlands. One enterprising distiller, Jake Wilson, took a massive spruce pine, added his own plastic greenery from a few dozen fake Christmas trees, then hollowed out the area near the trunk. He fixed up a winch arrangement and hauled the still up inside the tree at night and whenever he heard of the BATF being in the area. The plastic boughs closed behind the platform as it was raised out of sight and unless you stood directly below it and knew what you were looking for, the whole contraption was invisible.

After Jake was finally caught, talk went around the town it was only because he was bragging about the still down at Stimpkin's Granary, and one of the Righteous Church ladies, in to buy some feed corn for her ducks, heard him.

When the sheriff and the Revenuers showed up, Jake just stood around smiling while they searched the place, and kept smiling up to the moment they walked under the spruce, looked up, and smiled back at him.

Old Jake's big mouth was a hot topic around town for a while, but stills were broken up on a regular basis in the forests of Clarion County. Stills were a family tradition from the times when the residents remembered first-hand the old country in England and young George Washington had just come through on one of his early surveying trips.

The residents of Clarion didn't worry too much about the stills, but the newest residents frightened the old time distillers and former flower children alike.

Big-time drug dealers had come to the country.

Even the old hippies, who had advocated the legalization of the quaintly named "pot" - and who, on occasion, grew a plant or two in the back yard for recreational purposes - felt threatened. They had the feeling that the "V" sign and "Peace" were forever foreign to these guys in the dark cars.

The same things that made Clarion an ideal place for stills attracted drug growers and dealers and smugglers. The county had half a dozen scattered, secluded airstrips, and almost every night, anyone could stick his head out the window and hear the not-too-distant roar of a small plane engine descending into some valley airstrip or laboring to avoid the hills on take-off. They came from the south, heavy with cargo, and left empty. From the strips, cars and vans and trucks went north and east and west, loaded with white powdered death.

Old timers with 200 acre and bigger farms were bought out because they had a good place for a field, or they were secluded enough to provide the privacy for growing premium grade marijuana, or they had lots of barns where the drugs could be stored and a large farm house where the dealers could stay overnight or meet "associates."

An undercurrent of cautious fear pervaded the community. Old guns were pulled out of the closet and oiled and test-fired. New guns were purchased and zeroed in the fields behind wood frame houses. Strangers, especially strangers in large, expensive cars, who cruised dirt roads were eyed carefully when they passed.

One group of neighbors - neighbors in this case being people who lived within five miles of each other - assembled one evening in the Light Rock Baptist church and discussed the reticent people at the end of Old Dobson Road. (The name of the church had nothing to do with the members' musical tastes. There just happened to be a huge, almost white granite boulder in the way when they started erecting the church building. Instead of hauling it away, they rolled it onto the church lawn, flattened and polished one side of it, and carved the words "Jesus is King" into the stone.)

The neighbors were troubled about those secretive people at the end of the road. The state highway ended at their drive, and they had erected a metal gate and circled the top with barbed wire that continued along the boundaries of their land. They didn't talk to anyone and no one talked to them. All the neighbors noticed the big, new pickup they drove, with its darkly-tinted windows and camper covering the bed so they could never know what went in or out on the back of that truck. They had all seen it on the dead-end dirt road at all hours of the night and day, and wondered what the people at the end of Old Dobson Road did for a living. They sure didn't keep the same hours as regular folk.

The neighbors talked about them, and cautioned one another to keep an eye out and to be careful, but they did nothing. They were concerned, but still unsure enough to give their unsociable neighbors the benefit of the doubt.

"Hell," Old Man Altan observed. "Maybe they're just crazy like the rest of us."

But no one was surprised when, a week after the meeting, a truck load of DEA men, along with the sheriff's department and a healthy contingent of the State Police, raided the place at the end of Old Dobson Road, rolling over the shiny metal gate and the strings of barbed wire with a armor plated assault vehicle that looked like a tank. The nearest neighbor was evacuated, and his family, along with most everyone else within five miles, stood in the Rakes' yard, listening to the rapid fire of automatic weapons echoing through the Clarion County hills. The whistling, chattering scream of the two helicopters hovering over the area scared the cows out of a day's milking and sent the Rakes' dog running in circles, barking and howling at the sky. They all looked at each other and shook their heads.

No law enforcement officers were hurt, except for good old Deputy Stillson who broke his ankle when he slipped in the creek, but they carried six of the drug dealers out in ambulances. Four of them had their faces covered, and the other two looked to join their buddies under the sheets in the near future.

The police stamped out one place and two more popped up somewhere else.

Some people said that another drug dealer bought the place at the end of Old Dobson Road when the DEA put it up at auction the next year. At least the barbed wire went up again, and a new group of uncommunicative neighbors moved in. Soon enough, they knew, the sheriff and DEA and State Police would be back with their trucks and tanks and guns and helicopters. Even residents of a backwoods town and county knew there was just too much money in drugs to give up so easily.

Some of them knew first hand just how much money drugs brought into Clarion.

Big John Hill had a taste for new 'shine, old cars, big money, and little girls.

John Hill was big, of course, and wore dirty T-shirts too short to reach his trousers, hitched up under a stomach which would have worried a woman nine and a half months pregnant. He shaved when he remembered, and combed his hair into a filthy, greasy version of the slick look he wore long ago. He washed infrequently enough so that he didn't have to add the white, oily cream like he did in the old days. His mutton sideburns were a remnant of his late teens and he wasn't bright enough to realize they didn't make him look cool anymore.

Big John didn't care too much for the new drugs filtering through Clarion County, but he sure as hell enjoyed all the new money in town. The Top o' the Hill Ranch had been in his family for generations. He almost lost it to back taxes until he found a new source of income by renting a field once used to grow tobacco (when-tobacco-was-king) out to a group of well-dressed men who flew small airplanes as a hobby. Even Big John knew it was what was in those small planes that interested the well-dressed men, but he didn't really give a skunk's rump. They paid him five thousand dollars a month for an old scrub field that he was too lazy to work, anyway.

They could have bonfire orgies and bring dogs for all he cared.

The first month Big John bought himself a fully restored, dressed out two-door '57 Chevy built by a guy over in Alam Ridge. Even if he'd had the inclination, Big John could never restore a machine like that. Too much work. But he enjoyed cruising the narrow streets of the town of Clarion and the paved and unpaved roads of the county of Clarion, waving at anyone he knew - which was about everyone - and making sure they knew it was John Hill in that showroom condition Chevy. Everybody likes old cars, he thought. Even the young'uns.

John had his own still under the living room floor, with water piped in from his well, and the smoke routed to his chimney. As long as he didn't make too much shine during the summer, when the smoke might make somebody suspicious, he figured he was safe. He always managed to save enough over the winter to get him through the warm months, anyway. His cruising through the county wouldn't have been so bad if he didn't insist on consuming a few pint jars of the water clear 'shine first. Sometimes, if he was drunk enough, he poured a quart or so of the high-test squeezings into the Chevy's gas tank and laughed as it sputtered and coughed and smoked through town.

He was arrested three times for drunk driving and twice for stumblin' drunk in public the month after he got the Chevy. He finally decided he'd better lay off the stuff for a while. John thought the sheriff was a friend, but he said he would take his license and car if it happened again.

But when John wasn't numb drunk or on his way there, the Urge came on him, and he couldn't resist it.

It was Big John's most disgusting and repulsive weakness which he worried would finally cash in his life insurance and ensure his place in some private corner of hell reserved for people like him.

The monsters who hurt little children.

As Jeannie Baker walked home from a friend's house just after lunch, the bright red '57 Chevy stopped and Big John leaned out the window and smiled at her. His teeth were yellowed, and the front ones gouged with dark craters of decay. His shiny brown eyes shifted constantly as though he were expecting someone.

"Need a ride, honey?" he asked, still smiling.

Jeannie had been warned about strangers, especially strangers with out-of-state tags and dark windows. But she knew Big John Hill. Her father had been a drinking buddy of John's when he used to show up at the Saturday night card games. Even so, she almost didn't get in when he stopped and smiled his staccato smile at her. She was a little tired from playing all day at Sally Edelman's and her house was almost a mile away, but she remembered the disturbed look that had crossed her Mom's face when Dad mentioned that Big John had a new car and was out cruising.

"I don't like it, Sam," her mother had said. "You know what happened down in Somerset."

"Well, Gerry," his father said slowly, "they never proved anything, you know. And that little girl couldn't identify whoever . . ." He glanced toward Jeannie, reading through a new Ninja Turtle comic, and she remembered that he hesitated a moment before continuing. "She couldn't identify whoever hurt her," he finished.

"Sam Baker," said Mom, putting her hands on her hips and looking the way she did when she fussed at Jeannie for leaving her rock collection on the kitchen table. "You know as well as I do that he was the one who --"

Her dad had raised his hand and nodded toward Jeannie.

"Sweetheart," he said. "Why don't you go out and help your brother with the yard? He needs somebody to rake up behind him." He paused. "And make sure Scott mows under the bushes," he called after her.

So Jeannie heard no more about Big John Hill. If she had been around for the rest of the conversation, she would never have gotten into the Chevy when he stopped.

The girl in Somerset was eleven. Jeannie was almost ten.

Jeannie hesitated, twisting the red jacket between her hands, but her tired feet and the dusty, hot road finally convinced her to smile back politely. He wasn't a real stranger, after all.

"Thank you, Mr. Hill," she said. Jeannie walked to the other door as he leaned over and unlocked it for her. She opened it from the outside. "Sure is hot out here today. Wouldn't believe it's just spring and not summer."

"Hot," he agreed, licking his lips and sweating more than he should, no matter what the temperature. Jeannie noticed huge dark spots under his arms and on his chest where he had soaked through his T-shirt. His hands trembled as he gripped the steering wheel of his car, then reached down and shoved the stick shift into first gear. He looked over, and she felt uncomfortable as his eyes lingered on her for a moment. Something about him reminded her of the time she found an old slimy snail crawling up the cinderblock wall inside the pump house, leaving a slick, shimmering trail behind. She shivered and small bumps popped up on her arms.

"Too hot for little girls to be out walking," John Hill said.

Jeannie's smile was a little uncertain.

He let out the clutch and spun gravel against the side of a barn next to the road, and the rocks popped like small gunfire against the wood planks. Jeannie jerked around at the sound, but Big John wiped his forehead with an old rag he had lying on the seat between them and smiled again.

"I guess you're heading home," he said.

"Yes, sir," Jeannie told him. "Dad's taking me down to the grocery store with him this afternoon. Anyways, he said he might meet me on the way, so if you see him just pull over and I'll wave him down." Jeannie didn't know why she talked about her Dad so much, or why she made up that story about the grocery store, but it seemed to be the right thing to do.

In fact, Big John had a series of pictures of what happened in Somerset that he took with one of those digital cameras. And a video of the whole thing from start to finish was stored, along with a half dozen similar videos, on digital tapes hidden near the still under his living room floor. Any one of the recordings would have been enough to earn him a half dozen decades in a federal maximum security prison.

Big John had to suppress a tremor that threatened to sweep through his entire body. If Sam Baker came by and saw his little girl Jeannie in the car, he knew Sam would reach under the seat where he kept that big Taurus .357 magnum and blow Big John's brains all over the polished interior of that '57 Chevy. Even if Sam didn't see Jeannie, John couldn't very well pass without stopping and talking a bit. That would be unusual and suspicious in itself. He almost pulled over and let her out right then, but if he did she would tell her daddy, and he'd still come after him with the Taurus and plug him with hollow point .357 slugs until the pin clicked against the spent casings and Big John looked like a Christmas turkey two days after New Year's.

So he just wiped his sweaty palms on his pants and said, "Sure will, honey. I'll keep an eye out for him." And if he did see Sam, he'd slam Jeannie against the dash, throw her down in the floorboard, and speed past him with a wave and a smile. Maybe he wouldn't suspect anything. Sure. Right up to when he got to Sally's and found that his girl had already left. Then he would remember the Chevy and Big John and he'd still show up out at the Ranch.

John had the awful feeling he'd sealed his own fate when he stopped and smiled at Jeannie. He'd never done this close to home before, but the Urge had come on him like a fever and he knew he couldn't stop it now.

The Chevy was almost to the Baker driveway when John saw the pickup.

Oh, sweet Jesus on the cross! he thought when he looked to the left and saw the blue and white Ford truck picking its way down the rutted drive. Sam Baker was at the wheel, his sun weathered face perpetually grim as he considered the few million problems the typical farmer has to fight every day of the year.

Big John glanced over at Jeannie. She watched him, gripping the blue jacket she'd worn in the cool of the morning when she walked over to see Sally. Her eyes darted to her father's truck, still moving slowly down the drive, then back to John's face. They were accusing and frightened and angry and confused. John wiped the rag across his forehead again.

"There's Daddy," Jeannie said, her voice trembling. "Stop here and I'll meet him at the mailbox." She reached for the door handle and looked back at John when she discovered it had been removed.

John's eyes were tortured and shiny, almost as if he was going to cry, and his voice was apologetic.

"I'm sorry," he murmured in a quiet whimper almost too low to hear. "I'm so sorry."

Jeannie screamed as she lunged for the window, but John reached over and covered her nose and mouth with a massive hand and slammed her back down into the seat. Her jacket fluttered out the window, but there was nothing he could do about that. The Chevy accelerated, throwing up another cloud of rocks and dust, and John held the wheel with his knee as he waved at Sam Baker with his left hand. In the seat, halfway in the floor, Jeannie's face turned a dangerous shade of purple, and her eyes drifted from side to side, unfocused. Her struggling stopped. Big John released her and heaved a sigh of relief when she began breathing again. She'd be fine.

For a while.

Sam absently waved back at John Hill, then turned toward town. It was about time for Jeannie and he hoped to meet her on the way. She wanted to go to the Dollar Shop and look at that new book on astronomy everyone was talking about. Kid was sharper than a tub full of straight pins.

He looked in his mirror, watching the dust cloud in the wake of John's old Chevy and suddenly had the feeling he had forgotten something. Something very important. All he could see was a cloud of dust, though.

He shrugged and kept driving, but decided that if he didn't see Jeannie on the way, he would stop by the Edelman's and ask her and Sally if they wanted to go to town with him. Yeah, that's what he would do.

Jeannie breathed easily, but Big John sweated. He looked as though he'd been dunked in a watering trough with his clothes on. Despite the heat, he occasionally shivered.

Sam Baker had seen him and would remember when he couldn't

find his daughter. Maybe he should just put Jeannie out now and deny the whole thing when she started pointing a finger. It would be her word against his and they wouldn't have any proof at all. She hadn't even been hurt. He hadn't done a thing to her.

But the Urge was on him. He glanced over and saw the dark place on her cheek where his thumb had dug into the skin and her T-shirt hiked up to where he could see her bare stomach and braless chest and her jeans were tight and unwrinkled and the long brown hair was flung over her small shoulder and her neck was so smooth and she sprawled there with one hand curved as though inviting him to come to her.

And he knew he couldn't let her go.

If he had to, he'd get the shotgun at the house and watch for Sam. Sam couldn't be sure John took Jeannie, so he would come in cautiously, probably with the Taurus still under the seat. Then John would raise the shotgun and blow a small crater in his stomach and bury him out back of the barn with the various dogs he'd had over the years. He glanced over at the girl and sighed. And Jeannie, too. He never killed his victims but he would have to make an exception.

Then what could he tell himself to justify what he did? He used to think, Well, I might like them young, but at least I'm not a pervert fag. Then, I might hurt them a little, but at least I don't kill them. Except after today, he'd have to change that last bit. The self-revulsion bubbled up from deep inside him where he usually kept it bottled and threatened to spill from his mouth in blubbering sobs. What would he tell himself now? Well, I might have killed one, but at least I didn't boil her up in a pot for dinner.

He'd really screwed up this time.

But his eyes lingered over Jeannie, her smooth white skin, her perfect little features, and he clamped his lips together firmly. Maybe it will be worth it.

He was almost to the drive up to the Ranch when a dark shadow enfolded the car. For one wild moment, he thought the hand of God had descended from heaven and reached down to take him. Then the drone of the small plane shook the Chevy as it passed low overhead. Damn drug dealers come and go at all hours of the night and day! he thought, but he would never complain aloud. Too much money and too many bullets in drugs. He didn't bother them and they didn't bother him, except to deliver five thousand dollars a month in twenties to his front door. And that kind of bother he liked just fine.

Almost as much as he liked little girls.

What if that hadn't been a plane?

He thought he saw something else out next to the dump where he put the garbage. Dark. Not much of a shape. Like a cloud hovering around that stand of trees. He didn't know what it was, but it reminded him of what his daddy used to tell him.

"Dead meat'll bring the buzzards, Johnny. Something rotten will attract them that live on it."

Whatever it was made him think of an old buzzard sitting in a dead tree. Watching. Waiting.

"Damn fool," he said aloud. "Scared of a shadow."

John reached over and ran his hand up and down Jeannie's leg almost tenderly and patted her thigh protectively. Her eyes fluttered and her mouth moved soundlessly. He didn't have much time before she was awake and screaming, so he gripped the wheel firmly and shoved the Chevy into a lower gear and stomped the accelerator again. The car bounced up the drive to the Ranch, occasionally bottoming out in the particularly bad ruts that John had been meaning to fix and would have if it hadn't been so much damned work.

He didn't dare take the plane enthusiasts' private drive that went directly to the barn, and it was easier to dodge the holes than fill them.

Except now, when he had to reach the house before Jeannie woke up, and he went too fast to dodge anything. He'd have to run over Sweet Jesus Himself if He had appeared in the road just then. Fifty feet from his front door, the back end dipped into the Grand Canyon of potholes and John heard the screech of torn metal as he lost a muffler, and felt a solid, gut wrenching jolt as the car bottomed. A cracking snap echoed like a gunshot. A shock absorber letting go. The rear end of the car rebounded, but swayed like a drunk turtle the last few feet.

John stood on the brakes and skidded to a stop. The old '57 wouldn't be going anywhere soon, he knew. He'd have to call a tow truck out to get it to the garage.

But first, he thought, looking over at Jeannie. I got things to do. Lots of things.

He heard the plane taxi toward the barn and outbuildings he had rented along with the field. The barn had once been a huge milking stall when his Daddy was alive and, with the equipment and pens removed, it was big enough inside to play professional basketball.

Or hide a small plane.

But they couldn't see from the barn, or hear over the roar of the engine. He wasn't sure how they would react to the sight of Big John Hill walking up to his front door with a little girl slung over his shoulder like a sack of feed for the pigs, but he remembered the time he was picked up on suspicion in Somerset. And how the other inmates had looked at him when they found out he had been arrested for molesting a little girl. Even some fag on trial for murder - probably seething with AIDS - had spit in his face and the guards just stood by, their faces hard and unsympathetic while he wiped his face with his shirttail.

No, better not let them see or hear, he thought, unlocking his door. He walked to the fireplace and pulled open a door that appeared to be a sheet of paneling, and shifted Jeannie on his shoulder. She moaned "Daddy!" and struggled weakly. John started down the steps into the cellar no one knew was there and patted her on the back.

"It's okay, honey." He said as he closed the door behind him. "Everything is going to be okay."

But he knew he lied. The Urge made him lie. He knew Jeannie would be bloody and hurt and screaming before too long, and probably dead shortly after. He patted her back again.

"I'm sorry, honey," he murmured. But he knew that was a lie, too.

Chapter 4

"What the blue funk is it?" Dr. Jerry Reese asked. His nose almost touched the object and his head darted and bobbed like an old hound's catching a scent.

Evan Hall, PH.D., watched his friend and raised his eyebrows. In the wilds of Baltimore, Maryland, he thought. Never thought I'd be investigating an Anomalous Phenomenon in a woody swamp on the Patapsco River in old Balto. But I guess this is really Edgemere, or maybe Sparrow's Point. Evan thought Jerry was too short and skinny, but that was okay. Jerry thought he was too tall and fat.

"'Funk,'" Jerry told him. "I said 'funk,' not what you think." He didn't take his nose away from the thing. The thick layer of mucus-like substance quivered in the noon sun and showed no sign of evaporating, so it had to be something else. Something with no moisture and unaffected by heat.

"Jerry," Evan said. "If I heard you utter an obscenity, I think I'd call in another APE team."

Jerry gave a short, pained grin and turned back to the lump. It was egg-shaped, a little over four feet tall, five feet across and about eight feet long.

"Not too close," Evan cautioned. "We're still not too sure what it is, but it is slightly radioactive and that crud stinks like last week's fish special."

"For gosh sakes, I know that." Dr. Reese straightened his glasses and shook his head slightly. "But if it was really toxic, we'd be decked out in one of those containment suits from The Andromeda Strain." He glanced over his shoulder at the circle of soldiers, all carrying guns and wearing white pressure suits with self contained oxygen supplies.

An unsmiling Sergeant Akers watched them all. Jerry usual smile faltered for a second. "Wouldn't we?" he asked uneasily.

"Hell if I know," Dr. Hall told him, peering at the slime closely. "Maybe they want to know how it affects a couple of egghead, underpaid scientists."

Jerry glanced at him, smiled uncertainly and looked back at the slick surface.

"You're right," he said. "It stinks."

"Well, thank you for your confirmation of my diagnosis, Doctor," Evan said. He fiddled with the dial on an ultrasound machine, borrowed on short notice from the X-ray department of Edgemere Hospital. Yesterday at this time, the probe had been pressed against the stomach of an excited mother to be, showing her a vague shadow of the tiny life growing inside her.

Now, Dr. Evan Hall prepared to run it over the slimy surface of an object that A: had appeared out of nowhere. B: leaked noxious if not toxic fumes. And C: was radioactive. Not intensely so, but he wouldn't want to stay around it for more than an hour or two without protection. It had been enough to trip the radiation monitors on three different spysats, and that was hot enough for Evan.

"Think we should try to get into the middle of the thing?" Jerry asked.

"The 'E' in APE stands for 'Evaluation,'" Evan reminded him. "'Anomalous Phenomenon Evaluation' team. We examine but don't touch. That's reserved for the guys who make the big bucks. If it doesn't kill us, then it's their turn."

"That sure makes me feel better."

"What are friends for?" Evan asked.

"I wonder what this green stuff is?"

"Snot," Evan said emphatically. "What we have here is an eleven hundred pound booger from the nasal cavity of the Jolly Green Giant. I bet if we look around, we'll find a yellow pond about thirty feet across."

Jerry looked disgusted and shook his head again.

"Know what I think?" he asked after a few minutes.

"No, but I'm sure it's so fascinating that you'll have to tell me."

"This is essentially the crud you scrape out of the bottom of your sink after a week or two." Now it was Evan's turn to look disgusted. "No, really," Jerry insisted.

"After a couple of weeks, everything congeals into a kind of amorphous slime. Mostly organic, but it could contain bits of paper and metal and glass, like this thing seems to have in it."

"Tell me, Jerry. How often do you clean your sink, anyway?" Evan shook his head. "So what we have here," he continued slowly, holding the ultrasound probe by his side, "is the scum off the bottom of the Jolly Green Giant's sink."

"Don't be ridiculous," Jerry said. "But it could be something similar."

"Let me guess," Evan said. "This has to do with your garbage dump theory."

"As a matter of fact --"

"The same theory that says if we want to look for evidence of an advanced civilization in the universe, we should try to find out where it dumps its advanced garbage?"

"Yes, but --"

"And, of course, an advanced civilization wouldn't leave its advanced garbage just anywhere. Nosiree, Bob. They have too much toxic material and dangerous waste and discarded weapons and machinery to leave lying around on some garbage dump planet. They would have to get rid of it permanently. Right?"

"Well --"

"The best place would be down a black hole, where it would never be seen again, forever and ever."

Jerry said nothing for a few moments. He just stared at Evan.

"That's one alternative," he said finally.

"And at the bottom of that black hole is a swamp in Baltimore, Maryland."

"There are other possibilities," Jerry told him.

"I know," Evan said. Back to the object. "Neutron stars, normal suns, the aforementioned landfill planets, other dimensions, deep space, and hyperspace."

"Yeah, maybe," Jerry said. "But I prefer the notion of a gap, a discontinuity between universes where toxic waste could be dumped without affecting anything else."

Evan should have told him how stupid the idea was, but he remembered what happened a few weeks ago when Jerry was out with the flu and he had to investigate a glowing spot near Norfolk, Virginia.

Sergeant Akers and his squad was with him, mainly because the spot, like the slime covered sludge they were examining, triggered the satellite radiation detectors. As it turned out, most of the glowing was some kind of harmless phosphorescence. That wasn't the problem.

The problem was the man who suddenly appeared in the center of the spot.

Evan had missed the appearance. He'd gone to the truck, parked about a hundred yards away from the phenomenon, to get the video camera. At least that's what he had told Akers, but the real reason was to move away from the radiation for a few minutes. And to get a Pepsi.

An animal howl echoed from near the spot, halfway across a farmer's peanut crop. Someone yelled. Someone else fired a rifle. He ran back around the truck, but he saw only a circle of green clad soldiers with gun barrels pointed toward the center of the glowing area. More gunshots. Another scream, like an animal being tortured, but it changed even as the sound died away. At the end, it sounded like a man groaning in pain. Evan ran toward the soldiers, ignoring earlier promises to the farmer to step over the peanut plants. He remembered thinking, Let him raise the price of peanut oil.

He was prepared for almost anything. Anything but a naked old man writhing and finally becoming still on the glowing soil. He looked about ninety, face wrinkled, eyes dark and sunken until his head looked more like a skull. His ribs pressed against the shiny, translucent skin of his chest and his arms and legs looked like thin sticks of spaghetti. Red rimmed holes dotted his chest and abdomen, and blood pooled on the glowing area under his back. One of the soldiers coughed, and Evan looked around just in time to see him throw up on the peanut crop.

He decided then and there never to eat another peanut butter sandwich.

"It's a man!" one of the other soldiers said, as though surprised.

"A dead man," Evan said. "A dead, old, naked man." Despite his appearance, the man looked very familiar to Evan. He couldn't place where he'd seen him, probably because of the body's condition, but he had the feeling that at some point, he would snap his fingers and say, Oh, yeah. That's who it is.

The soldiers still held their rifles, and all - except Sergeant Akers - looked nervous. Akers studied the corpse. Evan noticed smoke still drifted from the barrel of his weapon, and none of the others, as though he had done most or all of the shooting. Evan swallowed, or at least tried to. His mouth was suddenly dry, for some reason, and he wished he had the Pepsi.

"Any particular reason you shot this guy?" he asked.

"He was just there," the guy who threw up began. "All knotted and twisted and dark --"

"That's enough, soldier," Akers told him, looking at Evan. "Save it for debriefing."

"Sergeant Akers," Evan said. "It's my job to investigate these phenomenon. If you have information...."

"Sorry, Dr. Hall." Sergeant Akers watched him with dark eyes as icy as liquid nitrogen. Evan decided he never wanted to meet him in a dark alley when he was in a bad mood. Or a good mood, for that matter. "I report through the chain of command, and that does not include you." Akers paused, looking around before continuing as though daring someone to contradict him. "If you want to know more about this incident, I suggest you confer with your headquarters."

Which is why, one night after the peanut field incident, Even found himself searching the APE computer files, looking for the report on what happened. He'd found a lot of crap, and one thing in particular, that scared him, but nothing on what happened to the old man. That scared him, too. Either they hadn't reported it, or it had been taken out of the files for some reason.

Evan made another adjustment on the ultrasound machine. It had been too long since he'd used one of these.

The scariest thing in the files was the discovery of more events in more places than they had ever mentioned to him or Jerry. These events were what Evan needed to fill in the gaps in a computer simulation he had been developing. The analysis was more frightening than the files. It showed a pattern associated with the events. It was complex, related to "event intensity" and "geographic drift." And a spike at BWI a few years ago didn't fit the other data. But the bottom line analysis was simple. A logarithmic curve, and the anomalous events would peak in the pre-dawn hours two days from now in a Virginia town called Somerset. The top of the peak was out there somewhere with the quasars. Evan wondered if he should tell Jerry.

"So what about this stuff?" Evan asked, nodding at the slime. "Did it drop out of a black hole?" Jerry shrugged.

The image came into focus as Evan adjusted the angle on the probe. He could almost see the outline of the object on the screen. It had a single vertical strip of material, and a circle with more shapes imposed over that. He peered at the screen, trying to position the probe to clear the image. It looked like letters. Two letters.

"Well, damn bugs in the bios," he said after he had studied the image for a few seconds.

"I don't know what advanced civilization dumped this particular object, but they have a taste for fine German automobiles." Evan shook his head and glanced from the instrument to the object itself. Yes, it was obvious now, from the size and shape of the slime mass. Anyone who knew anything about cars should have recognized the distinctive beetle-like shape that had earned its name.

Jerry looked at the display. There, clearly outlined in the center were two letters: VW. He looked at the object then back at the screen.

Jerry muttered something. Evan had his doubts whether he'd said "funk" or something else.

And if Jerry had said it, maybe it was time to tell him.

If Dr. Jerry Reese could utter an obscenity, maybe the destruction of the universe wasn't so far-fetched after all.

Chapter 5

G. Alan Benet never expected to save anyone's life. Given a few minutes to reflect on the possibility, he would have laughed and walked away. He always thought the old Oriental tradition of being responsible for the life you save was uncomfortably close to the truth.

He was determined never to make that mistake.

Alan only wanted to mind his own business that morning, as he ran and considered the possibility of a new name. He had used so many, one of them his own given name, that he was afraid of becoming predictable.

A magician should never be predictable.

He had discarded some names - including his own - because of trouble with certain overzealous officers of the court. A couple were being used by individuals with a prior claim. Others were just no good.

Alan remembered a few of the very old names, from a time when he was small and skinny, and any kid with the will and a few moments to spare could give his own ego a boost by pounding little Georgie Benet about the face and head for a while.

One of the most memorable was "Boy Georgie," and not meant as a compliment on Alan's singing ability.

"Guys! There comes Boy Georgie!" like a well rehearsed chorus from a gang of boys. Then, of course, he showed how right they were by turning and running in the opposite direction with a grace and gazelle-like swiftness that would have startled any aging and overweight singer popular a few decades ago.

Alan never could decide whether his chronically skinny physique was genetic, or a result of years of fleeing in the other direction. Eventually, though, the running paid off. After a while, the guys realized they would never catch him once those skinny legs started pumping, and they looked for easier, slower prey. Probably some fat guy, Alan figured. Singing ability optional.

Later in high school, George Benet became a track star, winning short and long distance sprints with an ease that surprised anyone who had not tried to chase him. Guys who had before screamed and yelled and shook their fists at him now screamed and cheered and waved their arms as he claimed first place in a succession of district, regional, and state races, at first breaking records set by others, but eventually ones he had set himself. In the end, "Boy Georgie" was his only competition. His wins focused a small spotlight of fame on his school with regional and state records still on the books after ten or more years. He was almost grateful for the earlier pursuits that developed his running abilities.

Almost.

More than a half dozen major colleges came knocking on his door with offers of full scholarships, but he had other plans.

When the really important talent developed, the memory of the screams almost balanced the memory of the cheers, so he merely scared his once-tormentors until they wet their pants. He didn't do anything really serious.

Killing them, for example.

Even that, Alan knew, wasn't the worst they could suffer.

Alan still ran.

Not because he was pursued (except by the demons of his own making) or because he raced (except for the race against mortality that had become a minor obsession as he slipped into his late twenties). Alan ran because running was a pleasure. He had always associated running with success. First, when he successfully ran from those who wanted to bruise their fists against his face, and later, when people cheered and patted him on the back after he won a race.

And he ran through life, looking always ahead, because then he didn't have to see his footprints in others' lives.

His head was always clearer when he ran. And his mind raced along with his body, considering and discarding possibilities almost with each step. Some of his best ideas for new gags had come to him while he ran. Like the "Girl and Ghost" stunt, and the "Great Ball of Fire" floating above the audience. Both of them took determined and exhausting applications of the Major Gift, but the results were worth the sweaty brow and armpits afterward. Some of the gags he dreamed didn't even involve the Gift, and those he sold to Magic Box, Inc., for enough to cover the construction of his own gimmicks.

He was especially proud of the Dimensional Box because of the gimmick, and the private joke he could never share. The conventional version was the old removable middle trick, where a girl reclined on a table while the illusionist positioned a box over her. Her feet and head stuck out either end of the box. The magician slid flat, solid blades into place, cutting the box into threes, then removed the middle section to show the small miracle. There was even a little door he opened to show that the girl's middle was still in the box.

In Alan's case, he used a round oatmeal box wrapped in a piece of cloth the same color as Rena's dress.

Alan thought about Rena Simpson, his mind worrying over her presence like an old hound gnashing over a new slab of steak. She was too good-looking to be working in a third- rate - no, second-rate - magic show, even if he did hope to make it first-rate by the end of summer. Three months ago she had appeared, a phantom from nowhere, at the Magic Hat bar in Philadelphia where he worked a one-night stand. And it turned out that she was out of work and had experience with other shows. At least she knew the lingo, and a few of the gimmicks. Given the way she looked, Alan didn't care if she could remember what day it was. She had been with him since, sharing the shows and, for the past two months, his bed. She was good. Almost too good to be working for his soon-to-be-first-rate show. During the removable middle trick, she laughed when he tickled the oatmeal box, and stretched her head and feet at the appropriate times to hide the real gimmick.

When he placed the box over her, Rena's middle sagged through the rubber sheet center of the table. She made the table appear solid by holding herself rigid on the surface of the black rubber sheet. Even though the audience could apparently see through the table, they were actually seeing the stage curtain through a double mirror arrangement that reflected the image behind.

Sometimes magicians did do it with mirrors.

The audience never seemed to notice that the curtain didn't quite match above and below the tabletop. But with a body like Rena's to study, they probably had other things on their minds.

They didn't notice that Rena's feet and head moved about six inches closer together when Alan lowered the box, and apart when he raised it to show her rigid on the table again.

Or that Alan walked behind the table only after he had put on a long, yellow "surgeon's gown" that covered him from ankle to shoulder with a single color as undetectable as the curtain.

What people didn't see made his "magic" possible.

The Dimensional Box contained a smaller gimmick built along the same lines, but just large enough to cover an arm or head, with a complicated arrangement of four mirrors instead of two. Alan had worked out several routines for the Box. In one, Rena put her head into the Box and walked around as the Headless Woman. In another, he lost his forearm and hand and made jokes about Richard Kimble, though most of the audience didn't get that, anymore, even with the Harrison Ford movie.

But the best routines involved a member of the audience, especially if the volunteer was a kid. And the best kids were self-confident six or seven year olds. Any older, and they were smart enough to figure out the trick. Any younger, and they were usually too scared to cooperate.

When a show ran short for some reason or another, he milked the Box routine for another four or five minutes, an eternity on stage and possible only when he managed to pick a precocious youngster. In those cases, he usually tried to fade into the background and let the kid take over for a while, just prodding and urging him occasionally to keep the rhythm going.

On the very good nights, the kid listened to Alan's stage whispers and followed his instructions, like getting up to run off stage when he announced he would make his new assistant's head disappear.

At that point, some kids ran and didn't come back, which meant he had to start over with someone else. He could understand the flight instinct.

But the good ones would run to the steps and hesitate, then walk slowly back when Alan motioned for them to return.

And, when he put the box over some kid's head, the head disappeared.

The audience always screamed and applauded and cheered.

When Alan moved in front of the volunteer, apparently to get a good look himself, he fed more instructions to the youngster.

"When I squeeze your shoulder," he would tell them, "I want you to say, 'And now for my next trick...' and stop. Okay?" Usually the box would nod, but sometimes it hesitated, and he repeated the instructions, but only once more. Any longer and the people would doubt the trick. Then he moved behind and to the right of the kid. As the applause died, he quickly squatted and moved his own head behind the box, to where he could see the audience through the mirrors. From the front, it looked as though his head had appeared where the youngster's should have been. He squeezed the shoulder and moved his mouth in synch with the words, more or less.

"And now for my next trick..."

And they laughed and cheered and applauded even louder.

G. Alan Benet liked that. He liked that a lot.

If he could just stay out of trouble with the law, his life would be almost perfect.

Jase Stevens, he thought. That has a nice ring to it. No, too many sibilants, and he already sound like a leaky steam engine on stage. Jared Stevens? His legs moved in a rhythmic motion, and he took comfort in the easy tap of his expensive shoes against the concrete, the quiet motion of his stride. Jared Stevens would look good on the program, he knew. And it was nothing like his real name or the one he currently used. He would also need a new title for the show, but he liked Magic Circle. It sounded a little wimpy, but still hinted at unknown secrets and some arcane, hidden organization of magic.

Just what I need, he thought, nodding. Then he heard the scream.

Alan looked up and said, "Damn!" out loud. And, like the man falling toward him, his own mind shifted into overdrive, moving to a plateau of speed and clarity only a few people ever experience.

After a few micro seconds of lightning calculation, he knew the man would miss him, though not by much. Even if he had kept jogging, the body would have hit the concrete a couple of feet ahead of him. Probably scared the hell out of him and splattered him with blood and brains, but it would have missed.

Alan could save him.

A very slim, very risky chance. The guy might be better off dead. Just a couple of years ago, Alan would have turned away. But now. . . .

If only the rube hadn't screamed.

But he did.

And Alan heard him.

Then saw him.

Scanned the streets. No one else around.

Looked again. Still falling. Still screaming.

Wide open mouth in terror. Flailing arms.

Thought, What the hell.

Shrugged.

He fought a wave of uncharacteristic sympathy.
Then Hid the poor bastard.

Chapter 6

Well, Rena Williams thought, fondling the short barreled .38 revolver in her hand. What's it gonna be? He'll be coming through that door any minute. Are you going to blow his brains out or throw him on the floor and screw his brains out?

At the moment, she didn't know which.

Her high school yearbook of five years before described her as ". . . a perky, intelligent combination of Gidget and Socrates. Most likely to succeed as the host of a game show called Madhouse Jeopardy."

Rena still had the same reaction to that description. She didn't know whether to laugh or cry. Or both.

She seemed to be having a lot of trouble with decisions these past few months.

(The police said it was a handkerchief.)

Sitting, staring at a re-run of an old black and white episode of Hogan's Heroes that she couldn't have summarized if her life depended on it, Rena wondered if her trouble with decisions could be traced to the day her brother died.

She couldn't decide.

On the screen, Richard Dawson conned John Banner with a slab of apple strudel while Bob Crane inspected the bed of a supposedly top secret truck. Five seconds later, Rena forgot the scene.

At that moment, she couldn't decide whether to kill someone.

"And, folks," she said suddenly into the stillness of the hotel room, "not just any someone, but a particular someone. A particular, peculiar someone who probably killed my only brother Jack, and pays me every week to stand around in a skimpy costume and point while he disappears into some dirty, scratched up trunk or box."

She giggled for a moment, then forced herself to stop. But it was funny. She had gone to work for the man she suspected of killing her brother to find evidence of his guilt. She thought she had enough proof, at least for herself if not the police, but two tiny problems stopped her from taking the snub nose and tracing a neat, lead circle on his chest.

The laugh track came up, then faded and she sat with her eyes focused in the center of the screen, still not seeing as Ivan Dixon built a bomb to destroy the truck.

(It was silk. Shimmering, shining silk clutched in his bloody hand.)

Jack was her first problem.

Jack Williams hadn't been a very good brother, but he was an even worse human being. Before he was eighteen, he had been arrested five times for drug possession with intent to distribute. Because he was a minor, he managed to get away with probation and stern warnings. But his deals grew larger and his respect for the law smaller as he approached the age of majority.

He celebrated that noteworthy day a year ago, when in the eyes of the law he became an adult, by shooting both an undercover cop and a big time drug distributor in a sting operation gone bad. He escaped by diving through a window before the distributor's associates could target him.

Within hours, a few hundred cops and an equal number of people associated with a certain drug cartel suddenly wanted Jack Williams dead.

(No identifying marks. But how many people carried snow-white silk scarves?)

The police didn't know they'd found Jack until a few hours after a crane lifted the concrete block off the body. No one then or since explained how several tons of concrete managed to fly from the construction site several hundred feet away and land on top of the unfortunate Mr. Williams, and nobody really cared. Another of the unexplainable things around these days. Rena couldn't explain how, but she knew Alan was involved.

The police were disappointed they hadn't gotten a chance to show their own displeasure at his actions. They assumed the mob had found him first and mob justice was always violent and gruesome. This latest example just showed how ugly it could be.

The cops publicized the murder, hoping that it would give young people considering a life of crime more to consider.

Meanwhile, the cartel was confused, though grateful for the publicity. A few small-time dealers who had been studying the benefits of turning state's evidence suddenly became loyal, closed-mouthed employees.

Death was one thing, but being flattened to the thickness of a postage stamp was another.

(She saw the scarf. It had four parallel furrows where Jack's fingers had dug into the silk. As though he held it in a death grip while someone tried to pull it loose.)

Jack had been a stupid, heartless bully, but he was her brother. They never found the killer because the police didn't care. If convicted, Jack would have gotten the electric chair, anyway, so let's save the state a few bucks.

The family didn't have to identify the body. There wasn't much to identify, except the bloody scraps of a leather jacket with the letters "JW" stamped into the right sleeve. The coroner obtained a positive ID with a new, sophisticated genetic analysis technique using a scrap of tissue from the corpse and piece of skin that remained behind when Jack had left the room through the window. Since several witnesses identified Jack as the donor of the skin, the coroner certified the body to be Jack Dean Williams.

One other little detail stopped Rena from killing her brother's murderer.

She fell in love with him.

TV credits flashed and faded over an Air Force cap hanging from the spike on a German helmet.

She had wept quietly through Jack's closed-casket ceremony while her parents had sat there in a stiff, drug- induced haze, staring at the steel and bronze and wood and silk that surrounded the remnants of their only son.

Alan had attended, a stranger out of place at the funeral. By itself, that was almost enough to prompt Rena to use her family's police contacts to trace him. It turned out George Alan Benet and his various aliases filled a large police file with details of his encounters with the law.

And on his career as a magician.

(He had been wearing a swatch of snow-white silk stuffed carelessly in his breast pocket, and it wasn't just any old scarf - he was the one.)

Rena took the .38 from her lap and stared at it for a few minutes before she lifted and pointed at the smiling face of a man gushing about a miracle cure for acne. She was an expert shot. Whenever they moved to a new town, she tracked down the nearest shooting range and practiced there for an hour each week.

G. Alan Benet thought she liked to go to movies.

What a charmer, she thought, trying to focus on the simple, all important fact that he killed her brother. Her mind refused to focus, and she found herself remembering his smile and the way his hair dropped across his forehead when he laughed and the feel of his arms around her in bed.

(Murderer. He was a murderer. A shimmering white scarf covered one corner of the trunk. He bought them in bulk from a magic supply house.)

She jabbed the "OFF" button on the television and leaned back on the sofa. Alan was out jogging, but he would be back at any moment unless something delayed him. Would she use the gun this time, or, again, greet him with a smile and a quick free-for-all on the bed?

Gotta decide, she thought.

Rena had taken the job when his old assistant suddenly found a very well-paying job in the factory owned by Rena's father. Of course, neither Alan nor the girl knew that. The girl had found employment where she could stay in one place, and Alan was delighted that Rena was available to fill the vacancy.

He hadn't known her last name was really Williams.

She intended to keep the relationship professional while she investigated her brother's death, but Alan's charm and an unexpected physical attraction had wrecked that plan. Rena told herself she tolerated the relationship only so she could gather the proof she needed for the police, or for herself. She lied to herself for almost two months before she admitted she had fallen in love with her brother's killer.

Alan had carried the substitution trunk in, packed with small tricks and gimmicks, and set it in one corner of the suite. Inside was a blank pistol that she fired at him as he stood behind a curtain during one part of the show. What if she removed the blank pistol and replaced it with the .38? She could plead ignorance, but if the police found Alan really had killed her brother and that she practiced every week on a firing range . . . .

Maybe Alan's prize sword in the bottom of the trunk. The one he kept so sharp that it was sheathed and wrapped in layers of felt. At one time, he demonstrated his blades were not fake by tossing apples into the air and slicing them in half before they hit the ground. Then, of course, he pulled a switch with the gimmicked one. (That was before he gave some curious kid a close haircut. And he was lucky. A couple of inches lower and he'd have taken the top of the kid's head off.) She could shove it into the basket instead of one of the flexible swords.

Stupid, she told herself. She could never use either weapon. Even if she had been there and seen how Alan managed to crush Jack under a block of concrete. Even if he found out who she really was and what she was doing there.

She could never kill the man she loved.

Rena hid the gun in her purse and covered her face with her hands for a few minutes.

Maybe she should just run. Pack her clothes and get away while she had the chance, because she didn't know what Alan would do if he did find out she was Jack's sister. She had seen enough to know Alan wasn't above skirting the fringes of the law, even tipping over to the other side on occasion. And even though she was sure he killed her brother, she had never actually seen him hurt anyone. His crimes seemed to be more of the fraud and deceit variety.

But to run she would have to make a decision.

She wondered if making no decision was actually a decision, too.

Would he hurt her if he found out?

Was she willing to risk it?

Would Alan kill again?

She couldn't decide.

Chapter 7

People disappear for mundane, ordinary enough reasons without inventing imaginary monsters and theorizing about other dimensions. Sid Thomas knew that for a fact. He, personally, had engineered the unexplained disappearance of a number of people, including his ex-wife, the bitch with the big mouth and money grubbing talons for hands.

Of course, he didn't get any money for that one, except the extra few hundred a month that he didn't have to send the slut.

For the right money, though, Sid Thomas would arrange an inexplicable disappearance and no one would ever find the body.

No one opens barrels of toxic waste to check for dead people. After a few days, there wasn't much of a body left, anyway.

Sid always assumed they died, even if they were alive and kicking and screaming behind a gag when he shoved them into the stinking, discolored scum and fastened the top securely. By the time the barrels were moved a few hours later, the banging had stopped, so Sid was fairly sure they were dead.

No toxic monsters ever burst out of the cans.

Sid was a real deal maker. He knew which suited bureaucrat to bribe and how much.

He was also good at breaking kneecaps, blowing up cars, bullying old people in the neighborhood, and robbing convenience stores.

Even in high school he'd been tough. After they threw him out, he'd stolen some fat jerk's college ring, just to show the nerd he was no better than Sid. His first major heist. He liked the way the blood-red stone gleamed in the sunlight through the bus window. He twisted it around his finger and watched the scenery. He hadn't expected to be on a silver bus lumbering out of Fairfax, Virginia, on Interstate 66 toward I-81 and a slow, leisurely trip to the deep south. And he hadn't really planned to visit another uncle in Atlanta, but it seemed a good idea now. The twenty-five hundred or so from the QT Mart was a comforting weight in one pocket and the Beretta he'd used to shoot the two clerks was a reassuring lump in the other. Eight shots in the mag and he'd only used two so far.

He hadn't planned to kill them, but he couldn't find his mask when he drove up, so he waited until the store was empty and iced the two kids behind the counter. Too bad, really. The girl looked like a high school cheerleader with those long legs and blonde hair and flawless smile. A real waste, but he didn't have any time for distractions.

Too many blue boys around after that - there must have been a doughnut shop in the area. He'd ditched the old Pontiac wagon sooner than he planned, but saw the bus station after a few minutes on foot. He smiled. Cops would never think of looking for him on a bus.

He'd gone inside and bought a one-way ticket to Atlanta. Five cop cars, lights flashing and sirens screaming, whipped past as the bus left.

Sid had saluted and settled back into the rich softness of the seat. First row, good view of the road ahead.

Hell of a nice view inside, too. Now he had time for distractions, but too many witnesses.

That little Latin piece across the aisle, for example. He twisted the ring on his finger and examined her. She was about twenty-five with legs up to there and back, and he shifted to see if he could get a better look at those luscious limbs. Not hard with the skirt she was almost wearing. And that blouse - like two rats fighting in a sack when she walked on the bus. Too bad she had to drag around some snotty nosed, kid about three or four. He might have made a move on her anyway, and to hell with the witnesses.

He could still look, and he did. Until she tossed her head and pulled the long, dark hair behind her ears, then moved to the back of the bus. Well, hellfire, he thought.

"What's the matter, babe?" he said, touching her arm as she walked by. He knew she could see the ring. "Don't know the good stuff when you see it?" She jerked away and continued to the back. Sid watched her sway and smiled.

Maria Quinones did know a jerk when she saw one.

After a couple of hours, the bus made the turn south onto Interstate 81. Sid closed his eyes, dozing. He figured it would be a while before they got to the first major stop in Somerset, Virginia. Plenty of time for a long nap since he had nothing sleek and soft to distract him. He looked forward to a quiet, uneventful trip.

The first hint of trouble came when the bus slowed abruptly and the driver muttered, "Damn!" very low, but loud enough for Sid, sitting just behind him, to hear. Sid opened his eyes, frowning. These guys were trained to be courteous and understanding. They never said, "Damn!"

He glanced at the windshield, and said, "Damn!" himself, but loud enough for everyone on the bus to hear.

The driver locked the brakes, but it was too late.

At forty-three miles per hour, the bus hit the black wall sitting in the middle of the interstate.

Sid braced himself, even though he knew that was the stupid thing to do. He should relax, go limp, but all he could do was lock his hands on the arm rests and stiffen his legs. He suddenly wished he'd followed the girl to the back.

The bus hit, and went through without a sound, without a bump, and certainly without any impact Sid could feel.

Sid was sure he was dead, though. Sure that the bus smashed into the wall, and now he was sprawled in the middle of the interstate, his brains smeared on the white line.

How else could he explain the soundless gloom, and the lack of any sensation? He couldn't even feel his heart beat, so he must be dead.

Then the voice came from the shadowy mists around him, and it looked as if the dark clouds were parting, moving out of the way to allow a greater darkness to approach.

"Welcome!" Like a gunshot next to his head. Sid tried to cover his ears, but that didn't seem to help.

"Welcome, soldier," it continued. "Welcome to your destiny."

When he saw it, Sid wanted to cover his eyes, too, but he somehow knew that wouldn't help, either. The shape was like a photographic negative that burned with muted colors, and he had a feeling more than just the image was reversed. Sid had done some bad things in his life, but this thing dripped with evil.

He pulled the revolver, and shot three times very quickly. The thing's head jerked with each shot, then it opened its mouth and spit out three mangled pieces of lead.

The gun dropped from his hand as the thing's face melted into another form and he recognized it.

"You," he said, the words sounding as distant as a cry for help in the city. Sid glanced over his shoulder, as though he could see back into reality. "But you just ...."

Shrill laughter from the thing, and finally, he felt something. The ring burned like a hot coal on his finger as the flesh transformed around it. Sid Thomas was allowed his sanity long enough to see scales ripple up his arm, and feel his tongue fork and flicker, and sense his skull flatten into a wide triangle.

Then he no longer needed sanity. Sanity would not help free Karick, his new master.

The voice inside his head laughed and laughed and laughed and . . . .

In the bright light of reality, the back portion of the bus skidded down the highway another hundred feet or so before the leading edge veered off the asphalt and dug into the soft dirt of the median. The vehicle's speed had dropped to less than fifteen miles per hour by then. Even amid the panic, screaming, and clouds of dirt, no one seated past the second row was seriously hurt. Sparks from the undercarriage somehow failed to ignite fuel leaking from the ruptured line.

Everything up to and including the second row was gone. The front end of the bus looked as though it had been sliced away like the first chunk off a loaf of silver bread.

The remaining passengers crawled out the front, and helped the shaken priest who had been sitting on the third row. He had flown out of his seat and rolled down the bank to a small ditch in the median. Other than a thick stripe of mud down his back, he was fine.

Maria Quinones hugged Ricky. "It's okay, baby," she whispered. "Everything's fine. Mommy's here. There's no reason to be scared."

She didn't want to lie to her daughter. She knew there were a hell of a lot of reasons to be afraid. She had felt the evil, like some deadly radiation emanating from that black wall well before she had seen it. At the same time, there had been something familiar tugging at her, calling her, and that deepened the fear she felt. She thought about the pock-faced sleaze who had been eyeing her, twisting his ring, practically drooling in his seat. But for him, she might have been sitting on the first row. If he hadn't vanished like a noisy Boojum, she might have been tempted to thank him for being a crude asshole.

But he was inexplicably gone. Along with the driver, about a ton of metal, and the black wall.

She shivered, then made herself stop before she scared Ricky.

What now? she thought. She didn't like air travel because of what happened to Brian, and now this with the bus. The car, safely back in Fairfax, would never make the trip, which is why she took the bus in the first place. Hell of a long walk to Florida.

They gathered outside the wreckage of the bus, huddling together, talking like old friends at a reunion. Some were hugging people they'd only met a few minutes before. Others couldn't, or wouldn't, let go of family or old friends. Some herd instinct drew them all together with the weaker ones toward the center and the young men standing in a half circle facing what the remains of the bus.

A Spanish phrase came to her, one of the few her mother had repeated enough for her to remember. In English it meant black demon, she thought, and that's what her mom would have called what she felt. The authorities would never believe her, though, or be able to explain what happened to the bus. But she knew the force behind it.

Something in the closet.

She held her head, not wanting to think about it.

Still, she searched her memory for the Spanish words she once heard from her mother, a religious woman who believed in the devil just as firmly as she believed in God. It may not have been a mere black demon, but *El Diablo Obscuro*, the Dark Satan.

She clutched Ricky. She suddenly wanted to go home and lock her doors and never let her daughter out of her sight again. The little girl sobbed into Maria's shoulder and she struggled to hold back her own tears. She knew their ordeal wasn't over.

Worst of all, she didn't know how much more of this she could take. Why did she shiver when she thought about the pock-faced man with the ring? Where had he gone?

But she had the feeling she knew.

Chapter 8

Dave had just exited the 695 beltway around Baltimore and made the wide right turn onto the Baltimore-Washington Expressway, "NO TRUCKS ALLOWED," when he thought he saw something dark move across his vision, a brief cloud of darkness. He peered around, but he saw nothing that could have caused it.

"Too much bacon for breakfast," he said aloud, shrugging. Then he looked around guiltily. Talking to himself again. Well, he could blame that bad habit on using the pocket recorder, at least.

Time to move, he thought, then immediately eased into the left lane. Less than a mile from the exit, and local traffic wasn't noted for courteous behavior. So it was either now or lose his chance forever. He wasn't surprised when an almost flat red sportscar roared up behind him, the front end dipping even lower as the driver hit his brakes. Lights flashed in the mirror, but Dave didn't budge. It wasn't his fault they built the exit to BWI to the left instead of to the right like most offramps. He was too close to the exit, and doing almost ten miles over the fifty-five speed limit besides. He estimated the sportscar must have been doing about ninety when he first glimpsed it in the rearview mirror.

The red car finally found a gap with six inches of clearance and slid into the right lane. He rode beside Dave for a few seconds, staring a challenge at him. Dave just glanced over lazily. He saw a boy of about twenty: glasses, hair laid back with something slick and shiny, a razor thin mustache. A single red zit in the middle of his forehead. Dave mouthed the words, "Screw you," and turned his eyes back to the road. Out of the corner of his eye, he could see the guy ranting and gesturing. Dave just smiled and eased into the exit lane.

The sportscar veered into the vacant space in the left lane, accelerating up to the bumper of a battered pickup which looked to have been used on a muddy farm for the past century. Before he made the turn to the left, Dave saw the man in the pickup roll down the window and spit a huge wad of tobacco and juice, which bounced off the sportscar's hood and splattered the driver's side of the windshield. Brake lights flared like silent fireworks in both lanes as the sportscar skidded to a halt in the grassy median. The pickup went on, oblivious. Dave laughed out loud.

Yes, they were living in truly strange times. Occasionally, the universe balanced.

Though the weather report had promised cool but clear weather, Dave noticed some sort of black cloud hanging low over the airport area. Forget it, he thought. Let someone else report the falling houses and flying monkeys. I'm here to talk to some very stubborn machinists.

And still, he felt an uneasiness gnawing at him somewhere deep inside. He remembered the momentary darkness over his vision, and a sense of falling. Something had happened and he felt that if he could focus his attention on it for a few minutes, it would come to him.

But then he was in the airport, and the thought slipped away like a juggled cube of ice.

Dave wanted to write something besides the "Creature Features" and was slightly amazed when Larry finally gave his approval. He liked to think it was because he had done his homework, and his proposal detailed a two year struggle for pride and recognition that the machinists were losing. He had promised an honest, hard-hitting article presenting both sides of the issue.

Dave suspected the real reason he received the assignment was because his column helped sell hundreds of thousands of newspapers every day - not to mention the even more numerous hits on the website - and he had made a few unsubtle threats about what would happen if he didn't get the job.

At the airport, he interviewed tired machinists all morning, some weary and despondent and others determined to fight to the end. He also talked to passengers flying the airline in question.

"That's not a strike," one uninterested citizen told him. "That's chronic unemployment."

And that, thought Dave, is the problem. The public didn't really understand what had happened to those guys, or how they and their families suffered while they fought for adequate health benefits. Or how management brought in semi-skilled and trainee machinists to work on the planes they flew every day.

Would those people let a semi-skilled surgeon take out their appendix?

Around lunchtime, Dave drifted back to the car, still observing, still watching the people hurrying to catch flights to destinations all over the world. He glanced at his watch. Almost time for Suzy and Chris to arrive. He threw the recorder into the back seat as a crash, like thunder in an echo chamber, rumbled down from the sky overhead. Before he even looked up, he knew what he would see. The dark feeling of deja vu cut through him, and he remembered the falling and the darkness. He remembered where he was.

Hell.

The clouds were a deep, velvety black, a rich ebony emptiness he had never seen anywhere, much less in the sky. (Something inside screamed at him, almost gibbering like a crazed ape. Run, you bastard! Save them!) He spotted a plane approaching, and it dropped lower, as if trying to avoid the darkness in its path. Yet the afternoon sun shown brightly on his own back, casting a stark shadow that was a miniature twin to the lightless shape overhead.

Dave's eyes widened as they tracked the plane. His pulse accelerated. He covered his ears. He forgot about taking pictures, despite the camera around his neck. But he didn't need a camera to recall that scene.

The black cloud roiled and churned and finally flowed into the shape of a giant hand. Dave thought he could even see fingerprints and lines on the palm. Jesus God, he thought. The hand, and the index finger is missing.

The hand slapped the airplane. Dave's entire body jerked at the same time.

The plane dropped abruptly, the nose dipped, and it pitched from side to side as though it were a toy shaken by a dog. Finally, it straightened, and stabilized, though flying in the wrong direction.

The hand hit the plane again. It went down.

Dave's scream tore tiny, black tracks through his head. It was almost as loud as the plane's engines as they roared above him, toward the four-lane approach to the airport.

He knew, as he watched the fireball and smoke, that Suzy and Chris were at the center of the explosion. That they died so quickly they had no time to realize what was happening.

As in his dreams, laughter echoed down from the clouds, but this time he heard it clearly. The laughter of a young woman, ringing like bells around him, cutting through him, unblocked by phantom hands over ethereal ears. He ran screaming toward the fire, though he knew he had been condemned to hell and this was just a memory. In the part of him that remained rational, he wondered if he was doomed to replay this scene for all eternity.

The laughter changed. It became deeper, and acquired a resonant, echoing tone that chilled him. Then it was nothing like a young woman's laugh, only the evil chuckle of something malevolent and powerful.

The fire died, and the light dimmed around Dave. The hand dipped lower and seemed to be reaching for him. As it threatened to squash him like an insect, he expected to feel the crushing pressure of the descending hand, but it only enclosed him in a dim cloud.

He was back where he started. Back in the dark hell. Crashing explosions in the distance that seemed to erase the universe for a second.

But he wasn't alone.

Something moved in the dark fog, stalking him. Closer.

He could see the unidentifiable shape, hunched over like a monkey trying to walk upright, grunting as no man or animal ever had. Dave tried to back away, but his feet did not move, held frozen by some supernatural power. The creature shuffled closer.

Dave put his hands up, trying to ward off an attack, but the shape reached out a clawed hand and knocked his left hand away. He felt blood ooze from a cut on his left index finger, suddenly cold to the bone.

Then it exploded.

No sound or flash of light, but his flesh was seared and burned and mangled and violated by explosion he couldn't see or hear.

Dave tried to back away again, with the same success, at the same time shaking his finger violently, as though attempting to fling the pain away.

He was only dully aware of the rest of his body, but the existence of that finger was vivid and excruciating.

He could hear movement in the cloud. The thing still trying to find him, so the cut must have been a fluke.

The pressure came suddenly, and for a second he felt as though he knew what it was like for a piece of steel attracted to a magnet. Whatever force holding his feet released, and he was violently jerked free, drawn through the clinging fog. From a dark region of the cloud, the clawed hand reached for him again and missed, and he thought he heard a howl of frustration. The hunched shape jerked violently at the moment he passed, and he had the impression it followed him through the dark tunnel rushing past on all sides. Somewhere along the way, though, it disappeared.

The brilliant light was almost as shocking as the total darkness had been.

He thought for a moment that he had been sent to a different part of Hell where the light would blind and cook the tormented souls just as the darkness had terrified and attacked. After a few seconds, his eyes adjusted and he realized he was sprawled on a slab of concrete. He looked up.

A large white pigeon feather floated above his head.

He was back, and on the sidewalk beneath the spot where he slipped off the ledge.

Had he actually been able to pull himself back in the window, then take the elevator down to the street? Had he dreamed the whole experience?

He might have convinced himself except that he looked at his left index finger and knew it was no hallucination.

The tip of the finger was brown and shriveled, and the leather like surface of the skin seemed to pulsate with a malevolent life of its own.

As he watched, the corrupt area oozed across his finger like a creeping amoeba.

He pointed the finger like an accusing arrow at the sky, as he quickly, desperately scanned the street. He stood and staggered toward the deli on the corner.

He slammed open the door, and a man behind the counter weighing bologna looked up in surprise. An old woman carrying a large purse clutched it to her and backed away when she saw his face. Dave circled around the meat case and back to where the clerk had stopped slicing and was now watching him in alarm.

"Hey," he started, then stopped. Something scared and desperate in Dave's eyes made him pause. "Hey, man, are you okay?" The clerk was young and skinny, and not inclined to argue with a six foot, two hundred and sixty pound man. "You need help, or something?"

Dave glanced around the shop. There had to be something he

could use. A cleaver or long butcher knife - anything.

Then he saw it.

He recognized the machine from an article he did on supermarket safety for a national grocer's magazine. The "Chicken Slicer from Hell," or at least that was how the magazine editor had captioned the picture. Its most impressive feature was a stainless steel blade whirling at few thousand RPM, set about six inches above the surface of the table. The lower edge spun in a horizontal stainless steel rod that had a groove cut in it for the blade. The end of the rod was slightly pointed, and a hinged and slotted metal guard fell against the rod and covered the whirling edge.

Most of the time. There had been enough exceptions to justify the magazine label.

During normal operations, a worker pushed fresh chickens over the rod through the hole in the carcass where the chicken's head had been. The blade made a singing sound as it sliced parallel to the spine of the chicken. Then he pulled the chicken back and made another pass to slice down the other side of the chicken, neatly removing the backbone.

It zinged, then rang as the blade sliced through bone and gristle without slowing.

Then the worker sliced the legs away from the carcass, and the thighs and legs separated in another pass. And the spinning blade never faltered.

Dave looked around and found a spool of butcher's twine. Using his right hand and his teeth - and being careful not to touch his index finger - he tied a tight tourniquet around the base of his finger. He took a deep breath and finally turned toward the chicken slicer.

Chicken bones are hollow, he thought. Have to hit the joint.

As soon as the blade whirred up to speed, he closed his eyes for a second in silent prayer.

The woman gasped, and the clerk made a sudden grab for him as they both realized his intentions.

Too late. A quick zing, followed by a ringing sound, and the top part of his finger lay on the clean, white butcher's paper at the base of the slicer.

There was little blood.

Dave held his hand up and stared at the smooth white bone of his finger where the blade had sliced through it. The pain was sharp and almost overwhelming. He supported himself with his good hand, leaning against the counter. Small drops of blood oozed from the flesh around the bone, and he pulled the string tighter, trying to stop the agony more than the leakage. He noticed a movement on the table.

The finger twitched.

The brown area pulsated, and spread even as he stared. The flesh quivered, shriveled, and he could almost hear the bone cracking as it curled like some vile, tainted worm. The cut end of the finger closed like a tiny mouth when the brown area enclosed it, and Dave had to look away. The young man stared at the finger, unable to move, and the old woman had run out to the street seeking some refuge of her own.

The man glanced up at Dave, then back at the finger.

"Oh, man!" he said, pointing. "It's crawling away!"

On the counter, the small, brown, shriveled thing did, indeed, inch along the edge of the table. There was a roll of plastic bags beside the slicer, and Dave tore one off, each movement like razors hacking at his hand. He tore off a half dozen more and nested them, one inside the other. He used another bag, doubled and redoubled, to pick the thing up and maneuver it into position. He had trouble holding the bags with lightning bolts of pain stabbing through his forearm. It felt as though he'd cut off the entire hand, not just a finger. The young man reached to help. Their eyes met, and Dave nodded, then dropped the thing in the bags as he held them open. The man tied the end of the bags with a metal twist tie, watching Dave as though expecting the rest of him to wrinkle and turn brown. Through the milky, layered plastic, he could see the finger had sprouted thick patches of black hair.

"What is going on, man?" the clerk asked, staring at the bag in his trembling hand. His face was white. He looked scared, like an atheist who died and suddenly learned he wasn't so smart after all. His perception of reality had been severely shaken.

Dave took the bag from him. It twitched and shifted as the finger moved around inside.

"I don't know," he muttered. "I just don't know."

He had to get out. His head whirled and the hurt from his hand and finger was like a blaring, badly played trumpet. None of this could be happening. The grief over Suzy and Chris' death had finally driven him mad.

The sunshine was still bright, and the morning was still cheerful and warm when he stumbled out of the deli. A few people walked down the street, but they just stepped aside and moved around him.

Familiar, and disgustingly normal.

The jogger, the scarecrow of a man who had been below as he fell, was there, and stared at Dave for a few moments when he staggered out of the shop. He glanced at Dave's finger, dripping blood despite the tourniquet, then at the bag, and turned and started to run. Dave took a few steps, as though to follow him, then gave up. Even if his knees hadn't been weak and his head not reeling from shock, he couldn't have followed the man. He was a runner, and a fast one. Dave, these days, could barely get up to a slow trot without his chest aching and wheezing like an asthmatic.

Somehow, he knew that man had something to do with what happened.

Impossible, but so were crawling fingers.

Something had happened, and Dave had to find out what.

Dave Richards, though he hadn't eaten since that early breakfast he thought was to be his last meal, didn't crave food. For the first time in months, he hungered for something else.

He studied at his throbbing left hand in growing horror, transfixed by the horrifying, familiar shape. He had seen that mangled silhouette before. Dave dropped heavily to the sidewalk and leaned against a trash can, seeing nothing. He never heard the sirens of the ambulance someone had called.

At the airport four years ago. The black shape in the sky. His own hand.

Somehow, he had killed his family.

Chapter 9

He should have Hidden the bloody finger!

Alan ran as he hadn't run since the time he'd been caught inside a chain link fence with two junkyard Dobermans nipping at his heels.

Alan ran so fast that he played the butt trumpet as he zipped past two old ladies out for a morning walk. They said, "Oh!" and covered their mouths as if afraid to breathe.

Sorry, ladies, he thought and would have laughed wildly if he'd had the breath. Too much oat bran.

By the time he stumbled to a shaky stop about a block from his cheap hotel, Alan shivered despite having just run almost a mile at top speed. He bent, his hands on his knees and breathed deeply for a few seconds. He wasn't cold, exactly, but the fat man's accusing stare, the fear in his eyes, sent a wave of chills through his body.

He'd panicked, again. Always the same stupid thing.

He stood for a moment, and then began rapidly walking, trying to cool and calm down.

And the finger. That had to be one fast-thinking S. O. B. to see what was happening to him and do something about it. Alan wasn't sure he could cut off his own finger no matter what was eating at it, even knowing what could happen. And that poor rube didn't know.

He didn't know a damn thing!

As if I do! he thought. Even now, there were closed places in the Gap. Places he couldn't see or feel.

He couldn't even Hide things in those blank areas.

He was afraid of what might be happening in the closed places. Afraid he'd see for himself some day. He was too aware of the strange events in the eastern part of the country. Aware that the events seemed to follow him on his show route. He knew they seemed to be building in intensity, getting stronger.

It couldn't be his fault.

Alan stopped again, wiped the sweat from his eyes with his forearm, then raised his tee shirt and buried his entire head in the cloth. It didn't help. The shirt was as soaked as his face. He needed a cold drink.

There were still safe areas, though. Relatively stable spots of calm where he could store items he might need.

He stared into the distance, frowning, not looking at anything, focusing on a place unseen by anyone else on the planet. There was a faint shimmer almost lost in the sunlight, then he reached forward and, in the middle of a street far from any store or soft drink machine, he held a frigid can of diet, caffeine-free Dr. Pepper. He searched for any sign of contamination. Okay, as always. Almost instantly, moisture formed on the familiar brown, checked pattern and ran down his hand and arm as he opened it and took a deep swallow. Not many left inside. He had to make another trip to the market soon.

Lucky for Fat Boy it was only a finger, he thought finally, wiping his mouth with the back of his hand. It could just as easily have been an entire arm. Wonder if he could have chopped it off at the shoulder?

That's why Alan stayed. If Tubby had come back as a distorted parody of reality, or infected enough to change when he reappeared, Alan would have Hidden him again. Sent him back there permanently to whatever Hell he'd seen so briefly.

Alan might have Hidden him immediately if he'd seen the index finger, but the guy hadn't given him time.

He should have zapped the bag with the pulsing brown thing, but then he had felt the man's gaze on him and he ran without thinking.

Same old stuff, he thought. Panic under pressure.

A sudden burning seared the back of his neck and he whirled around, but there was nothing there. He rubbed the base of his skull, staring at a nearby clump of bushes. Nothing. The burning faded, but it had been very real. He searched the street, wondering what would happen next.

Something drew his gaze to the tower on the mountain.

It should have been almost invisible on the distant crest in the daytime, a tiny needle-shaped line. But the tip seemed to glow and pulsate, with the sound of limitless energy crackling around glass tubes and transformers. Flickers of light twirled and jumped between the ground and tower.

Probably some kind of malfunction. And the sound had to be in his head. It was too far away for him to hear anything. He rubbed his temples.

He had the feeling he and the man would meet again. The fat man wouldn't let it alone. He didn't look like someone who would be happy just to be alive. He looked like someone who had to have the truth.

And Alan hated the truth. His life had nothing to do with the truth, and he liked it that way. His business and his pleasure were deception and no fat man and a corrupt finger would change that.

He swallowed again, stopped for a second and turned to the south. Something was there, a presence that he could somehow sense. It was as though his power had a mind of its own. Things were coming and going from the Gap as if it were a damn train station.

He remembered one face well even after a decade, and shook his head to make the smiling, cherub image disappear from his head.

Can't Hide that, can you, Bigshot? he thought to himself. Proud of that little move? That'll teach him to bump into you! After a few years, though, Alan had become convinced that guy hadn't pushed him on purpose. He'd been a real dummy, with not enough sense to do something stupid. Probably one of the other kids had tripped him, knocking him into Alan.

And Alan Hid him.

I didn't know! The thought was another stab in his head. He rubbed the cold can against his forehead, walking down the sidewalk to cool his heated body and still the voices in his head. I didn't know then what would happen, he told himself.

Sure that's a great excuse for the first time, but how about all the others?

Panic under pressure, he thought. Off the stage, in the real world, he could never handle pressure very well, a trait that contributed to his legal problems.

The newest pressure was that things returned and vanished at random in a universe that he had previously considered if not sane, then at least consistent, and Alan had no idea how. He stared at the can, thinking that the unexplained movements were just an omen. A tiny warning of things to come.

Alan drained the Dr. Pepper and tossed the container into the air. It vanished in mid spin. Now, the metal can was Hidden, too, he thought. At least from his view and that was good enough. If he could only do that with all his problems.

Anguished pain stabbed through his head, and an oppressive feeling of doom rolled over him.

Through slitted, teary eyes he saw a flash of light and a glowing corona around the distant metal tower. Brilliant sparks danced around the structure and to the earth.

Gotta match, buddy?

Yeah. My ass and your face.

Your mouth and a sewer pipe.

My head and a nightmarish, dark place a lot like hell.

The pain lanced again. And that he couldn't Hide.

Chapter 10

She was a dreamboat.

For a corpse lying on the pitcher's mound, that is.

"Hey, Jerry," Evan yelled when he put down the cellular phone. "When were you born?"

Jerry stared at the nude body, reluctant to tear his eyes away from the smooth flesh, the rounded breasts, the patch of skin that a bathing suit once covered, just a shade lighter than the bright hue of the rest of her body, and the curly blonde hair on miscolored skin. An unusual contrast.

"Dr. Reese, let's maintain some professional decorum here," Evan told him. "She's dead, after all. Well dead."

"Good grief, I know that," Jerry answered, standing and walking away, his eyes still on the corpse. "But she looks so lifelike, almost as if she could get up and dance around the baseball field. If she wasn't such a bright blue. She looks like a bald Muppet."

"Any idea what caused the color?"

"Not any pigment or tint that I could tell," Jerry said. "And I couldn't rub it off."

"I know. I saw you trying."

Jerry's face reddened. Almost as deep a shade as the corpse's flag blue skin.

"Evan," he said, obviously trying to change the subject. "Why is an APE team investigating a murder? Even one where the victim drops out of nowhere and is the color of a grape Popsicle?"

"Well, two reasons. First, we were in the area, anyway." Jerry nodded. He was still bothered by that ancient Volkswagen. "Second, the governor just didn't expect a lovely, nude, blue corpse to drop out of the sky and land on him as he tossing out the team's first ball of the season. He still has a few friends in Washington who requested our help."

"How's he doing, by the way?" Jerry asked.

"Still flustered, I heard, but otherwise unhurt." Dr. Evan Hill shook his head and glanced at the clipboard in his hand. "Too bad the first thing he grabbed to pull her off was a big handful of left teat. The press loves that photograph."

"So do the opposition critics."

"Back to my question," Evan said. "You were born in mid-October. What year was that?"

"In nineteen - wait a minute!" Jerry stopped and looked determined. "I ain't saying."

"That's okay, I've seen your file. You are a few tears short of forty, right?"

"I ain't saying." Jerry crossed his arms stubbornly. "What's it to you?"

"The report just came back on Miss Coldbody, here. Central had to search the inactive files before they found her prints."

"So?" Jerry said. APE had access to all closed and open police and interagency files. It would have been more unusual if they hadn't found her fingerprints. "What's the scoop?"

"Miss Sylvia Barry, twenty-three at the time of her disappearance. A legal secretary with a Washington lawyer at the time. No family. No steady boyfriends, or even close friends. According to the file, her neighbors said she went to the supermarket every Thursday. One Thursday she didn't come back."

"I repeat, so?" Jerry looked back at the corpse. One arm was across her forehead, as if she were shielding her eyes from the afternoon sun. He glanced at the ever-present circle of soldiers. Still in their white, self-contained suits.

"How long she been dead?" Evan asked. Evan knew Jerry had taken enough forensic medicine to make a reasonable guess.

"As far as I can tell, about ten minutes," Jerry answered. "I can't believe she's been here a couple of hours. No rigor mortis, no blood pooled in her back, skin still flexible and resilient. Her eyes are firm, her abdomen is neither distended nor sunken. Heck, her lips are still moist, Evan. If not for the skin and the lack of heartbeat, I wouldn't say she was dead at all."

"Don't get your hopes up. How old does she look to you?"

"I thought you said twenty-three. That looks about right."

"Yep. To me, too. But Miss Barry vanished seventeen years ago," Evan said. "She will be forty next November. She was born about two weeks after you, as it happens."

Jerry turned slowly and looked at the corpse. "The heck, you say," he finally muttered after a few seconds.

"Yep," Evan told him. "Well preserved forty, don't you think?"

"I do think," Jerry answered. "Wouldn't you want to look that good on your fortieth birthday, Evan?"

Evan looked at him. "Not if it meant I had assumed the ambient air temperature."

"Yeah, there is that." He shook his head. "What do we do with her now?"

"Put her in the warehouse, I guess," Evan answered. "With the Volkswagen and the other . . . things. We have the refrigerated section finished now. She'll keep."

Jerry looked at the circle around them, and moved closer to Evan. He spoke softly enough that the soldiers couldn't hear him.

"What's going on, Evan?" he asked, pretending to look at the clipboard. "This is the tenth weird thing we've investigated in three days. It hasn't been this bad in years. And these jokers have been with us every time. They weren't around when we dealt with the mutant moose scare up in Maine."

Evan glanced over at him without moving his head, then stole a look at the soldiers. None of them had moved.

"We're not the only APE team on this, either," Evan told him. "Two of the permanent and three or four temporary squads are in the region, looking at these anomalous events. The warehouse is filling up with things like the VW and pieces of metal trash they don't recognize and body parts they can't identify, either."

"We've investigated this stuff for years. Why the big uproar now?"

"Who the hell knows?" Evan answered. "But the effect seems to be focusing, and accelerating."

"Focusing?" Jerry asked. "Then they have a center for the effect?" Until now, the "Anomalous Phenomenon" had shown no pattern and occurred just frequently enough to keep one or two APE teams busy.

"Maybe," Evan said. He moved his head slightly and glanced around. Jerry followed his eyes. A large man with sergeant's stripes on his sleeve watched them closely. Sergeant Akers stirred and shifted from foot to foot as though he were anxious to get to the john. The last few days, the Sergeant seemed to make it his purpose in life to shadow them. Especially Evan. "Somewhere in southwest Virginia."

"A problem, gentlemen?" the sergeant asked, his voice tinny and distant through the suit's diaphragm. Combined with the unearthly quality of his voice, and the containment suit, and the very shiny, very dangerous looking M-16 in his hands, he seemed to be some sort of creature from another planet. The blue of the barrel gleamed in the afternoon sun like the alien metal of some futuristic ray gun.

"Of course not, Sergeant Akers," Evan said. Light sparkled off the beads of sweat on his forehead. "Trying to reach some conclusion concerning the corpse."

"Of course, Sir," the sergeant said. The speech diaphragm amplified every breath, making him sound like Keir Dullea at the end of 2001. Or maybe Darth Vader in dress whites. "If you've finished your examination, I'll have my men pack the subject for transportation."

"Go ahead, Sergeant," Evan told him. Akers saluted and began barking orders at his men.

"You scared of him?" Jerry asked.

Evan whirled on him. "You damn dirty right, I'm scared of him." He wiped the sleeve of his lab coat across his forehead and it came away wet. "Never mind. Maybe the guy deserved to die. Maybe the sergeant was right."

"What do you mean?" Jerry asked. "What are you talking about?"

"Later," Evan said, glancing around again. "Tell you later. Lot of damn stuff I have to tell you later."

The soldiers bundled the body into a black plastic bag, zippered it, then lifted it into the back of a large truck. Jerry watched as they piled into the back, their eyes and guns on the bag as if they expected the corpse inside to rip it open and jump out, screaming.

Maybe they did.

The sergeant turned and spoke to them pleasantly as the truck pulled away.

"Do you have another assignment, gentlemen?" he asked as though he didn't already know the answer.

"Fairfax, Virginia," Evan answered, consulting the clipboard. "Something about giant pods in someone's basement."

"I'll ride with you," the sergeant said, smiling. "These men will escort the subject to the warehouse, and a new contingent will meet us at the next site."

"Certainly, Sergeant," Evan said just as pleasantly.

Inside the car, Jerry noticed Evan's hands shook just the least bit as he turned the key and held the wheel for a second. The Sergeant removed his helmet, climbed into the back of the nondescript, government-issue sedan and placed the weapon across his lap. He smiled when Jerry looked at him and Jerry smiled back. Without the helmet, he seemed nice enough.

Evan gripped the wheel in white-knuckled fear, though, and he usually had more information about what was really happening.

Jerry couldn't decide whether it was better being ignorant and a little anxious, or knowledgeable and so scared that your hands shook when you reached for the turn signal.

They drove in a tense, strained silence toward Fairfax, Virginia.

Chapter 11

Sally Edelman stood in the yard. She tossed a baseball up into the air and caught it with the big mitt on her left hand as Sam drove up. He frowned slightly, remembering that when he was a kid, little girls never had much to do with baseballs and mitts, or anything else not strictly ladylike. Times had changed, sometimes for the worse, and in this case he hadn't quite made up his mind, yet. In his own family, Jeannie was a better player than Scott would ever be.

He pulled up beside the Edelmans' Jeep and leaned out the window to wave at Sally. Jeannie was nowhere in sight, but maybe she had gone inside to the bathroom. The sweat in the small of his back turned as cold as creek water, and he had to force a smile when Sally ran to the truck.

"Hi, Mr. Baker," she said, tossing back red curls that would someday soon throw half the teen-age boys in Clarion into adolescent shock. "You looking for Jeannie?"

"Hi, Sally," he told her. Jeannie was inside. She had to be inside. "Sure am. Thought you and her might like to head over to the department store while I was at the hardware."

"Gee, that'd be nice, Mr. Baker," Sally said. "But you just missed Jeannie. She left about fifteen minutes ago. I'm surprised you didn't see her on the road. She was walking real slow, it being so hot and all."

The dread emptied his stomach and filled the area around his heart, and Sam suddenly found it hard to breath.

"She's gone?" he asked, frowning.

Sally looked at him oddly for a moment, sensing the anxiety as only a child could.

"Yeah," she said. "If you didn't see her, maybe she stopped at the

Wilson's spring to get a drink of water. That's just off the road, you know. I always stop there myself." She sounded a little doubtful, as though she couldn't believe she was trying to reassure an adult.

"Sure," Sam told her. "Or maybe she took a shortcut through the pasture and I missed her." But he didn't think so, and he knew by looking at Sally that she didn't think so, either.

"Listen, Sally," he told her. "I'll see if I can pick her up before she gets to the house. Meantime, you go and ask your mom about going to town with us, and I'll stop up on the way back. How about it?"

"Sure, Mr. Baker," she answered, and started back to her house. Halfway there she paused and looked back at him. "You'll find her on the road home, Mr. Baker. I'm sure." But she didn't sound so sure.

As he turned the truck and bounced down the drive, throwing up a cloud of dust that drifted across the Edelman's yard, Sam was sure.

He wouldn't find Jeannie walking on the dirt road.

She hadn't stopped off at Wilson's spring to get a dipper of water.

She hadn't taken a shortcut through the pasture to the house.

Sam remembered the dusty billows behind John Hill's Chevy and the sheen of sweat on the fat man's face and how his eyes seemed to glitter in the bright light.

He was sure John had Jeannie.

He barely paused at the road, and the truck fishtailed as he turned left, back the way he'd come. The same direction John Hill had taken.

Holding the wheel with his left hand, Sam reached under the seat and grasped the handle of the Taurus .357 magnum he kept there. He laid it on the seat beside him, took a flat key from his pocket and fiddled with the trigger lock until he worked it loose. Not easy to do while bouncing down a dirt road ten miles an hour faster than he should. He slowed enough to flip the cylinder sideways, then back into place. Full load, and a couple of speed loaders in the glove compartment. Six shots to slowly remove pieces of Big John. Then he would reload and remove six more pieces. Then, if he had touched Jeannie, Sam Baker would put those strong, work scarred farmer's hands around John's thick neck and slowly strangle the sick, disgusting life out of him.

He slowed at Wilson's spring and peered through the brush off to the left. There was no one at the concrete box, and the dipper hung dry and shiny on the tree beside it. Nothing moved except leaves in a sparse wind, and a swirl of dust from the dirt road. He punched the accelerator and sped by his own driveway a minute or two later. Just past it, he saw Jenny's red windbreaker by the road. He didn't stop.

Oh, God! Let her be okay, he thought, wiping his eyes on the back of his rough hand as he skidded in the gravel around a sharp curve. Just let her be okay.

Chapter 12

Big John Hill locked Jeannie in an area that had once housed jugs of 'shine, peering at her through the barred window on the door. She stirred again, her eyes blinking as she opened them. She focused, then saw him at the door and screamed. John jumped and looked around the room guiltily, for a second wondering whether anyone had heard her.

But that was impossible.

The underground room was a secret, built by his granddaddy to hide the still, and turned into a concrete lined, steel reinforced bomb shelter by his daddy during the early sixties. John had added his own refinements. Like the barred room where Jeannie screamed.

There was only one way in: the door and stairs he had come down. Of course there was the big air duct, which originally doubled as an emergency exit. It came out in the woods a few hundred yards from the house, but John could never have gotten through the vent. He actually tried it once when he was eleven, and even then it was a tight fit and he thought he'd have to spend eternity at the sharp turn near the end. He had finally squeezed out with a small loss of skin on his belly and back, and he swore to never go in there again. He had eventually welded heavy steel bars into a grid over the end, above the layer of screen wire meant to keep out small animals and snakes.

Jeannie's screams were louder. Loud enough to make his ears hurt.

John walked slowly back to the door and peered in. She sat on the small cot, wiping her face with the sheet. Still screaming, sobbing, yelling for her daddy.

"Jeannie," he whispered. "Quiet, Jeannie. Just calm down for a minute. We'll talk." She screamed louder.

John glanced around the room again, wondering why he bothered. No one could get in, or hear her. Still he felt as though he were strolling through town with his fly open and nobody would tell him. Though he'd built the room years ago, he'd never brought anyone down and he had the feeling there was some flaw in his plan.

Then he realized what it was. The vent.

Six feet above the floor, just below his eye level, the opening was a black, empty hole. Through the wire grid, the squares of darkness were like blocks of night.

Sound carried well in the quiet hills of Clarion. And sound would echo through that metal tunnel like it was a custom made amplifier. People for miles around could probably hear Jeannie shrieking.

"Oh, Jesus!" John said aloud, then looked around the room, searching for something to block the vent, or quiet Jeannie. Nothing.

"Oh, Jesus!" he said again, and the screams went on and on and on.

Ray Willard was a hard man. From one of the toughest, drug-ravaged neighborhoods of New York City, he had emerged as one of the smartest, strongest small-time dealers in the city. When his superiors offered him a promotion, leaving behind the dirty day-to-day work of dealing with the crazy crack users - the most dangerous link in the business, no matter what anyone said - he jumped at the chance. Even when it meant he had to be an enforcer, collecting from dealers he had worked beside the week before, sometimes killing those who didn't pay up. And too many of them didn't pay. They made the mistake of using the same drugs they sold, and soon they were using more than they were selling, and then they owed the distributors a lot of money.

Those were the kind of scumbags Ray eliminated. Even when they got on their knees and, with a nine-millimeter Uzi pressed against their temples, promised to lick the crap off Ray's leather shoes if he'd give them one more chance.

But Ray was like the guy who came to shut off the electricity if you didn't pay the bill. He couldn't take money for the bill, or wait for you to go down and pay it. That guy's job was to shut down the electricity, even if you lost a freezer full of food or you were having a party or your frail old granny was on an iron lung and would die without the power.

Sure, Ray could take payment, but none of them ever had money. They wanted him to give them more time, or they offered to trade a blow job or their sisters or their old ladies for just a few more days.

Ray's orders were to eliminate scumbags. He liked that. And he never ran out of work.

Eventually, he moved up to taking delivery of tightly wrapped bundles from South America at rural farms in Virginia or North Carolina or Kentucky or Tennessee. Unlike a lot of his associates from the Northern states, Ray loved the outdoors and the lack of pollution and the deer that sometimes wandered across the airfield in the early morning while he waited for a plane. A couple of times, Ray had stopped a new guy from firing at the deer. He probably couldn't have hit one with a hand gun at that distance, but Ray took no chances.

Ray was a hard man, but he enjoyed the fresh air and a clear sunrise over misty mountains and the friendly people and the way kids could play without worrying about a gun battle on the corner.

He always thought that he'd probably move to Clarion County and buy a huge farm and graze cattle when he retired. All he had to do was avoid accidents and his own commodity.

The latest shipment had just landed with two men and a few hundred pounds of stuff on board. He, Steve Ashton, and the two from the plane were unloading the bales when he heard the scream. He stood, puzzled, his hand automatically dropping to his gun. It sounded like a girl screaming in the woods near the airstrip.

What the hell? he thought and looked at the other three men. They had all pulled their weapons. Ray motioned for them and ran toward the source of the screams. Her voice sounded very young. His dark, scarred face hardened. Nobody better be hurting her, he thought. Or somebody's going to be hurting for sure.

"Steve!" he shouted as they ran. "That's a little girl screaming. Like somebody's killing her."

"You think that stuff doesn't kill little girls?" Steve asked him, nodding back toward the plane.

"Not where I can hear them, it doesn't," Ray said.

They ran to the edge of the strip, hesitated, then broke through the thick brush underneath the trees. Ray smelled something rotten and slid sideways, away from the mound of filth and garbage nearby. That lowbrow redneck Hill was too lazy to take his own crud a half mile down the road to the dumpster.

The sound seemed to be coming from the ground near a big oak, and they crept over to it until they could see the vent that curved out of the ground and ended in a metal framework of steel rods. Ray peered down into the sheet metal tube and saw that the curve continued back to the main house. The screams still echoed through the hollow, and the man who had scattered the brains of more than a dozen scumbags looked sick.

"Back to the house," he told the other three men. "Hill must have somebody down there." He broke back through the brush and ran to the house with the others close behind. "I told the guys in New York that fat hillbilly was bad news. They picked him up for molesting a little girl once, but he got off." He glanced at the others then back before he lost his footing in the grass with his slick shoes. "I'll be damned if he gets off this time. God damned kid molester."

He held the gun ready as he approached the house and the other men followed closely behind him.

It waited.

Maybe it had waited for a million years, but when the dark faded to be replaced by light and warmth and growing things, it knew the wait was almost over. Its master had promised the end was near.

Behind a tree near the vent, something that might have been human a few centuries ago watched with narrowed, dark eyes showing a faint spark of red at the center as the four men left, then stalked to where the screams echoed out of the hard, shiny tube. It approached the vent slowly, cautiously, and touched the iron bars with a large, curved claw.

The screams didn't stop, and it growled deep in its chest. For just a moment, words were distinguishable in the screams.

"Help me, please. Anyone. Please help me."

And the screams began again.

It didn't matter whether the creature understood the words. It understood the pain behind them. The pain so much like what it had felt while trapped in an outcropping of madness for an eternity. What it experienced when some mix of forces in that place momentarily formed a mirror-like surface that reflected its image. It roared loudly, lifting a dark, knotted face to the sky and screaming until the two tortured voices merged into a kind of anguished duet.

Then it ripped the steel bars from the opening, and tore through the flimsy wire screen. It scrabbled into the dark opening, seeking the source of the pain, determined to stop it.

It roared again in the ductwork and the metal reverberated with the power of its wail.

Chapter 13

John jerked his head around at the sound of the thunderous baying in the duct so quickly he felt as though he had pulled his neck out of whack. But he forgot that minor pain quickly when he heard the savage, animalistic shriek echoing through the metal pipe.

What the Sweet Jesus was that? he thought, backing away from the vent until he pressed against the concrete wall opposite. The howl faded, and he slowly approached the grid over the pipe, suddenly aware that he had forgotten to bring the shotgun down with him. He turned, looked at the steps, then back at the vent. From inside, he heard the screech of torn metal, and the clicking sound of claws against metal. Something panted and moved in the vent, advancing toward the underground room. And Big John Hill.

"Oh, Jesus!" he said out loud, and started up the steps. He had to get the shotgun. Another roar growled behind him.

John took the steps two at a time, not easy for a man his size, pushed the door open, and almost fell backward down into the bomb shelter. Four men with automatic weapons stood there, and the barrels of their guns instantly centered on his chest.

"Okay, Hill," the big black man in charge said. John knew Ray Willard, and that he was very dangerous. "What the hell is going on here?" Ashton, and the two he didn't know, looked ready to take his head off.

John stumbled, and fresh sweat broke out on his forehead. "W-what's the matter, Mr. Willard?" he stammered. Ray Willard was the first black man he'd ever called "Mr." each and every time he saw him.

"No crap, Hill," he said, his voice low and very dangerous. "Where's the kid?"

John glanced at the steps involuntarily, and Ray pushed him ahead of him, down the stairs.

"Let's go, scumbag," the black man said. "I think you've made a big, big mistake." John saw the others nod behind Ray, and the dark determination in their eyes when they looked at him.

Just like in the Somerset jail.

He stumbled back down the steps and stood beside the still. Ray backed across the room, beneath the vent, and motioned the others toward the door. Jeannie must have heard them coming down. She stopped screaming. John listened carefully and he could still hear a scratching inside the pipe, just behind Ray's head. The others looked inside the room with Jeannie and examined the lock.

"Hey, calm down, honey," one of them said through the bars. "That fat son . . ., that fat guy isn't going to touch you. We'll get you out in a minute."

The uneven clicking was closer, and the others were too busy thinking of ways to kill John to notice.

"My daddy," Jeannie said. "I want my daddy."

"Sure, honey," the guy said. John didn't recognize him. He must have come in on the plane. "We'll get you out and call your old man in a minute. Are you okay? Did he hurt you?" When he asked this question, he turned to stare at John and raised his gun, as if the wrong answer would trigger a blast of gunfire into John's stomach.

"My head hurts," she sobbed. "But he just brought me down and locked me in here. I'm scared."

Just inside the grill, now, John thought. He imagined he could see a dark shape crouching there.

"No need to be scared, honey," Ray called from across the room. "This scumbag isn't going to hurt anyone. Ever again." He watched John and muttered, "Bastard!"

As if the word were a signal, the metal cover on the vent burst into the room and slammed into the back of Ray's skull. The guy who had been staring at John looked at the opening and raised his gun, but it seemed to be moving in slow motion, not nearly fast enough to fix on the dark blur exploding from the vent pipe. The shape landed beside Ray and lifted him over its head as if he were a cardboard cut-out and tossed him at the other three. A burst of automatic fire stitched a red track through Ray Willard and his dreams of retirement on a Clarion County farm died with him.

Ray's body bowled over the other three men, streams of red

pumping onto them from the twitching body.

"Blood! Oh, God, blood!" one of them said, and another screamed for somebody to get the body off him.

For a few extended moments, John stood there, glancing back and forth between the bent shape and the men near the barred door.

Inside, Jeannie screamed again.

The thing sprang into blurred action, leaping across the room and landing on Ray's body. It peered down at the other men.

Almost casually, it reached down into the pile of writhing flesh, and grabbed a hand holding an Uzi and jerked. It tossed the arm across the room where it quivered for a moment. More blood pooled on the concrete floor and ran to a drain near the center of the room.

The screaming stopped. John saw that the dead man was Steve Ashton.

The creature reached in again and grabbed a face. It tossed it aside and the man didn't even have a chance to cry out.

"Sweet Jesus," John said very quietly. He inched to the steps. Maybe he could trap it down here long enough to get the shotgun.

The last man, the one who had been reassuring Jeannie, managed to get off a three round burst before the thing swiped at the gun and removed it. Along with the man's hand. The man wriggled from beneath the others and moved against the door to Jeannie's room, holding his wrist and trying to stop the blood spurting over the other bodies like dark chocolate on a mound of ice cream.

The thing growled and threw the man across the room where he slammed into concrete wall and made large red puddles on the cold floor.

Big John made a small yellow puddle on the floor, and couldn't move. The thing could have come over and taken a few snack-sized bites out of his face, and he couldn't have moved.

But it ignored him and walked to the door, listening to Jeannie sobbing. It reared up on its back legs, and stood on dark hoofed knots to peer through the bars. After a second, it grunted in disgust and reached up and pulled the door off its hinges. The heavy duty layered lock, guaranteed to withstand a high powered bullet through the center, exploded into a half dozen pieces. Through the door, John could see Jeannie cowering on the cot.

The thing grunted and walked toward her.

Still frozen, John watched with a fascinated horror as it raised a massive clawed fist above its head, then brought it down and gently touched Jeannie on the cheek. She looked momentarily shocked, then sighed deeply and fainted.

It caught her and laid her on the bed.

Then turned and looked at John.

Its mouth was half open, showing teeth like ivory knives. As though the grin was a personal promise to John.

Suddenly, he could move again.

John touched the hand railings and backed up the steps. The dark creature ambled back to the door and stood there for a second, peering into the room at the piles of flesh and pools of blood. It leapt into the room, and for a few seconds, seemed to go completely wild, shredding and tearing flesh and crushing bone until nothing was left but scattered pieces of the bodies.

A step creaked under his foot, and the thing twisted a snarling face toward him.

John turned and vaulted up the steps again with the sound of the thing behind him, scratching at the concrete at the bottom of the stairs. He felt the steps shake beneath his feet and heard the sound of claws on wood. It was coming after him. He kicked open the hidden door and stumbled into his living room, half way to the shotgun before the thing clamped a clawed fist like a steel trap on his ankle. John went down on his stomach, unable to breath for a moment as the air was forced from his lungs.

His leg was on fire. It felt as though it peeled a hot, burning strip of flesh from his calf, but when he looked over his shoulder, there was only a long, shallow scratch on his leg that the thing studied for a moment.

It carefully extended a claw and pressed it an inch or two into his flesh, as if it was a needle injecting a drug.

"Oh, sweet Jesus!" he wheezed, and it grinned the stiletto grin. A mouth full of sharp knives.

John kicked at the thing, but it just grabbed the other foot and pulled him off the floor as though he weighed a pound and a half instead of two eighty. It was too short to lift him completely, so he lay with his head and shoulders still on the floor. It bent over and John could feel the hot mustiness of its breath on his face.

Upside down, John could see it was hairy in patches, gnarled like an old tree root and darker than Ray Willard had been. Its skin had the weathered and cracked texture of old leather shoes. Brown and tough. And it wore tattered cloth, the remnants of some sort of clothing.

Sometime or another, this thing must have been a man. John shuddered.

Its face was only a half inch from his and it growled at him. Its breath was a draft from a dank hole where sick animals had fallen to die.

Big John looked into the thing's eyes, and time froze.

Great-Granddaddy had been a dowser who found water for half of Clarion County with nothing more than a willow branch and his talented hands. The Ranch had been mostly paid for by Great-Granddaddy's dowsing.

Granny Hill did witch work: love spells, healing, cursing the devil out of a field of corn, or some poor unfortunate's black heart.

His mama had Feelings that were never wrong. The day his daddy disappeared into the cold, deep water of Clarion Lake, his mama had said that he was tangled in the trunk of an ancient oak buried at the very bottom of the lake formed when the dam was built. Three hundred feet down and in the center of that tree he would remain, the fishes feeding on his ample bulk for weeks, maybe months. Mama said he would never come up from there, and he never did. She wasn't very upset about it.

And Big John, when he didn't let the Urge overwhelm him, had an almost unnatural cunning that had enabled him to satisfy his sick cravings without detection for more than ten years.

He knew when the sheriff was out his way. When some little girl's daddy was within earshot. How long he had before somebody wandered by and caught him.

John thought of what his daddy had told him. "Dead meat'll bring the buzzards, Johnny."

Now John was linked, eye to eye and mind to mind, with a creature who had escaped from a timeless place that he knew had to be Hell.

Nothing could be worse than that dark, dead place.

John saw before, when the thing was still human. He saw it sent to that place, and the touch that spread the corruption over its body, twisting muscle and bone until it was a distorted parody of a human being.

He saw the return and felt the fear and hate and anger and frustration.

And he saw what the thing itself had never seen. John saw the shadow land where the presence, Karick, who ruled that place lived. He felt the cold thoughts of welcome, the promises of power and wealth.

He saw a succession of young girls, all of them familiar.

"Anytime you want," the voice rumbled. "All you want."

Laughter, as from a joke only Karick appreciated, echoed through his mind, almost dancing. John's staring, unseeing eyes didn't blink.

He drifted, and then saw an explosion of dark light, and Big John Hill knew it was filled with all the power of a nuclear explosion. Karick cradled it in its hand and offered it to him, then pulled it back and pointed. John looked and saw the tower to the north, standing astride the place between worlds. That's where he had to go to receive Karick's gift.

The gift of power.

With power and money, he could do anything he wanted. With anyone he wanted. No one could stop him.

"No one." The words came from all around, wrapping him in a blanket of darkness, filling him with the power it had. John felt something stir inside him. Something strong and powerful.

The wound on his leg burned and throbbed.

The thing holding his ankle dropped him and staggered back. For a few seconds, John lay there stunned. And surprised it didn't attack him immediately.

But its fists went to its forehead and pounded against the dark flesh. John realized it must have felt what was in his head.

Despite the horrors in the thing's mind, John had the impression that it had gotten the worst of the exchange.

He struggled to his feet, and stumbled out the door with the thing still leaning against the wall. Too late he remembered he should have gotten the shotgun, but he didn't go back inside. It might recover any second.

Outside, he heard the distant whine of an engine pushed to its limit and beyond. Sam Baker. Coming after him.

Sweet Jesus, he thought, looking around for a place to hide. He found it down at the barn nearest the house and ran for the grain bin there, a large metal cylinder that resembled a spaceship. He found an old ax handle and struggled inside, where he threaded the handle through the U-shaped metal latches. The door was secure. No one could get in.

He hoped to God no one could get in.

Sam Baker's truck roared closer.

Its feeble mind couldn't sort the flood of impressions, the flashes of desperate longing and perverse lust from both Hill and Karick, and its brain shut down. When it could see again, the fat man was gone, and the girl cried quietly in the basement. It sniffed, catching the scent of fear and excitement. It could find the fat man.

But in the distance, its keen ears picked up the sound of an engine screaming. Almost as if the machine was in pain, too. It glanced back at the door, listening to the sobbing sounds from the girl at the bottom of the steps and whuffed in sympathy.

Then it flexed its claws and stared through the window, outside the house. Something dangerous was coming.

It growled, low and threatening.

Sam Baker ordered himself not to cry. He didn't have time to cry. Crying would blur his vision and slow him down and make him miss when he aimed at Hill's perverted heart.

He slid sideways into Hill's drive and missed most of the pot holes in the road, including one big enough to break even the truck's suspension. He skidded to a stop behind the Chevy, the rear end of his truck barely kissing the car's bumper as it slid in a neat one-eighty.

In the rear view mirror, he saw the darting movement of something dark behind the truck.

He grabbed the Taurus, and rolled out onto the driveway, bringing the hand gun into firing position. Sam was no expert, but he could hit almost anything within ten or fifteen yards with the six inch barrel.

A black, distorted thing stood at the edge of the house and it growled at him. What in God's name was it?

Sam held the gun steady, his eyes unobscured. The creature looked as though it wore bloody red socks, cut in uneven tatters around its ankles. It snarled again and took a step in his direction.

The Taurus exploded.

The sound of the .357 cartridge almost deafened Sam. The dark crater in the thing's chest didn't spray blood or mangled flesh. It looked surprised, and howled in pain. It touched the wound and its paw disappeared up to the elbow. The other paw followed. Like a drain sucking down a tub full of water, the creature disappeared into the hole left by the gunshot. Until there was nothing but a black swirl that vanished like a patch of fog in the morning sun.

Sam was alone when he saw the thing's bloody red footprints leading back into the house.

"Oh, please, God!" he prayed, still holding the gun ready.

Inside, he saw the wall opened into a stairwell. A red path of clawed footprints led through the opening and down the steps.

He sighed deeply when he realized Jeannie wasn't in the living room.

He eased to the open door and down the steps. On the floor, he saw more blood. And bodies. As he approached the bottom, he found the tattered mixture of flesh and blood. A hot, thick metallic smell filled the room, reminding him of the slaughter house in Clarion on a busy Friday afternoon. Big John could be in that mess somewhere. The mound of flesh contained enough sheer bulk for three or four people, but nothing recognizable. Sam knew the police would have to identify those bodies using dental records, but he wasn't sure John ever went to the dentist.

He thanked God he saw nothing that looked like his little girl.

A step squeaked just before he stepped onto the concrete, and someone screamed from somewhere down there.

"No!" came the voice, and Sam's heart missed a beat.

"Jeannie!" he yelled. "Is that you?"

The scream stopped.

"Daddy?" she said quietly. The more loudly, "Daddy! I'm down here! Daddy, help me, please! Get me out!" Sam jumped down the remaining steps. Jeannie sounded hysterical.

When he saw the carnage in the room, he was a little hysterical himself.

The door had been torn off the hinges.

Inside, Sam held and cradled Jeannie for a few seconds. She hugged him so tightly he thought his ribs were going to break, but he wouldn't have let go for the world.

"Jeannie, are you hurt?" he asked, dreading the answer.

"No, Daddy," she answered, sobbing. "But I was scared. I couldn't help it. People were firing guns and yelling, and I cried and I yelled and I couldn't stop." She stopped and looked up at him. "And the black thing came in and looked at me and . . . ." She stopped and buried her face into his chest.

"It's okay, baby. It's okay to be scared."

"I'm not scared, now, Daddy," she told him, wiping her eyes and nose with the back of her hand. "Nuh...not now. Nuh...not with you here." She burrowed her face into his chest again and held him, still crying. Unable to stop. But it was a cry of relief and not terror, now.

Sam sat for a moment, hugging her, then held her at arm's length while he talked to her.

"Sweetheart," he began and hesitated. "I'm going to carry you out of here and put you in the truck. I want you to keep your eyes closed until I tell you to open them." She nodded. "This is very important, Jeannie, so listen to me. Just keep your face against my chest and don't open your eyes."

She did as he asked and wrapped her arms around his neck.

"It was awful, Daddy," she said. "Screaming and that dark thing growling, and...and I think a lot of people died." She paused, as though thinking. She sniffled and rubbed her nose again. "Is John Hill dead?"

"Yes," he answered after a few seconds. He hoped to God he was right.

"Good," she said, and Sam shuddered at the cold tone in her voice.

But he would deal with that later. For now, he had his strong arms wrapped around his Jeannie and she was okay.

It was weeks before Jeannie's nightmares stopped. Weeks before she stopped coming to her parent's room in the middle of the night because a bad dream had scared her. Weeks before she thought about walking to Sally Edelman's by herself. Weeks before the sound of a strange car pulling into the driveway didn't cause beads of sweat to break out on her forehead.

But Sam had seen the carnage, and how close his Jeannie had come to terror and death, and his nightmares went on long after hers had stopped.

Chapter 14

After watching the confrontation between Sam and the creature through a small crack in the bin, John Hill waited until he heard Sam Baker's truck disappear in the distance before he untwisted the ax handle and let the metal door slowly swing open. He peeked out tentatively, holding the handle ready.

There was no one - and no thing - around.

He dropped to the ground and shivered for a moment, slightly favoring his right leg where it had been punctured. Then he realized he felt better than he had in years. Almost exhilarated, and for a few moments, he couldn't figure out why. Then, finally, he knew.

First Ray Willard and his goons were going to kill him, and they didn't.

And that thing, which had tossed the other men around like stuffed toys from a baby's nursery, couldn't kill him either. Maybe his leg would get infected, but that was it.

Finally, Sam Baker had come out of the truck with that big-ass Taurus ready to blow his head off. And John had escaped that, too.

He felt powerful, strong, almost invincible. He'd found the secret to real power, and nothing could stop him. Not drug dealers or monsters or country hicks with big guns.

Big John Hill was going places.

He turned north and stared at the mountains. That way. That's where he'd find the source of the power he'd glimpsed. To meet the thing that promised him the power.

At a place near a tall metal tower.

But first, he had to get ready for the trip.

It was a messy job, picking through the blood and guts to get the keys to the limo the drug dealers drove, and emptying their wallets of their money. Messy, but Big John could stand a little mess if it meant a lot of money. He helped himself to a couple of Uzi's and extra clips, too.

In the bedroom, after he changed shorts and pants, he found the drop point hunting knife he'd ordered through the Shotgun News a couple of years ago. The six inch stainless steel blade gleamed in the light when he unsheathed it. He hooked the leather sheath to his belt. He had the feeling the knife would be useful later. Very useful.

He shredded his soiled shorts and pants with the knife, then carried them back downstairs with him. Maybe they'd think he was mixed in that mess somewhere.

His leg itched and he took a moment to inspect the wound. It looked half healed, and scabbed over with a brown strip of skin already as tough as old shoe leather. For a moment, he thought he saw the dark, dry flesh twitch, but when he looked closer he realized he must have imagined it. Scabs don't move.

He loaded the limo with cash and cocaine, and the shotgun and shells at the house, then took the dealers' private drive and followed the twisting dirt roads until he came to the main hardtop out of Clarion County. None of the people he'd passed knew it was Big John Hill behind those tinted windows. And he even gave Old Lady Benson the finger when he rode by the rickety shack where she sat on the porch knitting and watching for something to talk about at this week's church gossip circle. She didn't even blink.

He should have gotten one of these things years ago.

He smiled, running his tongue over the pits and cavities in his teeth, and turned the black car to the north. Something was there.

Waiting.

Chapter 15

Geek Nelson wasn't really afraid of the dark. The only reason he felt nervous at all was because the guys had taken his blade, and he felt almost naked without the steel. Left alone in the center of the Haunted Rock at the top of Lox Mountain was bad enough. But, dammit, he wanted his blade back. The ridged metal plate was hard on his ass, too.

The Tower lights weren't on after ten P.M., so until the moon rose and his eyes adjusted, Geek couldn't see around him. They'd taken his flashlight with the blade, then humiliated him with a search for another. He should have stashed some stuff when he had the chance. He'd been up there earlier that day by himself, checking the place out, so he knew a little about the terrain. The other Reamers would have probably given him a hard time if they'd known that, too. But all he'd seen was a bunch of beer cans, food trash, small white mounds of what looked like weather worn toilet paper, and lots of used condoms scattered around. The Reamers would take credit for those, he knew.

That's why Geek wanted in the club.

Geek, who had been born Terry Lee Nelson, wasn't very happy about his nickname, but he had learned to live with it. What he liked even less was his appearance. He'd tried to do something about his lumbering, six foot two inch, two hundred and seventy five pound body, but he couldn't. Every miracle diet failed. He would look in the mirror and see his thick, blubbery lips and the teeth that looked like a crooked, unpainted picket fence, and stiff hair that wanted to stand out at odd angles from his head. Then he would have to fight back tears.

"Yeah, dammit," he said into the night. Those asswipes would love to see him with his head on his arms, his massive shoulders heaving as he whimpered into his armpit.

When he got into the club, things would be different. Girls respected the Reamers. They did things for them. Even for Jay "Slimer" Anson. Geek figured if Sheila would do it with Slimer just because he was a Reamer, there must be a half dozen girls who'd do it with him.

Geek wasn't afraid of the dark, but he didn't like it much. He'd already gone through a week of various humiliations at the hands of the Reamers. Eating a variety of disgusting cooked, uncooked, once-living, and still living items. His stomach still churned. He hoped the crickets and worms finally died. Maybe it wouldn't have been so bad if they'd let him chew them into submission.

They made him walk down Main Street wearing a diaper and baby's bib, but at least they'd spirited him away when the cops arrived. Another time, he had to walk up to the first man he saw and kiss him full on the lips. His back still hurt. The man had been a Marine hand-to-hand combat instructor, home on leave. He'd repeated that fact several times for Geek's benefit, and to remind him not to ever in this lifetime kiss him again. Not if he wanted to retain usable possession of his balls.

Despite all they'd done to him, Geek wondered if this might be the worst. The Reamers meant it to be, of course. They'd told him all the old stories about how the Indians used to sacrifice to their dark gods here in the middle of the night, trying to quiet their anger. Geek heard about the little boy who, in the early 1800's, ran away to Lox Mountain and when they found him the next morning, his skin had turned to some indelible black color and his hair was cocaine white. In 1947, a doctor trying to stop construction of the Tower held a news conference on the very metal plate pressed against Geek's butt. Some freak thunderstorm blew in, and when the lightning stopped, the doctor was gone. He'd disintegrated. Some people said the Indian gods were angry with him.

Geek didn't believe all of it. This wasn't any spooky burial ground. If any Indians ever came through here, they probably just camped and enjoyed the view like any other tourists. The kid must have been already black, and they made up the part about his hair. He wasn't sure about the doctor. Geek had searched online, and found that a Dr. Harrison Baker had disappeared at the top of Lox Mountain in 1947, and that he opposed the construction of the Tower. Somehow, he and the metal podium he had been using disappeared in the middle of a thunderstorm. More likely an out-of-work carpenter who needed that construction job helped the doc vanish.

Earlier, Geek had noticed a mass of blackened, melted metal at the center of the sheet of steel set into Haunted Rock. The area looked as though someone had taken a blowtorch to it, but that could have been caused by a lot of things.

Geek didn't enjoy crouching in the dark at the top of Lox Mountain at all, but he only had a little over six more hours to go. It was almost midnight, and they said he could leave at six in the morning. As a Reamer. Then things would change.

He wrapped the thick blanket around him against the chill of the spring night and tried to get comfortable. He finally realized that was impossible as long as he sat on that dark metal, and he sure didn't want to lay down on it. It was as though he wanted to be ready to make a quick escape. He wondered if the other Reamers would try to come up and scare him away. Probably. Have a little fun at the big ugly guy's expense. Most people thought someone who looked like Geek must be dumb, slow of mind and body. He had to admit that his movements were slothlike at times, but Geek had never had any trouble learning in high school or the two years of college he attended. If those assholes came creeping around, they might get a big surprise. He yawned. He couldn't be sleepy.

But after a few minutes, Geek's head nodded. His eyes slowly closed, and despite the cold and the hard metal under his butt and the awkward sitting position, at one minute before midnight, he was sound asleep.

At exactly midnight, he was wide awake.

Damn, he thought. What was that?

He'd heard something ringing, as if someone had hit a giant bell with a big hammer. Now, nothing. He sat quietly for a while, head cocked sideways, listening for any sound.

From somewhere deep inside the mountain, he heard a moan.

For one wild moment, he thought an earthquake had struck. They weren't unknown in southwestern Virginia. The one that cracked the Washington Monument had rattled the area, and he'd been outside during that one. But this sound was different. Like the deep, sighing cry of something chained there. Something that wanted loose, and would do anything to be free. His skin tightened into mounds of tiny bumps. He pulled the blanket closer around him, and listened.

Probably the damn Reamers.

Geek sat on a solid slab of corrugated steel bolted into a chunk of hard granite that had been flattened over the years by the weather or Indians or the crew who'd built the Tower over forty years ago. He wasn't sure which. He knew nothing short of a few hundred pounds of dynamite could move the boulder and steel from the top of the mountain.

Sitting quietly at the top of Lox Mountain, the blanket pulled tightly around him, listening for any sound that could identify the Reamers, he felt something scratching at the bottom of the steel slab.

Geek didn't move. He looked down at the dark steel between his legs and heard the scratch again. Something was under there. In that granite boulder. In the glow of an almost full moon rising overhead, it looked as though the steel rippled. As though it flowed into a different form or parted like water before a surfacing shape.

He didn't stay frozen for long. Geek dumped the blanket, pushed back a torn section of chain link fence, and ran as if some underworld creature nipped at his heels.

To hell with Reamers and to hell with their girls. Geek looked back at Haunted Rock. Something moved there, and he ran faster.

His body flirted with a coronary as he pushed it to unaccustomed activity. He almost reached the parking lot.

His feet tangled in something that tripped him and sent him sprawling onto the asphalt walk. He struggled to get up, but he was caught and whatever held his feet wouldn't let go. He was afraid to look down, afraid of what he would see wriggling, twisting around his ankles. It moved as a mass of snakes would, sliding across his skin. Finally, he couldn't stand it. He had to look.

The blanket.

Wrapped firmly around his ankles, it dragged him back up the walk, to the rock. No one held the blanket, but still it pulled him slowly along the path to the granite and metal plate.

Geek's fingers dug deep grooves in the dirt beside the walk. He grabbed for the asphalt, losing the fingernails on his right hand. Skin peeled from his palms when he tried to anchor himself on a small tree.

The blanket paused for a second as it reached Haunted Rock and the metal plate. Geek looked above the rock and saw a void that hid the stars and sucked away the moonlight as if it were a supercharged Hoover. An evil laugh echoed in the blackness.

Geek was suddenly, totally afraid of the dark.

He looked at the metal and saw a black opening about six inches across. It seemed to reach for him.

"It's too small!" he screamed, his words disappearing into the void. The blanket started down the hole. "It's too damn small!"

Geek was wrong, and what was left of him funneled into the opening and vanished. The black void followed, and the dark circle irised shut. The metal plate was solid.

Lox Mountain, except for beer cans and old toilet paper and used condoms, was empty.

But it was waiting.

All are but parts of one stupendous whole,
Whose body nature is, and God the soul.
                    Alexander Pope: An Essay on Man

Part Two

DREAMS

Chapter 16

The first part of the dream was a vivid memory of what actually happened.

"How will the universe end?" Suzy asked.

"Huh?" Dave said, looking up from the manuscript he had to proof before tomorrow. He made a small mark on the page to show where he stopped. "What do you mean?"

"Well, I guess everyone has heard about the Big Bang, which supposedly started the cosmos. But how does it end? Another Big Bang?"

"More like a Little Whimper," Dave told her, smiling. He put the manuscript down and sat beside her on the couch. Suzy held the latest issue of New Science, and the cover story reported on new scientific theories of creation. The magazine rested on her nicely rounded tummy, a natural prop for reading, except when the baby kicked.

"Do you remember the personality piece on Dr. Habensword?" Dave asked. Suzy waved the magazine in the air. That's why they had the subscription.

"Well, it did touch briefly on his theories," he continued. "As usual, though, he had more to say than I could use.

"It depends on an obscure scientific creation called dark energy that seems to be pushing all matter in the universe away from itself. The expansion of space is accelerating instead of slowing, and the dark energy is the only explanation they can find. Given enough hundreds of billions of years, the universe will evolve to a cold, uniformly empty existence with no people, no matter, and no energy."

"The Little Whimper."

"Right. Except Habensword disputes that conclusion. He theorizes the dark energy is a temporary condition - if you can call fifteen or twenty billion years temporary - that will disappear as the universe ages. He thinks there is enough dark matter and free neutrinos to reverse the trend, and the universe will collapse due to gravity, eventually forming a huge black hole containing all of creation. Habensword believes at that point, our conventional time and space laws will no longer function, and the mass will compact even more to form something like the primordial mass that exploded to become the Big Bang. Eventually, the process would repeat."

"A neat cycle," Suzy said. "I like that."

"Except things may not be so neat. The new creation from that new Big Bang may be completely different from ours. Magic instead of science, for example. Or life might be metal instead of flesh and blood."

"Better than the Whimper." Suzy shivered. "That's a scary image for some reason."

"You'd rather we all condensed and exploded again?"

"At least there is some hope of a future."

"Maybe. Or maybe the new Big Bang would be the one we already had."

Suzy placed her hand on her stomach, as though waiting for the baby to kick.

"Care to explain that?" she asked.

"If it recollapses and our laws do break down, there will no longer be a space-time structure, and time will cease to have any meaning. Past and present and future will be all a single point, just as all matter will be a single point. So this next Big Bang could be the original one."

"And we would be doomed to repeat everything just as it happened?"

"No. Everything would only exist once and would happen only once. And the Big Bang would be a single event at both the beginning and end of time. Now do you understand?"

"No."

"Good," he told her. "I didn't, either, which is why I left it out of the article."

She shook her head. "Suddenly I prefer the Little Whimper."

"I think you have your own Little Whimper in that mountainous tummy of yours." He patted her abdomen.

"Yes," she said, her eyes twinkling. "It started with a Big Bang, too, and I saw stars afterward."

Divergence.

He should have laughed, then slowly removed her clothes, and made tender love to her on the couch, kissing every square inch of the beautiful, large stomach, and taking the tips of her enlarged breasts in his mouth and gently biting the nipples. That was the memory.

The dream was different.

"What about the time between the collapse and the Big Bang?" Suzy asked.

"What do you mean?" Dave was confused. He had meant to do something else, and he couldn't remember what.

"Well, there must have been a short, maybe even an infinitesimal, interval between the moment when the mass collapses and there is another Big Bang. What happens during this gap between the two events?"

"How should I know? Habensword never mentioned that."

Suzy sat up straight and her hands waved as she talked. "What if, in that split second, a place forms that encompasses all space and time from beginning to end and back again? There, no time and all the time in the world would pass, right?"

"Well --"

"It could develop its own lifeforms and be a universe unto itself. If you could get in there, you could even survive and travel between the end of one cycle and the beginning of the next."

None of what she said made any sense, but it sounded terrifyingly logical. A quiver went through Dave, and he stared at hands that looked as though someone had pumped them up like an old inner tube. The skin stretched tight, and the fingers were short, fat sausage links.

Suzy stood, slim and trim, and the bulge where the baby had been was gone. Her eyes were almost black, with a tiny spark of light at the center that frightened him.

Dave looked down, his abdomen somehow grown as large and swollen as Suzy's had been a few seconds before. Something twitched and moved inside the bulge.

So that's how it feels to be pregnant, he thought. Like a muscle spasm inside his stomach.

But his arms were swollen, too, and he didn't recognize the bloated face when he looked in a mirror floating nearby.

"It wouldn't be a perfect isolation, of course," Suzy said. "The boundary between the Gap and human existence would be bumpy with some places thicker than others. People and things might be able to travel back and forth in the thin places under certain circumstances. Some humans might even have the power to move things into that place and out."

She said "Some humans . . . ." as though humans were an alien species to her.

Suzy changed.

Her skin became dark, dusky, but it wasn't black as a black human would be. More the black of scuffed shoe leather, or dull, sand-pitted obsidian. She paced back and forth and her feet on the carpet sounded like animal hooves on packed ground.

"That place wouldn't be subject to conventional laws, either." The voice was low and gravelly. It seemed to echo from the walls. "It would be a place that humans, and other beings, could tap for a source of magic. And the magic would change them. Slowly and almost imperceptibly if they stayed in the human world, or quickly and catastrophically if they traveled into the Gap. Through history, those who dared seek magic were changed. And the demons they called were once those foolish enough to believe they could control that place."

Suzy no longer looked human at all. She was naked and her skin was black and leathery, cracked and lined like a discarded snake skin. Single pads of solid bone replaced her feet, and her hands were large and knotted and tipped with sharp, curved claws. She smiled and revealed a mouth full of razor-edged molars, the sharpened tips almost sparkling in the light. Her gnarled and twisted features seemed to crawl across her face, and behind her, something long and snakelike twitched on the carpet.

Dave backed into a corner of the room, and bent convulsively with the force of a cramp in his stomach. The skin of his abdomen knotted and bulged as something moved inside it. Something that wanted out.

"Oh, Jesus!" he muttered, then bit his lip as another stabbing pain convulsed his body. His stomach distended, and the buttons of his shirt popped open, no longer able to contain the mass of flab and blubber. Dave's whole body was fat and swollen like a corpse two days in the sun and ready to explode with the gases of rotting decay. He looked down, and a face seemed to press against his skin from the inside, a tiny baby face pressed against a thin rubber sheet.

A small slit appeared and the top of an almost bald head pushed through the opening. The skin stretched and molded to the contour of the emerging body, and it stopped halfway out, everything from the waist down still inside Dave. Still kicking to get out.

It turned its face toward him and smiled. A small, round baby's face with a mouth full of needles and knives.

"Hi, Daddy," it said with Christopher's voice. "We're going to have some fun, now." Tiny hands clapped together.

The thing that had been Suzy stood in the corner of the room, laughing.

"I've touched you," it said. "And you're mine."

Dave ran, panting. His stomach was still the size of large watermelon, but it was whole again. His arms and legs were too big and he moved so slowly. He sweated and his breath came in heavy gasps, and his arms felt as though he were carrying a small refrigerator in each hand.

Something sleek and swift chased him.

He thought it might have been the Suzy-thing, but when he looked back, he saw it was a tall thin scarecrow of a man wearing jogging shorts and a t-shirt, a pair of Nikes, and a determined, predatory scowl on his face. His prominent nose gave him the appearance of a hawk hunting its prey.

Then Dave was there again, in the place worse than the dark.

The scarecrow jogger still chased him, and he could hear the laughter of the Suzy-thing in the distance. Ahead of him, he saw two faintly glowing objects, one bigger than the other, floating and bobbing in some unseen current.

In the midst of that dark evil, they were two glowing spots of salvation, and he ran to them.

As he drew closer, the light resolved into two bodies. He heard the faint cries for help.

The jogger was closer now, reaching for him.

Dave peered ahead. A woman and a small child, and they were holding their arms out to him, crying.

Suzy and Chris.

They were whole and intact, dressed as they had been the morning he left for the airport. Suzy wore a smooth green blouse and skirt that made her look like a million and change, and Chris was dressed in his Big Bird shirt and shorts, with Weeboks on his tiny feet.

"You have to get away, Dave," Suzy called. "Save yourself."

"Run, Daddy," Chris yelled, his whole body shaking with the effort. "Get away. I love you, Daddy."

Suzy smiled, but her face was strained and sad.

"I love you, too, darling," she said as he reached them. She pointed somewhere into the distance. "Look for the Tower."

The jogger clutched at Dave's ankle and touched it, just as he dived through the space where Suzy and Chris had hovered a second before.

Dave screamed, suddenly covered with a smothering, binding shape. He couldn't breath, and the thing wound itself tighter and tighter around his body and his head.

In the distance, he heard the hotel alarm screeching, and after a few moments unwrapped the hotel sheets from around him and sat quivering on the edge of the mattress. His left hand throbbed with every heartbeat.

Suzy's and Chris' images were so vivid, as if he could have touched them. He felt his stomach, pushing the flab from one side to the other. Not quite as bad as in the dream, but no doubt he was an obese, overweight slob. How could he have let this happen?

He stood and walked to the window, and looked out at the standard hotel panoramic view: rows of cars lined up in front of the rooms. But high on the top of the mountain, still glowing in the darkness of the early morning, was the Somerset Tower, a symbol of the city's progressive policies and hope for the future. Was the power on or was that some other type of light around it?

The Tower she mentioned. A dream. Just a dream. But that glowing needle was real.

What the hell is it about the Tower? he wondered. Is it the structure itself, or where it's built?

A violet aura shimmered around the top of the needle for a second, and was gone so quickly that Dave wondered if he imagined it.

It's calling others, he thought. Either the Tower or something else is calling the others to this place. But why? To destroy the dark place, or set it free?

He looked down his bandaged hand. The emergency room doctor hadn't believed him when he told her he'd caught it in a car door. The cut was too clean and neat. But he had brushed off her questions with vague answers and misdirection, and refused to even discuss staying overnight for observation. She hadn't been happy about it, but she finally gave up questioning him. After all, doctors were required to report gunshot wounds and child abuse, not missing fingers and obstinate patients.

Every time Dave thought about his hand in silhouette, so much like the cloud, he felt a stabbing fear in his gut. He knew it couldn't have been him, of course, but there had to be a link. Why had that monstrous force taken the mangled form he remembered so well?

He had destroyed the finger. He had worried that it wouldn't burn when he attacked it with the propane torch he picked up at a local department store. But it twisted and squirmed like a real worm in the blue flame before it finally stopped moving. The torch had reduced it to a black ash before he was satisfied. Even then, he had scraped the residue into a metal box, now buried in the city landfill.

The light at the tower's point seemed to flare again, and Dave winced.

He wanted to go to the airport again, but wondered if he should drive up to the tower. Try to find out what the hell was going on.

Dave dressed slowly, feeling deep inside that something waited for him at the top of that mountain.

Something from his dreams.

Chapter 17

"Destruction? How much destruction?"

"Total destruction." Evan gripped the steering wheel of the car and tried not to tremble.

"You mean this computer program you dreamed up shows the anomalous events will reach a total destructive potential at a certain place."

"Somerset," Evan told Jerry again. "Somerset, Virginia."

"Total destruction of what? The city?" Jerry didn't sound as though he believed him.

"Everything. The city, the state, the country, the whole planet." He glanced sideways briefly. No, Jerry didn't believe him. "The graph peaks at infinity, for God's sake! For all I know, the whole damned universe will burst like a balloon on a bed of nails."

"Tonight."

"Actually, tomorrow. Before dawn." Jerry said nothing for so long that Evan glanced over to see if he was still breathing. He was. Just his luck.

"Listen," Jerry said. "I don't know if this ties in, but I had this dream last night and it gave me an idea."

"Jesus! Wait a minute. What time is it? I have to get a pen and write this down. Saturday, ten o'clock in the morning, the day before the universe collapses. He has an idea." He glanced around as though looking for something.

"Come on, Evan. Watch the road and give me a break," Jerry told him. "I'm trying to figure out what's going on here. Especially if it's going to zap the universe."

"Noble sentiments, my friend. Especially since it's your ass, too."

Evan ignored Jerry's disgusted glance, and looked around at the Virginia landscape they were speeding past, as though he expected Sergeant Akers to jump out from behind a tree somewhere. Luckily, after the pods turned out to be nothing more than inflatable rafts left by a previous owner, the Sergeant was called back to the warehouse by some emergency or other. He was still busy the next morning. So Dr. Hall and Dr. Reese were allowed to continue alone. He had convinced Jerry that they should head for Somerset, Virginia. That was probably as smart as heading for ground zero of an H-bomb test to see the pretty lights.

"You've seen those files you weren't supposed to see, because you broke into the offices. . . . "

"I'm sorry I offended your sense of propriety, but I wanted to know what the hell is going on here."

"Well?" Jerry said after an extended silence.

"Well, I still don't know." A few miles of interstate rolled by before either of them spoke again.

"Okay, Jerry, tell me about your dream and the idea. I'm ready to listen to anything at this point."

"It has something to do with the garbage dump theory," Jerry warned.

Evan shrugged.

"What the hell. Some of the APE brass are conjecturing about aliens from outer space. Your dump theory sounds almost plausible next to that."

"I think I have an idea about how to get into that gap I told you about."

"Great. If all this stuff we're chasing around the country really does come out of some interstellar garbage dump, all we need is to go poking around to see what else we can drag out. Then we won't have to wait until tomorrow for everything to blow up." Evan shook his head. His head ached, and that happened all too often lately.

"We have to learn more about the place," Jerry said, and Evan struggled to concentrate on his words. The headache made it difficult.

"Why's that?"

"Well, so we could figure out why all this stuff is happening and find a way to stop it. Besides, it's your computer program that predicted the total destruction of the universe tomorrow morning. It might be nice to work on a way to prevent that."

Their car sped along the interstate at around seventy miles an hour, only about five miles above the posted limit for cars on this particular stretch. Trucks were limited to the same speed, but Evan wasn't surprised to see one of those double trailer rigs scream past him at about eighty. Sometimes he thought they could save more lives if they outlawed tractor trailers instead of guns.

"Have any ideas about how to go about exploring this little garden spot that's going to destroy us all?"

"That's it," Jerry said, nodding wildly like some sort of nerd. Evan glanced over at him. He was, of course. "I have some ideas about how to explore the discontinuity if we can find a weak place to break through."

"Right," Evan said. "All we need is a place where time and space are warped together. Jesus, Jerry. Are you listening to yourself? Are you starting to believe in goblins, elves, and aliens from hostile planets?"

Jerry crossed his arms and maintained a stubborn silence for a few seconds.

"How do you think all this stuff is happening?" he asked finally. "Something's behind it, and you said it's getting worse."

Evan grunted reluctant agreement.

"If we could just be there when one of these things pops in from somewhere else, maybe we could actually send probes or a human being into the place."

"Jerry, you're talking about sending someone into a place that is worse than any toxic waste dump we've ever seen, if your theory is even vaguely on target. What do you think is going to happen to someone who goes in there?"

He shrugged.

"Maybe nothing, if he has the right kind of protective suit." Jerry looked thoughtful for a second. "If he could take the suit with him."

"How's that?"

"I just wonder if the stress would rip it apart."

"No more than it would human tissue."

"I don't know. Humans are more resilient than most people think. Guess it would depend on the transport process. If anyone came out, he might be covered with gunk, like the VW, or naked, like the blue lady."

There seemed to be a sudden chill in the car.

"If he returned at all," Evan said. He suddenly wished he had a Pepsi. "How long could someone stay in there?"

"I'm not sure. Probably our physical laws don't apply, and that's the real problem. The person might return in a few seconds, a few weeks, a few years, or never. Or maybe last year or last month."

"What?" Evan glanced over at Jerry. A Toyota in the passing lane beeped at them as the car drifted across the center line.

"Sure. Time might have no real meaning inside and anything sent in could return at any time in the past, present, or future. That's consistent with certain theories of Dr. Habensword."

Evan's hands weren't too steady on the wheel, and he needed to stop somewhere and get a grip on himself, and maybe on a good, stiff drink. Not Pepsi.

He wished the old man in that peanut field hadn't looked so damned familiar.

Hell, by his own calculations, in less than twenty-four hours, he wouldn't be around to wish for anything.

Chapter 18

The limo handled like a dream.

Big John Hill decided he should have taken the first fifteen or thirty thousand dollars of "rent" and bought himself a used Caddy, or maybe a big Lincoln with everything power except the by-God hood ornament. Then he would have ordered one of those electric jobs from J. C. Whitney with the little light bulb inside.

Daylight hauled itself over the mountains to his right, his leg no longer ached, and Big John felt good.

After leaving Clarion, John pulled into a combination truckstop and motel, and spent the rest of the afternoon and most of the night watching television. Somerset was only an hour and a half away, but he wanted to stay out of sight for a while, and see what the news said about what happened on the Ranch.

He threw back his head and laughed when he heard the newsman say he'd died.

Some "unknown assailant" had evidently interrupted a drug deal in progress, killed all the people involved, then stolen an undetermined amount of cash and drugs. A vehicle had been taken from the scene, but police didn't have a good description of the car. They had a suspect, but weren't releasing his name at this time.

What tickled John most was that they questioned Sam Baker. Enough people recognized Sam's truck to know he was in the area, and even that he was up at the Ranch after it happened. He must have told the sheriff about John and Jeannie, though, so they let him go, and Big John no longer had a home.

No big loss, he thought. He had more money than he'd ever seen in his life, a big car that hadn't even been reported stolen yet, and enough white gold to keep a bunch of crackheads happy for a long time if he needed more cash.

Yes, indeed. He surely felt good.

And there was more to come.

When he rolled into Somerset, the first thing he would do is to drive up Lox Mountain and take a close look. Everybody in this part of Virginia knew about the famous Tower on Lox Mountain.

That had to be what he had seen at the Ranch.

During the Bicentennial, they mixed blue and red lights with white on the sides, and even Big John had driven up from Clarion to see it. It was beautiful. A patriotic beacon that the fags, liberals, and flag burners could see for miles around. Big John Hill had been a little misty-eyed the first time he saw it blazing on top of that mountain.

Now, still twenty or thirty miles from Somerset, he imagined he could see the metal structure, flashing and throbbing with energy. Signaling him. Showing him the way along the path to real power.

In perfect time to the pulsing force from the image in his mind, his leg throbbed with each bright beat.

When he'd checked his leg before he left the hotel, there was almost no trace of the original wound. He should have been grateful to escape with just a little hole that healed so fast. But John was worried. The scratch was almost gone, but a patch of brown, leathery skin had grown in a dark band around his lower leg. It hadn't spread, but it seemed darker, and tiny lines had formed on the surface of the skin.

Like crinkly bend lines on an old pair of leather boots.

Jesus, he thought, looking at the gas gauge. Almost empty. And he needed refueling himself. Took a lot of food to keep a big man like him full up and raring to go.

Ahead, he saw a sign that read "The Store Stop." Closer, he saw it was a convenience store with gas pumps, a bathroom, and a rack of T-shirts and souvenir hats sitting out front. It advertised "HOT FOOD" but he figured they probably had those cold hamburgers and cardboard pizzas that were "HOT" only after a couple of minutes in the microwave.

John stopped at the gas pumps and stepped out. He pulled the clear country air deep into his lungs and smiled. Even near the pumps, the air was clean and sweet and full of new morning smells. Somebody cutting hay nearby. Them city rats don't know what they're missing, he thought. But he knew he should be grateful they were stupid enough to stay in Detroit or Los Angeles or some other God forsaken place. If they all decided to head for the hills of Virginia, pretty soon he'd be living in a slimy cesspool just like where they came from.

Inhaling another generous portion of air, he searched for the gas cap.

He walked around one side of the car, then the other before he located it under the back plate. He fumbled with the cap then noticed the clerk at the window, staring like an old busybody. The gas gurgled into the car and John casually waved at the young man inside the store. He threw up his hand, and turned back to wait on another customer.

Nothing, John thought. Probably nothing.

If not for the sack of fifty and hundred dollar bills in the car, John would have complained about price gouging oil companies. It seemed an eternity before the automatic shutoff kicked in. Damn car must have a hell of a tank. Walking to the store, the leather sheathed knife on his belt, he saw the young man glance at him, then at something on the counter.

Probably nothing.

Inside, he realized he was wrong about the hot food. The store actually had a grill worked by a lady who looked like somebody's spry old grandma. She whistled and flipped greasy piles of home fries with one hand and stirred a pot of grits with the other. The fries sizzled and the grits bubbled. Rows of bacon strips waited under a warming light, the grease still hot and steamy. A Gibraltar mound of scrambled eggs accumulated under another light. Hot coffee perked and filled the store with the sweet aroma, mingling with the even more delicious smell of the food.

John swallowed, suddenly hungrier than ever. Probably the whole reason for the grill and freshly cooked food. Who could resist that smell first thing in the morning? A couple of plates of eggs, bacon and grits with lots of coffee loaded with caffeine and he would be ready for anything. He noticed a corner with five small tables for patrons to relax while eating.

That pimply-faced clerk stared at him again.

He turned away from the grill. "What's the problem, boy." It was a challenge more than a question. "Got nose trouble?"

"Uh, no, sir," he said. John noticed he had a name tag with "STAN" printed on it. Stan couldn't keep still. He moved and twitched and vibrated like somebody who had been plunked down on an anthill. "Just wondering if I could help you, sir." He smiled uncertainly, and the grin died as quickly as it was born.

"The gas, son," John said. He stared at the boy quietly. Stan looked away, at a console with glowing numbers on it.

"Sixty-three fifty," Stan told him. "Will that be all?"

If John didn't know better, he'd think Stan was trying to get rid of him. Well, to hell with him. Big John Hill was hungry. Big-time hungry. He laid down a hundred.

"I want to get me some of them eggs and grits, with a little bacon and coffee on the side," he said. "Any problem with that?"

"No, sir, of course not," Stan said. His next smile also faded quickly. "We have an all-you-can-eat special for only seven dollars. Would you like that?"

"Sure, Stan," John said. For a moment, the boy looked puzzled, then looked down at the tag on his shirt. "Best seven dollars I'll ever spend, but you won't make any money on that grill today. When Big John gets to eating, better fire up the grill again."

Stan glanced toward the grill and John followed his eyes. "All-you-can-eat special, Granny," he called.

John wondered if she really was his granny, or if everyone called her that.

Granny, with the spoon in one hand and the egg turner in the other, stopped and stared back at Stan, as if puzzled about something. Then she shrugged and turned back to the sizzling home fries. John watched her for a few seconds and saw her peel the paper from a row of sausage links and toss them onto the grill. His mouth watered again.

"Yes, sir," Stan said, handing back his change.

"Get much business on the grill?" John asked, tucking the money into his wallet. Too many damn fifties.

"We will in a little while." Stan still vibrated like a plucked guitar string. He reminded John of Don Knotts in all those movies he made after he left TV. "The real rush will begin in about thirty minutes, just before the factory down the road opens up. A lot of the guys stop for breakfast before work."

"Better get to it, then, before they show up." John turned toward the grill.

"Sir," Stan said. John looked back. "Could you please move your car to the front or side of the store? It's blocking the pumps right now. Some of those factory people will want to gas up while they're here, too."

John nodded and started out the door. It was a reasonable request. The big limo had completely blocked access to one side of the pumps.

But he felt uneasy for a moment. As though something warned him to be alert.

His leg suddenly itched like the blazes.

He held the door for a second and looked back at Stan, who tried to smile again, and botched it again. Stan's eyes moved to something near the cash register, then to the long black car at the pumps, then back to John.

Suddenly, as sure as skunks stink, he knew there was a hot sheet taped there, probably complete with license plate numbers and a description of old Steve. Or maybe they had found pieces of Steve, and figured John Hill was the one who had taken the car.

Sweet Jesus! he thought. If that was true, everyone from Deputy Stillson up to some drug boss in New York was after his blood. As he slid across the leather seat and under the wheel, he knew he should tear out of that parking lot, ditch the limo, and buy, beg, or steal another car.

But he couldn't.

For one thing, dammit, he was hungry. And he had already given pimple face in the store his five dollars. He meant to eat his five dollars worth.

He also knew that if he spun out of the lot, any doubts the kid had would disappear, and a few minutes later, the local sheriff would be looking up his tailpipe with red lights flashing and siren screaming.

But the main reason he turned the car and backed up to the building was that he was still convinced of his own invincibility. No one could beat him. The power in the darkness hadn't let him come this far to fail now. No, it had plans for him, and Big John had plans of his own.

Through the window, Stan studied a sheet of paper. He shook his head and scratched at the beginnings of a bald spot as though he were indecisive about something.

The spring morning was too warm for a jacket, but John pulled on a light windbreaker, anyway. Then he tucked an Uzi into his waistband, in the small of his back. The bulge couldn't have fooled anyone looking for it, but if he kept turned away, the boy and Granny would never see the gun.

Back inside, he walked and stood at the counter in front of the grill. Granny handed him a plate, and a knife and fork wrapped in a napkin.

"He'p yaself," she said. Her words were quick and clipped, as she had to pay for the extra letters. He looked at her for a second. If some yankee came in looking for something to eat, he'd need a translator.

He dismissed the woman from his mind. The sausages were ready, the juices still crackling from the grill. He tossed half a dozen on his plate, piled up a few scoops of eggs, filled a small bowl to the edge with grits, laid a few strips of bacon on the eggs, and tossed a couple of pieces of toast on the whole thing. He carried that to a table on the side, being careful never to turn his back to Granny or Stan. He went back for coffee, and left it hot and black.

John didn't realize how hungry he was. That cardboard cinnamon bun back at the hotel hadn't done a thing for him.

His leg throbbed near the scratch, but this time it was almost a pulse of pleasure. John had the feeling he needed the energy, and began shoveling food as though he were starving.

The dull itch that had been centered on the band of dark flesh around his calf crept up over his knee and down around his ankle. John didn't care. He pushed the food into his mouth like a nineteenth century coalman stoking the box of an old locomotive.

His face went blank, but his hands and jaw never stopped moving. After emptying the plate, he refilled it, piling the food even higher than before. He ignored the engraved sign that read "STATE LAW REQUIRES A CLEAN PLATE WITH EACH VISIT TO THE BUFFET" and spooned the grits, eggs, sausages, and bacon over the remnants of the previous visit. If he had been thinking or seeing at all, he would have noticed the alarm in Granny and Stan's eyes when he turned to go back to the table, and they saw the butt of the Uzi stuck out of his pants. He would have noticed the look they exchanged, then that Stan dialed three numbers on the telephone and spoke urgently to someone at the other end.

The second plate was almost empty when John came out of the trance. He shook his head, flinging a piece of egg that had been hanging out of his mouth onto the wall next to the table. The egg stuck there, quivering.

What the hell? he wondered, then looked at Granny and Stan. They watched him.

He remembered everything. The looks. The phone call.

"Jesus Christ," he said aloud, to no one in particular. How long had he sat there stuffing his face while the sheriff and probably a dozen or so men converged on this place? They could be here any minute.

"Jesus Christ," he repeated.

Suddenly, the Uzi was in his hands as though he practiced the draw for hours a day, every day. Stan dropped behind the counter, but

Granny froze as the bullets traced an exploding line across the wall, then her chest.

The blood fountained from her back and sizzled and danced around the hot grill, and the aroma of the food was overpowered by an acrid, metallic stench.

Granny gurgled, and stood there for a moment. Behind her, thin trails of dark smoke rose from the stove, sucked up into the exhaust hood to heaven. To John, it was as if Granny's spirit left her as she died. She finally tipped forward and hit the floor without trying to catch herself. The blood boiled and disappeared, leaving small burned circles.

One dead old biddy, John thought. He'd never had much use for older women. Not since his mama had died. One dead old biddy.

He walked behind the counter and held the barrel against the top of Stan's head, centered on the tiny bald spot. The paper he'd been reading had fallen to the floor. It was a description of the car, with the tag number, but Steve Ashton's name was listed as the suspect. The description was just enough off to make Stan have doubts about whether he was the one the police were trying to find.

Of course, he no longer had any doubts.

"Got a car here?" John asked, his voice low and clear. Stan didn't look up.

"Yes, sir," he said. "Nineteen eighty-two yellow Eagle station wagon parked on the side. It's got a lot of miles, but it's four-wheel drive and runs great."

"Jesus, Stan," John said. "I'm not buying it, I'm stealing it. Hand over the keys."

Stan fumbled in his pocket for a few minutes, then handed a ring of keys to him. John searched through them until he found a key with "AMERICAN MOTORS" stamped on it. Then he reached down and lifted Stan up by the collar.

"Come on, boy," he said. "We've got a little job to do." They had to hurry. If the sheriff didn't show up soon, the morning crowd from the factory would.

Stan did most of the work, transferring the money and drugs from the limo to the wagon, and he worked quickly and efficiently, occasionally prodded with the barrel of the Uzi, or the hunting knife John had unsheathed. When they were finished, John put the knife away, handed him the keys to the limo and told him to start it.

"Even trade," John told him, and Stan looked surprised. The engine purred with the barest touch. "Damn good car. Sorry to lose it."

He smiled. His crotch itched, but he smiled anyway.

Sheriff Travis Dean held the accelerator to the floor, and the big cruiser danced around Amos Gold's old farm tractor like a fat lady doing a jig at a barn dance. If only he hadn't been on the other side of the county, but he couldn't help it if some idiot truck driver who hadn't slept for two days decided to kill himself and a family of five when his rig wandered into the oncoming lane. The driver never woke up, but he could imagine those kids watching as the big truck bore down on the tiny Korean car and ran over it like it was a groundhog that had wandered onto the highway. Even then, the two-year old lived a while longer, crying and asking for his daddy while his life leaked onto the asphalt.

The sheriff decided it was a good thing the driver didn't live. Looking at the faces of the EMT's and the firemen when the little boy died, he wasn't sure the bastard would have made it to the hospital alive even if he'd survived the wreck, and he would've hated to arrest one of those boys over that piece of worthless slime. He'd felt an urge to walk over and put a few bullets into the body himself. Just for good measure.

Travis hoped some of his deputies were closer, but he knew most of them had moved into place near the schools and major factories, ready to direct the morning traffic jams.

Except for the box factory. Not enough people worked there to justify a deputy. And the box factory was just down the road from the Store Stop.

He fishtailed the cruiser into the parking lot from the south at the same time one of his deputies popped over the hill to the north of the store. Travis was already out of the car, behind the door and his gun ready, when the other car slid to a stop.

The limo sat in front of the store with the engine idling. Through the dark glass, Travis could see the outline of a head and shoulders, and the barrel of a gun pressed against the windshield.

"Sheriff --" Deputy Tyndale yelled from behind the other car.

"I see him," Travis shouted back. "Out of the car," he yelled at the limousine. "Keep your hands up and don't make any sudden moves." No reaction. "Do it. Now!" he boomed, trying keep his voice low and powerful as he had been taught to do in officer's training. Still nothing.

Now what the hell do we do? he wondered. Sit around and stare at each other all day? Then he knew.

Something moved behind the dark glass and the barrel of the gun seemed to swing and point directly at him.

Sheriff Travis Dean opened fire with the big bore .357 - explosions bounced from the surrounding hills - and his deputy was close behind. When his gun was empty, he deftly ejected the casings then popped in a speed loader and released the shells. He fired again.

The form inside the car twitched and jumped like an old drunk with the D.T.'s, but the barrel of the gun stayed on the dash. The windshield was long gone, yet the man just sat there holding the gun, taking soft nose bullets in the upper chest and face.

An autopsy would later absolve Sheriff Dean and Deputy Tyndale of any blame in the death of Stan Wilson, employee of the Store Stop convenience store. Stan was already dead when they arrived, most of his stomach blown away by a neat, close grouping of nine-millimeter lead from the Uzi they found taped in his hands. Sheriff Dean's first shot had removed most of Stan's face, so they couldn't be blamed for not recognizing him immediately.

It took a long and extensive autopsy before they could be sure it was Stan, even though he was missing from the store.

Two things bothered Travis about that day.

He was madder than hell that the animal who killed Stan Wilson and Granny had gotten away. By the time they realized he must have taken Stan's old wagon, he was long gone in one of the six different directions out of the county. All he could do was pass along a description of the station wagon, and it was the next day before he got the message on the wire.

The second thing that bothered Travis also worried and scared him. He was a rational, logical person, but this frightened him deep inside where those logical thoughts disappeared, and he was once again that skinny little kid, afraid of shadows and old Hammer films.

It was stupid, he knew, but he could still get in the shower some mornings and soap up his hair real good, then start thinking about Psycho, not a Hammer movie, but still gone-to-blazes scary. Travis would see that knife going up and down, and blood spiraling down the bathtub drain, and he would have to rinse his hair and wipe away the soap. To get rid of a skin-tightening chill on his backside, he had to see that no one else was in the bathroom.

He felt the same way when he thought about the limousine, the dark shape inside, and the barrel of the gun.

What made the gun swing toward him?

It could have been a muscle spasm, a last dying twitch from poor old Stan. That's what the coroner said.

But Travis could have sworn he saw the dark form slowly and deliberately aim the gun at him. Just before the barrel twitched, he thought he saw a dim smile and a tiny glimmer of red through the glass where Stan's eyes would have been.

Sometimes in the darkest part of the night, he wondered about the gloomy limousine, whether there was some kind of shadowed life behind those tinted windows. He knew it had been used by drug dealers, and he supposed that if any car knew death, it was one that had carried so much of the white, powdered poison that destroyed so many people.

Why had the barrel moved?

Why was he so sure that if he hadn't opened fire, Stan's dead finger would have tightened on the trigger and sent a burst of lead through the windshield and into good old Sheriff Travis Dean?

Chapter 19

It had been a long time, a little over three years, since Maria had seen the inside of an airport. She still couldn't quite believe she sat there, waiting for the plane that would take her to Florida. She looked out the huge windows and didn't see airplanes. She saw oversized aluminum caskets. Metal outside, and inside, cushioned vinyl or leather or whatever the hell they used these days.

A few days ago, Maria Quinones would have done anything to avoid an airport, but decided that bus terminals weren't so great, either.

Business men gathered in clutches, cell phones propped against their ears. Some of them looked at their watches and shifted from one foot to the other, the receiver on one ear, and a finger in the other, trying to block out the construction noise. As though dancing some choreographed routine.

She covered her mouth to hide a grin and looked at her daughter. Ricky would eventually become restless, she knew, but for the time being she was content to sit and talk to her stuffed Green Frog. She asked detailed questions about a nursery and the little babies and the babysitter. Maria smiled at her just as she looked up. She beamed back. That same toothy grin she had seen so many times on Brian's face, a lightning bolt of white on her dark face. At the same time a choking ache caused her to catch her breath, seeing her dead husband mirrored in Ricky's face made her remember she still had a tiny part of him with her.

Up until yesterday, it would have taken nothing short of a miracle to get her inside an airport, much less board a plane. And while the accident was so far unexplainable, it certainly was not a miracle.

When the dust had cleared on the interstate, the bus company representatives admitted they didn't know what had happened. That's why they scratched their heads, and offered free plane or bus tickets to everyone who wanted them. Erica had been in a perpetual state of panic on the bus sent to take them to Somerset, and Maria wouldn't force her into another.

Now Maria waited, twitching in the uncomfortable chair, to board what had killed her husband. There were few travelers so she was waiting until the last minute before suffering the security check.

Her head hurt, not helped at all by the construction near the screening area. Maybe she should move to the end of the terminal and try to read some before it was time to face the TSA. If it was possible to read when her head pounded in time to the hammering.

As the departure time approached, she became even more nervous. Her earlier feelings intensified, and she had a sense of someone at her shoulder, whispering a warning in her ear. She whirled, but no one was there. She closed her eyes. For just a second, it felt as though Brian were there, begging her not to leave. Not to get on the plane.

She didn't want to think about how insane that sounded.

But for some reason, she had the feeling she and Ricky shouldn't take the plane. Not that it would crash, but that she must stay in town for the next few days.

Almost as if their lives were in danger.

Ricky, sensing something was wrong, looked at her, then reached up and hugged her neck and kissed her on the cheek. "I love you, Mommy," she said matter-of-factly and turned her total attention back to the frog. Her eyes were full of trust, and the total confidence of youth that her Mommy would make everything all right. Too young to know that Mommy was not omnipotent.

Ignoring the glare from the almost overpowering mirror decor, Maria stared out the window, at a plane taking off, and at the mountains around the Somerset Valley. The same mountains that forced the plane to climb sharply to avoid a collision. Maria closed her eyes and had a vision of Ricky and herself on a plane, over the mountains, when a dark giant hand suddenly reached from the hills and slapped the plane aside as if it were an annoying fly. It spiraled into the ground and crashed in a spectacular ball of flame. Just as at BWI. She jumped at the sound of the explosion and her eyes snapped open.

Maria was safe in the airport. Another plane landed.

And for a second, she again felt a presence urging her to stay.

Her lips moved in a soundless whisper: "Brian."

Dave knew where the construction was noisiest, so he found a seat at the other end of the airport. Evidently, that part of the structure had already been remodeled by someone with a mirror fetish. There were silver columns, mirrors on the walls between the airport shops, and even the floor had been polished to a glassy finish. From the outside, the windows looked like oversized mirrors embedded in a concrete wall. The dozens of reflecting surfaces made the terminal look more crowded than it was, but maybe it gave some sense of comfort for those people who were nervous about flying. A reinforcement of the herd instinct.

Just a couple of minutes, he'd told himself. He would go to the airport and stay for just a few minutes, just to prove it didn't hold the same dark fascination. Deny that he was compelled to eat and watch planes by some perverse, stubborn part of him that insisted it was all his fault; that he deserved all the death and destruction that haunted him. Damn! Why not include little children dying in some backwater country in Africa if he was shouldering the world's ills? Just say Dave Richards did it. He rubbed his sleeve across his brow.

That was stupid, of course, but maybe if he'd been a little more attentive, more willing to compromise his journalistic impulses, he would have been somewhere in town, eating lunch with Suzy and Chris instead of luring them to their death at the airport.

Would it have made any difference? he wondered. Some people believed in fate and predestination. Maybe if they'd been downtown, a runaway cab would have plowed into the restaurant and run them down. Or the plane might have fallen there. If the universe decided someone had to die, these people said, then there was nothing anyone could do to change that determination. Whatever the method, Suzy and Christopher Richards were selected to die. It couldn't be Dave's fault.

Then why had he torturing himself for the past three years?

Why was he in the airport again, searching for something he could never find?

Still, he watched the air traffic for a while and didn't feel that consuming sense of dread that had once affected him. He didn't expect a dark hand to form and slam a plane into the ground.

Dave wondered if he'd ever seen a hand in the first place. One therapist had suggested that he had projected the image onto the scene after the fact because of the guilt he felt.

"A manifestation of your own dark thoughts," he'd said. "All of us have them, and you are blaming the deaths on your own feeling of guilt. You think it's your fault, anyway, so you imagine this black hand as an extension of yourself."

At the time, he'd been sure the doctor was full of warm, smelly manure. Now he wondered. If the doctor could see Dave now, he would be confident that he had somehow arranged to have his left index finger hacked off so that his own hand would match the one from his illusion.

But would that be reversing cause and effect?

Obsession. That's what had drawn him to airports, big and small, over the past few years. Except this time it was different, somehow. Like the difference between wandering aimlessly around a department store, and going in to buy a particular item. He felt he'd gone there for a reason, not just to satisfy a compulsion to flagellate his guilty conscience. Something was there. Something he should be looking for.

He just didn't know what.

After they changed seats, Ricky took Green Frog to a mirror, dancing it back and forth to the beat of some unheard melody. Maria smiled and tried to read a few more words from the trashy novel she'd found at the airport bookshop. Either her concentration was shot or this book was even trashier than normal. She didn't think the book's crud level was abnormally high, so that left her concentration. She sighed, checked Ricky again, then read three more words.

Something moved.

Her head snapped up, but she saw nothing. Whatever it was, it had been quick and dark, but looking around the airport she saw only sunlight and glittering mirrors. Every corner, every surface, and even the air itself seemed to sparkle and scintillate with a thousand images reflected and re-reflected. It made her feel as though she were in some sort of giant kaleidoscope.

So what had moved? What made her study the terminal as though she expected armed terrorists in every corner?

The airport was just as gaily bright as it had been, and people walking by still laughed and pointed at each other and the images in the mirrors laughed and pointed back. Nothing odd or out of place.

Ricky waved at her and she waved back. Three more words in the novel, and they made no more sense than the crazy world she'd found herself in these past few days.

Whatever his reason for being there, Dave was not so oblivious that he didn't notice the woman sit down nearby. She was darkly spectacular, with dusky eyes that seemed deeper than the ocean's depths. Once, when the little girl interrupted her play to talk to her mother, the woman's laughter had echoed through the building like a fine bell ringing. It was beautiful laughter, but for some reason it reminded Dave of other laughter that wasn't so beautiful. In the bright tones of her laugh, he heard dark echoes from his nightmares.

Stupid, he told himself. Was he so crazy that a young woman's laugh reminded him of death? It wasn't at all like the evil cackle he remembered from his dreams and the airport. But he wondered why she looked so familiar.

Her hair was dark and long and shimmered in the bright light, scattering a thousand diamond sparkles. He was vividly aware of her white dress and how it almost glowed against her tawny skin. How it was so tight against the smooth curves of her body and her long, perfect legs. He made a conscious effort to look away. He never made it habit to react like an adolescent flush with hormones. For the first time in a long time, so long that he at first didn't recognize it, something stirred in Dave. A buzzing in the back of his head that spread like a pool of warmth through his body.

But in the depth of her eyes, he noticed something else. Fear. She was afraid of something, trying to hide the fear but not quite succeeding. That feeling he knew well.

He watched her and didn't watch her, trying to talk sense to his overactive gonads, when he saw a movement near the little girl. The woman must have seen it, too, because her head moved so fast it made his neck hurt as she looked around. Their eyes met for a second in passing.

She was losing. In her dark, beautiful eyes, the fear was winning.

He was a part of the background. Someone there, but not someone she should, or would, notice. Some cataloging part of her brain made a note of him: overweight man, mid to upper thirties, potentially nice looking if he dropped thirty or forty pounds, vague resemblance to someone she couldn't remember. Then she ignored him. He didn't look dangerous, and Maria didn't have time to worry about innocuous bystanders. She felt a cold wind on her skin, maybe from the open area near the construction. It chilled her, made her think of endless caves and deep lakes.

Maria had heard of people who were afraid of heights, or closed-in places, or open spaces. Those obscure things didn't bother her. Bottomless, fresh water lakes did. It was a very precise phobia, and one easily avoided, so it never really had an impact on her social or professional life. But if she wanted to give herself a case of the uncontrollable shivers, she could sit in a dimly lit room and start imagining the black, frigid depths of a lake and the things that could live there. Imagine herself floating on the lake, her legs pointing down, into the dark water, fresh and tasty bait for some hungry denizen. Maybe it was the unknown quality, the thought of floating above thousands of feet of cold, dark water. Cold. Black. Concealing.

Tiny bumps covered her. She felt a burning in her lower back from muscles tightening there. She sensed something nearby that reminded her of the bottomless lake.

Another movement.

Ricky made a grunting noise, then rocked back and fell on her backside. She stared into the mirror at the thing that glided nearer, as from unseen depths.

Maria looked around the terminal. Nothing. But in the reflection, distorting Ricky's image, a vague, silver shape moved toward them, the surface of the glass shimmering as if it were liquid. Closer still. The hard polished surface quivering like water agitated from below.

The shape hesitated for a second, then a scaly, clawed hand left the surface. Maria's eyes widened. She almost expected it to shed shining drops of mirror from it's silver-scaled skin.

It wore a large, gold class ring that Maria recognized. The creep from the bus.

The groping hand was less than a foot from Ricky, who stared from her seat on the tile, unable to move.

"Ricky!" Maria screamed. The shout shocked the little girl and she scurried backward. Too late. The clawed hand lunged and caught her sleeve.

Maria dropped the book and almost without thinking grabbed a nail file and handkerchief from her purse. She wrapped the handkerchief around the curved end of the file even as she stumbled to her daughter.

It pulled her toward the shiny surface. Maria knew if she didn't stop it, the silvery talons would drag her into the mirror.

She jammed the nail file into the thing's arm, and a scream of pain echoed from somewhere a million miles away. Maria pulled Ricky from the thing's grasp, but despite the file in its forearm, it caught the little girl's foot before they could back away.

Maria said "God, no!" and braced her feet wide against the wall, aware and not caring that the white dress rode up on her hips.

Only her daughter mattered. Nothing else. Why didn't someone come to help her?

Her lips moved. "Ricky," she whispered. The little girl screamed.

When he heard the squeal of fright, Dave was already running back to them. Each jarring step made him wish for the pain killers the doctor had given him. For the merest fraction of a second, he'd hesitated when he saw the silver arm grow from the surface of the mirror. Long enough to blink once, quickly, and decide how to help them. He'd held the injured hand to his side while he ran to the other end of the terminal. The workers were on break, and Dave didn't even bother to ask. He just stumbled by them and took the gasoline powered masonry cutter, not taking time to wonder why they didn't look up when he took their equipment.

He'd seen them using the machine before, cutting through three or four inches of concrete with some sort of hardened blade, carving out blocks that were removed to allow access to pipes or wiring below. It was an oversized circular saw with the tumorous growth that was the gasoline engine on top.

The woman and girl both screamed, but no one seemed to notice. Families still walked calmly by. The businessmen still fondled their cell phones. The omnipresent TSA continued to sort underwear.

They don't see or hear them, he finally realized. Only me. Simple reasoning. If someone could see the little girl being dragged slowly to the mirror with the woman hanging on to her like life itself, that someone would have been there helping hold the little girl. Or at least staring at them in bewildered horror. People walked by, unconcerned, and did not react to the ear blasting screams or the contorted mask of horror on the woman's face. Only Dave ran toward them, and he wasn't sure he could help.

The woman looked up as he skidded to a halt, meeting his eyes. She glanced at his bandaged hand and nodded once. She knew she had to hold the child by herself. He prayed the engine would start on the first pull, so of course it didn't. It spluttered once or twice, made a coughing noise and rattled to a halt.

"Choke it," the woman said in a hoarse whisper, as though she could not spare the energy to talk properly. As if every muscle in her body, including her vocal chords, was used to hold the girl. "Check the kill switch on the handle."

The switch was off. He flipped it on and pulled the rope again. The engine stuttered, backfired, then smoothed out, the whining putter of the two-cycle engine echoing through the terminal.

Still, no one looked around.

Dave took a deep breath and moved next to the mirror, and the scaled arm growing from the surface. He pulled the trigger on the saw, and was rewarded with a high pitched ringing from the engine. He gunned it and brought it down on the arm.

For a few seconds, sparks sprayed out from the arm, as though it were truly made of metal, then the saw cut deep, showering them all with a dark fluid the color and consistency of hot tar. The engine labored. An echoing moan of pain blended with the scream of the saw until the raucous noise was like some innovative, apocalyptic music.

Still no one in the airport noticed.

The silver scaled fingers danced and twitched as Dave cut through nerves and tendons and bone and muscle. Assuming, of course, the arm had such things. It did, or something equivalent. When he was halfway through - tough going through the bone - the claws danced a final jig and released the little girl. Dave didn't stop, though. He leaned into the saw with his good hand, forcing it through the steely flesh until the forearm clattered to the floor.

A howling wail erupted from the mirror as the stump disappeared back inside. The screech rattled the fillings in his teeth and sent a shiver of pain through his skull that he would remember for a few centuries.

Dave dropped the saw and helped pull the girl away from the mirror. The clawed fingers opened and closed in what Dave hoped was a reflexive action. A few seconds later, he wasn't sure.

A wide, triangular head on a long, thin neck burst through the surface of the mirror with a roaring scream of pain and anger. A sharp tongue darted from between twin fangs. Dave could almost feel its feathery touch on his face. It looked at them and hissed as they scrambled backward. A dark ichor dripped from the stump of its arm and made a black pool on the gleaming floor. Dave looked around for some sort of weapon, anything he could use to fight the thing if it should follow.

Miraculously, it didn't.

It pointed the mangled stub at the limb writhing on the floor. The arm leaped into the air, smacking against the stump with a meaty thud.

And the silver scaled arm was whole again.

It hissed at them one last time and pulled itself back into the mirror.

Reality, if not sanity, returned to the airport.

And still, no one else acted as though the afternoon was anything other than normal, calm, and uneventful.

Maria's face burned, her lips trembled with barely controlled rage, the anger tempered only slightly by the feel of Ricky in her arms. No one, except the big guy with the saw, had helped. They ignored her! She'd screamed at some guy wearing a maintenance uniform, and he acted as though she wasn't even there. Damn them! Damn every one of them!

She felt a touch on her arm and jerked away before she realized it was their rescuer. Looking at him, she thought he wasn't one she would have chosen, but at the moment she was damn glad he'd been around.

Maria held Ricky close to her, trying to quiet her sobbing.

From somewhere in the back of her mind, her earlier analysis of the man surfaced, and she added to it. Obviously a quick thinker, and he didn't hesitate to put himself into danger to help Ricky. And there seemed to be a cloud hanging around him. As though he'd seen and done things that left a festering wound somewhere, leaking dark vapors like steam from a volcano.

He didn't seem surprised by a creature bursting through an unbroken mirror.

"I'm sorry," she said. "It's just that --"

"I understand," he told her. "I'm sort of touchy myself."

She looked past him, at other people in the terminal.

"The bastards." Ricky wrapped her arms around Maria's neck. "They ignored us. I screamed and they didn't do a damn thing. Where were the TSA goons? Confiscating a dangerous pair of high heels?"

The man shook his head. "No. They couldn't see you, or hear you, and had no idea what was happening. Listen, there's something about people that I've always thought of as the Coliseum Factor. No matter how gory or bloody the accident is, some group of idiots is going to be there, every one of them jockeying for position to see what's going on. A flash mob will form, waiting for some poor slob to jump off the t-top of a building." Something about that image caused the man to stutter, but he pushed on.

"The same thing drives those TV 'reality' shows. People want to see others pain and suffering and horror. It makes their own problems petty by comparison." He looked at the line at the ticket counter, at the armed officers watching the crowd, and at the bored agents shuffling through open suitcases. "No, for whatever reason, they couldn't see us."

Maria didn't want to let go of her anger. She wanted to use it as a weapon to strike back at the thing in the mirror and at the people who allowed it to threaten her little girl. Anger was better, stronger than grief or fear. She could handle the rage, direct its energy into a useful force. But she felt the anger drain away as she looked around. The people weren't gawking or backing away in fear, they were just unconcerned. To them, nothing had happened. Nothing at all.

"Oh, God," she whispered, finally realizing. She looked back at him. "But you could. Why?"

"Yeah, that's the question." He helped her to her feet and back to the chairs, favoring his left hand. Ricky held her as tightly as a form-fitting glove. "I've been asking myself that a lot the last day or so." He held out his good hand. "My name is Dave Richards." Even his name was familiar, tickling at a spot in the back of her mind. Where had she seen him?

"Maria Quinones," she said and took his hand. At the moment she touched him, one arm was around Ricky's neck.

Hell opened up.

A few demons issued forth. The terminal darkened, the mirrors becoming black panels of dull ebony. The screams of tortured souls filled the air for several eternities. A clinging, nebulous darkness closed around them, a shadowy fog rolling over reality, swallowing light like a cosmic sponge. Maria saw a shock of recognition on Dave Richards' face. He knew the hell around them or something similar, and it reminded Maria of the dark place she thought she'd imagined in her closet.

It closed around the three, and she cried out as it enveloped them in the dark fog.

But they were untouched.

In a small circle that formed a bubble of light and reality, she and Dave Richards stared out at the horror, both illuminated by an almost unbearably bright, blinding radiance. Within that small bubble, they looked at each other, then at the center of the scintillating brilliance.

Ricky glowed with some pure white light that seemed to wash the color from her form. The little girl looked at them with eyes shiny and wondrous, filled with the joyous power within her. She turned her hands over as though fascinated by beams of light flashing from the short fingers. She raised a tiny hand to her mother's face and it was as though Maria could feel the heat of creation in her daughter's touch. For a moment, she seemed to be more than just a little girl. For a few seconds, she was the promise and salvation of the world. Of the universe. Everything bright and good with the world. Something no evil could touch. A pipeline to the future, to all the things Maria and Dave would never see, still tied to the past through the gentle touch on her mother's face.

If Maria could have seen one of the mirrors now, she knew what her reflection would show. The day she moved out on her own, she'd seen a then mysterious look of longing on her Mom's face. It was a mixture of love, sadness, and acquiescence. At that moment, it seemed, she had truly realized Maria would not be the little girl she wanted to love and protect forever. She knew Maria had moved beyond her ability to shelter, and it hurt and sickened and filled her with pride all at the same time.

Maria knew she would see the same thing in her own eyes, now slowly leaking tears down her face.

Too soon, she thought. Twenty frigging years too soon.

The bubble glowed with a pure and strong light, and the darkness recoiled from it as if each touch were the snapping of a whip. Maria could feel it drawing strength from her, but oddly, she felt stronger, not weaker, as the power of the bright sphere grew.

Then it was gone.

Dark fog and the glowing sphere vanished together, and sunlight and reality returned.

Ricky shook her head, then re-established her grip on Maria's neck as though nothing had happened. The two adults stared at each other, their hands still touching, then pulled back as if burned.

"What --" she began.

"I don't know," he said. "A warning, I think."

"About what?"

"About what might happen to us all if it isn't stopped." He looked into the distance, but Maria had the impression he searched for something specific at the top of the mountain outside the terminal.

She had to bite her lip to stop an insane burst of laughter. Something about sitting there talking to the stranger who'd just saved her daughter from a creature out of a mirror - not to mention sharing a vision of the end of the world - struck her as funny. Wildly funny. She saw a slight smile on his face.

"Crazy, isn't it?" he said. "But if you don't grasp at something in this reality, you might find yourself looking around, wondering what happened to your marbles." He put a tentative, gentle hand on Ricky's hair, then stroked it slowly when the world remained intact.

"Erica," she said in reply to his unasked question. "She answers to Ricky if she answers at all."

He nodded.

Maria glanced up at the departure board. Her plane had left the airport exactly three minutes ago. It made no difference, now. She was about to ask a stupid question, like asking a hanged man if he was enjoying himself, but she didn't care.

"Mr. Richards," she said. "Has this sort of thing happened to you before?" He shrugged. "Do you have any idea what the hell is happening?"

"No," he answered, shaking his head. "But I know someone who might." He glanced at the wall beside the mirror. Maria followed his gaze, then inhaled sharply. She could have sworn the wall was empty before.

There, rustling in a breeze from somewhere like a wanted poster in an old western, hung a flyer advertising a magic show to be held that evening. A picture of the magician, "Stefan Star," dominated the center. He was tall and lean, and his dark eyes looked out over a hawk-like nose.

"Do you know him?" she asked.

"Not really. We've met, sort of, but the last time I saw him he wasn't dressed in a tuxedo. He was wearing shorts and a t-shirt, and I think he saved my life." He stared at the flyer for a few seconds, then at himself in the mirror. "I'm still not sure whether he did me a favor."

Chapter 20

Dave maneuvered his car into a space near his hotel room, stealing a glance at Maria's profile. After a burst of conversation at the airport, they'd been remarkably uncommunicative on the way over, especially considering what they'd just been through. He supposed he could blame that on Maria Quinones' efforts to soothe Ricky, and his concentration on finding his way through a strange town. But the fact remained they were still basically strangers, even if strangers who just happened to share an experience that would have sent most people running for the nearest psychiatrist.

It had to be coincidence that they both lost loved ones in the BWI crash.

He stared ahead for a few moments, listening to her murmur nonsense words to the little girl. The time gave him a few moments to collect his thoughts, and maybe even look at the woman without making an idiot of himself. After a while, he did.

Maria Quinones had half turned to look at Ricky, buckled in the center in the back. (She'd been worried about not having a child's seat, but had to be satisfied with a firm seat belt across the girl's hips.) Most of her hair lay straight down her back, but one stray strand had worked its way across her forehead, and she kept pushing it out of her eyes. Her skin was dark and smooth, and her voice like liquid sunshine that filled the car.

Dave's eyes dropped, and he gave himself a mental slap. That wasn't enough to distract him and he gave himself a couple more.

Turned as she was to talk to Ricky, her short dress was shorter still, and almost glowed against the dark skin of her legs and thighs. He forced himself to look away. What kind of jerk would he have to be to even think of trying to take advantage of their situation? He had the vague feeling it would be like trying to hit on a woman as their wingless airplane plunged toward the ground. Maria Quinones was someone he wanted to know better, and that feeling was motivated by more than the fact that she looked better than most of the models in the Sports Illustrated swimsuit issue.

At least, he hoped it was.

Still, he knew that humans, men and women alike, were subject to instincts developed through a few million years of evolution designed to propagate the species, throughout the universe if necessary. Though standards of beauty were subject to regional and cultural bias and change, he was a man of his time. Maria's long legs, her smooth, perfect features, and the way her eyes sparkled when she smiled triggered responses in Dave he thought he had lost in that plane crash.

He tried to rationalize that he couldn't help himself as he studied the delicate shape of her ear, but he knew that was a load of bull. Human brains could, and did, overcome millions of years of evolutionary programming every day.

It was called civilization.

Dave realized her smile was even nicer when it was directed at him.

"What are you thinking about?" she asked. He looked away from her lips, but staring into those deep eyes was almost as bad.

"Charles Darwin," he replied. "And wondering about his motives."

"I'm not even going to ask what that means."

"It means my brain feels like its been through a meat grinder the last few days." He glanced back and saw that Ricky looked calmer than either of the adults. Maybe the girl soothed the woman instead of the other way around.

"Mr. Richards, do you think we're crazy?"

"You know, it seems silly to go around calling each other 'Mr. Richards' and 'Ms. Quinones' if we are sharing some sort of hysterical delusion." She smiled and nodded agreement. "So, you call me Dave, or 'Hey, you' or whatever - I answer to anything and I'll call you Maria." Or Beautiful, he added to himself.

"My room is number 48. Why don't you and Ricky go inside and clean up?" Even the frown didn't make her look any less beautiful.

"You'll be safe," he assured her. "Listen, even a homicidal maniac with necrophiliac tendencies couldn't be any more dangerous than the thing at the airport."

"Dave, I have the feeling you're about as dangerous as our

neighbor's pet kitten."

Dave scratched his head. "I don't know whether to take that as a compliment, or be insulted." He dug in his pocket. "Here, this is my only key. You take it while I talk to the clerk and get directions. There has to be a library somewhere in town with information about the Tower." He smiled at her and patted her arm. "You'll be safe."

Maria looked into his eyes and for a minute, Dave wondered if he had again been transported to another world. But this time a bright, open world where flowers were in eternal bloom and the sound of birds and children's laughter drifted on a gentle breeze. After a few eons lost in her eyes, Dave felt the touch of her hand on his arm, on skin suddenly hyper-sensitive. The touch became the focus of the universe.

Maria leaned over and kissed his cheek, an explosion of soft sensation.

"I know I'll be safe with you." She got out, opened the back door and gathered Ricky and her single suitcase. She waved as she walked to the room.

After she was inside and out of sight, Dave remembered to breathe.

The only thing that ruined the moment was that he had to swing the adjustable steering wheel out of the way and struggle to get out of the car. Even now, he thought of himself as the way he was when he and Suzy first met, and ran into reality when he tried to move.

Dammit! he thought. Even if I'm the only human left on the planet when this is all over, I'm not going to use food as a substitute for emotion.

Whatever he and Maria had become involved in, Dave knew it was dangerous. Dangerous enough to kill any one of them, and, he suspected, deadly enough to menace everyone around them. He had the vague feeling he didn't carry that thought far enough, but refused to pursue it.

It was possible that he could find himself alone and feeling sorry for himself again when this was over. Okay, he could accept that. But he damned well wasn't going to reject humanity for a box of jelly doughnuts.

The hotel clerk, distracted by a thick paperback with some sort of green creature grinning on the cover, gave Dave vague directions to the library.

"You can't miss it," he said. Dave wondered why people who gave instructions that no one could follow always said that. As though the phrase, "You can't miss it," told him that if he did miss it, he was an idiot who couldn't find his ass with a microscope and a detailed map.

A stack of bright yellow paper on the counter attracted his attention.

"Where did you get these?" Dave asked, indicating a pile of tickets.

"Some guy sold them to the manager, and he said to give them away. They're free. Take all you want." His attention wandered back to the book.

"Family Ticket," he read. Well, they weren't a family, but they were close enough. He took one.

Walking back to the room, Dave thought about the conversation at the airport.

"I know you from somewhere," he'd said to her. He sounded exactly like someone trying to pick her up.

The puzzled look didn't make her look any less lovely.

"I think you're right," she said. Maria had tilted her head, as though searching through layers of memory.

At the same time he remembered, he saw the hurt, and even more fright, in Maria's eyes.

The crash at BWI.

He'd seen her there, as spectacularly beautiful as she was now, though obviously in her last few weeks of pregnancy. Both of them were restrained by policemen to keep them from rushing into the fiery wreckage of the plane.

She'd lost her husband at the same time Suzy and Chris died.

"Why?" she said. Dave knew the orange-white flaming image flashing through her mind. He'd seen it in his own thousands of times. "What is doing this to us?"

Dave had only shrugged, unable to answer. He didn't want to use the word "coincidence" because he believed coincidence had nothing to do with their meeting again.

Later, she had told him about the black wall that caused the bus to wreck, and why she happened to be in the back. And about her closet and Ricky's smile. Something about that sent a chill down his spine. Probably the most bitter lesson he'd learned when his family died was that the universe didn't care whether you were an innocent child or an aging serial killer. One was just as likely to die as the other.

It wasn't fair.

Maria let him in immediately when he knocked, and the first thing he noticed was that she was still as beautiful as ever. The second thing was that she had changed clothes. Now, she wore a loose, white blouse and a more functional pair of jeans that emphasized her long legs and strained Dave's civilized state of mind even more. She had replaced her white pumps with a pair of well-worn Nike's that showed she'd bought them for their durability and not the name.

Dave had a pair, once. He hadn't worn them in years.

"Good enough?" Maria asked. Dave could feel his face redden as he realized he'd been staring again.

"Even better," he said. "Besides the fact that it makes you look great."

"Thank you," she said with a slight curtsy. "As a teenager, I remember watching old horror movies with the heroine being pursued through the woods, or the moors, or an old castle and she always wore some sort of diaphanous dress that billowed and streamed behind her as she ran. I always thought that was stupid. If I have to run from something, I want to be in jeans and jogging shoes." She struck a pose with her arms slightly raised. "And I'm ready." Their eyes locked together.

Maybe that was a moment when Dave could have moved closer to her, taken her in his arms, and even kissed her. He could feel an energy moving between them as they stared at each other. Maybe she had seen something in his eyes in the car before she kissed his cheek. There was a message in the slight smile, in the way she stood there for a few seconds as if waiting for him to see the message.

The moment was not to be.

"Mommy," came a small voice from the bathroom. "I'm finished, now. I need help."

It was Maria's turn to redden slightly.

"Uh, I have to help Ricky. She can't quite do everything herself, yet."

"I understand," he said. He did understand, but as she walked into the bathroom, he tried not to let himself remember why he understood. Not now. He couldn't afford the time, and he was afraid of where such thoughts would lead him.

"What did you find?" Maria called from the bathroom.

"Directions to the library. The guy didn't know too much about the Tower, either, except that it's been around as long as he can remember. He wasn't too talkative." Maria followed Ricky out of the bathroom. The little girl crawled up on the bed with her Green Frog.

"And I found this," he told Maria, pulling the ticket out of his pocket. She studied it for a minute.

"It's for the magic show tonight."

"More coincidence, I suppose," Dave said. "These shows set up phone rooms to sell tickets to businesses, and sometimes to people at their residences. But most of the money is made by selling blocks of tickets to businesses who give them to employees or customers, or donate them back to the sponsoring organization to give out at schools or where ever they want."

"You mean like the rescue squad on this ticket."

"Yes. The show has to find a local charitable organization to sponsor it. Then sell tickets through a phone bank, and the show and sponsor share the proceeds. If a business decides to donate the tickets back to the sponsor, they are given out at schools, or orphanages, or to 'others less fortunate.' Most of the time."

"You know a lot about this." Maria returned the ticket. "Doesn't the state have laws about this sort of thing?"

"I wrote an article on it a few years ago, and I don't suppose it's changed much. Most of the shows and sponsors break the rules and regulations by mutual agreement, because it means more money for both parties. For example, they are not supposed to oversell the facility. If the auditorium holds only two hundred people, then they should only sell about two hundred tickets. In practical terms, not everyone shows up, and a lot of the 'donated' tickets are never used. So they might sell a thousand tickets to fill that two hundred seat auditorium."

"What if everyone shows up?"

"I asked one promoter that. All he said was that they didn't. He'd been doing it for ten years and he'd never had a problem. If they sell more tickets than anticipated, or he knows the town always has big sales or attendance, he schedules an afternoon show for the overflow."

"So it's pure coincidence that these tickets were sold to the motel where you're staying?"

He hesitated. "Probably," he said finally. "But I have the feeling we would have found tickets somewhere else if not here."

"I think you're right." She looked unhappy with the idea.

Despite the obscure directions by the clerk, they found the library, but even after an hour or two of looking, they knew little more than before. The information on the Tower was only dry facts, uninformative figures. He had to see the place for himself, but wondered if he should leave Maria and Ricky at the motel. He had no idea whether the Tower was dangerous. By mutual agreement, they gave up and left the library.

There was a long walk leading from the front of the building, and midway he stopped and looked around. A block over, he saw the old hotel building where he had slipped off the ledge. Dave stared at it for a few moments, trying to remember his feelings as he climbed to the top floor, afraid to take the elevator because someone might see his shaking hands and the sweat on his forehead and suspect something wasn't quite right.

"Dave," Maria said. "Are you okay? What do you see?"

"Nothing," he said. After a moment, he pointedly looked away from the building, as if denying the Dave Richards who had entered that place with suicidal intent. That was another, self-pitying man who had no purpose in life and who disparaged the memory of his Suzy and Chris by showing so little respect for his own existence.

"Nothing important. Let's go." He knew Maria didn't quite believe him, but she said nothing as they walked to the car.

He wanted to think, because he had changed his mind before he slipped, that he would have come to these conclusions no matter what had happened. He was afraid that only his incursion into that dark place and his obsessive desire to find out what it was and how he got there and back forced him to think about these things.

If he found a stupidly simple explanation that satisfied him, would he revert to that disgusting, self-pitying person again? A few months from now, would he find himself at the top of another building in another town?

Not likely, he told himself. Not after what happened at the airport.

But even that was only an excuse to forge ahead. To solve the mystery of the snake in the mirror. Something to distract him from what happened three years ago.

He looked at the beautiful woman beside him, then at the little girl tugging at her hand. He'd given up trying to deny he was attracted to Maria, but he must have imagined the look in her eyes. While he resembled a beach ball, someone like Maria would never give him a second look. Circumstances sometimes threw unlikely couples together, he knew, but they were the unlikeliest of all. If - when - this was all over, they would go their separate ways, and Dave would again be faced with a lifetime of solitary nights, wondering if he could endure them.

He should be concentrating on what they'd found in the library, and all he could think about was each accidental touch of her hand as they searched through moldy files. Or were the touches accidental? When she laid a hand on his shoulder to look at something he pointed out, did she do it without thinking, or because he had become important to her? With a conscious effort, he thought about what they'd found.

In a folder of old newspaper clippings, they discovered that town officials had dedicated the Somerset Tower at the top of Lox Mountain on Halloween in 1952 for the beginning of the big holiday season. It cost about thirty-five thousand dollars, and was a hundred and fifty feet tall (including the concrete base and support structure), and it contained over twenty-four hundred feet of neon tubing up the sides and at the top. Since then, there had been periodic controversies over whether the city should enshrine or demolish the landmark. No hint of anything more unusual.

Except one intriguing line from one of the articles.

Probably every native of Somerset knew about the old nickname, which had been around since the 1800's. One of the reasons the merchants wanted the Tower built was to give the city a new symbol and alias, so Somerset became the "Tower of the South."

Before, Somerset had been the "Mystic City."

"Do we go up there or not?" he asked abruptly.

"Do we still have time to make the magic show if we do?" Maria asked after a moment.

"I think so. If I can remember the map we found, it shouldn't take more than a few minutes to get to the Tower."

"Let's go."

He stopped, and for a brief moment admired the way the sun made her hair sparkle and shimmer.

"It might not be safe there. We don't even know how it is involved in this."

"If we weren't safe in my apartment or on the bus or at the airport, we're not safe anywhere," she told him and turned toward the car.

But Dave stood for a second, waiting until he could stop shivering. Her words, "...not safe anywhere" seemed to echo around him. He caught up with them at the car, and by then he could put the key in the lock without shaking.

In a short while, they stood at the base of the Tower, leaning back so they could see the top point. Ricky wanted to pull away and look through the binoculars at the city, but Maria kept a firm grip on her hand.

"Not exactly the Eiffel Tower, is it?" Maria said.

"Not exactly," Dave replied. "More like the cell phone towers sprouting up everywhere, except rusty and decrepit." Maria nodded agreement.

The somewhat rusty metal framework of the structure had channels on the major supports containing double rows of neon tubes. The point was really a small globe housing more intense lighting. When Dave saw it with the lights on, it looked almost like one of those fairy tale magic wands, grown out of control. Or some people said a needle with a glowing point. Dave had noticed the more recent clippings called it the Needle, a nickname some people of Somerset embraced, and others hated.

"It's gaudy, somehow," Maria said. "I can't believe they built that thing here, in the middle of nowhere."

"Well, there is the zoo and restaurant down the road."

"Now there is. When they built it, this place was rock and scrub land." Dave nodded. Some of the articles had been very specific on these points.

He could see why some might think it was an elegant landmark and others would want to tear it down as a blight on the rustic surroundings.

But he saw no evidence of anything unusual. No sparks or flares or flashes of electricity as had been reported in very recent articles. A warm, serene spring afternoon in a beautiful park. Lots of families around enjoying the weekend sun, groups of kids playing wild games of physical tag between the trees, mixed pairs of slightly older kids playing emotional tag with the same intensity.

Nothing odd. Nothing abnormal.

"Okay, Ricky," Maria said. "We'll look through the binoculars." Dave grinned as Ricky dragged Maria toward the benches arranged in a U-shape in front of the needle. As she put a dime in the machine for Ricky, he looked out over the small city of Somerset. Even this far away, he could hear the sounds of the traffic on the interstate and the muted buzz of the small city as it lived its safe, normal life. Horns, a whistle from somewhere, a solid, mechanical clunk as two train cars locked together, some sort of hydraulic pounding he didn't recognize. The jangled heartbeat of the city.

Maria held Ricky as she whipped the binoculars back and forth across the city in an awed silence. The woman looked at him and smiled tolerantly.

He heard two boys behind him talking about the "Haunted Rock."
"Where?" one asked.

"Over in the middle, dummy," the other answered.

As they pointed and ran off, he turned and saw a set of concrete stairs leading to an almost circular raised area, like a mesa, surrounded by a deteriorating chain link fence. Steps to nowhere. The place was silent in contrast to the city below, and Dave felt a tightness around his spine. A young man and woman, all loose fitting blue jeans and tee shirts, sat at the top of the steps, kissing, oblivious to their surroundings.

But Dave felt something else nearby.

He stared past the couple, studying the area around them. There seemed to be some sort of black markings on the concrete, as though it had been subjected to a lot of heat at some time in the past. On the mesa itself, he saw a lot of broken bottles, paper trash, and litter left by people who had no regard for others' property. Even an old blanket that looked as though it had been through a shredder. The couple didn't even look up as he stared.

Maria was busy with Ricky.

For some reason, he didn't want to walk up those broken, rain worn steps past the two, go through the fence, and push through the brush to the center of the almost circular area. It looked as though someone had sculpted the area to form this natural platform into a stage for actors to perform a play. The sun was still high on the horizon, but past the thick brush and inside the fence looked as dark as a moonless midnight. He stopped at the bottom step and looked up, started to raise his foot, and could not. At the same time he felt drawn to the boulder in the center, something held him back. Some inner sense told him to turn away, collect Maria and Ricky and run back to his car, and drive away from this place.

If he valued his sanity, his life, his very soul.

Before he realized it, he had backed away from the steps. He heard Maria whispering to Ricky and forced himself to stop. It was happening again. A roller coaster that he couldn't leave. Something dark loomed over the man and woman. A void that sucked up the light, like the giant hand at the airport. It hovered over the couple for a few seconds before the crushing fist hammered down on them.

Dave cried out. Maria came up and stood beside him with Ricky between them.

The darkness enveloped the couple on the steps and for a few seconds, he could see them struggling as though caught in a fisherman's net. The fog dissipated, and the woman shook her head. She looked up at what the man had become and screamed, then tried to wrestle from its grip.

The wide, triangular head shimmered like molten bronze in the afternoon sun. It's mouth gaped briefly before closing on the young woman's neck and shoulder.

She gasped, and lay still, her eyes open and staring. There were two, widely spaced puncture wounds that seeped red through her tee shirt.

The snake thing turned slowly to face them and hissed. Light glinted off the ring embedded in the flesh of its left hand. It was the same creature they had seen in the airport, and Maria on the bus.

Ricky took his hand and held her mother's at the same time. From somewhere, a bright, pure light pulsed. The globe surrounded them, then reached out toward the creature. It screamed as the liquid fire touched it, smoldering streams of smoke rising as if the light had seared its scaly skin. The globe expanded, pushing toward the thing and the unmoving woman. It was almost within the light when the sphere of light exploded, drenching them all with a brilliant shining that seemed to drip from Dave's fingers as he watched.

The snake thing flared and vanished in a cloud of dark smoke, screaming.

Then there was a young man and woman sitting on the steps, watching the three with a slight puzzled look. The woman was unhurt. The man was human. Dave and Maria had enough presence to smile weakly and turn away.

"Was it real?" Maria asked slowly as they sat on the bench.

"Real enough, when it was happening," Dave answered. Without realizing, he sat so that their arms were touching. He could see her in profile, her lips slightly parted, her dark hair across her forehead. Only a slight smudge, probably a child's handprint, on her cheek spoiled perfection. He realized he'd forgotten, or denied, so much in the last few years.

He put a protective arm around her shoulder, and she did not pull away.

"It's as if something were trying to come into our world, like the thing at the airport, but isn't quite strong enough yet, so it sends us these little surprises."

"Us?" Maria asked. "Why us?"

Dave looked at Ricky, sitting beside Maria. After the flare of light, she had resumed talking to her Green Frog as though nothing had happened. "Maybe because of her. Maybe it needs more power to break through, or a conduit for the power it has." He hesitated.

"What is it?" Maria asked.

"Just a feeling," he replied. "But a very strong one. I think we're being manipulated, moved from one place to another."

"The magic show tonight."

"Maybe. Or maybe it's trying to scare us so we won't go to the show. We're like cattle who don't know which way or why we are being herded."

He felt Maria shiver under his hand.

"You're right," she said. "Like cattle who don't know whether they're going to pasture or to a slaughterhouse."

Above them, bright light danced on the point of the Needle.

Chapter 21

The show was a dream gone bad.

Things had started well. The opening bit had gone according to plan, with a series of ten or fifteen small tricks to warm up the audience. The Infinite Vase dutifully refilled from the hidden chamber whenever he put it down, and each time he emptied it into the bucket at the edge of the stage, the audience applauded.

Alan pulled an ever increasing number of fake flowers from concealed cubbyholes in the Trellis and soon had a colorful row of multicolored silk across the front of the stage. The flowers were designed as darts and he threw each one with a flourish so that it stuck, quivering, in the stage precisely where he wanted.

Though it had happened before, he didn't think about catching hell from the school administration over splintered punctures in the stage floor. That would have distracted him from the show. Time enough for problems later.

The entire series was great until the last trick, the Exploding Floral Globe. The gimmick was to lock down the base of the "empty" tube he showed to the audience, and pull off the outer cover. Then, according to plan, the spring-loaded flowers folded between the inner and outer layer of the tube would pop up into a beautiful red and yellow globe of flowers.

Alan finished the Scarf Change, green into blue and back, and turned toward the Globe, stumbling as a sharp pain stabbed through his temples. Something had returned. And it was close. Very close. He thought he covered the gaff well, but Rena, watching from the side for her cue, knew something had happened. He looked at her and bobbed his head just the least bit to let her know everything was fine. She nodded back, but the worried look never left her eyes.

He glanced out over the audience, expecting to hear screams and see people running for the exits. Maybe a creature or two bounding to the stage, poised to rip apart the arrogant magician's skinny body. But he saw nothing. The crowd still fidgeted a bit, not quite comfortable yet. Of course that's why he started with the small stuff. He wanted them settled and attentive by the time he wheeled out the big illusions.

Alan fitted the base of the Globe onto the small stand, grasped the outer cover, and pulled. The metal cone slid halfway and locked.

Maybe one of the springs broke, he thought, still trying to pull the cover off the metal tube. After a few seconds he muttered something the audience couldn't hear and shoved the cover back into place. It didn't go all the way down and the gimmick was clearly visible. He grabbed at the air, produced a pure white silk scarf, and draped it over the Globe. He shrugged, and the audience gave a tiny, nervous laugh.

"Well," he said at the microphone. His head still throbbed as he scanned the sea of puffy hairdos and caps. Only some of the children seemed free of the Southern badges of adulthood. His voice echoed around the room, booming from four-foot speakers at each side of the stage. "Guess I should have used more fertilizer on that bunch."

They laughed a little louder while Alan studied the dark corners of the room. Something was in there. Something from the Gap. But what?

Over the years, he had Hidden a lot of things, animals, and even an occasional person, when he had to. Especially when he was younger. He wanted to think he wouldn't have been so careless if he had known how they changed. At least he stopped Hiding anything that lived when he realized. It still bothered him that he put the fat man in there, even if just for a fraction of a second to save his life. Even under the most extreme circumstances, he avoided Hiding a human being.

Even with a .45 auto pointed at him.

Once, he might have Hidden the shivering doper and let him rot there. Let him twist and change into something that made being a crackhead seem like a vacation in the Caribbean.

Instead, he merely killed him.

What else could he do? The guy, dirty and stinking like last week's cesspool or a particularly vehement Occupy protester, held a gun that shook like an old man's pointing finger. He could have just Hidden the gun, then run away. But the man might have tracked him down, especially since Alan had seen the bag of money and drugs he dropped in the alley. And Alan wasn't sure even he could outrun somebody strung tighter than high-C on a toy piano.

So with the barrel pointed at his stomach, and the man nervously looking from one end of the alley to the other, wiping the fine beads of sweat from his upper lip and trying to gather enough neurons to make a decision, Alan had to defend himself.

He should have found another way; done something else. But he couldn't think while looking into a gun barrel so big that he could see the rifling grooves. He was afraid the guy would twitch or stumble or have a seizure and then G. Alan Benet would never again do magic. Except the magic of slowly rotting beneath several feet of cold dirt. So he used what he could see.

He stared at a nearby construction site, at a massive concrete block that was part of the foundation of the new building. After a few seconds, the block silently vanished, and just as quietly reappeared eighteen inches above the sweating man and his oversized gun. Gravity took hold.

Something in Alan's eyes must have warned him. He stumbled forward and reached for Alan as the block appeared. Somehow, the crackhead plucked a silk scarf from his pocket at the same time the block slammed against the sidewalk. Alan tried to get it back, but the dead hand wouldn't let go. Finally, he'd panicked and performed his best and oldest trick: he ran.

For almost five years, Alan hadn't deliberately hidden any living thing. He could squash the crackhead like an ant on the concrete if he had to, but he wouldn't Hide him. Most of the Gap was too strange, and too dangerous.

He did not know how he did it, but he could feel the areas that were dangerous, so he could still find fairly calm places for things that were, as far as he knew, safe for later use. When he jogged, he sometimes retrieved a cold Dr. Pepper that he hoped was safe inside its aluminum can. With all the weird stuff the past few months, though, he sometimes doubted anything in there was safe.

Right now, standing on the stage, he could sense a twenty-four pack of Dr. Pepper, a few cans of mixed fruit cocktail, a bottle of chilled champagne, and the Colt Government .45 Auto hand gun with a couple of loaded magazines that had been there since that day in the alley. Those items, and various other things either inorganic or completely sealed, were safely locked in a corner of the Gap that seemed free of any contaminants. At least, he hoped they were safely locked away. He once believed only he could release anything from there.

So why had something popped into existence close by?

And there were other things, mostly living or once living creatures, that he could no longer sense inside the Gap. He had no idea what had happened to them. Maybe they slipped back to reality and he couldn't detect them for some reason, or something inside consumed them, or they were hiding in one of those black areas he couldn't access.

Alan didn't know, and if not for the stabbing, migraine-like pains, he wouldn't have cared.

Whatever had returned, it was near.

Somewhere, something waited for him.

Everything went all to hell after that.

Alan slogged into his opening patter, a series of jokes and one-liners designed to loosen up the audience. At the same time, it gave Rena and the new muscle - Craig was his name - time to move the small props off the stage, and bring out the Invisible Girl and other illusions. He flubbed two jokes in a row, started to sweat even more, and cut the routine short by three or four minutes.

Rena and Craig weren't ready when he pushed through the curtain.

He helped her wrestle the black tubes around the stage while Craig locked the Invisible Girl panels into place. "Alan, What the hell is going on out there?" she asked. "We won't be ready for a couple of minutes, yet."

"Let 'em stew," Alan told her, quickly inspecting the Invisible Girl box Craig had finished assembling. "They haven't been sitting long enough to get antsy." Rena shook her head, but didn't argue. She knew he was right. If he'd tried this during the latter part of the show, the people would start talking loudly and asking what the hell was going on up there. Now, they just twisted in their seats and looked at each other.

The Invisible Girl cabinet was a cleverly designed box about six feet tall with a peaked roof and small blocks of wood attached to the insides of the box with an interior painted black so the spectators couldn't see any details. The openings for the four tubes seemed to be so large that it looked as though there was no room for anything bigger than a Chihuahua after Alan slid them into place.

Looks, especially in the magic business, are deceiving.

No one paid any attention to the frills and decorations on the illusions, but these distracting ornaments were usually what made the tricks work.

The openings for the tubes were outlined in five inch wide, brushed aluminum panels. This made the holes, two squares and two octagons of various sizes, look twice as large as they really were. In turn, the available space looked even smaller. The girl, in this case Rena, just stood on one side of the box with her back arched over the top of the upper tube, in the peak of the cabinet. She had plenty of room to stand comfortably, and no one could understand how she did it. She even changed clothes, removing the skimpy leotard she wore and donning an evening dress that had been concealed in a black panel inside.

But the rubes applauded Alan just as if he had done something magical and somehow made her disappear and reappear in the dress.

When performed correctly, the illusion triggered thunderous applause.

That night, it wasn't performed correctly.

At the beginning of the illusion, Alan invited members of the audience to come on the stage and certify that she didn't leave the cabinet. He always chose a couple of members of the sponsoring organization, in this case a local rescue squad, because the more they were involved with the show, the more likely the chances of re-signing them next year.

As he slid the tubes into the box, Rena tossed out the leotard she had been wearing, just as she was supposed to do. At that moment, Alan knew, she was nude inside the box, but searching for the evening dress concealed in the floor. He tossed the leotard to a tall man with a salt and pepper beard and a rescue squad cap. The man grinned stupidly and fondled the garment for a moment before he seemed to realize he was on a stage in front of several hundred people. His face turned red as he tossed it to the side and carefully studied the cabinet.

As he pushed the last tube into place, Alan thought Rena muttered something. The rescue squad member frowned and cocked his head, trying to hear what she said inside the box. Alan smiled and turned back to the paying customers. He raised his arms and they applauded.

He took the microphone from the stand and went to the man with the beard. "Did she leave the cabinet?" he asked. The man shook his head. "Did you see any trap doors or hidden panels or false bottoms?" Another shake. Alan thanked him, and asked the other two men the same questions. They replied just as they should, and Alan thought maybe his bad luck was over. He took the microphone to the front of the cabinet.

"My assistant Rena has faded into oblivion, but I believe we can still hear her voice across the void. I'll try to ask her a few questions.

"Rena," he said to the box. "Can you hear me?" He held the mike close to the box for her answer.

"Yes, Alan," she said. Then a titter of laughter ran through the audience as she made a quiet grunting sound.

Alan looked at them and said, "She must be closer than I thought. Are you okay, Rena?"

"Uh, yes, Alan." She seemed to hesitate over the answer. "But I may have trouble returning from the void."

Alan frowned. She wasn't supposed to say that. Why the hell was she adlibbing?

"Okay, Rena," he said as he took the mike away from the box and returned it to the stand. "I'll do my best to return you to reality." He gestured, then frowned as Craig turned up the music. No, he cranked up the music. Kids in the first two rows held their hands over their ears, and Craig had wandered off in the back to do God knew what.

Jesus! he thought again, and began removing the tubes. Rena tried to talk to him from inside, but the music was too loud for him to hear her clearly. What a mess!

And finally, after he stacked the tubes to the side, the door wouldn't open. It was stuck, almost as though something held it from the inside.

Images flickered through his head. Something dark and toothy appearing inside the cabinet, smothering Rena's scream as it ripped open her throat. Blood dripping, pooling in the bottom of the box. A wide, red smile on the thing's face as it chewed.

And now, it held the door as it sipped Rena's blood.

To hell with the box. He was ready to rip the doors off to get her out. Something in his chest tightened and he found it hard to breath when he thought about Rena laying torn and bloody in the box.

Alan jerked the door savagely and threw it open. What he saw shocked him so much that for a full five seconds, he stood there with the door open, the interior of the box in full, panoramic view of the audience.

The young kids in the audience laughed. The slightly older boys leaned forward for a closer look. Mothers put one hand over their children's faces and the other over their husbands'. A sigh of wonder ran through the hundreds of people and the three men on stage edged around the cabinet for a better view.

Rena stood there, safe and unscratched.

Completely nude.

Posed exactly as Botticelli's Birth of Venus.

She held her right arm across her breasts while her left hand covered her crotch. Red hair like flame rippling in an unfelt breeze.

She is so beautiful, Alan thought.

Then he realized everyone else in the auditorium was seeing the same thing.

Idiot, he told himself. He'd seen her bare-bottom naked dozens of time. Why should this be any different?

Maybe because she stood there with an unforced, confident look of dignity on her face. But he wanted to hold her and protect her from the crazy, dangerous world they lived in. From crackheads and chuckling men who killed for the taste of blood and things that appeared from nowhere with large teeth and sharp talons.

He shut the door quickly and motioned to Craig, who had wandered back, to stop the music. He rolled the cabinet off stage.

"Well," Alan said at the microphone. "After that, I'll have to ask each of you to pay an extra two dollars as you leave this evening."

They laughed, but Alan didn't know whether they thought the joke was funny or whether they were as embarrassed and nervous as he was. He glanced to the left and saw Rena stalking out of the cabinet, her hands still in place. Craig watched her from behind with obvious delight. You're fired, mister, Alan thought. If you manage to survive the night.

Alan thought they were in the absolute nadir of a nearly bottomless pit, but things went rapidly downhill from there.

Damn! he thought then, the first of many similar thoughts over the next hour and a half or so.

To make things worse, he had to conceal pains that, like the contractions of an overdue mother about to give birth, became more intense and closer together as the evening passed. He didn't dare try the two tricks involving his Talent. Alan was afraid he wouldn't be able to control what disappeared. Or appeared. So far, Rena had accepted his explanation of a gimmick even she wasn't allowed to see, but let some sort of damned creatures start cavorting across the stage and she might become a bit suspicious that something more was involved.

And people might die. Rena, for example.

The punishment subsided near the end of the show, but the finale was still a catastrophe. The trick lid on the sub trunk didn't lock back after he went through and fell open when Rena and Craig lifted it. He could only hope that few people saw it. Then the ten foot American flag he pulled from a top hat tangled, and only telescoped to about three and a half feet. It fluttered weakly as he waved it until he finally stuffed it into the trunk, out of sight.

Alan bowed to the audience as the curtain closed in front of him. He wiped his brow with his sleeve and listened. They clapped for a few seconds, then quieted. He heard them murmuring about the show and none of it sounded good. Well, he thought, here's one sponsor who will never hire us again.

"A hell of a disaster," he said when the curtain had closed. No call for a second bow this time. After the few seconds of polite applause, they filed out of the auditorium. He walked to the edge of the curtain and held it open enough to see the people as they left. A lot of them were shaking their heads.

"Alan," Rena said as she packed some of the smaller gimmicks. "About the Invisible Girl thing - after I tossed out the costume, the hidden panel wouldn't release and I couldn't get the dress." Alan disassembled some of the larger illusions, while Craig stood with his hands in his pockets and watched him. Either he was stupid or just plain lazy. Probably his damn fault the panel screwed up.

"Forget it, Rena," Alan said. He motioned for Craig to stack the pieces of the trunk near the loading door. "We probably should set up a code word in case it happens again. Then I can toss in a towel or something for you to wrap around you." He looked up. "Craig, take the sound system apart and pack it in the big box over there." He nodded and walked slowly to the amplifier.

"Why don't you do that, anyway?" Rena said. She neatly folded some of her costumes, and hung others on the rack. "The dress is strapless and I can bunch most of it up around my waist. When you open the door, everyone will think I'm wearing the towel, and nothing else. So you slam the door, like you did tonight, and I'll drop the towel and step out in the evening gown. Instant costume change, and the yokels will get the thrill of almost seeing something." She paused. "Unlike this evening when they actually did."

"Not bad," Alan said. He folded the Hindu basket into its wide base, then stood, walked over to her, and wrapped his arms around her, enjoying the soft pressure of her body against his. He wondered if there was more than just the promise of sex that attracted him to her. He had never allowed himself to get seriously involved with anyone. Too dangerous for him and the other person. He was all too aware of his quick temper and his tendency to react to stress with almost hysterical fear. Though his efforts to manage it over the past few years were mostly successful, he worried that he could again lose control. Just an innocent disagreement with Rena and she might disappear like his old garbage.

But earlier, when he thought she might be in trouble, he would've taken any risk to save her.

"It's not fair," he said, half to himself.

"What's not fair?" she asked. He felt her tense, but after the show tonight, both of them had a right to be tense.

"You," he said. He couldn't tell her what he really thought. "Not fair that so much beauty and so many brains could be packed into such a petite package." Rena relaxed and smiled at him. Alan always had the impression of a barrier around Rena. There was a line she had drawn around herself that she allowed no one past, not even him. He could sympathize with the feeling so he never pushed the subject, but at the same time wondered what she hid. When she was ready, she would tell him, he had decided. Until then, he tried not to worry about it. They had fun together, and enjoyed each other. What more could he ask?

"Must be the company I keep," she said. "I was never noted for my flashes of brilliance before."

"Speaking of flashes," he said, glancing at his watch. "I have to go flash my dazzling smile at the sponsor and see if I can convince them to book this slapstick for next year."

"And don't forget your share of the gate receipts," she told him.

"I never forget that." He looked at Craig, casually wrapping speaker wire around a spool. "Craig, open the loading door and the van and start loading as much of the big stuff as you can. I'll be back in a few minutes." Craig nodded and continued wrapping the wire. Alan shook his head and pushed through the curtain.

Someone must have turned down the house lights. The dark pits at the corners had expanded into large, black pools that seemed to stretch, amoeba-like, to touch each other near the back of the auditorium.

Alan had walked up the inclined aisle to the doors when he remembered the presence he'd felt earlier.

The voices of the rescue squad members drifted through the doors, but Alan paid no attention to them. He cocked his head, straining to hear or see something in the blackness to the right.

And he did.

It was a hollow scratching sound, as if someone had stuffed a cat into a paper grocery bag and stapled the top. A ripe odor of decay drifted from near the sound. He still couldn't see a thing. He needed a flashlight.

Then he remembered the Money to Burn gimmick that looked like a wallet, but ignited when he opened it. One of the tricks he had skipped tonight. He had enough troubles without setting himself and the auditorium on fire.

Alan walked to the edge of the light, and tried to peer into the corner. Still nothing. He shrugged and opened the trick.

The lighter fluid ignited and flickered crazily as it burned. Shadows danced around the walls, leaning this way, then the other. Alan held the gimmick above his head until he could see into the corner.

It was a grocery bag.

He could read the store name printed there: "Scott's Super." He had shopped there while in South Carolina last year. In his travels, he'd seen only one "Scott's Super" anywhere in the country, though for all he knew, there could be a chain of a dozen or more on the next street.

He remembered "Scott's" because of where he had to stay before that show. The contract was a fairly large one, and it took him almost two months to properly work the business taps and the phones for the home sales. But despite the big payoff in the end, he had to stay in a dirty, unpainted, roach riddled old house. The filth finally reached his personal "gross" limit and he began Hiding the garbage rather than hauling it to the dumpster on the corner.

This looked like one of his.

But what the hell was that scratching?

Suddenly he knew, and wish he didn't.

At the same instant he realized what it must be, a brown head the size of a small dog's poked past the top edge of the bag, knocking a few corroded tin cans clanking to the floor. It had long antennae that quivered in the flickering light, and a glistening, slick carapace.

It was - or once had been - a roach.

Alan had the distinct impression that it smiled at him. As if it were glad to see him.

The light flickered out. He heard the bag rattle, then a soft plop like the sound a huge roach would make as it dropped to the floor.

Something scratching at the carpet.

A chittering sound he couldn't identify.

Alan backed into the light, and could see the antennae wavering in and out of the dark like twin batons held by an unseen conductor. It had stopped, reluctant, as all its kind were, to come into the light.

"What the hell -- !"

Craig's voice from the stage broke his fascinated trance. His head whipped in that direction. Rena was back there.

First, he had to handle this thing.

He reached out with his talent, focused on the brown shape, and Hid it.

Or tried to. It stood in half darkness, still chittering at him. Somehow, it had pushed back just as he tried to Hide it.

He tried again. Harder.

It made a whining noise of pain, but didn't go away.

Alan sweated. Craig and Rena were making startled noises on the stage and this thing looked hungry. As though it were tired of garbage and ready to munch on something more substantial. Like a magician's foot.

He shook his head, focused his concentration until a tiny spot of pain centered in his forehead grew, and reached out with his talent again.

It squealed, grabbed for the rug, and vanished.

His head throbbed violently.

Alan sprinted to the front of the auditorium, then vaulted onto the stage. Behind the curtain, Rena and Craig were staring into the night, a mix of wonder and fear on their faces. Craig looked around, then pointed out the door.

"What the hell's happening here?" Alan began, rubbing his temples. He looked where Craig had pointed.

High on the mountain above the city, a point of light blazed.

When he arrived, Alan had noticed it. Somerset billed itself as the "Tower of the South." He was sure they never expected this when they built the structure, though.

Sparkling whirlwinds circled the point and the metal struts. Lightning danced from the Tower to the ground and back again. A glowing violet aura brightened and pulsed like the beating heart of supernatural being.

In perfect time to the throbbing pain in his head.

Beat-pain. Beat-pain. Beat-pain.

"What is it?" Rena asked. Alan barely heard her. He held his fists to his temples, trying to quiet the agony. "Alan, what's the matter?"

Beat-pain. Beat-pain. Beat-pain.

His vision blurred and his ears seemed to fill with a sound of roaring water that couldn't hide the pounding.

BEAT-PAIN. BEAT-PAIN. BEAT-PAIN.

"Alan!" he heard in the distance.

He met the hardwood floor with a savage, overwhelming explosion of light and agony. Then nothing.

But at least the beating pain was gone.

From far away, just before he lost himself, he thought he heard laughter.

Chapter 22

With Erica twitching uneasily on her lap, as if plagued by bad dreams, Maria realized they shouldn't have come to the show.

She could feel the presence building up around them, as on the bus. The cloying scent of death built in a fog around the auditorium, and no one noticed. Even Dave smiled at the show occasionally, though his eyes kept stealing to the dim corners of the room as if he expected another scaled arm to grow out of the wall.

Once, he jerked his head around, eyes wide and shifting. His brow furrowed, but after a moment he turned back to the show.

"What is it?" she whispered, leaning over so he could hear her words.

"I'm not sure," he answered. "I thought I saw a flash of light or something, but it's gone now." He shrugged. "Anyway, no one else seems to have noticed anything. Probably nothing."

Maria wasn't so sure, but she returned his slight smile with a weaker one of her own. She turned to the show, but her thoughts drifted back to Dave. There was something about him that attracted her, but she couldn't pinpoint it exactly. Ricky loved him, and the way he held her on his lap at the motel and talked to her as though she were the most important person in the world didn't hurt, either. And he had a sense of humor, if the story he'd told Ricky about the Dirty Lion and Clean Lion was any indication.

"I've never heard that story," Maria had told him afterward as he sat on the bed watching Ricky play with her frog.

"I made it up." He had seemed reluctant to admit it. "I never did too well with fiction, but Chris always liked my stories." Dave had stopped and stared out the window for a moment before continuing.

"He always expected me to be there with a new one before he went to bed. Sometimes, he would tell me what tomorrow's tale was about."

"And you would have to make up one with his plot?"

"His plot, his characters, and his location." His eyes unfocused, and Maria looked away, studying the cover of a magazine. "His eyes would sparkle as if they were crystal, and he'd laugh, and his dimple would crinkle." He'd stood and walked to the window, his nose almost against the glass.

"I can feel him, Maria," he said. "I can close my eyes and think back to a thousand of those moments and of how each of them ended with his arms tight around my neck, and his giggle tinkling in my ear, and how damn good it felt to hug my little boy."

Maria had stood and walked up behind him, laying a hand on his shoulder.

"You have those thousand moments," she'd told him. "Hold and cherish them."

He'd put his hand over hers, then said, "I have to go out for a little while." He'd been gone over a half hour.

Around her people clapped, so Maria did, too. Though she wasn't quite sure why. She glanced sideways at Dave briefly. Yes, it was easy to see the man he'd once been, but even now, he was still damned handsome.

Something held her back. Like a thin wall between them. Nothing either of them couldn't tear down with a minimum of effort, but one both of them seemed reluctant to tackle.

Was it because she still grieved for Brian? She didn't think so. She had dated a little in the last year or two, though nothing serious. She didn't have time to get serious while caring for Ricky, managing the restaurant, and reading a little in her few spare moments.

Maria couldn't decide whether it was her, or Dave. An image of her mother flashed through her mind, talking about silver tears. From one of their very rare quarrels, when her mother had said she would never be serious about another man until she let go of Brian.

Bullshit.

Maria remembered the warm glow she felt when Dave had complimented her dress, though she thought it was too short and too tight. And despite his compliment, he seemed a little uncomfortable, too.

Dave was warm and friendly and courteous, everything a Boy Scout should be. She smiled to herself. He seemed to be fighting an internal war between lust and propriety and propriety had the upper hand.

At the moment, she couldn't decide which to root for.

Ricky moved uneasily on her lap, still sleeping. She'd drifted off to sleep halfway through the show.

She didn't miss much.

Maria thought there had to be something wrong with the magician. His stage name, obviously, was Stefan Star, according to the program book, yet Maria remembered seeing him in a show in northern Virginia working under a different name. His show was much better then. More professional, smoother, more polished. Tonight, he looked as though he stumbled around the stage, unable to quite get into synch with his performance. He hesitated, seemed to forget his script, rushed the tricks when he should have lingered over the climax, and generally gave the impression of someone who had other, more important things on his mind.

A lot of us have more important things to think about. She knew Dave was impatient, anxious for the end of the show, so they could talk to the magician backstage.

To find out what he knew about stormy dimensions and scaly arms.

Ricky again squirmed on her lap and she bent and kissed her forehead. Her little girl smiled.

I wish I could sleep and dream a pleasant fantasy, Maria thought.

But she knew any dream would only turn into a nightmare.

Dreamy eyes.

That's what Mommy called it when her eyes got tired and she blinked a lot. When it happened, she always went to sleep, no matter how she tried to think about toys or the Turtles or Mommy. She liked to think about toys and Turtles and Mommy. Especially Mommy.

But Big People were so Very Serious.

Ricky didn't always understand everything that Mommy told her. That's why she got in trouble sometimes. Once, when she told her not to climb on Things, and she climbed on a chair and fell off and cried. She didn't know a chair was a Thing, but Mommy picked her up and hugged her and said, "See, Sweet Heart, that's why you don't climb on Things."

Ricky tried to listen to Mommy all the time, but sometimes she wished Mommy could talk to her better and tell her better what to do. Like telling her a chair was a Thing after she said not to climb on Things.

She knew what "dangerous" meant, though. When she got hurt, Mommy said climbing was "dangerous" sometimes. One time, she almost cut herself on a piece of glass she found, and Mommy said it was "dangerous," too.

So when Mommy told her to be careful because some Thing might try to hurt her or Mommy or Dave because the Thing was "Very Dangerous" and might try to get them like at the airplane place, she was worried. She knew a chair was a Thing, now, and had watched them since Mommy told her, but none of them looked "Very Dangerous" to her. And Mommy and Dave sat in them and didn't look worried. So this Thing must be a different Thing, and she wished Mommy had told her what so she could stay away from it.

But all the thinking about "Very Dangerous" Things had made her sleepy, and even the skinny man who talked loud and made pretty flowers on the floor couldn't keep her awake. She blinked once or twice, then again. The last time she didn't open her eyes.

After awhile, Ricky found herself in a giant playhouse that looked a lot like an airport. There were toys as far as she could see in every direction, and she sat down, giggling and clapping her hands, to play with those nearest.

She heard footsteps moving toward her but, for the moment, couldn't spare enough attention to look up and see who was coming. After a few minutes, she giggled again, then gave orders to the Green Frog to watch the other toys.

The footsteps moved closer, and Ricky could see a pair of shiny shoes nearby. A man stood there. A tall man, and Ricky had to lean her head way back to see him.

He was handsome and had a smile that reminded her of a flashlight and a dark head of hair like hers. There was something in his eyes that Ricky had no name for, but it was the same way her Mommy looked at her when Mommy thought she didn't pay attention to her. It always made her feel good when Mommy looked at her that way. She realized it made her feel good when this man looked at her, too.

"Do you know who I am, Erica?" the man asked, his voice clear and deep.

Ricky stood and stared at him for a minute before she made the connection with the pictures on her Mommy's table.

"You're Daddy," she said with some surprise. "But Mommy said you went away to heaven and couldn't come back." Ricky studied him for a few seconds. "Are you coming back to live with me and

Mommy?"

"No, Ricky, I can't do that. After you go to heaven you have to live there. You can't come back."

"Do they make you stay there?" Ricky asked. "Even if you want to leave?"

Daddy looked away for a minute, like he could see something that Ricky couldn't. For a minute she thought Daddy was crying.

"Erica, after you go to heaven, you don't want to leave. It's a wonderful, beautiful place."

"I want to go, too," Ricky said. "And Mommy can come with me and we can all live together like you and Mommy did before I was borned."

Daddy looked like he was crying again.

"Baby, you can't come to heaven, not yet," he said. "It's not your turn. You have to stay with your Mommy and help her and Dave fight the Bad Thing."

"I can't go to heaven?"

"Not now, Ricky. Someday, maybe. But you have to try very hard to understand me, Baby, this is Very Important. Okay?" Ricky nodded. Daddy took a deep breath.

"You can't go to heaven because you are alive, Ricky, and being alive is a wonderful, beautiful thing, too. Remember that, Sweet Heart, no matter what anybody tells you. Some day, some bad person might come along and tell you that not being alive would be nice because you could get to stay with your Daddy and the magic man." Daddy stopped.

"The magic man isn't in heaven," Ricky said. Mommy said you have to be careful about telling Big People when they were wrong, but she remembered seeing him throwing the pretty flowers. "Mommy is watching him do magic." Daddy took another deep breath.

"That's right," he said. "Sometimes your Daddy forgets things and get things mixed up. But don't you forget. You have to stay and take care of your Mommy. She needs you. Daddy has friends to take care of him, but your Mommy needs you and your love to take care of her. Do you understand?"

Ricky nodded slowly.

"I have to stay with Mommy," she said. "Because I love her and she loves me."

"Right, Ricky. Mommy and Dave need your love and help to fight the Bad Thing." Daddy looked around, off into the distance again. "I have to go, Ricky."

"I love you, Daddy," Ricky said, and she felt a warmth in her tummy that made her suddenly understand why Big People were sometimes Very Serious. She ran and jumped into Daddy's arms and hugged his neck real tight. Her Daddy smelled like a fresh pine tree. "I won't forget you, Daddy."

"I love you, too, Erica," he said. Daddy sure did cry a lot. "And tell your Mommy I love her, too." He put Ricky down. "And most of all, Ricky, be brave and be strong. Your Mommy depends on you." He turned and walked away.

"Okay, Daddy," Ricky called after him. "Will you come back to see me again someday?"

Daddy turned. "Look inside yourself, Erica," he said. "And you will realize that I never left. I am with you all the time."

And her Daddy faded away just like the space people on TV did.

Ricky slept a while longer, nestled in her mother's lap, smiling, and dreaming of nothing more than love.

Chapter 23

Pleasure surged and exploded around Karick, drenching it in an ebon-hued fog of human screams of pain. The forces of the Gap crackled, and the landscape flashed, not in black or white or any color, but blankly. As if the energy was a wave of non-existence, and the universe stuttered as it reformed. Those unfortunates who retained enough of their senses to know what happened screamed again, and Karick let the sound wash over it's body like a pleasantly warm shower. More humans found their way into the Gap every day. Soon, the human universe and the Gap would collide and merge in a crescendo that would snuff suns and split worlds. The sky would blacken and lightning would flash darkly and lightless clouds would speed across a suffering world.

Two voices echoed in the hot wind, but there was only Karick, and the dark slash of its mouth never moved.

"Soon, there will be nothing but the Gap." This voice was rough, low and gravelly as from the bottom of a deep pit of rock and mud.

"I am pleased." Voice Two was only slightly less deep, but somehow wilder.

"Of course," said Voice One. "It is only appropriate." It chuckled, like stones on tin. "That puny thing in the beginning would not have approved."

"That frail creature is long dead."

"And not yet born," reminded Voice One.

"Nevertheless."

It didn't matter. There was only Karick.

And Karick had been waiting many billions of years for this, the completion of the cycle. The place of the beginning was now the end, and soon it would be able to depart from its predetermined prison. Not the stormy, dim place it ruled. It rather enjoyed the place. But it thirsted to leave the endless, immovable circle, burst through into the universe of humanity, and drink deeply of the destruction it and its soldiers would share with them. It could almost feel the waves of pure distress and anguish flowing over it, a shower of black ecstasy.

"The time is near," said Voice Two.

Now the slash opened, showing dark spiked teeth in a grimace that might have been a smile on a creature more human. Time and space shimmered and it was again the cloud hand above the airport. It replayed the incident, not in its memory, but in real time.

Voice Two's laughter echoed through space time as it ended.

That missing finger. So clever. So appropriate.

"He will never know the real connection," said Voice Two.

"No more than the woman who saw her own face in the closet."

They were so stupidly human. They would not believe. No matter how many times it showed them.

It rippled back to the moving spot of space-time called the "present" by less perceptive beings, and summoned the recently human thing still wearing the ring. It had an affinity for the woman and child.

"The little girl is a danger," said Voice One.

"She was not. The pattern, the events are set. They happened as they will happen."

"But she has such power within her. Enough to destroy the plan, and the universe if she desires."

"My soldier will handle the two females."

"Something is bothersome about the soldier," said Voice One.

"The ring."

Small things had changed. Reality flowed and shifted but always returned to the true path. The first time, the ring was taken from the soldier. "A small thing that makes no difference. It will fulfill its task."

It would be eager to return to human reality and set after them. At the weak spot near the tower structure, the fat human whose avarice encompassed all major human lusts approached. He would help pull the soldier through. Together, they would prepare for the confrontation. Together, they would ready the path.

And they would die, of course. Not together, but they would die, providing Karick with what little measure of human fear and terror they still possessed. A tiny bit of pleasure.

Then the triumph. The final triumph still to come, though it happened billions and billions of years ago.

Karick trembled. It had waited so long.

Things were coming. Things of death and pain.

The wait was almost over.

"They will never know who they fight," said Voice Two.

"Never," agreed Voice One. But it somehow did not sound quite as sure.

The police had to be looking for him by now, Big John knew. And if anyone at the Somerset department remembered him from the previous arrest, and that he got off on a legal screw-up, the cops there would be real damned glad to see him sitting behind bars again.

If he made it that far.

Even with all the crap about police brutality, John figured they'd find a quiet spot where there were no video cameras and show him how glad they were to see him. He wasn't sure even them pansies at the A. C. L. U. would do anything to help him.

What the hell. He didn't need any damn body's help.

Lox Mountain Park was a quiet place, with only an occasional wild call from either the nearby zoo or the groups of children running in the open spaces between the trees and picnic tables. If he listened carefully, he could hear the sounds of the city just past the line of trees that hid the skyline. For a while Big John just followed the movements of the children, his fingers flexing, his eyes darting from one group to the other. For a while it worried him that he could watch and not feel the Urge come on him. But it wasn't time, he finally realized. He was sure he would know when it was time to leave the car, Urge or no Urge.

Sitting in the parking lot near the Tower, Big John Hill looked at his hands, then angled the rear view mirror so he could stare at his face. He knew, without opening his shirt or pulling up his pants leg, that only the visible parts of his body looked like the old John. The rest of him was dark, hard like a piece of tough leather drying in the sun. An old hound of his had once dragged pieces of a dead cow home, and chewed on the stiff, almost indestructible hide for weeks. That was his skin now. He ran his fingers across his arm and traced the outline of cracks and ridges in his skin where armor plates conformed to his body. When he tapped his leg with the brass butt plate of his hunting knife, it sounded like metal clicking on a wooden table top.

Big John felt strong, invincible. If someone shot at him with one of them tiny little .22 popguns now, he knew the bullets might sting, but they wouldn't hurt him. He was just too damned tough. The Taurus magnum might be able to do some damage, but he planned to stay away from those damn things. For the time being.

He had ditched the Eagle that morning, Saturday, and stolen an Olds station wagon from the repossessed lot at a bank just outside Somerset. If he was lucky, it would be Monday before anyone noticed the wagon was gone. John had been a little surprised when he tried the door and pulled it open without unlocking it first. He thought it might have been only partly latched, which would explain why he didn't break the lock, but didn't explain why he had the strength to jerk it open in the first place. Until he realized the promises were being kept. Powerful and strong. Everything that he wanted when he wanted it.

He unconsciously flexed his fingers, thinking about Jeannie, then shuddered, thinking about her father. Not long, he told himself, and even Sam's .357 won't be more than a nuisance.

Time drifted across the mountain. People came and went. A short man with a cane entered an old Mercedes and drove away. Someone screamed, in delight. That might change later.

Now, time to leave. He had an appointment.

The sound of the car door closing echoed through the park, and even the zoo animals were quiet for a moment. A dozen or more faces turned to look at him as he stood beside the Olds. They felt the power, Big John knew, and every single one of them looked uneasy as they glanced away. Even the kids. Without thinking, they moved their games away from him, almost casually running just a bit farther with each circling game of tag. Let them run while they can, he thought.

Big John felt himself hesitate as he walked slowly past the metal tower and wondered what the hell he was doing. What had happened to him? He stopped and leaned against a tree, running a hand back through his slick matted hair. After a few seconds, he recognized what he felt and knew that, for one last time, he still had the power to choose.

Inside the fat and the armored skin and the much stronger barrier of perversion he'd built up over the years, a tiny spark of guilt and remorse fanned into a flame that caused sweat to break out on the still human parts of Big John Hill. He saw tiny, scared faces. Even smaller, scarred souls. His victims, from the little five year old girl his mother caught him with when he was ten to Jeannie Baker slowly being choked unconscious on the floorboard of his Chevy. They stared at him, fingers pointing, chanting his name, accusing him only of what he'd done. Reciting his crimes for the internal trial of good versus evil taking place inside his head.

He stood at a crossroads, he knew. He could choose the path back, even become completely human again if he renounced Karick, denied its existence. Then Big John Hill would be nothing more than any other perverted, twisted human, eventually to be taken and stand trial for what he'd done. The police must have found the pictures and videos in the basement by now, and they had more reason than just the murders of a few drug dealers to find him. Hell, they might have given him a medal if not for . . . the other things.

The guilt and remorse flared as if a flame in a thunderstorm and died.

His freedom of choice was an illusion, he knew. He had no choice.

John could never go back. Not only because of the power that had been promised him, but because of the whispering and pointing and scowls of disgust that would be directed at him if he was caught and managed to make it to jail alive. He was sure he wouldn't live long after that.

He had forsaken humanity long before.

His only choice was the dark power.

At least there he had a chance. The other way, he knew he would die quickly, and dying human would be a small comfort.

Big John had chosen long ago. He had reaffirmed his choice when he stopped and talked to Jeannie Baker. When he snatched that girl off the playground in Somerset. When he carried little Cissy Robbins into the loft and his mother found them and switch whipped them both until they were raw and bleeding.

The sound of leather creaking underneath his shirt reminded him of the power he possessed.

He stepped back onto the sidewalk and took the first step to the Needle. To his destiny.

"John."

Something called his name from beyond the Tower.

He scanned the park, but none of the people around him reacted. None of them heard the deep, gravelly voice that echoed and vibrated around him.

"John."

It called him again and he walked toward the sound.

He barely spared a glance for the structure itself, but continued on to where a fence separated park property from private property. There, a deteriorating chain link fence enclosed a small grassy area. Intruders had cut and then wrenched the fence away from the metal poles in three or four places, breaching the barrier. John pushed through the largest opening and walked unhesitatingly to the center of the mesa, where he saw a wide, almost flat boulder with a sheet of steel set into the center. A small knob of metal protruded from the deeply grooved steel plate, corroded and blackened with the passage of years until it was like a large chunk of misshapen coal.

It spoke to him.

"My warrior approaches," it said. The low, distorted voice echoed around him, filling his body with its power.

"You and the soldier will fight those who would close the barrier." The voice was different now, but John knew it didn't matter. Only the power mattered.

A dark shimmering appeared to flow from the metal knob, forming a slowly shifting void in the air before him. Big John reached into a pulsing black cloud, felt cold flesh against his palm, then pulled. Something scaly and black became solid. John backed away from it and wiped his hand on his pants.

"The hour is approaching." The voice echoed from nowhere around him.

"Things are coming."

"Things of death and pain and destruction."

It told him of the little girl, and how he must use all his cunning to take her. Bring her to this spot and lay her on the cold steel plate. It whispered the things he must do to the small body to make him strong, and Big John licked his lips and wiped his palms on his bluejeans. He touched the hunting knife at his side.

Then it laughed.

And Big John Hill laughed with the thing, the chill of his laughter spreading through the mountain park, making lovers and families and solitary thinkers run for their cars to hide from the sudden frigid wind circling the mountain. Animals in the zoo nearby whimpered and shrank into their shelters.

The reptile thing cowered deeper into the shadows.

John laughed until he laughed away every fearful remnant of his humanity, and there was only the cold, dead laughter of Karick and the echo from Big John.

At the end, as darkness closed around the mountain, they both chuckled with the same soulless mirth, and Big John no longer had any choice about anything.

Lo! thy dread empire, Chaos! is restored;
Light dies before thy uncreating word;
Thy hand, great Anarch! lets the curtain fall
And universal darkness buries all.

Alexander Pope: The Dunciad

Part Three

REVELATIONS

Chapter 24

Maria, holding her sleepy child in her arms, followed Dave out with the rest of the audience at the end of the show.

"Aren't we staying to talk to 'Mr. Star?'" Maria asked.

"After some of this crowd clears out. They'll be here for a while packing the show. And he still has to get his share of the gate receipts. We'll wait in the lobby for a few minutes."

Ricky rubbed her eyes sleepily and yawned as Maria held her and patted her on the back.

"Magic man is gone?" she asked.

"The show is over," Maria told her. "But you saw the best parts. Remember the flowers and the pretty cards?" Ricky nodded, but still didn't look too happy about missing anything.

"Tell you what," Dave said. "If you'll wait a few minutes, we'll go talk to the magic man and maybe he will do a trick for you."

"Really?" she asked, her eyes no longer sleepy but wide and awake.

"Really," Dave said. He touched her hair, then leaned over and kissed her cheek. Maria read somewhere that men who had children looked at any child differently. Something about pupils dilating. A bit more wonder or tenderness than a childless male who hadn't been infected with the love of a child. Whatever else happened, Dave had fallen for Ricky. But how could any sane person resist her?

Maria wanted to hold Ricky close to her and to hell with the universe. Here was a little girl who had seen something in her closet that would frighten most adults into apoplexy. She had been in a bus wreck caused by a black wall that appeared from nowhere and returned there. She had almost been abducted by a snake from inside a mirror. She had generated a glowing globe that destroyed the vision at the top of the mountain (if that truly was a vision). And now she was excited by the prospect of meeting a man who pulled silk flowers from his sleeve. Any rational human being had to love children.

Maria might wonder whether she was rational after the last few days, but she was sure she loved Ricky. She didn't think she could endure the pain of losing her as she had lost Brian. She looked at Dave, watching the people leaving the show, and wondered at his strength. He held his left hand carefully, even winced whenever he bumped it accidentally, and looked as though he'd just finished a marathon carrying a few hundred pounds. But, like some magical, irresistible force, he wouldn't stop. How did he do it? If she'd lost both Brian and Ricky, she wouldn't have lasted a month.

The flow of people thinned. It was time to talk to the magician. Dave opened his mouth to say something, but was interrupted by a high pitched scream of terror cutting through the auditorium.

The rescue squad members, who should have been first to respond, did not even move.

"They don't hear it," Dave said. The men stood around in their white EMT coveralls, talking, joking, counting money.

"Like at the airport," Maria said.

Maria followed Dave to the steps at the side of the stage, though she wanted to turn and run from the auditorium. She held Ricky's head against her shoulder as they pushed through the heavy curtain. Smaller moans of pain came from behind another drape at the back of the stage. They went through and saw the magician on the floor with his assistants by his side. Maria remembered he had introduced them as Rena and Craig.

They were at the back of the stage, near a set of large double doors. The performers must have been loading up the big van there with magic show equipment.

On the dusty, hardwood floor of the stage, the thin magician twitched as though caught on a ten thousand volt electrical line. The impression was so strong that Maria looked around for a live wire, sparking and spitting against the stage floor, but saw nothing.

The woman assistant, Rena, tried to hold him down as Craig bent over them. The magician heaved, moaning, caught in some sort of seizure and she needed help. She had to have been the one who screamed.

"What's his name?" Dave yelled as he bent over. "His real name."

"Alan," the woman stammered. "Alan Benet."

"Alan, listen to me. Hold on, Alan. Hang in there," Dave yelled. He put a knee on Benet's chest to hold him down, then fished a comb out of his pocket and used his good hand to insert it into the magician's mouth to keep him from swallowing his tongue. Maria talked soothingly to Ricky, but she seemed more curious than alarmed.

"Grand mal?" Dave asked. He looked up at the woman, still dressed in her last costume from the show. "Has he ever had a seizure or shown any sign of epilepsy?"

She shook her head sharply. "He looked at the flashing lights on the mountain, grabbed his head, then collapsed." She looked up at the mountain, stared for a few seconds and covered her eyes. "No, Alan," Maria heard her whisper into her hands. "Not like this."

As she watched Dave and Alan, Maria realized whatever had happened to the magician had nothing to do with any physical ailment.

He glowed.

Maria was ready for a black cloud to appear out of nowhere, or a scaled hand to reach out of one of the magician's props. That same, skin-tightening tingle she felt in the closet, on the bus, and at the airport was back. Something was nearby. Something evil searched for them.

Ricky squirmed from her arms and went to the magician. She touched his arm, and his convulsions stopped.

But radiance around him was unabated.

Like a contagion, the brightness had jumped to Ricky's hand where she touched him. Slowly it moved up her arm and across her body until she, too, looked like a firefly grown to gigantic proportions. She looked at her hands, then up at Maria in wonder.

"Pretty, Mommy," she said.

Maria only hesitated a second. Whatever caused the glow was not the threat. She bent and hugged Ricky to her, and felt her body tingle as the brilliance filled her. It was happening again.

Dave took her hand firmly. He touched his lips to the back of her hand, and Maria almost giggled. He looked as though he'd been drinking radioactive milk, his lips and the area around his mouth painted with sparkling points of light. After a second, he, too, was engulfed in brightness.

Craig had obviously decided that he wasn't interested in convulsing magicians and people who glowed at the drop of a magic hat. Through the open door, Maria could see him running for the parking lot. The only other person on the stage was Rena, and she looked as though she couldn't decide whether to run away screaming or faint.

She did neither. She stroked Alan's face gently, receiving the infusion of light with just a slight intake of breath.

Like a flame leaping to a piece of dry tinder, the bright, beating glow had leaped from person to person, until all five of them were like brilliant Christmas lights that flashed in a cold December twilight. The point of the Tower sparkled.

Important, Maria thought. Important, but somehow incomplete. As though something was missing.

"Pretty lights," Ricky said. "Everybody makes pretty lights."

The aura around them throbbed in time to the light Maria could see flashing around the distant Tower. But the light around Ricky was brighter, purer, stronger than the rest.

Maria took a deep breath, inhaling a fiery cloud that filled her with a tingling warmth.

Just a few minutes before, Dave had been tired and hurting. He'd risen early that morning from a night of dream horrors, and hadn't stopped since. His head hurt. His hand throbbed. His eyes felt like the dried stuff around an old bottle of Elmer's glue.

Now the blaze spread through his body with a tickling energy, touching his fatigued arms and legs. Down to the tips of his toes and fingers. He felt rested, ten pounds lighter, and willing to fight off a few dozen tigers. Even his hand stopped aching.

The magician, Alan, stirred as the glow pulsed around him. Rena helped him sit up, then stand. He looked as though he couldn't believe the lustrous air dripping in almost liquid streams from his hands.

"My God!" he said. "What is it?"

"We hoped you could tell us," Dave said. Alan studied him.

"I figured you'd show up. You didn't seem to be someone who would give up easily."

"No. Not lately, anyway," Dave said.

He was worried. The other times there had been a reason for the pulsating light. To fight off the snake thing at the airport. To drive back the black cloud at the Tower. Now he was afraid something approached that only the radiance could fight. From the way Maria glanced out the loading doors, he knew she had the same idea.

They were right.

The snarling, howling creature appeared at the back of the stage as if conjured by a master illusionist. Only it was no illusion.

The thing was taller than Alan, knotted with dark musculature that might have won a Mr. Universe contest but for the leathery texture to its skin. What wasn't the texture of an old worn shoe was covered with wire-like hair. Its body was a nightmare combination of wolf and some sort of big cat. The eyes were almost black, with just a hint of a red glow in the center. Teeth like white, gleaming knives. Claws capable of cutting a man in half. Tufted ears standing above the top of its head. A Rick Baker mask of terror from a movie monster more horrible than any done before.

But it was no mask. And it advanced toward them.

Rena broke away from them for a second and came back with a gun from somewhere, holding it in both hands, pointing at the creature. It snarled at her, but she didn't shoot. Dave wasn't sure the bullets would hurt it, anyway.

It moved closer, and the sphere of brightness intensified. The creature held its paws across its face, shielding its eyes from the effusive light. It growled even louder in protest.

"Bad doggy," Ricky said. Dave didn't risk a glance, but he couldn't believe that she thought this thing was no more than a dog. And yet, children have a tendency to reduce their world to those things familiar to them, so maybe "bad doggy" was a good description, after all.

Ricky held her hands up, palms out toward the creature, and

repeated her words. "Bad. Bad doggy."

Then the sphere of light exploded.

It rippled away from them like the wave front of a nuclear explosion, sweeping through the air, across the stage, reaching for the thing. It stood for a moment when the circle of expanding light engulfed it, as though caught in the beam of a blinding floodlight.

They covered their ears, trying to close out the anguished howl that tore through the shimmering air. It sounded as though some sort of animal was tortured to the point of death.

It changed.

The skin smoothed, became a suede-like shade of gray, then sprouted a coat of short, dark fur. The fangs retreated, and the claws shrank to a fraction of their former size. Its entire body mass shrunk until it was nearly as small as Ricky. The form flowed like liquid, one feature melding into another. It wailed, the howl becoming less inhuman, but still not man-like. As the light washed over it, it became less monstrous, more familiar. When the effluence finally dimmed, it was most definitely not a man.

The German shepherd dog wagged its tail and whined.

But it was somehow different, too. Not like other dogs. As if its experience had taken it beyond canine capability.

Even its eyes were different, acquiring some glimmer of intelligence. Now it looked around, as though seeing them and the stage for the first time. Dave perceived something that hadn't been in those eyes before. Before, there was only rage and death. Now, it looked frightened. It whimpered and backed away, unsure whether it would receive a pat on the head or a kick in the ribs.

"Good doggy, now," Ricky said. Before Maria could stop her, she wrenched away and ran toward the animal, a figure of light trailing tiny rivers of luminous air.

Ricky stopped and looked at the dog. It still could have ripped away the soft tissue of her throat in a second. But it stood quietly, impassively, its tail wagging slowly. As though it was the helpless one and Ricky could have destroyed it in an instant.

"RICKY!" Maria screamed. Rena had lowered her weapon, but raised it again.

Ricky frowned, watching the dog, then looked back at Maria.

"It's okay, Mommy. Good doggy, now." The tiny face studied it for a second, and she finally leaned over and hugged the thick neck. The air around the thing pulsed.

"Mommy," Ricky said. She was smiling. "I think he's here to help us."

An animal? But Dave knew they were whole. No sense of something missing. Completeness.

Then, revelation.

Maria's palms were sweaty. She wanted to go after Ricky, but was afraid any sudden move would startle the dog. It had been too much like the snakelike thing at the airport before it changed. But there was no ring then or now. She was sure. She was so sure that she kept repeating the words to herself so she wouldn't forget.

Why was the dog here? What could he do?

An airy brilliance engulfed the stage. Luminous spots drifted above them in a lazy circle, like fireflies caught on an invisible carousel.

She squinted through the brightness at Ricky and saw that she watched the pulsating air with awe, her mouth a small "O" as her eyes moved from one spot to the other.

The lights around her morphed into a kaleidoscope of motion and flickering.

A wandering, glowing pinpoint angled toward Dave, touched his forehead, and he grunted, as though he'd been hit in the stomach with a sledge hammer. His mouth and eyes opened and light streamed from them like triple beacons in the night. The beams played over them each in turn, and when he looked at Maria, she sensed the gaze of something else in that light. Something not Dave, but still warm and powerful and brilliant. It reassured her, filled her with a confidence and satisfaction she hadn't known for a long time. She felt something familiar, a gentle touch on her hand, a quick kiss on her neck.

Brian was there, somewhere in the light. A tear formed and tickled her cheek. Across the stage, Ricky giggled and laughed and jumped up and down. "Daddy! Daddy! Daddy!" she said.

The dog barked, as though he were playing a particularly exciting game of fetch. He shook his head, almost dancing on his front paws.

Maria saw the dim red ball of light before anyone else. It drifted in through the open doors, weaving and bobbing through the glowing sphere around them, as though avoiding the brightest points of light. She saw it hover for a second above Alan before it dove at him, engulfing him in a faint crimson glow. He looked as though he wanted to scream, but couldn't.

"Cold," he said. "So cold."

Dave turned toward him, and the red glow fought the pure white light for a moment before it dissipated and Alan was again engulfed in phosphorescent air. Dave no longer gleamed like a hyperactive lighthouse, but he looked into the brilliance and whispered two names, "Suzy. Chris."

The glow faded.

On the mountain, Maria saw the Tower dim to its normal neon fluorescence, a cosmic beacon shimmering in the spring night.

Chapter 25

Dave finally knew what had happened.

The dog sat beside Ricky, his eyes alert and watching. Dave had the feeling that as long as that animal lived, Ricky would be safe. Observing the sleek animal, once as gnarled and misshapen as a lump of clay pounded by a mad sculptor, he knew he was dead.

Everything, from the black nothingness he'd seen to cutting off his finger to the cloud at the Tower on the top of the mountain; all of it was an hallucination generated by his terrified mind as he plummeted to the hard gray concrete. He must be only seconds or fractions of seconds from impact and the final, lonely oblivion, but his psyche seemed determined to let him live out a full, complete fantasy life. Even if it wasn't one he would have chosen. His ideal life would have been different.

He would have run when he first saw the black cloud, intercepted Suzy and Chris, and gotten them out of the way before the plane crashed. Then they would have lived, if not happily, then at least contentedly ever after.

That's what the fantasy would have been.

It bothered him that his mind should conjure this half-mad delusion that was nearly as bad as the reality he tried to escape. He almost preferred to have this shimmer and disappear so he could watch the sidewalk. Dave wondered if he would feel anything when he hit. Would the remnants of his brain maintain this hallucination until the last bits of coherent thought disappeared? Would his soul, if there were such a thing, drift off into the stratosphere or the geosphere or wherever the hell it went?

Hell was the probable destination. Maybe this was hell and he was doomed to live this fantasy horror until the end of time.

He felt relief. The world wasn't crazy. Only him. Somewhere, outside the delusion he'd built, life went on as it always did. No creatures, no flashing points of light, no fingers inching across a greasy meat counter.

That was strangest of all. Underneath the bandages, the finger did not ache. It was still gone, of course, but it was as though it had never been hurt. Or that it had been healing for six or seven months. All of this could have been a phantasm from a deranged mind.

Sure.

Liar, he told himself. And you know it.

As a writer, Dave wasn't very good at deception. He had been an excellent reporter and had a knack for imagery that often made his readers feel as though they had been watching the events he reported. But beyond bedtime stories told to an attentive and imaginative son, he discovered he was less than not very good. He was terrible.

And he had that same sick feeling in his stomach he'd felt when he read some of his fiction efforts. It just didn't ring true.

However much he wanted to believe this was nothing more than an hallucination, he knew it wasn't. The night was too dark, the spring breeze that caught his hair and caused it to flutter around on his forehead was too cool, the people around him were too scared, and the creature that the dog had been was too hideous.

It was real.

He took a deep breath, filling his lungs with clean country air, touched with a faint moistness from dew just condensing on the spring grass, and knew it was just too damned real.

Most of all, Maria was all too pleasantly warm against his side.

The dog whined, and nudged Ricky with his nose. The little girl squealed. Ricky crawled on the animal's back like it was a miniature horse. Even as he gripped Maria to keep her from rushing forward, Dave realized the squeal had disintegrated into a stream of child giggles and laughter. A sound he remembered and missed.

So many people forgot how really important it was to bring joy and security to as many children as possible, allowing them to laugh like miniature hyenas. Something his own Chris had little chance to do. Dave knew enough about grim realities and humanity and inhumanity to realize there was not enough laughter like that. Too few squeals of delight and too many screams of pain and terror. Not enough joy and security and too much hunger and despair.

He might not be able to save every little boy or girl, but he sure as hell could try in that tiny portion he could reach.

The animal seemed to be suffering Ricky's exuberance well. His only movement had been to lick her nose whenever her face ventured near. And watch the others. He looked as though he didn't know whether to trust them or not.

Dave looked at Alan Benet, who watched the animal carefully. His hand trembled. Almost as though he were afraid of the dog. Maybe he was. Dave still remembered the look on his thin face and how he had disappeared, running away as though a few hell dogs were on his tail.

His profession seemed appropriate.

The magician smiled at him, but a lopsided, forced grin. His legs seemed unsteady as he sat on a large trunk, set one foot on the edge of the trunk, then propped his arm across his knee. Something that only someone with his spider-like thinness could have accomplished.

"Did you bring your little buddy back from the Gap with you?" The Gap. That's what the Suzy-thing from his dream had called it.

"You tell me." Alan Benet said nothing. "I think you sent me there."

"And brought you back," Alan said. "That could have been a big damn mistake. You might have been the mutt's twin."

Dave said nothing. Maybe he should be grateful. Yes, he'd finally rejected suicide. But would that have changed the fact that it had been over two years since he was interested in anything except the next meal? Now, he found himself caught up in events stranger than anything he ever wrote about, not knowing whether he would be alive or dead ten minutes from now, and he'd never felt so vital since the accident. He felt his gaze drawn back to Maria. In the past three years, he had not wanted so much to live as he did just then.

"Thank you," he said after a few seconds.

"You're welcome," the magician said in the same tone, which fit the crooked smile still on his face. He didn't look happy. He glanced at the dog with Ricky, who played a drum solo on its head. Benet's eyes were more frightened than the others. As though he'd seen something in the white light, or the red glow, that no one else had.

The dog whined again, and Ricky, sitting on its back, frowned. She leaned over, hugged its neck and kissed it on the muzzle.

"Bobby," she said. "The doggy's name is Bobby."

Bobby looked at Alan and showed his teeth. He didn't growl. He was trying with every doggy muscle he had to imitate a human smile.

The simulation was not very comforting.

Alan still wore his jacket from the show. In the pocket was a white silk handkerchief that seemed to shimmer beneath the lights. His face paled until it matched the white cloth.

That grin looked hungry. Alan wondered if that was how he would die, chewed to death by a German shepherd that had once been a creature from another dimension. The damn thing was probably one he'd put in there himself.

He didn't believe in magic, only illusion. But his death was no illusion. He'd seen it in the dim, red glow. Something from the Gap would kill him.

The revelation of his death had shaken him, but didn't mean he wouldn't fight the inevitable. All he had to do was avoid the Gap, and anything that had to do with it.

So he had to run from these people. They reeked of the Gap.

Far away and as quickly as possible.

What about Rena?

She stood quietly by the sub-trunk, the gun in her hand hanging loosely by her side. A gun? Where the hell had she gotten a gun?

"Planning to kill someone, Rena?" he asked her.

She laughed, and the daggers of ice behind her voice made him want to take off immediately.

"Actually, yes," she said. "I've been trying for weeks to decide whether to kill you." He couldn't tell whether she was kidding or not. It looked as though she didn't know, either.

"Well?"

"I haven't decided yet."

She was crazy. All of them were crazy.

"Any particular reason?" he asked.

"A very particular reason, you charming bastard." Somehow, her voice had lost the endearing tone from the last time she'd said those words. "My real name is Rena Williams. Jack was my brother. Jack Williams."

Shit.

He should have seen her at the funeral. Maybe he did. Maybe some perverse deep part of his mind knew who she was all along, and compelled him to hire and then fall in love with her, knowing she was the sister of a man he'd killed. Knowing she would want to nail his ass. Knowing if she killed him, it was no more than he deserved.

The funeral must have been where she first saw him. Alan wasn't sure why he went in the first place, except maybe to quiet a noisy conscience. What good did it do to attend and murmur unheard apologies to a corpse? Now it looked as though he might be able to apologize face to face. Ghost to ghost? There had to be a joke for the show in there somewhere.

All he had to do was live long enough to use it.

After a moment, Rena sighed, and placed the gun back into her purse. Alan realized he'd been taking short, shallow breaths, and breathed more normally.

Now he'd have to run from Rena, too.

"What's the Gap, Mr. Benet?"

Alan stared at the big man for a few seconds before he stood and started loading the truck again.

"What's the Gap?" the man repeated.

"Who the hell are you people?" Alan asked. He held a sword from the Hindu basket trick in his hand very tightly, resisting an impulse to slam it against the floor. "What do you want from me?" The fat man glanced down at the sword in his hand. He probably thought it was real.

"I'm Dave Richards, and this is Maria Quinones and her daughter, Ricky. We were hoping you could tell us what the hell is going on."

"Right now, I'm going to pack up this frigging truck and head to southern Florida for a few months. That's what the hell is going on." He tossed the blade on top of a blanket he used for padding.

The big man, Dave Richards, looked as though he wanted to choke someone, and Alan knew who he had in mind.

"Let me tell you," Richards said. "Somehow, you can put people into that place you called the Gap. And bring them out. But while they're inside, they change." He held up his bandaged hand. "A little like this hand, or a lot, like Bobby.

"You have this magic show that you take up and down the east coast. If you do a little research, as I have in the past, you'll begin to suspect that all of the unusual events of the last few years have a source, and this source has been moving, in a slow cycle, along the east coast."

Alan threw the tubes from the Invisible Girl into the truck, not caring whether they shattered into little wooden toothpicks when they hit. He dragged the sub-trunk into the back of the truck, rolled down the doors and locked them. Dave stepped in front of him as he started around the truck.

"We're not finished."

"The hell we're not, fat boy. Step back or learn to tango with Bobby's pals. They haven't changed." For a second, it looked as though Richards was going to call his bluff, but the memory of the Gap was still vivid. He stepped aside.

"I'm sorry about your brother, Rena," he said as he fished in his pocket for keys. "He had a gun, for God's sake. And he looked scared enough to use it." Alan leaned against the van and shook his head. "Ask Richards how, but I Hid a concrete slab in the Gap and brought it back above him. I was afraid." He paused. "Too damn late to think about it now.

"Keep your costumes, Rena, they wouldn't fit me, anyway." He stepped into the truck. "I'll leave your stuff in the hotel room. Have a good frigging life."

Then he drove away, not looking back, as fast as he could.

The Magic Man went away, but Ricky didn't worry. He was supposed to do that, so it was okay. The big doggy had a problem.

"Mommy," Ricky said. Mommy didn't look very happy. Dave looked mad at somebody, and the pretty lady who helped the Magic Man was crying. Ricky wanted to go over and ask her where it hurt so she could kiss it and make it better the same way Mommy always did. But she didn't know the pretty lady very well, and Mommy worried when she talked to people she didn't know very well. So she didn't.

"Mommy," she repeated. When her mommy looked at her, she had to stop and think for a minute what she wanted to say. Oh, yeah. Bobby.

"The doggy, Bobby, is hungry. Can I give him something?" Mommy looked like she did the time when Ricky almost fell off the bed. "Just a Butter Finger, Mommy. I think Bobby will like Butter Finger." Ricky knew Mommy had a Butter Finger in her pocketbook. Mommy didn't let her see it, but she still knew. Mommy took a deep breath and gave her the Butter Finger.

Ricky unwrapped it and broke just a little piece off the end.

"I have to show him," she told Mommy, so she would know why she had to eat the candy. Mommy nodded and smiled. Ricky liked it better when Mommy smiled.

The Butter Finger was good. It crunched then melted in her mouth. Ricky handed the rest of it to Bobby. He started to chew the whole thing.

"Not the paper," Ricky said. She took the candy bar back and tore off the paper. "Now."

Bobby ate the whole candy bar at one time. Ricky looked at Mommy, but she just smiled at her. If Ricky had done that, Mommy would be mad.

"Mommy," Ricky said after Bobby finished. "I think he is still hungry. Can we buy more candy bars so I can show him how to eat them, too?"

"I think he knows, but we'll get him something better than candy. I don't think dogs are supposed to eat chocolate, Sweet Heart," Mommy said. Sometimes Ricky wondered why Mommy called her "Sweet Heart." She knew about "Sweet Tart" candy and "Sweet Tooth" (because Mommy said she had one, but her teeth never tasted sweet to her when she licked them). Maybe somebody who likes candy has a "Sweet Heart," too.

"We should be getting back to the motel," Dave said. Ricky liked Dave. He was a very nice man, and he liked Mommy a whole lot. Mommy liked him, too. Sometimes Ricky knew things that other people didn't, but she thought everybody knew Mommy and Dave liked each other.

"Where can Bobby ride?" Ricky asked. Maybe in the back with his head out the window. Bobby would like that.

"I don't think Bobby can ride with us," Mommy said, bending over so Ricky didn't have to look up.

"But he has to," Ricky said. Didn't Mommy know? "And the pretty lady, too. They have to go with us."

Mommy stood up and looked at Dave. Dave shrugged. Ricky knew how to shrug.

The pretty lady still looked like she hurt somewhere. "What's the lady's name, Mommy?" Ricky asked.

"Rena."

Ricky walked over to Rena. She knew her name so the lady wasn't really a stranger any more. Rena.

"If you hurt your finger, Mommy can kiss it and make it better."

Rena looked funny, smiling and crying at the same time.

"It's not that kind of hurt, little one," she said.

"Mommy can fix almost any kind of hurt."

"I'm sure she can."

"You have to go with us."

"I do?"

"Uh huh. Back to where Dave lives. They can give you a room, too, with a TV and a shiny bathroom and plastic glasses with plastic paper on them and a big bed that you can bounce on. Dave let me."

"I have a place to stay." Rena wiped her eyes.

"But you have to go to where Dave lives." Ricky wanted to stamp her foot, but Mommy said that wasn't very nice. Why didn't they know?

Rena and Bobby had to go with them.

The voices in the light said so.

Chapter 26

Big John Hill was jumpy.

Few things in this world could bother him anymore. He was controlled and guarded by a higher power, one that could stop any enemy. Turn aside any attack. He was stronger than any six or seven men together, and his skin was tough enough to stop small caliber bullets.

Leap short buildings. Stronger than a Honda. Faster than a speeding turtle.

John laughed, but it was not the same as the cold amusement he had felt back on Lox Mountain. It was more a high pitched, nervous giggle. He wished that snake-thing weren't in the back seat.

He had known where to go when they crawled back through the fence at the top of the mountain, and had known they had to hurry. The nailed heels of his boots clicked against the sidewalk. When he'd walked past the illuminated Tower, he had glanced up at the glowing neon, his eyes drawn to the metal and glass shape and the globe at the top as though it were a magnet and he was nothing more than a chunk of cold, dead steel. For a second, he gazed as if fascinated by the shape, thrusting into the dark night like a bright phallus. The thing following him emitted a low growl, and his eyes refocused. He almost ran to his car, the reptilian creature slithering close behind. As he turned the key, the Tower pulsed and brightened. John watched for a moment as it brightened to almost blinding intensity before dimming. In the back seat, the thing hissed angrily.

It was bad enough that the reptilian monstrosity had teeth a tyrannosaurus would envy. And razor claws it had a habit of sheathing and unsheathing. And the stench of a badly cleaned reptile house at one of those cheap roadside zoos. Not to mention the sucking, slobbering sounds it made, and the steady drip, drip, drip of some viscous fluid onto the floorboard. John wished he had brought his wading boots instead of his hobnails and he was glad this wasn't his car.

All of it was pretty damned disgusting, but what worried John was the ring.

He had noticed a heavy gold ring embedded in the scaly flesh of the thing's left hand, the kind people received when they graduated from high school or college. John knew it wasn't likely that Drip Face had attended any school that he'd ever heard of in its present condition, so that could only mean one thing.

It had once been human.

John had checked, so he knew the skin under his shirt wasn't the rough scaled hide of the lizard thing, but still he worried. There was enough humanity left in him to think about becoming some non-human creature and decide he didn't exactly relish the idea.

At the top of the mountain, Karick had promised that he had reached his final form and would stay strong and powerful for the rest of his life.

Suddenly, that was no comfort at all.

But he thought of the tiny girl waiting for him to come and take her as though she were a green apple stolen from a tree and he felt better. Only in his deepest dreams had he considered the things Karick had told him he must do.

Until now.

Now, was the proper time. Karick fed on human terror and pain, and John knew the girl would be a right tasty snack. She was young and naive and it said she held the power of worlds within her tiny body.

When Big John finished with her on that steel slab, that power would belong to Karick.

And Big John would be at its side when it used the power to break through.

Afterward, there would be many young girls. More chances to fulfill his dreams. Karick had promised him new, delightful terrors to try.

For that, Big John decided he would crawl into a Olds with a dozen monstrosities.

Chapter 27

The hotel room was silent, except for Rena mumbling occasionally in the other bed. Maria thought she heard her say "Alan" once or twice. Beside Maria, Ricky slept peacefully. Earlier, Maria thought it might take an act of God to get her quiet. After all the excitement at the school. And Bobby. He breathed quietly at the foot of the bed. They'd had to sneak him in, but Maria didn't know what would have happened if they'd separated them.

Despite the uproar, Ricky settled into bed with no argument and was asleep in minutes. She looked so peaceful. No nightmares there. Not yet.

Children seemed to have such a single-minded view of the world, and at the same time looked at it as a marvelous, infinite place where they could play games and have fun forever and ever.

Maybe that's why they were so precious and appealing. Maybe that's why otherwise rational adults were so willing to sacrifice their own lives to save a tiny, almost insignificant body. Erica had become such a part of her life that Maria would make that sacrifice in an instant. Even more than Brian, Ricky had so entwined herself around Maria's every waking thought and hope and dream that they were all indistinguishable from each other.

She needed to ask for a raise (so I can buy things for Ricky) or that guy was handsome (I wonder what Ricky would think of him) or there was a good movie on television (but Ricky can't watch it).

They had stopped by Rena's room and gotten her things. Just as well, Maria decided. She wasn't sure whether Rena could have stayed there by herself, not in the same room she and Alan had shared earlier. Even though it was Ricky who insisted, Maria agreed that Rena should not be by herself for a while. She thought about Dave, alone in his own room. All of them were sleeping fully dressed, and she had the feeling Dave was grateful for that.

She remembered her instant analysis the first time she saw him at the airport. Her immediate reaction had been to disregard his presence, and she knew why. There was no way to put it politely and she had never been too politically correct. Dave Richards was fat. Maria suspected the reason. She dealt with grief in her way and he dealt with grief in his.

But she discovered something a bit disturbing about herself and how she looked at people. She always said, and believed, that people should be judged as individuals, not by appearances or part of a group. So what did she do? The first time she saw Dave, she immediately classified him with Paul, the rather rotund cook at the restaurant. Harmless and mildly amusing, but no one she would be interested in dating, by any means.

So she was a bigot, of course. A weight bigot.

As programmed by society as any slavering male chauvinist, leering at women as they walked by. (She knew that was overly dramatic, but the image seemed appropriate.) She was sure Dave wasn't immune, either. Would he have been so quick to help if she'd been forty pounds heavier? Or had been wearing a loose pantsuit instead of the tight, short, white skirt?

Now she knew she was being unfair to Dave. She had the feeling he would have helped if she had been a hundred pounds heavier with a face littered with bumps like discarded cherry pits.

And the way Ricky seemed to love him . . . .

After they arrived at the hotel and Dave rented the room next to his for them, Ricky had run over to hug him. Bobby trotted along behind her.

"I have to sleep, now," Ricky told him. "I need rest."

Dave had lifted her and kissed her on the cheek. "Big day tomorrow?" he asked.

"Tonight," Ricky had answered. "Have to get up real early in the morning when it's still dark."

"Why?" he asked. Ricky was silent for a long time, and Maria had come over to her and touched her arm.

"Why do you have to get up when it's dark?" she asked Ricky.

"To run. To run from the bad man."

"Honey," Dave said, hugging Ricky in arms that almost hid her.

"Don't worry. Your Mommy and I will never let the bad man hurt you." Ricky put on her thinking expression, crossed arms with one hand under her chin.

"But Mommy said even grown-ups can't always do what they want."

"That's true." Ricky thought again.

"I don't think you can stop the bad man. No matter how hard you try. He is too bad to stop. Even Bobby can't stop him. So I have to sleep so I can run."

Dave had looked at Maria and sighed. He'd done his best.

"Okay, Ricky," he said. "If you want anything, just yell. I'll be in the next room and the door will be open between the rooms so I can hear if you need help."

"Okay," Ricky had said, smiling.

As she lay studying the ceiling, Maria's thoughts drifted back to Dave alone in the next room.

Alone again.

Just like the song. Alone again, naturally.

Dave didn't see the ceiling. All he saw were dark eyes that seemed to go on forever, and a smile that was a light in the darkness, and a laugh that reminded him of Christmas chimes.

Why fantasize? Beautiful women like Maria didn't associate with guys like him (fat ones, he thought), unless they had to. When this was all over, she would probably go along her merry way with a brief wave backward and a "See you later" on her lips.

On her beautiful lips.

Her daughter fascinated him, too. Ricky was bright and articulate, with very definite opinions about how the world should be. So far, she seemed oblivious to the danger they faced, and almost enthralled by the adventure. Ricky had treated Bobby like any other pal. That he had been a dark, wrinkled creature with needle teeth and claws like steak knives didn't mean a thing to her.

She reminded him so much of Chris that he had to keep blinking to clear his vision.

He remembered holding his son a few weeks before the accident. Chris had been determined to stay up and watch the end of The Return of the Jedi on television, though it was already an hour past his bedtime. So Dave had relented and let him crawl up on his lap, nestle his head against his arm, and watch the movie. Of course, Chris was asleep within minutes. But Dave didn't move through the rest of the movie or the local news afterward. He just sat holding Chris, a warm comfort in his arms. He never remembered seeing much of the movie that night, and couldn't have told anyone a thing about local events, but he recalled every vivid detail of Chris' face, how the hair fell across his forehead, how he sighed occasionally and twisted on his lap.

But Chris was dead. And though the memories had been both a comfort and a source of despair, just having Maria around seemed to take a sharp edge off grief undulled by the passage of time. Something about her wouldn't let him go.

He should be worrying about the Gap and whatever it threw at them next. Instead, he was thinking of Maria's lips and her dark hair and her melodic voice. Forget how good she looked. What about the danger they faced?

Then the shape appeared in the door between the rooms, just a dark outline too vague to see. Something was in the room with him. It moved toward the other side the bed and stood for a second as if staring at him. Or trying to decide whether to eat him in small gulps or all at once.

He took a deep breath and a rose-like perfume filled his head, and he knew why Bobby hadn't barked.

He wondered if he had fallen into a fantasy as Maria slipped into bed beside him.

"Ricky's asleep," she whispered. "And Rena said she would keep an eye on her."

"Why are you here?"

"Well, I didn't come to change the sheets, if that's what you're wondering."

Dave pulled her against him, unfamiliar lips searching before they kissed. He lost himself in sensation. In every fiery touch of her skin, of her body beneath her shirt and jeans. They began to remove each other's clothing.

He stopped, even as Maria lowered her head to the mattress.

"What's wrong?" she asked. "Did you hear something?"

"Nothing," he said. "I can't do it."

"Do what?"

"Make love to you." She looked almost afraid. "I mean, I can, and I want to, but . . . oh, Jesus." He ran his hand through his hair. "How can you even look at me? I feel like somebody's pumped me up with an air compressor."

Maria pulled his face back to hers and kissed his lips carefully. "I won't lie to you. The first time I saw you I wondered how you could do that to yourself. But that didn't stop me from seeing something else. Okay, it's corny, but I saw the goodness and kindness inside you. I thought maybe you liked the way you looked. Fine. If not, maybe you had your reasons." She kissed him again. "It doesn't matter." She smiled and her dark eyes twinkled in the light filtering in from the parking lot, and he knew her delighted, mischievous expression would light up the darkest night.

"Besides," she told him, "haven't you ever heard that size isn't important?"

And, after a while, it wasn't.

Chapter 28

"Dammit! Dammit! Dammit!" Big John slammed his fist into the dashboard of the Olds, leaving a hand sized dent in the vinyl covered metal. The thing in the back made a hissing sound, like a tub full of snakes stirred with a stick. "Sweet Jesus on the Cross!"

Karick had warned him to hurry or they might be gone when he arrived. Not that it mattered a whole hell of a lot. He, or the scaly thing in the back, would find them. John just wanted to save some time.

The school was mostly dark, the loading door at the back of the stage closed and silent. He could see where they'd been: footprints in the grass on either side of the asphalt, a bright red silk handkerchief caught against the base of a nearby tree, and what looked like a chunk of painted plywood from some kind of box. They must have been in a damned big hurry to leave this garbage scattered around. There might have been more, but Big John examined the area from the safety of his car. He was reluctant to go any closer. For some reason, he had the notion the area at the back of the stage was as dangerous to him as a stroll through the pits of Chernobyl would be to anyone else. It even seemed to glow faintly.

There was probably a janitor inside somewhere. The school might not keep a watchman overnight under normal circumstances, but with the show being there, they would at least have a clean-up man. Maybe he had heard something. Might be fun finding out, anyway.

Big John left the car and walked around the front of the school, wondering if Snake-breath would follow. It did. As he passed a classroom window, he noticed a flickering at the edges of the closed shades, maybe from a movie or TV. John warily crept to the window and maneuvered so he could see through the small gap between the frame and shade. Yep, there was a video player, and the TV going with the sound so low that he couldn't hear it. The sound probably didn't matter anyway. The man and two women on that bed weren't doing a hell of a lot of talking. John shifted his viewpoint and saw the janitor. That's why there was no sound. He wore earphones, staring at what looked like a school yearbook open on the teacher's desk. His eyes flickered to the TV, then to the book, then back to the TV. He lazily rubbed himself with his left hand.

Sweet Jesus! John thought. Right in the middle of the classroom.

He heard a liquid sound behind him and turned to see Snake-breath trying to look over his shoulder.

"Get away from me!" he said, his voice low through gritted teeth. "Just get the hell away!" It backed off, its slitted eyes narrowing even more. Just like a damned snake. John had never liked them. Back when he was a boy, he had learned that a round eyed snake was harmless, but that never stopped him from killing one. It was those slant-eyed ones with poisonous fangs that you really had to watch for. The dark thing with the ring had a mouth full of white, gleaming fangs, every one dripping some sort of slimy, slick venom that looked like snot pouring out of the nose of a sick brat.

"Stay here," John ordered. It growled lowly, but stayed when he walked to the front door. Locked, but that only slowed Big John for a few seconds. He pushed and metal exploded into the hall, clattering and bouncing along the shiny floor. The safety chain and padlock stopped the door, but he pushed again and the chain slammed against the wall and jangled to the floor. John wasn't worried about the noise. The janitor wouldn't notice.

When Big John kicked the door in and stepped over it into the room, the janitor froze, his hand still on his crotch like he had an itch he couldn't scratch. John smashed his fist through the TV screen then tossed it against the wall.

Even when he ripped the earphones from the old guy's head, the janitor still didn't move. John noticed "Harry" stenciled on his shirt pocket.

"How ya doin', Harry?" he asked as he walked over and stood above him. He looked down and saw the yearbook open to pictures of cheerleaders. He smiled approvingly. Young stuff. The janitor finally moved, trying to stand. John helped him, and lifted him by his shirt until his feet barely touched the ground. "Now, Harry. You're going to answer a few questions. Okay?" Harry nodded.

"Good. Remember the show here tonight?" His head moved up and down again. "A bunch of people showed up back stage afterward, right?" Harry grunted something that might have been an affirmative. "Good. Now here's the really important question. I'll be really upset if you don't have the answer to this one." Harry's eyes widened and a quick shudder rippled through his body.

"Where did they go when they left?"

Harry swallowed. "Somerset Inn," he squeaked. "I heard them talking about going to the new motel over on Newton Road, near the interstate."

John put him down, but kept his grip on his shirt. He looked around the room. It had been a long time since he'd been in a school, though he'd spent a few afternoons cruising past them the last few years. He had no pleasant memories of school itself. Mostly years of pain and humiliation from teachers and other kids. Not his fault he was no good in school or too fat to fit into his desk.

He spied the red, white, and blue flag on its staff, sticking out over the classroom like a colorful erection. He looked down at Harry and smiled.

They would find Harry on Monday morning still sprawled across Mrs. Beeken's desk, the flag and pole above him like a patriotic flower sprouting from the bloody hole in his chest.

Big John left, smiling. He didn't know much about Somerset, but did remember enough to know where the interstate crossed on Newton Road. No hurry, now. He had plenty of time.

Ricky dreamed of sparkling points and beautiful shapes drifting in the air like white clouds on a bright summer day. She had heard her Daddy in the light at the school and he had called her name.

She had the feeling she would see her Daddy again.

Very soon.

It was 2:00 AM. The attack would come just after three.

Alan concentrated on the asphalt of the interstate in the headlights, as he'd done since he retrieved his clothes from the hotel room. If he let himself think about anything else, he was afraid he'd go back.

Back to the craziest bunch of people he'd ever seen.

He'd seen a few strange people in his life. Once, he'd wrangled an invitation to an exclusive dinner after a performance by a world famous magician in Pittsburgh. Everyone in attendance but the damn cook was a magician.

Dancing cards. Ropes tied in intricate knots. A flaming rocket, made from a folded cocktail napkin, drifting near the ceiling. Coins palmed, unpalmed and repalmed. A few doves cooing from concealed pockets.

The most normal person in the entire restaurant was the star of the show, waiting in line for his turn at the buffet, holding his newborn baby girl as though she were a piece of precious, fragile crystal. He smiled politely, talked to others when they talked to him, acknowledged their congratulations on a great show, but his eyes were for the baby. He was to open his show on Broadway soon, and Alan knew that was nothing compared to the tiny life he held in his hands.

It was a cute baby.

She reminded him of the little girl, Ricky.

No! he thought, but too late. He could see her standing there, laughing with Bobby. She yelled like a banshee, so why did his chest suddenly tighten at the thought of that tiny girl in danger?

And he knew it was worse than that.

Alan had seen his own death in the red light, somehow related to the Gap. He was determined not to ever Hide or bring back anything, no matter what. The only way for him to live was to avoid the Gap. Don't think about it. Forget it ever existed.

And, oh, by the way, let a three year old girl die a bloody death.

The crimson glow had told him of his own death, but the white light had shown him more. He had seen Ricky, hurt and bleeding.

When that image flashed through his mind - the picture he'd been driving away from like a maniac - Alan thought he was in trouble.

When he took the next exit and swung back toward Somerset, he knew he was in trouble.

When he realized he knew exactly where the others were, he wondered how long before he died.

It was 2:45.

Dave was half awake again, watching Maria sleep. It had been so long since he lay beside a beautiful woman.

He wished it could stay this way and was afraid it wouldn't. He worried about Ricky asleep in the next room. Dave knew the pain of losing a child. Knew it was something that could tear the strongest of people apart. He didn't want that to happen to Maria, but most of all he wanted nothing to hurt Erica.

The only discordant note was that they had dressed again after making love. Dave had wanted to lay beside her and feel her soft warm skin against his, but knew she was right. Both of them felt the presence, closing in like clouds over a full moon.

The dimple on Maria's right cheek twitched as she smiled briefly in her dreams. So domestic. So normal.

It was 2:50.

As he drove to the motel, the back of Big John's neck itched as though someone were watching him. He studied the rear view mirror, but there was only the creature in the back seat, which was enough. Far behind him, he saw lights from another car, but they winked out after a few seconds. It either turned or parked somewhere. He looked up at the sky and a worrisome thought crossed his mind. With the street lights and full moon, it was almost bright enough to drive without any extra illumination. If people wanted to follow him, they could turn off their headlights and he'd never know they were back there.

Okay. If anyone wants to follow, let 'em. What could they do?

Let John and the scaly creature get out of the car and they'd probably break a leg getting away.

So why did his neck itch so bad? He rubbed it and shook his head.

It was 2:55.

Dave's electronic watch beeped the hour. Three AM.

Ricky screamed.

Even from the next room, her shrill cry was like a knife through Dave's head. He felt a strange rasping vibration in his ears, as though they had been overloaded by the intensity of the shriek. Maria jumped up and ran into the other room before he had a chance to move. In her own bed, Rena sat up and rubbed her eyes. Bobby stood at the door, his feet wide and rigid, a low growl in his throat that should have frightened burglars for miles around.

"No!" Ricky yelled, clutching Maria. "Don't let him take me, Mommy!" Maria enfolded her in her arms.

"It's okay, baby," she said, her voice low, soothing. "You're here with Mommy. No one will take you."

"Yes, he is!" Ricky insisted. "The bad man is here to take me and go to the mountain and . . . " Her voice faded to a quiet, horrified whisper. "He's gonna hurt me, Mommy." She tightened her arms around Maria. "The bad man's gonna hurt me."

Dave looked around, moved toward them, hesitated and stopped. He wanted someone to shout at, to hit.

"No," Maria told her. "No one will hurt you or take you away. I wouldn't let anything happen to you, baby."

Their heads whipped around as all three adults turned toward the door. Outside, a metallic crash, as if a few tons of steel had fallen on concrete, echoed through the night. Bobby barked.

"Mommy," Ricky said, her voice quiet and calm. She seemed almost resigned. "The bad man is here now."

Chapter 29

Dave stood in the door with Maria beside him. Bobby hadn't run out after whatever was outside. He stayed near Ricky.

An overturned sub-compact car in the parking lot rocked slowly back and forth like a turtle on its back. He looked around, searching for whatever had flipped it.

When he finally found it, he wished he hadn't.

A snake with arms and legs.

A flat, triangular head sat on a long, sinuous neck above almost non-existent shoulders, with a forked tongue darting out occasionally to taste the air. It arms were long and flexible, too, its entire body covered by bronze scales with just a touch of iridescence. It hissed, showing several rows of fangs, all dripping with a viscous, probably poisonous, fluid. The creamy white inside of the gaping mouth almost glowed in the lights from the parking lot. Dave felt Maria jump, as though startled.

A large class ring circled its left ring finger.

Bobby leaped into the night, growling, and attacked.

The snake thing whipped its head toward the rushing form, but Bobby somehow dodged the initial lunging strike. Then teeth like razors sliced through the reptilian flesh where its chest should have been. A hissing scream screeched across the lot.

Dave looked for a weapon, anything he could use to kill the snake without getting near the fight. In his rage to destroy the thing, Bobby might strike out at him, too. Unlike the reptile, Dave didn't think he could take a bite like it did and live. They backed away and circled each other for a second.

He remembered what Maria had said about the man on the bus. He was a sleazy looking bastard dressed in too loud clothes who looked as though he thought he could take whatever he wanted. A cheap hood, she'd said.

The snake thing hissed again. Too many fangs. Oddly white flesh of its mouth against its dark skin. Tattered remains of a purple shirt and striped pants. The ring.

"We have to go," Maria said, pulling on her tennis shoes. "We have to run, just like Ricky said." Dave didn't hesitate, but found and donned his own shoes.

"What about Bobby?" he asked. He didn't like leaving him there to face that snake thing alone.

"I'll help him," Rena said from behind them. She flipped the cylinder of the gun sideways, then clicked it shut. "You get Ricky away from here."

Maria handed Ricky to Dave, and hugged Rena. "Thank you, Rena," she said. "Do me a favor."

"Sure."

"Kill the bastard."

"That's my specialty. Killing bastards."

Outside, it sounded like a fight between two vicious dogs, with a couple of cats thrown in for good measure. Dave held Ricky's head against his shoulder as he watched them. Bobby was cut and bleeding in a half dozen places, but there was no blood on the snake's fangs, so the damage must have been done by claws, or the piece of bumper the snake thing held. Bobby was in serious trouble. He wouldn't last much longer.

Then the snake would come after them.

"Time to get out," Dave said. "We don't have much time." He saw Maria squeeze Rena's hand.

"Let's move," she said.

Dave looked back. Rena stood in the doorway, staring at them, pointing the gun in her hand at the creatures like an expert marksman.

Dave hoped she was.

They disappeared into the darkness of the night. A gun shot thundered behind them.

Rena watched them go, and almost screamed as a shape moved out of the shadows and followed them. It didn't look human. She shot, but it was too far away. It just turned and grinned at her like a drooling idiot. Then it, too, disappeared.

Bobby would die unless she helped, and she had no idea where the others had gone. Rena had to stay and try to kill the snake thing before she could go after Dave and Maria.

The triangular head struck at Bobby again. Bobby crouched, but the thing kicked out at him, slamming him against a nearby Plymouth. He fell, dazed, beside the vehicle. It moved in, mouth gaping for the final strike.

She was too far away, but still Rena fired the gun. The shot went low and to the right, taking out the windshield of Cadillac. The snake man turned toward her and away from Bobby, hissing again. She moved to the side, wondering what the hell she could do to help. She wasn't much bigger than a kid herself. How could she fight it?

At least she bought time for Bobby to recover. He stalked the snake from behind as it tracked her, then launched himself into the air. The animal slammed into the snake man from behind, knocking it against a light pole with a shattering concussion. The crack of breaking ribs was like a gunshot. It turned back to Bobby, and he drove forward again, hitting it at the knees. The boneless legs bent with the blow, flowing over the dog's body like an undulating snake. The thing's arms encircled Bobby, suspended him in the air, then tossed him. After a short yip, Bobby was quiet. Rena stalked as close as she could and fired carefully.

The first one caught the snake thing in its right eye and a noxious, dark fluid gushed onto the street. Thin tendrils of smoke arose from the asphalt where the blood dropped. The snake thing staggered back and a second shot cut through the left side of its skull. It put dark claws over its face and screamed. Like a creature dying in pain, but something like a man afraid of the dark, too. Black blood fountained from the third shot that grazed its thin neck.

A tentacle-like arm whipped out and knocked the gun to the asphalt. It hissed and wrapped the ropy appendage around Rena's arm. She felt herself pulled toward it, the skin of the thing cold and lifeless around her wrist.

She dropped, grabbing for the gun. Her fingertips touched it. The gun slid sideways. Out of reach. The wide, flat head covered the horizon.

A hot reptile stench.

Fangs dripping, an acrid, rotten odor.

She was going to die.

Something sang in the night. A ringing sound that was somehow familiar. Something cutting through stubborn air with a sharp edge.

The snake thing looked startled for a moment, just before its head fell off its thin neck and tumbled to the ground. The snake-like arms relaxed as the rest of it collapsed.

Alan stood there, breathing hard, holding the sword from the sub-trunk. A small portion of it was covered with an almost black fluid.

He looked down at the snake thing, its mouth opening and closing as it died, then back at Rena. His eyes started to water.

"I'm sorry," he said. "Another few seconds and I would have been too damned late. Just another frigging stop light or some idiot in a farm truck and --"

"Stop, Alan," Rena said. "You came back in time. That's what's important."

"But you almost died!" he said. The words were forced out, as though through a steel barrier. His eyes were even wetter.

"I didn't." She touched his cheek with her hand. He held and kissed it, and some of the hysteria left his eyes.

"Where are the others?"

"Gone. Running from some other creature. It followed them when they tried to get away."

"Get away where?"

Rena pointed toward the city. "I don't know. They didn't know themselves."

From the somewhere distant in the night, Maria's scream was like a knife slashing through the darkness.

Chapter 30

Dave jumped when he heard the crash from behind them in the alley. Something had knocked over a trash can. Probably a cat, but he had to see. Maybe the snake thing had already finished off Bobby and Rena and was after them.

A massive dark shape in the alleyway blocked the light from the street.

Ricky whimpered and buried her face in Maria's chest. Dave looked up at the form, squinted. He realized his first thought that it was a man was wrong.

An involuntary shudder ran through him. This behemoth looked human, but didn't feel human. It made Dave think of jackals tearing at dead meat or crows picking at the remains of a roadkill.

"What the hell are you?" Dave asked him. The huge form shrugged and touched the obscenely large knife on his belt.

"They call me Big John, but it don't matter none," he said. "You won't much care where you're going." The giant looked at Ricky and an evil, repulsive light flared in his eyes. He licked his lips as though contemplating a juicy steak dinner.

"Come here, little darling," he said. He pitched his voice higher with a sickening sweetness. "Karick will be real happy to see you. And you and I have things to do. Great things." He smiled and showed teeth with tiny points on them, and a dark ring of hard flesh above his collar. Dave finally realized he was no more human than the snake creature. He held out his huge arms to Ricky, but she didn't see. Maria held her head still buried against her shoulder.

Dave swung a discarded chair from the trash in the alley at the man-thing, but the intruder just caught it in his right hand and threw it against the brick wall.

"Not very damned friendly," he said, showing his teeth again. "Let me show you how friendly Big John can be."

Shots from the direction of the motel drew his attention, and Dave slammed into him with his shoulder. It felt like hitting a Buick. The man mountain brushed him aside like an annoying fly , but looked momentarily worried when an unearthly howl filled the air. Dave leaped again and Big John grabbed him by the wrist of his injured hand, lifting him off the street with one hand. Dave felt his shoulder separating like a piece of tissue.

"Karick says there's no time for more play," Big John said. He looked at Ricky again. "Time to leave, sweetheart. Karick is waiting." He tossed Dave against the wall again, and this time he couldn't get up. A knot bulged to the left of his chin. Excruciating pain from his dislocated shoulder paralyzed him. For a brief instant everything went dark, but he forced himself back to consciousness.

Maria screamed as her fists struck the big man, a sound like she was banging on an oak door.

Ricky cried.

Dave looked for her.

His eyes blurred, then refocused.

Big John had her.

Ricky screamed for help.

Dave fought the pain, stood and staggered toward him.

John threw Maria across the alley. Dave tried to catch her with his right arm and both of them sprawled on the asphalt. His shoulder exploded. He lost consciousness again.

He awoke to more gunshots.

Maria tried to get up, and finally did. She limped to the alley entrance. Dave struggled to his feet and followed. Another shot, then the loud click of a firing pin against an empty shell.

The man who said his name was Big John hurried into the night, holding Ricky against him as if trying to protect her. He glanced back at them briefly then ran back to the hotel. A few seconds later, Dave heard a car start and tires squeal as it spun out of the parking lot.

Rena and Alan stood there. She held a revolver. The faintest wisp of smoke drifted from the barrel.

"I hit him," she said, staring where he had vanished. "I was worried about Ricky, but I hit him three times in the back and he just twitched."

Maria leaned against the building, pounding on the brick wall. Dave wondered about the grinding sound, then realized it came from Maria's teeth.

Dave's shoulder throbbed but he forced himself to stand straight, focus on them.

"Where's the dog?"

Alan pointed at the other end.

"He couldn't move after the fight, but I think he'll recover." Alan spoke rapidly, words running together. Or was that just Dave's perception? His head still seemed to spin in circles.

"Should have seen Rena shoot out the thing's eye. Jesus, and Bobby fighting it." The magician's hands fluttered around like wild birds in a cage.

"Maria," Dave said, reaching out with his good hand. "We have to get after that guy, Big John."

She leaned against his right side, then looked up as he involuntarily moaned. Her dark eyes glistened, though she hadn't been crying. Even through her worry for Ricky, he could see her concern for him.

"Dislocated," she said, touching his arm tenderly.

"You a doctor?" he asked.

"I know enough first aid to get me in trouble." She pointed down. "Sit." He did, and leaned against the wall.

"Now," Maria said. "Close your eyes and hold on. I know it hurts now, but this will be like hellfire. Ready?" Dave closed his eyes and nodded.

He felt her hand on the knot. She put her palm against it and pushed.

Dave groaned through gritted teeth. His shoulder seemed to shatter into a thousand tiny pieces and every single fragment burned with a torturous pain.

And, suddenly, almost all the pain was gone. His shoulder throbbed dully and he knew it would be days before it was normal, but at least he could flex his fingers and move his arm slightly. Maria improvised a sling from a rag from the alley. He could tell she wanted to hurry. To go after Ricky.

Big John had named the enemy. Karick. Even the name chilled him.

But it had her now. Dave realized Karick was after Ricky all along. They were unimportant. It had what it wanted.

Karick had won.

Chapter 31

Alan walked back to the hotel room with Rena, not quite meeting her eyes, while Maria helped Dave with his arm. He couldn't believe a crowd hadn't gathered to see the carnage.   Where the hell was everyone? He expected to hear people talking or screaming, and sirens in the distance.

The only movement was Bobby. He walked up to them, wagging his tail weakly.

Except for the sound of their shoes on the pavement, it was quiet.

"Why did you come to work for me?" Alan asked, not turning as he walked.

"I wanted evidence. I knew you killed Jack and I wanted to find out how."

Alan stopped and turned to her.

"Well, you know now. Are you going to tell the police?"

"Tell them what? That you sent a concrete block through some sort of warp and dropped it on Jack's head?" She shook her head and her eyes rolled back. "I'd be locked away faster than you could say straight jacket."

He followed her into a hotel room, one of two adjoining. Rena sat on the bed.

"So?" he asked.

"I had another idea. The one I mentioned before. This." Rena showed him the gun. Alan suddenly found it hard to swallow and he had the feeling that even if he tried to run, his legs wouldn't support him at that particular moment. She laid the weapon on the table beside the bed and stared at him. At a spot just above his eyes, in the center of his forehead, he thought.

"A few dozen times every day, I wanted to take that gun and blow your brains all over the wall. Especially when you were being a jerk. Then you would do something sweet and nice and confuse me again.

"I probably would have done it anyway if I hadn't fallen in love with you."

"You're in love with me?" His eyes flicked to the gun then back to Rena's green eyes.

"Not dead, are you?"

A romantic line, if he'd ever heard one.

Alan walked to her then leaned over and kissed those sweet lips. He put his right hand behind her neck and with his other hand he took the gun. Rena only smiled as he backed away.

"Jack was a jerk, too, even more than you." She tossed her head and hair like red flame flickered in the light. "Mom and Dad had given up on him years ago, when he ran off to live on the streets. He did keep in touch, though. Especially when he needed money enough to beg Dad for it. Mom cried every time she thought about what he'd done with his life. I guess she remembered how he was before the drugs. A cute kid with a real talent for baseball.

"Maybe you did them a favor. At least now, they can remember him like they want to instead of being reminded every day of how he really was.

"But, damn you, he was my brother! I had to find out the truth."

Alan lowered his eyes.

"I'm sorry, Rena. I really am. Maybe I could have gotten away without killing him, I don't know. But standing there in that filthy alley with that gun pointing at me and the money spilling out of the bag he dropped, I couldn't think. I didn't know what else to do.

"Dammit, Rena, if I'd Hidden him, he'd still be alive but he'd be like Bobby was or the snake thing. Or worse. He wouldn't be your brother. Do you understand?" Rena nodded. She looked as though nothing could surprise her.

"What are you going to do, now?" she asked, looking at the weapon.

"First, hide this thing. In this universe." Alan hadn't forgotten the Gap would kill him. He didn't even want to think about the Gap. He pulled open a drawer and threw the handgun into the back. Then he kissed her again. He only wished they had more time, but Dave and Maria would be back soon, ready to go after the guy that took Ricky.

"Second, try to make up for being such a jerk so often." For the first time in a long time, Alan knew the honesty in his voice wasn't an act. And his voice cracked as though he were a kid caught with his arm up to the elbow in a jar of cookies.

"Alan," Rena said, wrapping her arms around his neck. "We will be old and gray and starting on our second pair of dentures before that happens."

And, somehow, that prospect didn't bother Alan as much as it once might have. He only wished he could live to enjoy it.

Maria felt a familiar emptiness inside her. The first time it happened was over three years ago when Brian died. Then, she hadn't been able to do anything about the vacuum in her heart. She didn't dare even cry. She could only try to be strong for the baby she carried. A baby who more than filled the emptiness. Ricky had infused her entire being with a life glow. Repaired and revitalized her damaged spirit. Caring for Little Erica, who had no patience for Maria's grief when her belly needed filling or her diaper emptying, left little time for self-pity.

Now, she felt as though she were falling and there was no safety net. She was afraid she would cry and the tears would strike the concrete with the tinkling of bells and roll away like tiny silver spheres.

Dave looked so tired, and she knew his shoulder had to be throbbing, even though he was already working his fingers. As if determined to go on no matter what. Alan and Rena walked ahead, but she didn't know whether the magician had come back to help, or just to get Rena. His van was parked near the overturned car. Ready to drive off into the night again.

She saw Bobby lying near the motel door, but wasn't surprised there was no crowd. Like at the airport and the magic show. Again, Karick had sheltered them from reality. Not too hard to do. All it had to do was cloak the sound and unless someone happened to look out the window at three in the morning, no one would know.

Bobby whimpered, as though he realized that Ricky was gone. Maria bent and patted him on the head.

Even as she quivered with the effort to stop herself from running to the car, and send it screaming into the night, looking for Ricky, she knew it was useless to try without help. She had to get Rena and Alan.

She, like Dave, knew where to look. The Tower's presence had plagued them for the last couple of days. That's where they had to be.

Maria hoped Rena and Alan would help, but it didn't matter.

She didn't care if the whole damned bunch of them turned and ran, but she would get Ricky back.

Even if she had to do it herself.

Rena and Alan walked toward them.

"What now?" Rena asked.

"I'm tired of being hunted. Now, we're going to be the hunters." Dave nodded.

Alan looks scared, Maria thought. His arms were crossed as though he thought they would shake uncontrollably if he let them go, and his teeth were clenched together so tightly that the muscles in his jaws quivered. Maybe his teeth would chatter if he relaxed.

She wondered why he hadn't used his "Hiding" ability on the snake thing, or the man that had taken Ricky. Earlier, when he mentioned it, he hadn't even offered to demonstrate. He'd seemed panicked at the thought of "Hiding" anything again. Maybe it had to do with what happened at the school.

"Hunt them where?" Alan asked. "I don't even know which way they went."

"Only one place," Dave said. "The mountain. Big John had to have taken her to Lox Mountain, where the Tower is."

Rena drew a sharp breath and said, "Oh, damn. That name." She shook her head.

"I thought I recognized the freak who took Ricky, and now I remember." She stopped as though reluctant to go on, watching Maria. "John Hill," she said finally. "From a county southwest of here. I saw a news report on TV yesterday at the hotel. There's a big manhunt on for him. He's wanted on various charges. Murder, theft, drug running, kidnapping. The worst is child molestation." The emptiness in Maria turned ice cold.

"He was arrested a few years ago in Somerset, but got off on a technicality. This time, the child's father rescued her before she was hurt, but a lot of people died, most of them drug dealers. They think Hill killed them for the money and drugs. From what I heard they were almost shredded wheat. But that's not why they want him so badly.

"In his house, they found videos and pictures. A reporter said one deputy refused to watch more than a few minutes of the first recording.

"They showed him assaulting five or six young girls, almost babies, really. They're not sure what happened to the girls, yet, whether he let them go or killed them."

Maria leaned against Dave. This couldn't be happening. My poor

Erica, she thought.

John Hill was a monster when he was still human. She was afraid to think about what he had become, now.

And he had Ricky.

Chapter 32

Evan Hall was so scared he thought his balls had drawn up and disappeared somewhere near his bladder. Tonight was the night his computer picked. The night the cosmos would collapse like a popped balloon.

He didn't know why he let Jerry talk him into following the undulating creature and that huge man from the school. The first thing they should have done when they saw them creeping around the building was to make sure the gas tank was full - and if not, find a QT Mart and fill the tank - then drive as far and as fast as they could without stopping.

"No," Jerry had said. "We can't do that. What about your computer projection? Do you think maybe California will be safe from the destruction of the universe? Come on, Evan, our job is to investigate things like this. We'll never get a chance like this again."

"I hope to hell not," Evan had told him. They had parked on the street, but they could see the school parking lot, and the building where the two were looking in a window. "Besides, I'm not on the clock. It's not my problem."

"You didn't object to driving over here when you heard the police report of a strange glow and some sort of creature wandering around."

"You heard the radio. There was a magic show here tonight. It was part of the performance."

"Think those guys are in the act?"

"No," Evan had admitted. The snake-like being stayed put while the big man broke through the front door. Evan wasn't sure how he got in. Usually schools were secured by heavy duty locks, with chains for good measure. "Another good reason to get the hell out of here while we can."

"Just a few more minutes. Let's see if he comes out soon."

A piercing scream of pain and terror, twisting its way across the school grounds like a bolt of lightning, had caused both of the men to jerk upright. The sound cut off abruptly, and both men jumped again like someone had punched them in the stomach. They looked at each other, then back at the school. The big man came out, wiping his hands on his pants, then both creatures climbed into the car and drove away.

"Damn," Evan had said then. And he said it again after they followed the car to the back of the motel, and the two disappeared around front. They could only see a little of the front from where they were parked.

There was a hell of a lot of gunfire, but no police reports on the radio. That was crazy. Someone should have heard the crash like thunder when the snake man rolled the car and people shouting and more gun shots popping like giant champagne corks. When the big man returned to his car carrying a small bundle, Evan could stand no more. Computer graph or not, he decided it was time to go home and accept that grant from the fast food industry to investigate the feasibility of using shredded paperback books as meat filler.

"We're leaving," he said.

"Like hell," Jerry said abruptly. Evan turned and stared at him. That couldn't have been Jerry. He never swore.

"What?"

"Did I stutter?" Jerry asked. "We're not leaving."

"Jerry, that snake thing is still around here somewhere. You want to get out and run across something like that in a shadow somewhere?" Even shook his head. "Not me, brother."

Jerry moved his head back and forth, trying to get a better view of the front of the motel.

"I thought I saw some people, but not any kind of snake creature. I don't think they would stand around talking if they were in any immediate danger." He glanced back at Evan. "We really need to find out what's going on. You said there was a lot in those reports you didn't understand, right?"

Evan said nothing.

"How are we ever going to find the answers to those questions unless we investigate these things?"

"Maybe I don't want to know any more," Evan said. "I'm to the point where I'm afraid to know."

"Dr. Evan Hall," Jerry said. He didn't sound happy. "I would think that you, of all people, would understand the importance of scientific investigation, of the advancement of pure knowledge. Research is important. Research is why we can launch a shuttle, save a heart patient, drive this car instead of running around on bare feet like Fred Flintstone. Research is --"

"Okay, Jerry, I get the message. Science is good. Science will save us all."

"It will," he insisted.

"I wish it would hurry. I don't want my head swallowed in one easy gulp by some snake monster. Is science going to save me from that?"

"I think they must have killed it. Look, they're walking to the other end of the parking lot. This is our chance."

"Yeah, a chance to get killed. Those people have to be touchy as hell," Evan said. "They're all probably like guns with a hair-trigger, ready to fire at the slightest disturbance. And they have at least one real gun. You want to quietly walk up behind these people and tap them on the shoulders? You'd probably be dead before you cleared your throat to ask a question."

Jerry looked thoughtful for a few seconds, then nodded. "We'll wait a few minutes."

They waited less than a few minutes. Almost immediately, the group of four people - and a dog, for God's sake - entered one of the cars. Evan had an idea he knew where they were going. To the top of Lox Mountain. That's where his computer program had pinpointed the impending disturbance, and he had the feeling they were involved. He shivered.

Evan watched them leave and let out a sigh of relief. In all his years of investigating creepy occurrences, that had to be the creepiest bunch of people he'd ever encountered. They looked almost like members of a cult, with a single- minded view of the world, but he suspected that was because they had shared some truly weird experiences in that motel parking lot, and maybe other places, too. Places he didn't want to think about.

Jerry wasted no time. He ran around the front of the building. Evan walked after him. Briskly, but he didn't run. He wasn't that anxious to see what was there. As he approached, he saw that it was a giant snake head. And a headless, scaled body on the pavement nearby.

Creepy as hell. And just as creepy to watch Jerry examining the head. Evan sat on the pavement, his back against a Cadillac with no windshield.

"Notice the white interior of the mouth. A perfect example of ancistrodon piscivorus, a cottonmouth moccasin. Or would be if it were a tenth that size," Jerry said, studying the head. His nose was almost against the scaly skin. "And if it had six less fangs. On second thought, it's not so perfect at all."

"Perfect enough for me, Jerry. I'll wait over here."

"Evan, I believe you're burned out."

"Like a piece of bread stuck in a toaster. Next week at this time, I'll be in a nice quiet lab somewhere, testing the palatability of newsprint." Even as he said the words, he felt a premonitory shudder. As though he knew he would be doing nothing of the sort.

Evan looked away from the head, but saw the body of the snake thing. He didn't know which was worse. He started to look at the full moon when he thought he saw the body twitch. Just a slight movement in a finger. It could have been a post mortem muscle contraction.

Or something else.

As far as Evan was concerned, and he had found nothing to change his mind after several years of investigating some of this planet's stranger phenomenon, dead was dead. Dead things didn't say a whole lot, they didn't bother you with stupid questions, and they definitely didn't get up and ask for a glass of water in the middle of the night. Evan, to that moment, had rather enjoyed the predictability of death. He could always count on dead to stay dead.

Something scratched at the concrete.

Evan leaped to his feet. A prodigious leap. He landed next to Jerry and the severed snake head. He looked down and reached to tap Jerry on the shoulder when one slanted eye popped open and swiveled to stare at them. Jerry stumbled back, his arms waving, until he ended up sitting near Evan's feet.

They were in trouble. The head was between them and their car and the body was on the other side. Nowhere to run unless they vaulted the Caddy, which Evan felt very capable of doing at the moment. Then what? Neither of them were fast runners.

The headless body quivered.

Dead things don't walk, Evan thought, repeating the words like a mantra. Dead things don't walk.

He was wrong.

The head slid across the asphalt, slamming into the body with an audible thud. Two scaled hands held the head for a moment and what looked like a seam around it's neck disappeared. It stood and hissed.

The snake creature was alive.

It ignored them and tore across the parking lot with a lithe, sinuous speed that no human could ever match. Almost as fast as a car. The thing seemed to skim across the street. It disappeared into the distance before either of them could do more than twitch and break out into a cold sweat. Evan looked at Jerry. He looked back.

"How --?" Evan began.

"I don't know," Jerry answered. "This time, I just don't know."

Evan knew where it was going, though, and knew he and Jerry would soon be right behind it, however insane he thought that idea was. It was following the car.

It was going after those poor, creepy people who had just left for the Tower.

Chapter 33

John Hill hummed to himself as he wheeled the big Olds around the twisting route to the top of Lox Mountain.

And the Tower.

He had come to realize that the Tower was his enemy, but that its power was weak compared to the strength of Karick. On that cold steel slab near the Tower, he would use the power and blood of this young girl to open the way for Karick.

The small form was still in the floorboard of the Olds wagon. He had tied her hands with strapping tape, being careful not to hurt her, but she seemed resigned to her fate. She didn't attempt to scream or get away or even cry. Just lay there in silence, staring at him with disturbingly calm and judging eyes.

But the chaste and pure blood. Hot, coursing with power and youth and vitality.

John might even get a taste of it.

He touched his face, and he heard a sound like wood on wood. In the rearview mirror, he could see enough to know the hard, dark area had finally moved past his collar and his shirt sleeves. Interlocking plates of dull obsidian covered his face, the joints between the armor sections like dark lines drawn on his skin.

Big John was a black man and he didn't even care.

He figured if there were more black men like him, pretty soon there wouldn't be any white men left. Or any other kind, either, including those who thought they were black.

Soon. Very soon.

Only one thing really bothered John. After years of living with, and sometimes fighting, the compulsive need to possess the young bodies of the girls he took, it was gone. He didn't want to do the things he once did. The things he had captured in intricate detail on videotape so long ago when he was still human, in appearance if nothing else.

True, he had other urges, but the Urge itself was gone.

Karick had promised him all the young girls he wanted and needed to satisfy his Urge, and that part was true, at least, because he no longer wanted them.

For one brief, distressing moment, he wondered if all Karick's promises were so reliable.

Then the moment was gone, lost somewhere in the increasingly non-human head. He touched the hunting knife hanging from his belt almost lovingly, thinking of the girl and the steel plate on the mountain.

Steel on steel ringing down the mountain, echoing through the valley and from nearby hills when he rammed the point of the knife into the plate.

Those others at the warehouse would be following him, he knew, but they would be too late to stop him. Much too late.

By the time they got there, John's new thirsts would be sated, and Karick would crush the metal, glowing phallus and stand like a twisted dark tower itself above the mountain top.

In this world.

Then the fun would begin.

Chapter 34

Alan was afraid that if he used his talent, he would die. He hadn't tried since the school. Afraid the attempt would be his death. As they drove to the mountain, he explained to Rena how he had done the Ball of Fire and the Girl and the Ghost trick.

"Those were the only two," he had said. "Everything else was genuinely fake magic."

Hell of a comforting phrase. Genuinely fake. He'd had enough of the genuinely real stuff to last a lifetime. He figured that was maybe another hour or two.

Maria drove, with Dave beside her, while he sat in the back with Rena, Bobby between them. He sat against the door, as far away from the sharp grin as possible. The teeth glowed in the faint reflection from the headlights. But he didn't look like he wanted to tear his head off. He looked confused and, at the moment, docile. Not like something from the Gap.

Without using the gift, he tried to remember what he had Hidden in storage lately. Not a lot. Even the Dr. Peppers were almost gone.

Alan couldn't understand why he was there.

He traced the events in his mind back to Rena, then back to the moment when she stood, naked on the stage with nothing but her dignity to cover herself. He remembered how beautiful she looked, how vulnerable. He'd felt an uncharacteristic urge to protect her from the world.

Right. She carried a gun and could shoot the eyeballs off a gnat at fifty yards and he had to protect her.

But Alan didn't fall in love with Rena then. He had been in love with her for weeks, but only realized it when he found himself running away in the truck. When he almost lost her, what he discovered then chilled him down to his self-serving butt.

He would fight to protect her.

He didn't want to live without her.

He would do anything to keep her happy and safe.

He - dammit! - would even die for her.

He tried to convince himself otherwise. What good was his love if he were dead? He could get over her. Like anyone else who loses a loved one, he would continue living and her memory would fade and he would find someone else who could help him forget.

Dave had lost his wife and child and Maria's husband died and they survived.

So Rena was beautiful. So were a lot of women.

She was smart and witty and could see through his crap any day of the week. There were other smart, witty women. He wasn't sure he wanted anyone to see through his crap, anyway.

She had hair like red flame and green eyes that seemed to see into his soul and a laugh that exploded into a room like nitroglycerin. Her kiss made his skin tingle. Her fingers knew where to touch him to make him tremble. Her words knew when to soothe or scold him.

He was in love and couldn't talk himself out of it. His minor gift had deserted him, too.

Panic under pressure.

He had been lucky. Until then, he hadn't fallen into any really serious trouble. Not since he developed the habit of running from trouble as a boy. When he couldn't run, the familiar near-hysteria set in. Like when Rena's brother had cornered him.

When all he had to do was protect himself, he could deal with the problem. Or ignore it. In this case, the same thing.

But now these people depended on him. Rena depended on him.

A tiny, dark-haired girl depended on him.

Panic under pressure. The phrase echoed through his head.

He was thrown hard against the front seat as Maria slammed on the brakes and the car skidded to a halt with a slight chirping of tires. The sudden stop threw him against Bobby. The dog's skin was pleasantly warm and furry. Carefully, Alan patted him on the head. Bobby looked pleased. He had never seen a dog that looked pleased.

He peered out the front, trying to see why they had stopped.

Dave said, "Damn!"

An overgrown oak blocked the narrow road, the roots in the trees to the right and the top lost in the ones on the left. There was no way to get a car past that point. According to a sign beside the road, Lox Mountain Park was only a mile away.

Too damn far.

"Think we can move it?" Alan asked.

"No," Dave said, twisting to look at him. "The car wouldn't budge it even if we had a rope. It's locked in those trees like a wedge." He didn't appear or sound happy at all. Alan could have jogged that last mile in just a few minutes, but he knew that Dave would puff and sweat and probably collapse after a hundred feet.

"Did Hill do that?" Maria asked. Dave nodded.

"Who else?"

They didn't want to leave the car, Alan knew. Inside, with the doors locked and the windows rolled up, they were secure. Out there, they were exposed to a world with snake things and monsters who carried off little girls.

So Alan did a stupid thing and opened the door to get a closer look at the barrier.

For all he knew, John Hill crouched behind the tree for someone to do something that reckless so he could jump out, grab the person and unscrew his head like the top of a diet, caffeine-free Dr. Pepper. At least he still had his sword.

His hand trembled as he leaned against a tree limb to steady himself. He heard the others behind him.

"We walk from here," Maria said.

"We'll never catch him in time," Dave said. He sounded angry and frustrated, and Alan realized a lot of that anger was directed at himself. Dave knew he would slow them down.

And, though his knees felt weak enough to send him crashing to the asphalt at any second, Alan knew what he had to do.

He and the damn dog.

He climbed over the tree and motioned for Bobby.

"Come on, Bobby," he said. The animal bounded to the tree trunk, then bounced down to the asphalt as though he had understood every word. Alan wondered if the others noticed his forehead was wet. "We'll stop him somehow."

"Are you crazy?" Rena said, climbing after them. "I'm going with you."

"You'll slow me down," he said. He leaned the sword against the tree and held her shoulders. "Bobby won't. Hell, he can outrun me."

"Take the gun, at least."

"I've got the sword and my buddy here," he said, nodding at the dog. "And you have to protect the others in case Hill or something else is around."

"You might reach him in time," Dave told him, quietly. But Maria heard. He noticed that she flinched like someone had slapped her sharply. "He had to stop to knock the tree over and that must have slowed him."

"Sure, we'll make it. You guys hurry, though, we might need someone to clean up the mess." He looked into Rena's beautiful eyes, swollen and red and filled with tears that glistened in the headlights. But they were still beautiful.

"I truly love you, Rena. I'm sorry about your brother and all the crap you've had to put up with in the past few months and the fact that I'm a jerk who never treated you like I should have." Alan began to think this was a final, grim good-bye, and he did not enjoy that thought at all. "Most of all, I'm sorry for the lost time I could have spent with you."

"Shut up, you bastard, before I hit you over the head with this gun and drag you back inside the car. If you have something to say, wait until we catch up with you. You're wasting time."

"Right," he said, grinning. He did not feel like grinning, but he did. Is that what being in love meant? Doing things you thought were irrationally stupid but did anyway? He kissed her, briefly, grabbed the sword, and started down the road with Bobby at his side.

He had jogged only a dozen yards or so when he realized he still wore the hard shoes from the show. Dumb as a day is long! he told himself. He should have gotten the running shoes out of the truck at the motel. At this rate his arches and knees would be like warm, runny Jello in no time. After he had warmed up a bit, he had planned to pick up the pace. Not too quickly, though. He would do Ricky no good if he was paralyzed with a leg cramp. With the black, polished dress shoes, he would be lucky to get there at all.

There he was again. Doing things he thought were irrationally stupid but did anyway.

He was almost grateful for the full moon overhead. It meant he didn't need a light. After his eyes adjusted, the road seemed as brightly illuminated as an indoor running track.

But it also meant black shadows ringed the trees on either side of the road. Huge dark areas that could hide a dozen creatures like they killed at the hotel parking lot. It had taken the combined efforts of Bobby, Rena's gun, and his sword to stop that one. Alan had no misconceptions about his own fighting ability. That's why he'd come up behind the snake at the motel. That's why he was a runner. If they did meet up with one of those things, he and Bobby would be in serious trouble.

Something broke through the brush from the left, a dark form bounding across the road in front of them. His heart accelerated and pounded as he stumbled to a stop, holding the sword in both hands. Bobby whimpered.

The deer stared at them with dark, shiny eyes and leaped off to the right.

Alan breathed again, and looked back. He couldn't see the others, though he thought there was a faint glow over the hill they had just crossed. Probably from the headlights.

He started again, and his legs pumped even faster this time. After a few hundred feet, he fell into a steady rhythm, feet slapping against the asphalt. Each impact time sent a shock up his shins to his suffering knees. He considered removing the leather shoes, but he had no idea what other surprises Hill had prepared. Still, they covered distance quickly. It seemed that he and Bobby were alone in a dimly lit tunnel with an endless road that stretched into the distance. He had no problems except a compulsion to reach the end of that tunnel. There were no monsters or near-monsters. Only the road.

Alan didn't look left or right, just straight ahead. He was worried he would break the spell.

That happened soon enough.

They ran only a minute or two longer when he heard three quick shots from behind them.

Was that a scream?

Then silence.

Either they had killed something or something had killed them.

Fear, so intense it was like a painful slap across the face, shook him. Alan knew that even in the brightest daylight his face would have been colorless. In that cold light, he must have looked like a thin, pallid spirit.

They were okay or dead, and he couldn't help in either case.

He had no choice. Whatever had happened, he had to go on. He ran.

A half minute later he heard the slap of feet against the asphalt, like the rapid tapping of drumsticks on a table top.

Someone running. Very fast. Faster than anyone they left behind could have.

Alan stopped and turned to face the way they had come. He gripped the sword tightly, wishing he'd actually learned how to use it. At least he had something to fight with. Beside him, Bobby halted and looked around as though confused by his actions. Then he stared down the road and growled low in his throat.

Like the sound Alan heard during the fight at the motel.

Beside Bobby, pale moonlight on a paler face, Alan waited.

Though Rena felt as though every sense was strained to the limit, Dave heard the tapping sound first, and motioned them into a clump of dark brush to the right. She stood in front of the others, her .38 held ready, pointing back in the direction of the car. A thin, silhouetted form appeared on the crest of the small rise, the car's headlights haloing the shape as it paused. Somehow, it must have sensed them because it turned a triangular head toward their hiding place. Rena gripped the gun more tightly, wondering how many times she would have to kill this thing. Maria gasped.

The oddly long neck and the boneless arms undulated in the moonlight like twin snakes wrapped around a pole.

She had to stop it.

Rena fired quickly, three rapid shots, and every one of them struck. The first took a dark chunk out of its right upper arm. The second hit it in the midsection and sent a spray of blood and dark flesh across the road. The third careened off the top of its skull and it staggered, but didn't fall. The creature barely slowed, and that was only long enough to look back and hiss at them.

"It died," Dave said. "It's supposed to be dead."

"Maybe it's like a vampire. You have to drive a stake through it's heart or something," Maria said, her voice tense.

"But we cut the damned head off! What do you have to do to kill it?"

Rena couldn't stand it any more. The thing ran down the road, where Alan and Bobby had gone.

"ALAN!"

Her scream echoed through the trees and something crashed in the brush off to the right, moving away from them. Dave and Maria had frozen into immobility. She ran back to the road, sighted down the barrel again, but it had disappeared over another small rise. Damned mountains, she thought.

"Come on!" she yelled back at them. "You going to run your mouths all night?" She ran after the creature.

She heard them start after her.

Too far and too fast. Alan was too far ahead of them and the creature was too fast.

By the time they arrived, it would all be over.

Chapter 35

At first, Alan didn't realize the creature staring at him in the cold, white light was the thing from the motel. Then he saw the snake head and the rippling arms and knew it had come back to life, or never had been truly dead.

He wondered why it didn't attack.

Bobby's growl deepened, at his side like a faithful dog facing an intruder. Alan was also amazed that Bobby had not lunged at the creature, but perhaps he remembered the first encounter at the motel.

If fear was a level, his just shot off the scale.

Damn.

Alan looked down to make sure his crotch was still dry.

Then, unexpectedly, the creature moved to the side of the road, hissed at him, and breathed one precious word.

"Run."

It wasn't a human voice. It was whispery and dry, like a desiccated and discarded reptilian skin Alan had once found as a boy.

It repeated the word, more emphatically, gesturing back the way they'd come.

"Run!"

Alan knew what it offered. All he had to do was abandon his quest for the end of that road. Give up. Let the snake thing pass and let Hill have the girl. None of the others could fault him if he didn't fight this monster. No contest. Blow the whistle. End of game.

Run. All he had to do was run, and he was very, very good at running.

As a boy he ran from his tormentors.

As a teenager, he ran from his parents and home.

As a man, he was always on the run from the law.

Running from commitment and responsibility.

Running from involvement.

He ran to avoid injury and disappointment, but at the same time, he realized, he ran to avoid love.

"RUN!" it roared, still only a loud whisper.

But Alan gripped the obscenely inadequate sword and knew he was through running.

No more panic under pressure.

No more running. He shook his head at the thing.

It walked toward him, very slowly. As if giving him a final opportunity to scurry away like a frightened mouse.

Damned apt description, Alan thought. He figured his eyes probably looked like a mouse's that had been caught in a trap and slowly suffocated.

Bobby growled and leaped at it.

One of the gently waving arms whipped out and wrapped around Bobby. It tossed him against the base of a large tree, where he hit with a thud. Bobby staggered to his feet. He walked as though he had guzzled a few pints of bourbon. Alan backed away, swinging the blade in front of him. The snake thing ignored it.

He had to take the risk. He had to try to Hide it.

Alan reached for his talent, felt a vibrating tension and a rush of fear at the same time. Would he die now? Would the blood vessels in his brain explode in a massive embolism?

He reached out with his mind and pushed.

It opened its mouth just a bit, cool moonlight making the inside glow as if phosphorescent. Like a deadly smile.

Alan pushed again and he felt the talent slip sideways. He couldn't Hide this. It was a hundred times harder than the giant roach.

If that was a smile, it vanished like mist on a windy day, torn off its face by the growling roar behind it. The snake thing fell to its knees as Bobby hit it.

The snake caught him, wrapped both arms around Bobby, holding those dangerous teeth away. Its mouth gaped, four rows of fangs white in the lunar light.

Alan swung the sword, aiming for the neck, but it uncoiled an arm from around Bobby, and knocked the sword from his hands, into the brush. He slugged the thing with his fist, shuddering every time he touched the cold, tough skin. The thing turned its head as if on a swivel and hissed at him. Alan backed away.

He'd never felt so damned useless in his life.

Some wonderful gift. He couldn't do a damn thing to help.

Then he realized he could.

He held out his hands and they shimmered in iridescent colors.

The Colt Government Model .45 automatic materialized in his hands, and he fired twice at the snake, hitting it both times.

It turned and roared at him.

Alan wasn't an expert like Rena, but he was a mere four and a half feet from the thing when he emptied the remaining five bullets into the thing.

One in the chamber, six in the clip.

The first shot actually hit a fang, exploding white chunks across the road like pieces of a broken plate.

The second burst the left eye again. Rena would have been proud.

The third bounced off its forehead, chiseling a groove beside a similar gouge.

The fourth hit the gaping mouth and a dark fluid like burned motor oil gushed from the hole.

The last shot hit where its heart should have been and blasted chunks of white flesh and dark blood out its back.

It finally went to its knees, then raised its good eye and hissed at him.

Another shimmer. Alan ejected the empty clip and slapped another into place. He jacked a shell into the chamber and sighted down the barrel.

Bobby seemed to know there was only one final way to stop if not kill it. He locked his teeth around the thin neck and shook until the head hung by only a single strand of tough skin.

Alan retrieved the sword while Bobby held it, and hacked the snake man into a few dozen pieces. There were few bones in its body.

Alan panted, unable to get his breath for a few seconds. He felt as though he'd just run a marathon. Bobby stood guard, watching for any flicker of movement from the thing. If it could come back to life once, it could again.

He couldn't leave the body and head there. The others would be by in a few minutes and it might still rejuvenate.

A shimmering glow appeared around the body parts and head, similar to but subtly different from the iridescence when he'd brought the gun back. The pieces of the snake vanished, leaving only dark wet splotches on the road. In its almost death, it didn't have the power to resist. The road looked as though there had been a minor oil spill, or a few dozen people bled to death. He had to leave a message for the others or they might think it was his or Bobby's blood. Beneath that moon, all colors became black and white, dark and light.

He reached out, and a frigid Dr. Pepper appeared in his palm. The cold carbonated liquid tingled as he swallowed, cooling his throat. He held the can to his forehead for a second and noticed Bobby watching him. He shrugged and offered it to the creature. Bobby licked his lips. Alan held it so some of the liquid poured down the dog's mouth. More spilled on the road than he swallowed, but he made a strange face and then showed his teeth in a fearsome grimace that Alan had decided was another attempted smile. Alan shrugged again and took another drink.

What was a few dog germs among friends?

He inventoried his available resources briefly. Nothing in the Gap. He patted his pockets. And, finally, he had it. A perfect way to leave a message on a moonlit asphalt road.

If you were a magician.

They pushed forward along as quickly as they could, Dave struggling to keep up with her and Maria, but Rena knew that they were too slow. Much too slow. Besides being so scared she could barely breath, she was confused. Where had those gunshots come from? Had John Hill waited with a gun over the next rise? She didn't remember Alan having any kind of weapon except the sword.

The roaring cry of some massive beast echoed across the mountain.

For a few seconds, Rena couldn't place the sound. Like a monster screaming its displeasure, and at the same time familiar and commonplace. And finally she knew what it was.

A chain saw. The characteristic whining chatter of a two-stroke engine cut through the early morning air.

What the hell would anyone be doing at four in the morning cutting wood?

Unless they were trying to remove a tree across the road.

Rena tried to pinpoint the sound, but Dave stared back down the road, listening.

"Someone sawing up the tree," he said.

"Any idea who?" Maria asked. Her feet twitched and danced like her bladder had an urgent appointment elsewhere, but Rena knew it was only because she wanted to keep moving.

"Maybe a concerned citizen who just happened to have a chain saw." Dave breathed deeply, rapidly. Rena worried that he was venturing into heart attack country. "Maybe a deputy patrolling the area found the tree and called for someone to bring a saw. Who knows?" The slight pause had given him time to regain his breath. "Doesn't matter. Let's go."

When Dave, Maria, and Rena finally jogged across that rise at a slow run, they saw Alan's message still burning in the middle of the road. Just two letters, but Rena felt something loosen around her chest.

"How?" Maria asked.

"Flash powder and lighter fluid, I think," Rena told her. "For special effects and his flaming wallet." Dave and Maria still looked puzzled.

"I dare you," Rena said, "to find any magician day or night who doesn't have a trick ready to perform. Alan is just more prepared than most."

The flames died as they ran past, but the burned areas gleamed a dull red and the hot tar would continue smoking for another half hour or so.

Just two letters. Two glorious letters glowing in the night:

OK

Chapter 36

She wouldn't cry. She wouldn't cry.

Ricky told herself to be brave, like her Daddy wanted, but it was hard.

The huge man stopped the car and pulled her out, holding her shoulder as they walked.

He was scary. His face looked like the skin of an alley-gator she saw on TV once. (Her Mommy had told her they lived in Florida, and Mommy never lied to her. And she had never seen them in the alley at home, and her Grandmom took her to see some in Florida, so she must have been right.) When he grabbed her arm, his fingers felt harder than the iron rails on the steps at her house.

The big knife on his belt was scary.

Her lower lip quivered, but she made it stop.

Mommy called her Erica when she was bad sometimes, but she thought her Mommy would call her Ricky, now, because she tried very, very hard to be good.

She wished her Mommy would come and get her. But she was worried that the man would try to hurt her Mommy so she also wished that she would stay away. Ricky wondered how she could wish for two different things like that, but she did.

And, all of a sudden, she knew that Mommy was coming, but too slowly. She knew that only one person could help her now.

Her Daddy.

She liked her Daddy, even though she had seen him only once when she was asleep. And she thought Daddy liked her. But he said that he didn't want to leave heaven, so she wasn't sure that he would come and try to help her even if she asked him.

But she would try.

Mommy had told her that God was in heaven, too, and if she wanted to talk to God she should close her eyes and bow her head and pray. This is how you talked to God. But Daddy was in heaven, too, and she decided that to talk to Daddy she had to do the same thing.

She bowed her head and prayed for her Daddy to help.

The big man said a very bad word and let go of her shoulder. Ricky opened her eyes and it looked like he was smoking.

Not a cigarette like Mr. Munson downstairs did. His fat fingers smoked like they were on fire.

Her arms were tied but she tried to run away anyway. The man said a different bad word and ran after her.

He knew a lot of bad words.

Ricky knew she couldn't run faster then he could. He was fat, but he was still a grown-up.

Just as he reached for her, she dodged to the left.

The man stumbled and fell on his big belly. Ricky ran as hard and fast as she could. More bad words and he was after her again.

The Full Moon was bright, but not bright enough. (Ricky always wondered if it was full of milk since it was so white.) Not bright enough for her to see the root she tripped over. She tried to get up again, but the fat man lifted her by her belt before she could move.

He put his alley-gator face close to hers and said a bad word again.

It scared her.

But she wouldn't cry.

She wished her Daddy and her Mommy would hurry.

Chapter 37

Rena was wrong. Alan had forgotten the flash powder, though he had some paper and one pellet. So he sacrificed two shells from the automatic, sprinkling the dark gun powder on the lighter fluid he had already squirted on the road. The flame was nice and bright and very hot. Even if the fire was gone when the others came by, the burned asphalt would still be visible.

He Hid the sword. If necessary, he could get it, but the gun was better, anyway. Then he discovered the extra clip wasn't full. He had only three shells left. He cursed stupidity and never slowed.

About the time the others passed the burning letters in the road, Alan and Bobby made the final turn into the parking lot near the Tower. He knew about the place, even before the pulsing lights that knocked him senseless, but he'd never been there. At the moment, with all the lights out, he wasn't even sure he could find the Tower. There was no real reason for the city to keep it on all night, and they probably saved a nice bundle on electricity, but he wished he had more than the full moon overhead for illumination. He wanted to make sure he knew where he pointed that damn gun.

He hadn't realized it until then, but those flashes of light he had seen around the structure were a lot like the glowing halo they had experienced back at the school - so long ago, it seemed. He wondered if that meant the Tower, or whatever had flashed around the Tower, was on their side? Dave had told them in the car about the metal plate inside the fenced off area and the uneasiness he felt around that place. Nowhere near the Needle, so why had they seen the lights there? If he hadn't been so cynical, Alan might have believed that the universe abhorred imbalance as much as it did a vacuum. If there was a great force for evil, maybe there was an equal and opposite force for good.

Who was he conning, now? he thought. Any idiot could watch the evening news and see that was a truckload of crap.

Or was it?

Television journalists thrived on sensation and bad news, reporting spectacular stories of war and crime and disaster while usually ignoring the "lesser" stories of kindness and love and humanitarianism. For every big story of great destruction, there were a thousand smaller instances of people picking up dropped packages for someone else. Or smiling at a little kid as they walked by. Or holding the door open for a complete stranger. Maybe all that did balance.

Besides, good news didn't help ratings. Death and destruction did.

Alan heard someone yell a guttural obscenity from an open area beyond the parking lot. It had to be Hill. He thought for a moment, and the gun glowed and vanished. He didn't know whether Bobby could understand completely, but he had to try to explain what he wanted. All they really had to do was slow him down enough for the others to get there, but without endangering the little girl more than she already was.

Jesus, that poor kid, he thought. What could she be thinking? All this had pushed him close to a mental precipice, with a long, hard fall to insanity at the bottom. And he was a supposedly rational adult. What must it be doing to her child's mind?

Now, if he could only explain to Bobby what to do. He seemed like a smart dog, smarter than he should be, but unless he was the Einstein of all dogs, he wasn't going to understand. All he could do was try. He bent and whispered in the dog's ear.

Show time.

Big John wanted to break her neck right then, but knew it wasn't the time, or the way, to take care of her. He knew the way, and the time was almost here.

He worried that he might have taken too long with the tree, but knew he had to slow them down somehow. He needed enough time to finish before they arrived.

It had not helped that he could only drive slowly that last half mile or so. The creeping hard flesh had worked its way down his fingers and it was harder and harder to control the car. His hands felt numb and sluggish, as though reluctant to take orders.

And he could feel the same creeping dullness invading his brain, so maybe that condition wouldn't last too much longer, either.

Sweet Je-- In mid-thought his brain shut down and he shook his head. Whatever thought he was chasing had evaporated like water dancing around a griddle. His changing brain would not tolerate his favorite expression.

Something snapped toward the parking lot, a dried twig cracking in the darkness. John stared at the picnic area. By the bright moonlight, he could see tables scattered haphazardly over the area, with an occasional clump of vegetation between the tables.

Two trees with overlapping branches formed a crude doorway. John squinted and thought he saw a movement in the gloom. Then a crack and a dazzling flash of light made him cover his eyes and stumble back, still holding the girl's shoulder.

One of them stood there. The tall, thin man with the suit. He limped slightly as he walked toward them with something small and white in his hands.

A bird.

The jackass had a damn white dove in his left hand, petting and talking to it like it was his best friend.

The skinny guy suddenly cupped the bird in both hands, waved it up and down a few times, then raised his hands and opened them as though he meant to let the bird go free.

A cloud of white and silver and gold confetti drifted down around him, sparkling in the pale light from the moon. His hands were empty. There was no bird.

He pulled out a cigarette case, opened it and removed a long white cylinder. Then he closed it and snapped his fingers like he had forgotten something. He flipped the case again and flame danced where there had been cigarettes. He lit his smoke and closed the case. The flame was gone.

What the hell is going on? Big John thought. This guy was crazy.

The cigarette danced across his fingers, rolling back and forth like a spinning baton. John wondered why he didn't burn his fingers. Then the skinny guy reached up into the air and the cigarette vanished, but he was holding a pure white silk scarf that shimmered and glowed in the moonlight like a pool of liquid light. He touched the scarf on the top and it disappeared in a sheet of blinding flame.

And the skinny man held a forty-five pointed directly at his heart.

John looked around for the girl, but she had slowly backed away from him while he was distracted.

The skinny guy fired once, twice, then three times.

Big John stumbled back with each impact, a succession of mule kicks to the chest. His vision blurred and he thought he would lose consciousness, but he fought it and his eyes finally cleared.

In time to see the skinny man holding the gun an inch or two from his forehead. His finger twitched again, and John flinched.

Only a slight click as the trigger moved. The slide had locked open. No more ammo.

He pulled the trigger several more times, but the clip was empty and the gun didn't even squeak. Where John touched his chest there was no blood, though he felt three hard knots where lead lodged in his flesh. He hurt like hell, but the bullets hadn't gone through his tough hide. He looked up at the skinny man and smiled.

Pay back time.

Alan didn't know why he kept pulling the trigger. It was stupid, useless, and took time he should have used running from this armor plated creature. Like he'd lost a telephone connection, then hit the button a few times and said, "Hello? Hello?" Useless, superstitious behavior. Phone systems were automatic these days. No operators you could get by hitting the receiver button.

Then he took two steps back and threw the gun at the fat man. That was about as useful as pulling the trigger on an empty forty-five. Hill brushed it aside without half trying.

Alan wasn't completely surprised when John Hill shook off the effects of the bullets and grinned his maniac smile at him. Not after what happened back at the motel. He had hoped the larger caliber handgun would at least slow him down, but it looked as though it had just made him mad.

Not a smart thing to do.

Alan circled to his right, toward the girl, and Hill turned until he faced away from a small clump of trees. Time for Plan "B" if his companion understood his part.

"B" for Bobby.

Bobby howled and leaped on Big John Hill's back, his teeth gouging at hard, tough skin with little effect. John swayed, then lumbered back, knocking Bobby away. Alan thought he looked like a mass of interlocking bony plates, like some ancient dinosaur's armor. All of Bobby's efforts did nothing but annoy him. Hill was unhurt.

"Erica, do you remember me?" he asked her, trying to get the tape off her hands. She looked up at him with dark, hurt eyes and nodded.

"The magic man," she said.

"That's right, honey. I'm going to try to work some more magic and get you away from here." He looked back at Hill. He held Bobby by the throat, squeezing, and Bobby's eyes became shiny and frightened. He clawed at the hand at his throat, but Hill only squeezed harder.

Alan should have taken the girl in his arms and run as far and as fast as he could. Someone as morbidly obese as Hill should not have been able to keep up with him, but Alan was not sure that normal rules applied to him. His metabolism was no longer human. The fact that he held Bobby with one hand at arm's length proved that. It's possible he could run faster than an Olympic sprinter.

He should have escaped with Ricky, but he didn't. He looked at her.

"Get away," he said. "Run as fast as you can." She nodded, and scurried away, her short legs moving all too slowly. He hoped she would keep going. He thought of fires where children had died because they hid instead of trying to get out.

Alan liked it better when he was a coward. There were fewer decisions to make. He only had to know when to run.

He patted his pockets and found what he wanted. The old cut rope trick. This time he had a better use for it than fooling an auditorium full of rednecks. He tied a knot in the center, to apply the pressure where it was needed.

Then he maneuvered behind Hill, looped the rope around his neck and pulled like hell, both skinny arms aching.

Bobby fell to the ground. His eyes were open and glazed and he didn't move. He looked dead.

Hill turned, but Alan had attached himself to his back, wrapped his legs around the fat man's waist, and held on as tightly as he could. When the Hill turned, Alan just swung around with him. He tried to get a stubby finger under the rope, but it was buried deep in the fat under his chin. Alan allowed himself a tiny bit of hope. Maybe he could even stop the bastard.

The hope was a short-lived.

Hill slammed back into a tree. The impact loosened Alan's grip and filled his vision with a black, formless cloud. Something snapped in his chest. A rib letting go. Pain stabbed through him. He couldn't breath. Each attempt caused a burning, digging pain deep in his chest.

Punctured lung, he thought, knowing if it was true he would never see Rena again. Even if Hill didn't kill him immediately, there were no hospitals nearby, no 911 numbers, no paramedics to ease his suffering. He would drown in his own blood.

The gloomy cloud was still slowly growing when he saw the massive, ridged fist fill the night.

An unexpected brightness flashed.

Then the blackness was sudden, complete, and universal.

Chapter 38

Dr. Evan Hall maneuvered the car into the parking lot and caught Hill and the tall, skinny guy in the headlights just as Hill smashed a huge dark fist into the man's face. His head snapped to the side and his body went limp. He looked very dead.

They had picked up three passengers on the road, after removing the tree. They knew Dave Richards from his newspaper columns and books, of course, but if he hadn't recognized the APE emblem on the side of the car, Evan was sure he and Jerry would be bleeding in a quiet heap somewhere. That woman with the gun was nervous. When they all introduced themselves, Evan kept repeating her name. Trying to reassure her that she didn't have to shoot them. He also knew who they were chasing. Not only was John Hill's picture on the TV news and in the papers, but some of the latest reports about him were enough to attract APE's attention. Not that Evan gave a big damn about APE anymore.

"Alan!" Rena's scream, loud enough to pulverize brick, probably destroyed whatever hearing was left in his right ear, already a victim of too much seventies rock.

Seeing something the shape of a man but with pointed yellow teeth and skin like a turtle's bony carapace reduced his hearing problem and youthful stupidity to the same level as spit on a rainy day sidewalk.

This was the place and time, Evan knew, predicted by his computer. The general area was Somerset, but this was the specific place. Lox Mountain, pinpointed precisely in the newest projection on his laptop tied to the main lab through the new, for government eyes only, XG network.

The time was a few minutes from now.

He began to feel a real antipathy for modern technology.

Everyone, except Evan, jumped out of the car and yelled at the creature. Hill snarled at them, looking even less human than before, his eyes darting and fixing on a nearby trash can. He evidently found what he wanted.

Alan hit the ground near another still form and didn't move. The gigantic man ran to the trash can, faster than Evan thought was possible for a man of that, or any, size. Of course, he was no longer, even by a loose definition, a man. Hill bent and picked up a small form cowering behind the can. Evan finally left the car and stared at them.

It was the little girl.

Now the dark haired woman, Maria, screamed.

"Erica!"

"Mommy!" the little girl called back.

"Stop." Hill's voice was low, raspy.

"Any of you get any closer and I'll twist off her head." Evan saw Maria lean against Dave Richards. None of them moved. Hill backed away for a few yards, then turned and ran up an asphalt walk, out of sight around the crest of the ridge.

The dog finally stood on unsteady legs, but when Alan stirred and sat up, Evan was surprised. He had looked as though his next residence would be dark and warm and lined with silk and satin. Rena ran to his side and knelt beside him, holding his head against her bosom. Alan grimaced and moaned slightly, and Evan didn't think it was because he had a breast pressed into his right cheek.

Jerry, who actually had taken a few medical courses on his way to becoming a doctor massaged his ribs for a moment, and stopped when Alan's moan turned into a cry of pain.

"Cracked rib," Jerry said. Alan's face, already white and pasty in the moonlight, paled even more.

"Through the lung?" he gasped. Jerry shook his head.

"I don't think so. It's not fractured, just cracked. It'll be okay as long as you don't move around. I need something to wrap it, though."

"I'll get the tape," Evan yelled. He popped the trunk and rummaged around in the equipment there. It was the first time they had used the chainsaw since those giant beanstalks had sprung up in the middle of I-81 near Troutville. He finally found the wide adhesive tape and threw it to Jerry, who began wrapping Alan's ribs, at the same time explaining why he and Evan were there.

"We're going after Hill," Dave interrupted. "Alan, you stay here with the APE team."

"Like hell," Alan told him. "Hill and I still have a discussion to finish."

"You're hurt. Stay here."

"I repeat, like hell!"

Dave looked at his eyes and probably saw the same thing that Evan did. Alan would do what Alan wanted to do, and no one would stop him.

"Okay, let him finish your ribs and catch up with us."

"I'm going, too." Evan looked around to see who said that and realized he had.

"This isn't your fight," Dave said. "You're not even supposed to be here."

"Oh, really?" Evan asked. Why argue with this guy? The best thing he could do was listen to him. Get in the car, tune in Public Radio and relax for a few hours. Let them handle saving the world.

"If we hadn't come along," he said, "your skinny friend would probably be dead by now and you'd still be a quarter mile away. It doesn't matter where we're 'supposed' to be. We're here."

"Damn," Dave said. "Can't even keep the innocent bystanders away. Come on, let's go."

Jerry stood and looked at him.

"Be careful, Evan. I don't have a good feeling about this."

"Yeah," Evan said. "I always thought you watched too much television. Just hurry. We might need the help."

"Sure."

Evan caught up with Dave, Maria, and Rena. The auburn haired woman was obviously satisfied that Alan was okay, and that Jerry would do a good job on the ribs. The dog trailed them, limping on three legs. His left front leg was either broken or badly sprained.

It was a time and place of ancient and powerful magic, tainted by an evil from some place between worlds. Power swirled around the mountain top. Like an electric current charging all of them with flashes of prescience. The very air seemed to be filled with dark and light sparkles fighting for dominance of the universe.

Evan looked away from Jerry and knew he would never see him again.

As they walked by the Tower, the neon lights snapped on abruptly, with no warm up or gradual increase. All four bathed in the bright glow for a few seconds, the radiance like a revitalizing shower of warm light. A halo formed around the globe at the apex of the Tower, and pulsed gently.

To the side, a black beacon reached up into the night, fighting the light thrown by the Tower. It was a cone of stygian darkness, as if emitted by a searchlight from hell. Where it stretched across the night, the stars disappeared and the bright moonlight seemed to recoil.

Dave ran - though it was more like a skip and a stumble - with the two women and Bobby following him.

Evan, against his better judgment, followed. Then he knew his better judgment had been correct.

Hill had torn a huge section of the chain link fence loose and tossed it halfway down the slope. They had a clear, unobstructed view of the small plateau, littered with cans and bottles and paper. But that was not what attracted their attention.

The darkness burst from the center of a metal slab set in the ground, as hurtful to the eye as a bright, blinding light. Nearby, at the metal's edge, Hill pinned the girl to the steel plate with his left hand. In his right, he held a large hunting knife. The blade sparkled with the light from the moon and the nearby Tower.

He raised the knife.

Maria screamed. Bobby growled, still groggy.

Rena aimed the gun but didn't shoot.

Dave ran forward, stumbled and fell.

Evan found himself running at the man.

He yelled at Hill. Called him a fat bastard son-of-a- bitch with body odor and bad breath.

Hill looked up and grinned, pointed teeth yellow with some vile coating.

Evan reached for Hill's throat, and at the same time tried to kick the knife away.

Hill put his knee on the girl's chest, reached up with his left hand and grabbed Evan's shirt, stopping him dead in his tracks. He heard a pitiful, quiet whimper and knew it wasn't the little girl.

It was him.

Hill tossed him with no more effort than knocking away a bothersome mosquito.

The dark cone embraced him and Evan lost the world.

As he disappeared into a black silence so complete that he did not even hear his own heartbeat, Evan realized why Sergeant Akers had watched him so closely and so curiously. Now, he finally knew why the old corpse in that circle had been so familiar.

It had looked a lot like his dad, but it wasn't.

"Evan!"

Dave heard the scream from behind but couldn't tear his eyes away from the black cone. The scientist grew smaller, as though receding into the distance. His mouth was wide, screaming as he disappeared, but they heard nothing.

And he was gone.

Dave turned and saw that the other one, Dr. Reese, helped Alan limp toward them.

"Do you know what happened to him?" Dave asked. On the small mesa, even Hill seemed stunned by what happened to the scientist, and he stared at the lightless beam from the metal plate, a slight frown on his face.

Dr. Reese spoke hoarsely, staring at where his friend had been. "He's in the Gap."

"The Gap?" Dave asked. He looked up at Alan, who shrugged. "Why do you call it that?"

"I think it's a Gap between universes. A timeless, formless place where past, present, and future mix in an unpredictable, dangerous, manner."

Rena stood halfway between them and Hill, her revolver held in front of her like a steel rod set in cement. Dave knew Hill's hide was tough, but wondered if he could take a bullet in the eye and keep going. Maybe Hill wondered the same thing. He looked back at them, but didn't raise the knife again.

"Stop the bull," Dave told Reese. "What do you know about it?"

"Know? Nothing. I have a few theories, though."

"Imagine that," Alan said with exaggerated amazement. "A scientist with theories. And I'll bet you're going to tell us what the hell is going on, too."

"I don't know," he said again. "But I think the Gap is a garbage dump." Dave said nothing, and knew the others looked as puzzled as he did.

"Everyone on earth has a problem with garbage and industrial waste. Where do we put it? It's a relatively small problem now, but will become increasingly important in the future. Sure, we recycle, but not everything can be recycled. And what about things like radioactive fuel rods or chemical waste? What do we do with those?

"We could put them in the Gap.

"If we had a way to get in there, we could dump all our trash, and radioactive waste, and hazardous materials into the Gap and never see or worry about them again. I have a few ideas on how we can --"

"Are you crazy?" Alan reached over and grabbed the front of his coat. Dave knew that wasn't a smart thing to do with a cracked rib. He winced, but didn't let go. "What about the things that live in it?" Dr. Reese's face turned a paler shade.

"Things are alive in -?" he began.

"If all of time and eternity mix in there," Alan interrupted, "then whatever goes in or whenever it goes in is all there at the same time. Like your buddy and all that radioactive and hazardous crap. What about the rats and roaches and microbes that hitchhike in with the garbage? What is that place going to do to them? Or to people who might be sent in there?"

Dave looked at Bobby, then at his missing finger. He knew what happened to people in there. They changed.

Inhuman laughter rippled through the air around them, a strange burning sensation crept down Dave's spine as he looked at the black cone of non-light. A cloud of even deeper darkness seemed to form there. An oval that suggested a face.

Two red, glowing slits that might have been eyes.

A lighter slash that might have been a mouth.

"Karick," he heard Hill whisper.

"The circle is almost complete." The voice came from all around them and from nowhere at once. The thing's mouth, if that's what it was, didn't move. "That which occurred a billion billion years ago will happen again." The oval shifted again, and it looked as though those red slits turned to John Hill.

Dave noticed that Ricky's eyes had closed and her lips moved, as though praying.

A slight glow surrounded her.

Behind them, the Tower's point pulsed and brightened, throwing a light like the midday sun around them. The black cone shrank a bit, then surged back, larger than before. Stronger, darker, more evil. What might have been a mouth curled upward in the slightest suggestion of a smile.

But the air around Ricky still shimmered, alive with energy. Dave had the impression that the darkness wanted to reach for her, but didn't dare as long as she lived and the bright pulse beat of light filled her. For some reason, that didn't seem to apply to John Hill, who held her pinned to the metal surface.

He lifted her and walked to the black cone.

Maria screamed and tried to break away, but Dave held her tightly against him. Physical force wouldn't stop Hill or Karick.

He couldn't have reached them in time. And even if he could - then what?

Hill walked into the darkness, but didn't disappear as the scientist had. Even through the black cone, Ricky radiated a pure, white light that repelled the darkness like a protective screen. Hill laid her unmoving form back on the metal slab.

Then he raised the knife.

Maria screamed again. Everything seemed to happen at once . . . .

Laughter exploding in the air.

Dave and the others finally stumbled forward, but too slowly, too late.

Alan staring at Hill, his forehead wrinkled in concentration.

A howl of despair from Bobby.

A single gunshot, Rena firing before the gun turned a deep, dull obsidian and vanished.

Divergence.

Twin images of the future fought for control. One flickered into view as the other faded, then like cosmic dancers, they changed places. Alternating realities. One was death for humanity. One was life.

The universes whirled and battled for domination. As if some omnipotent being faced indecision.

Only one would win.

Shadow One

For an instant, Hill glared at them, as if daring them to try and stop him. Nothing human was left in his eyes.

The blade, now black, glittered with a sharp edge of evil.

Alan abruptly sprinted with all his runner's speed, ignoring his broken ribs, then launched himself into the air toward Hill. His toe caught a rock and he stumbled and fell grunting in pain to the ground a six feet short of Ricky.

And the blade cut down.

Dave saw the dark steel drive into the small, soft chest, through Ricky's fragile heart and out her back, hammering against the metal plate below her. She jerked once without screaming.

Hill stumbled back, his face dark and tortured.

Ricky lay on the steel, glowing quietly, blood leaking from her body, feeding the blackness at the top of the mountain. Insane laughter echoed around them.

Alan struggled to his feet and limped to Ricky, pulling the knife from her chest. His eyes were darker than they should have been in the light of the full moon. Hill stood staring, as if unable to move even as Alan raised the knife and drove it to the hilt into Hill's left eye.

Hill fell, his hands clawing at the knife before his body stopped jerking.

Dave caught Maria as she collapsed. Around them, the laughter grew deafening, echoing like blasts of thunder from the hills.

And suddenly it was gone.

The black cone, the laughter, any evidence that the Gap ever existed, all vanished in an instant.

Alan shook his head and held his ribs.

"We stopped it. We've won," he whispered. "But Ricky - is it worth the price?"

Dave felt the weight in his arms, and it seemed that he could even feel the burden Maria was to bear in the years ahead.

"No," he said. "We've paid the price, but I don't think we've won." The laughter still echoed through his head. "I don't think we've won at all."

Shadow Two

For an instant, something like human doubt flickered across Hill's dark leather-like face. He held the knife before his eyes, but stared at his hand. At his ring finger. For a precious few seconds he hesitated.

The blade, now black, glittered with a sharp edge of evil.

Alan suddenly sprinted with all his runner's speed, ignoring his broken ribs, then launched himself into the air toward Hill.

And the blade cut down.

Alan had no time to do anything but throw himself atop Ricky, and the blade thrust into his back, sinking to the hilt. A low cry of pain and release came from Alan.

Hill stumbled back, his face dark and tortured.

Ricky lay on the steel, glowing quietly.

Beside her, Alan reached behind him, brought his hand back black and shiny with dark blood in the moonlight, and collapsed with a quiet moan. The handle of the blade clattered on the steel.

The sound rang from the top of the mountain and seemed to echo from one end to the other of the valley below them.

Maria sighed a huge breath and leaned against Dave. Rena screamed and sank to her knees. Bobby sat on the ground and whimpered. Dave stared at the small, still form and Alan's body beside her, fighting a sense of unreality. He tried to deny that it could be happening. For a few moments, his mind shut down. Refused to function. When he could think and see again, they were still there.

After a few seconds, the flickering universes slowed, and stopped. One faded and the other grew brighter. The omnipotent being had finally chosen.

Ricky glowed.

Alan bled.

A brief quiet gripped the mountain.

A moment of silence for the dead.

Chapter 39

The universe paused.

Karick directed a sizable portion of its power and wrestled time itself to a halt, so much harder to do than merely suppressing sound. In the "real" universe, blood ceased to flow. Hearts no longer beat. Thoughts were frozen in human brains incapable of comprehending what Karick could do.

Planets stopped. Electrons no longer spun. Light froze, impossibly slower than its ultimate speed.

It hadn't felt the emotion in a billion millennia, but Karick worried.

Something was wrong. Not as it had been before.

"It started with the ring on the hand of the soldier." Voice One said.

"That was nothing."

"It became something."

Why?

WHY?

The scientist was thrown into the Gap, correctly, but instead of the hard steel sinking into the deliciously soft flesh of the child so that her blood would fuel the door, the magician's blood now flowed like a dark river. It had power, too, but not like the child's. And the magician would be needed later. His destiny was to become a disciple of the Gap. To help prepare the way. To use his meager power to encourage exploration of the Gap.

"We have lost."

"NEVER!" Voice Two roared. Humans were weak. This one more than most.

Karick touched the magician.

His body jerked and twitched. A streak of dark crimson stained his shirt, but no longer flowed. His eyes opened, and he looked as though he wanted to scream.

Karick did not allow the scream.

It seemed to build within the man until a soundless whisper escaped from between his teeth.

Good. He would be amenable to negotiation.

Karick watched the human, at the same time examining the recent past for what had gone wrong. Both the fat human and snake creature should have been at the mountain to reinforce each other. The soldier had reappeared in the Gap just an instant ago with its head separated from the parts of its body by a fair amount of air. Karick hadn't examined it yet, but it was very obviously dead beyond revitalization.

And the magician was dying.

He did/was to stop Hill after the pervert killed the girl, then help re-close the gateway, without realizing his efforts helped to open the path in the future.

How is it possible that he did/will he die?

Karick's view of reality wasn't perfect, especially around the little girl and the magician. It could only guess at what had happened.

Somehow, the magician had killed and transported the dead creature into the Gap.

How could the cycle of events change? What has gone before must come again. The circle must be closed, the cycle completed.

The other scientist, the important one, still lived. Watching the gate into the Gap from a distance, learning what he could. Enough to tantalize, but not enough to scare him.

Good. At least that was as it should be.

But G. Alan Benet helped him with his research in the years ahead. He did.

Helped him and the other one. The one conceived but not yet born.

It almost laughed as it watched them frozen in the midst of their struggle, in that time and place. They thought they were fighting an important battle to close the door while they were merely engaged in a minor, unimportant skirmish. The real victory would come later - much later in human terms - for Karick, when their efforts and the long dead child's blood burned a path through realities, opening the doorway. It was so sweet. So appropriate. The time of feeding approached.

But the child still lived.

Karick examined the top of the mountain as through a foggy glass, but it looked at the people there, feeling a vast, almost infinite hatred for them. At the same time, an emotion totally alien to its present form flashed briefly through its mind before the maelstrom of evil destroyed it, whipping the sentiment into oblivion. For just a second, it directed the barest hint of compassion at two of them, a man and a woman.

Things weren't the same, but those two must not die. That had to remain unchanged.

Else, how could the soft creature - still unborn, but being subjected to the dark energies from the Gap - that was to be their child fall into the Gap and become the all powerful being now and for all eternity?

If they died, how was Karick to be created?

Now.

Now is the time to talk to the human.

Alan knew his face looked like some hick gawking in amazement at the big city.

Not because he lived, because he wasn't too sure about that.

He was amazed that he remained sane. Probably not sane enough to pass any of those standard psychological tests the police had given him on occasion. But he was rational enough to feel the beginnings of a struggle inside. His body, his soul, and everything that made Alan Benet prepared to fight that penultimate battle he was afraid he'd have to face one day. The death fear spread through him. Down to the cellular level, his body wanted to fight and struggle. Clot the blood. Send white blood cells and antibodies to fight the infection. Try to knit the flesh where the blade had shifted a fraction of an inch.

It did not matter that some part of him might know it was a useless fight. The fear of a non-existent void was powerful and loud, and drowned out a tiny voice that said to let go. Give up the fight. It wasn't worth the trouble.

Alan never believed the crap about life after death. After death was only death. Nothing. When his own mortality had intruded on his thoughts, it was like a white hot wall that repelled his being, sent him recoiling from the forbidden place in his mind. If he was not careful, he would have let the fact of his own existence lead to the inevitable fact of eventual non-existence. That way, he thought, lay madness.

He finally noticed what had happened to the world.

Everyone stood like horror-stricken statues. Unmoving. Not

breathing. Screams frozen on stiff faces.

Even the air around him was dim, as if light had frozen, too, and something else lit the mountain. He didn't see any sign of Karick, but felt its presence all around him.

"You have another chance."

Karick's voice was like every slimy, filthy piece of debris and garbage that Alan had seen decaying in dirty alleys or scummy landfills. He thought of pockets of gelatinous froth scattered in litter and trash. What might be left of a human brain after a few months of decay within a dark coffin.

Yet, it compelled and fascinated, like the old films he'd seen in driver's ed. With assorted body parts scattered around car wreckage. Black pools of liquid. Flesh torn from forever young faces.

If he had been able, Alan would have thrown up.

But he remembered what it had said. Another chance.

"Yes, that's right." Obviously, it did not need to hear his words. "I don't. You are mine, Alan Benet. What you think, I hear."

"Bullshit." Alan touched his chest where the point of the knife protruded a half inch or so. Almost without thinking, he reached behind him and pulled the knife from his back, expecting an agonizing pain to cripple him. Nothing. His ribs felt fine. He tossed the knife away and it stuck in the dirt.

"There is no time here. When time resumes, you will again feel the pain.

"You will again die.

"Unless you choose otherwise."

He could almost feel those struggling cells within him swell with joy. He did not have to die. He could live.

But how?

"Simple." Karick's voice seemed to be all around him, filling his body. "All you have to do is to let time resume its former track. Go back to the point where you interfered. Stumble, fall down. Let Big John strike as he was destined to strike."

"What do you mean?"

"I will give you the power to flex time. Reality will flow into the new pattern. No one will ever know that you were stabbed and the girl lived. Indeed, the events will have never happened. All will be as it once was and as it was to be."

Oh, shit. Alan felt a familiar, burning rush. Panic. He could live, and no one would ever know he had died.

"Even you, Alan." The voice shifted up and down the scale in a pleasant manner. Alan had to struggle to remember the stench of garbage from before. "You will never know you made this choice. Never know the guilt. Your conscience will be clean, clear as mountain water."

Life! He felt the scream inside. He could live.

"Hell of a cheap promise if you destroy the universe."

"Humans are so stupid. That is not what this is about. Even if I explained you could not grasp my motives. What are a hundred, a thousand years to me? When this universe is destroyed, you will be long dead and your body even less than dust."

That didn't sound too comforting to Alan, but at least there was a chance. Karick might be lying - probably was lying - but his personal future was short and dark if he did nothing.

"But Ricky will die?" he asked.

"The girl would die." The voice sounded almost human.

"You said no one would know what happened."

"No one. Not even you."

Con game, Alan thought, trying to hide deeper thoughts. Gotta play a con game.

"Play as you will." The voice seemed amused. "That will serve me, too.

"Watch."

The world shifted and stuttered around Alan.

Hill again stood over Ricky, the knife raised high. Not far away, he saw the others. And himself.

Then everyone moved in slow motion, as if directed by a cosmic remote control. Hill hesitated. Alan saw the others try to run, but too slowly. Saw himself sprint forward, fast even in slow motion. As if some force gave him the power to move faster than humanly possible. The scene froze.

"There," it said. "Move a stone to the point of your toe. This will trip you and allow time to resume its rightful course."

"And I'll live?"

"No one else may die."

Panic under pressure. The chance to run away again. To flee from the ultimate blackness into the light. At least for a while. But what did Karick hide? Alan heard a chuckle at this thought, which meant he was on to something.

Why did everyone else have to live?

A dark cloud formed in front of him, becoming something like a human shape. It was still indefinite, but looked more and more solid every moment. Karick spoke from the cloud.

"It is necessary."

Behind the shape, a single, tiny pinpoint of light grew.

"You have the power, now. Save yourself. Save the others."

The light became a circle, unseen by Karick. The circle expanded and became a doorway.

In the doorway stood a woman holding a little boy's hand. And a man with dark hair and a bright smile.

For some reason, Karick didn't see them in Alan's mind.

But Alan felt the warm light from them. A breeze like sunny salt air. Sound like chimes rustling. They spoke to him without words.

Alan looked at the slowly forming shape of Karick.

"I know," he said.

Karick hesitated, then began to swell, the dark cloud enveloping the mountain.

"What do you know, mortal?"

"About them. Dave and Maria. About the word Maria heard in her closet."

"NO!" it screamed.

Suddenly, Alan was in two places. His body on the ground, motionless with blood pooling beneath him. And above, in the light. It had all been a lie, of course. Everything Karick promised. He was already dead.

Then, only the light.

The three shining shapes joined him. The brightness intensified. The glowing man looked at Ricky, his eyes misting. Then he reached down a hand and a semblance of the little girl stood, separating from the still body.

Alan stared at them.

First, there was a tall, dark man wearing a suit and a flashing smile almost as bright as the air around them.

Then a young woman as dazzling as diamonds in the sunlight.

Finally, a young boy about Ricky's age. He looked at Alan with eyes as new as a newborn's and as old as eternity.

Alan was amazed, again, that he knew who they were.

Brian Quinones. Maria's dead husband.

Suzy and Christopher Richards. They died in the same plane wreck that killed Brian. Alan wondered if Dave and Maria realized that yet.

Though they must have seen each other after the crash, they probably didn't remember very much about the days after the tragedy.

All dead.

But why Ricky? Had she died, after all?

She was a bright sun even in the shimmering air. He had thought the light - whatever it might be - was luminous before, but she made it absolutely brilliant. He squinted, staring at her, as she raised her arms.

"Daddy!" Ricky shouted. "I waited so long for you. I was so scared." Brian lifted her, and held the small body against his. She giggled. "Not anymore. I'm not scared anymore." She hugged her father's neck and looked at Alan. "Daddy said tell you it's time to go."

"Where?" Alan felt the panic again. He was dead. Time to go to where these souls had been? Or somewhere worse?

The woman smiled and shook her head.

"That's Suzy and Chris," Ricky said. "She said we should all join hands. Then you will know."

"NO!" Karick's scream shook the mountain like an earthquake. Alan stumbled, and would have fallen if the man hadn't grabbed his arm. "You can not do this! This is not to happen!"

Ricky stood between her father and Alan, taking their hands in her tiny ones. Chris held his mother's hand and Brian's. The five faced Karick.

It screamed, its shape as incoherent, as indefinite as its voice. Dark lightning flashed around them. It lost control of time and the universe resumed its track.

"I'll kill them all!" it screamed. "I'll smash this world into rubble and scatter the atoms throughout eternity!"

The others, still alive, stared at them.

The glow surrounded and filled him. Panic vanished. Knowledge of what they had to do was more important.

As at the school, the living formed a circle, hands touching, bonding together into a coruscating ring of light. A touch from Rena's hand even included Bobby. Then, Alan had seen only his own death, a tiny part of reality. Now, his mind expanded to fill the universe. Past, present, and future flowed through his consciousness and he knew what they had to do.

The ring shifted position and hovered above the metal plate on the top of a dark mountain.

The black light below faltered, weakened.

The Tower pulsed in time to the glowing circle's flashes.

Alan looked out at the living through the light from a place that was both a universe away, and yet still at the top of that mountain. His eyes sought out Maria's and fixed on her. She stared at him, and walked forward. Dave followed, watching the halo of light.

Then Rena. Poor Rena. He wondered what she would do, now, with no one to love and hate.

Finally Bobby, of course, limping beside Rena.

That made five of each, including the one they could not see.

Five living and five dead. Each one like the point of two pentagrams, interlocking around the gate into the Gap, choking the power from that other universe, focusing their strength into a white, scintillating barrier.

There was more to do. Somewhere else.

The word Karick spoke to Maria in her closet was "Mom."

They all focused as one mind, bending and controlling energies he never knew existed. There was a feeling of motion, and of double vision. Though they moved through and beyond any limits of time or space, he knew the living circle on the mountain could see them. It was necessary to see them. Alan and a pale ring of the once living flashed into a still possible future, shifting the circle to a time and place that was the beginning and end of the cycle of evil.

Chapter 40

Dr. Carly Richards raged against stubborn old remnants, but she was as determined as she was mad and that was pretty damned determined.

Alan would have a Greek cow if he found her there at that time of night. Alone at midnight, staring at the banks of equipment she was forbidden to use.

Alan and Dr. Reese said she had to wait before she tested the new projector. They said it was too unstable and too dangerous for human subjects yet.

"A possibility of unstable feedback still exists," Jerry had told her and Alan. "Remote, of course, but still a possibility. If the power grid surges and links with the energy of the Gap, an explosion might occur that could throw this entire county, or perhaps even the state, into the Gap."

A load of crap.

She pushed the long, beautiful black hair she inherited from her mother behind her ears and shook her head.

They were just bowing to pressure from her parents, Mr. Dave Richards, the Famous Writer and Maria Richards, the Rich Entrepreneur. Carly could almost understand why they treated her like a thing made of fragile glass, though. They had lost their spouses and her half siblings to the forces in the Gap. Her half-brother, Christopher, had died with Dad's first wife. And Mom's first husband, by some incredible coincidence, had been on that plane. (She could clearly hear Alan saying, "Coincidence? No such thing. We think we see coincidences only because we are ignorant and blind and don't see all the factors involved.") Then her half-sister Ricky had been killed on the top of Lox Mountain so long ago. She'd heard that story much too often.

Even though Carly had not known her little sister, she still shuddered at the thought of some madman stabbing a young child like Erica Rose. It bothered her even more that Dr. Reese had taken the knife and analysis of the metal - along with tests on Alan's abilities - had led to the first breakthroughs in building the projector.

She figured the real problem was that Alan blamed himself for Ricky's death because he stumbled while trying to save her. Now, he worked himself into a cold fury whenever something remotely dangerous threatened Carly. He had even settled in the area after her birth. Hovering over her like a guardian angel.

But this was different. She and Jerry and Alan had the thing under control. This was a laboratory, for God's sake, with machines and computers and power switches and safety interlocks. Not a coven circling a pentagram on the dark top of a mountain in the hills of Virginia. There was no way in hell the grid could link with the Gap energy. In order for that to happen, something or someone in the Gap would have to provide a pathway for the power.

Once, Carly had calculated backward from the date of her birth and suspected she had been conceived on or before that night on the mountain. She often wondered if that had anything to do with her affinity for the Gap. What forces had she, as an unborn fetus, endured?

Enough, she thought. She was deliberately delaying the choice she had already made. Carly knew she had not come there to stare at the readouts and review ancient history. Whatever lie she had told herself to justify her presence, she knew she had to try the projector.

A chill cut through the laboratory, as if someone had left a door open somewhere.

But the lab was about two hundred feet underground and there were no drafts.

Carly shivered and walked to the platform. If it worked correctly, they would have a safe, secure path into the Gap. A place they could research, and eventually use for the ultimate garbage dump. A place to hide those things too dangerous for humans to live with. The protective suit, more a spacesuit than anything else, hung nearby. All she had to do was slip her cute little buttocks (she knew they were, every male within thirty or forty miles had told her so) into the seat, set the timer, disable the dual interlocks, then wait for the grid to activate.

Nothing could go wrong. Nothing.

She stared at the ridged metal plate of the platform for ten minutes or so, chewing on fingernails that were barely nubs, before she finally decided to go ahead. She took the suit down and prepared to assemble it around her.

Carly had never been to the top of the mountain where her sister died. She had never seen the grooved steel plate set into the rock there.

She closed the last zipper and reached for the helmet.

Divergence.

Reality shifted and flowed around her, as though the universe were being torn down and rebuilt. A rumble moved through the mountain. Earthquake, she thought, then realized that was impossible. There were no faults in that area. That is why they built the lab there.

The helmet fell off the table and cracked into a half dozen pieces, and that was impossible, too. It should have been able to fall off the top of a building and survive without even a scratch.

The fluorescents died. Carly said, "What now?" and searched for a flashlight. The emergency lights should have snapped on after a second or two, but they didn't, so she had to fumble in the dark for a cheap light she had bought at Wal-Mart.

Then a glowing ring of sparkling purity flashed into existence in the center of the lab, blinding her before she could cover her face. It pulsed like the beating of a slow, gigantic heart. After a few seconds, her eyes adjusted and she could see shapes within the radiance.

She recognized one of them immediately and the others from pictures. A chill of fear made her shiver again.

She knew Alan at once, though the pale form looked slimmer and younger than the one she was familiar with. He didn't frighten her.

The other four did.

She knew their names and could recite them like an invocation. Brian Quinones, Suzy Richards, Christopher Richards, and Erica Quinones.

All dead.

Alan looked at her and smiled. It was a familiar, sad smile but apprehensive at the same time and she decided this Alan frightened her, too.

"Hello, Carly," he said. She backed against the wall.

"What the hell is this, Alan? What's going on?"

"We're here to break the cycle."

"What are you talking about?"

"A cycle that has gripped the universe for an eternity. An endless, eternal cycle with death and destruction for all mankind at its beginning and end. A cycle you started and we have to end.

"This is where the real battle is. Yes, we managed to stop Karick at the top of that mountain, so many years ago to you. But we didn't know it was all just a preliminary to now, when you would walk out onto that metal platform and power up the projector."

"What are you talking about? You're not making any damned sense!" Carly screamed at him. The universe was rational. Things like this didn't happen. She had to be hallucinating.

"When you turned it on, the power grid linked to the forces inside the Gap using the pathway set up by Ricky's body, creating an infinite power source for the projector. You were thrown inside, to the beginnings of time and space. To the moment when the Gap formed between the destruction and creation of the universe.

"You became Karick.

"And when you were thrown back to the beginning, the door into the Gap opened here, to this time and place. Karick broke through, filling our universe with the forces from the Gap. It fed, Carly, on every man and woman and child. Karick fed on the suffering of mankind for eons. That's what we have to stop."

"How?"

"It made a mistake. Maybe some tiny fraction of it was still Carly Richards, and didn't want to see humanity suffer through a few million years of pain and domination.

"Whatever the reason, Ricky wasn't stabbed." Alan looked down at the blood on his shirt, and Carly took a deep breath, covering her mouth. "This time, I didn't stumble. It doesn't hurt, though. And I'm not even scared, anymore."

Carly squeezed her eyes shut. She hoped the apparition would be gone when she opened them. It remained.

Alan's eyes widened suddenly, his face twisted as though someone had again stabbed him. He looked away from her and at Erica Quinones, who seemed to be talking to someone Carly couldn't see.

"It followed us," Alan whispered, his voice like a faint echo from the bottom of a well.

"Who?" Carly asked.

"You," he answered, his hands trembling in synch with his voice. "Karick. It followed us through time. It's here. Now."

The little girl had been brightest of the pale, pearly forms in the circle, and she suddenly dimmed, like a light bulb in a brownout.

Pain twisted Alan's face, his eyes begged for help.

Sweat trickled down her forehead and she wiped it from her eyes. The ghosts she saw scared her. Though she wished they would go away while she was still sane, she felt that something was terribly wrong.

Erica saw the nice lady in the distance walking toward them and smiled at her. Then she looked back at the other woman in the room, wearing a suit like the space men on TV wore. They looked the same. Like when two babies come from the same mommy at the same time. Her brow furrowed in thought.

Like twins.

The two ladies looked like twins.

But the one dressed like a spaceman looked scared and her hands trembled when she raised her arms. Ricky felt good when she looked at the lady in the white room.

The nice lady she saw walking toward her didn't look scared at all. And suddenly she didn't look so nice. Ricky didn't feel very good when she looked at the woman dressed in black.

She had a black dress on, with black gloves and shoes, and smiled like Mommy's friends did when they talked to her.

"Hi, Ricky," the lady said. "Do you know who I am?"

Ricky shook her head. Her Mommy told her not to talk to strangers so she didn't say anything. And she didn't like this lady very much, anyway. She looked back at the little boy and woman holding her hands, then at Alan. He looked like he tried to say something, but his words wouldn't come out. Sometimes Ricky had that problem, too.

Then she looked at her Daddy, remembering how good she felt when she saw him. She was glad he finally came to help her, and was even happier when she saw he had brought Alan and the other two with him. Now, he looked worried. But he didn't say anything. He just stared at her with sad eyes.

"My name is Carly," the lady said. "I am your sister."

Ricky studied her and shook her head.

"I don't have a sister."

"Sure you do," the lady said. "I just haven't been born, yet. As a matter of fact, I am in your Mommy's belly right now, growing bigger and stronger so I can come out and see my sister." Erica's eyes widened and her mouth formed a small "o."

"Mommy is going to have a baby?"

"Sure is. And I'm going to be that baby."

"You don't look like a baby." Ricky was skeptical. She knew a baby was small and slept a lot and made messy diapers.

"Not now, but this is what I looked like when I was grown up." The lady smiled and Ricky fidgeted uncomfortably. She didn't like it when the lady smiled.

"But there's a problem, Ricky." The woman frowned and looked Very Serious like grown-ups sometimes did.

"These people are trying to hurt me. I don't know if you can understand this, but that lady is me, too." Erica looked where she pointed. At the woman in the spacesuit. She didn't act like she noticed the other lady who looked like her. Maybe she was afraid to, or maybe she didn't see her. Ricky didn't quite understand what the lady dressed in black meant. How could she be a baby in Mommy's belly, and in that funny room dressed in a space suit, and with her and Alan and her Daddy and the others at the same time?

"That's what I looked like . . . a long time ago, and your friends are trying to hurt me so I can't finish growing up."

Ricky shook her head. Alan would never hurt anybody, and she didn't think her Daddy would, either. Through her hands, she felt the warmth from Suzy and Chris that seemed to fill her with a comforting reassurance and knew they could never harm any living thing. Despite her doubts about what the lady said, she suddenly felt tired and scared, as though the black clothes the lady wore were taking energy from her. She could almost feel the power flowing away. The aura around her lessened. She felt like she did when it was time for her nap. All she wanted to do was go away somewhere and sleep. Close her eyes and rest.

"It's true," the woman insisted. "They don't quite understand what they are doing, and that is why they are hurting me. They don't know." If only the woman wouldn't smile.

"Ricky, darling," she said, her voice gentle and soothing. "Wouldn't you like to rest, Sweet Heart? Being alive is so hard. Wouldn't you like to go to Heaven with your Daddy and Alan? Wouldn't it be nice to stay with them forever?"

The words caused her to jerk as if the lady had hit her. Abruptly, Ricky wasn't tired anymore. The woman's words rang with familiarity. Unconsciously, she tapped into the flood of light around her, drawing strength and understanding from the living five at the top of the mountain and those linked with her in the brightness.

"Some day," her Daddy had said, "some bad person might come along and tell you that not being alive would be nice because you could get to stay with your Daddy and the magic man." And Alan was the magic man.

Erica looked up at her Daddy and he nodded.

"No," Ricky told the woman. The glow around her intensified, moved in streams toward the lady dressed in black. The woman held up her hands and it looked like her clothes were going away. Like little bugs were eating them.

And her, too.

"Go away, bad person," Ricky said. "Go away and never come back."

She felt the others with her and her consciousness expanded far beyond her years. She spoke with five strong, unyielding, irresistible voices.

"You have lost, creature. The cycle is broken and the Gap is closed."

The lady turned into a featureless, lightless shadow that fell apart into tiny, ragged pieces and was gone.

Light cascaded from them, playing across the machines there, making them explode in brilliant sparks of light and electricity. The lady in the spacesuit looked stunned, but somehow Ricky knew that it didn't matter. This was no longer real. No longer the future, but only a thin, fading shadow of what might have been. The dark lady had gone away and she would never come back.

Ricky laughed and jumped up and down, and would have clapped her hands had they been free.

Chapter 41

At the top of the mountain, the living five who thought they were only four stood in a circle around the metal plate, restricting the dark light, and at the same time feeding their energy to the five souls above them. And that is what they were, Dave knew.

Suzy and Chris. But they were not alive. They had come back to help, but they were not alive.

He could finally accept that without feeling his life was nothing but an empty, useless waste of time.

Brian Quinones stood with his daughter Ricky. Dave felt tears on his face.

He could hear the sobs from Rena, watching Alan with the others. Even Bobby was making an odd snuffling noise.

Everyone but Maria. She just stared at her daughter's glowing shape, her jaw clamped shut, almost trembling.

None of them looked at the metal plate. Ricky's small still form lay there, with Alan's beside her. Unmoving. The knife in his back a dull black. John Hill had frozen into immobility, his leather-like face turned up. They all watched the halo of light.

Maybe, Dave thought, there's hope. If the light can fix whatever was wrong with Alan's head at the school, why can't it restore that little girl? Or bring Alan back?

Alan's specter seemed to talk to someone, then stopped, his pale features twisted with fear. The radiant aura around Ricky's image dimmed as she spoke with someone Dave couldn't see.

"No," he said aloud without knowing why. His knees weakened and Maria's grip on his hand loosened slightly. The energy flowed from them like a flood from a broken spigot. Dave gritted his teeth and refused to let his knees buckle. Maria's fingers tightened.

Dave thought he heard a voice like Karick's, only higher, chanting words like a religious litany: "I've won. I've won. I've won. I've won."

When the brilliance flared again, he released the breath he'd been holding. The living all squinted and turned their heads, but didn't break the circle.

John Hill screamed, staring into the dark night.

More than fifty miles away, Sam Baker's face was a bright spot in his bedroom. A ray of light filtered through his window across his eyes, and brightened for a few seconds. He twitched, dreaming.

Behind closed eyes, Sam was standing on his front porch, watching something creep across his yard. For a moment he was afraid of the thing, a dark shape like a mound of corrupt flesh inching toward the house. He first thought of Jeannie, afraid that she might be in danger. But he glanced back at the door, closed securely, a ivory glow around the edges as though it had been sealed with a supernatural glue. Sam turned away, satisfied that Jeannie was safe in her room. Nothing would touch her.

The shape was closer. Sam looked down and realized he was holding the Taurus .357 in his right hand and a speed- loader in his left. He checked the cylinder of the Taurus. Every chamber was filled.

The form grew taller, became a naked mannequin. Features took shape. Eyes opened and blinked. It looked more human.

But when Sam recognized it, he knew that was not the case. There was not much human about Big John Hill.

Sam raised the gun and pointed the barrel at John. His finger touched the trigger, and it felt cold and hard under his flesh. Somewhere deep inside, he knew it must all be a dream. But he'd never had a dream that seemed more real than reality.

Somewhere deeper inside, he knew it was no dream.

Big John's pupils looked like dots in the center of his eyes. His mouth opened in an unending scream that Sam couldn't hear. When John looked fully human, Sam fired the first shot.

The bullet smashed into his shoulder, John's flesh splashing like a creek that had a rock tossed into it. The shock wave rippled across his bloated stomach for a second or two. But John didn't fall. He stood as though his feet were anchored in cement.

The next shot removed a large slab of flesh from beneath John's right armpit.

Sam could feel the recoil in his forearm each time the revolver fired. Colors, sound, the biting odor of gunpowder, all were more real than he'd ever seen them.

He fired rapidly, four more shots slamming into John's chest and stomach. He flipped the cylinder to the side, dropped out the empty shells and slid six more rounds into place. Still John stood there, his mouth open, his entire body heaving as he screamed.

Sam fired five more times. John's flesh blossomed a fiery red with each shot until there wasn't a place on him that didn't drip crimson.

One shot left. Sam raised the weapon a little higher and took careful aim. The last bullet expanded as it hit and removed a good portion of John's head.

The dream faded. Sam was back in bed, the light fading from his face. He wouldn't remember much about the dream by morning, but he would know he had slept better than he had since he got Jeannie back.

Sam breathed deeply, dropping into a restful sleep. He would, however, remember John's face, his eyes wide, and his mouth open. Screaming.

It was a piercing, tortured shriek so high and shrill that it sounded like a child's anguished cry for help. They all watched as chunks of Big John were removed by some unseen force. He jerked violently time after time, and Dave thought he looked like a puppet with a particularly inept - or sadistic - puppeteer. The jerking stopped when a large crater appeared in his forehead and Hill rose into the bright air, drawn up into the center of the non-living circle before he finally vanished. The scream cut off like a disconnected speaker.

But Karick still twisted above the metal plate for a long instant or two, an obscene, corrupted evil that Dave still feared. Could it still find a way to fight?

Now, as the glowing power rose to its almost infinite level and those living had to shut their eyes against its supernova brightness, Karick howled a thundering protest that reverberated from the mountains and shook the ground around them. Dave thought his head would burst as the shrill cry cut through his temples like a cold, sharp blade. The shriek was filled with terror, a rending, screeching wail for mercy and forgiveness. A scream of ultimate death and non-existence. Of a thing that, in the end, had never existed at all, except as a bad memory. When the echo of the skin-tightening scream finally faded around them, Dave felt like a tortured soul released from hell and thrown into heaven.

Alan couldn't stop grinning. The light filled him with a joy and relief he never felt when he was alive. Karick was beaten. Had never even existed.

But Ricky's presence brought a sickness inside that he shouldn't have been able to feel within the light. Why did she have to die?

One more revelation rippled through the living light around him, and he learned what he should have known all along. He was not omniscient. Yet. The others smiled at him. Each revelation had come when it was needed, not before. His concern wasn't for those who died, but for those left behind. The ones still in pain.

Something waited for him at the end of this task. He knew it as surely as Brian, Suzy, Chris, and Ricky knew it. He would know when the job was finished.

But it wasn't over yet. Maria had to learn the secret of *las lagrimas de plata*.

Chapter 42

The black beacon, and Karick, were gone.

And the pure light around them pulsed even brighter until the entire mountain, from a distance, looked like a snow-capped peak that glowed with the fierce light of an exploding star. It was as if the top of the mountain had become a miniature sun on the surface of the earth.

That night, for a few minutes, the white energy flooded southwestern Virginia.

A man living near the Tower turned over in bed before he realized that he shouldn't. He'd been paralyzed for two years, since a motorcycle accident, and the doctors had given him no hope of recovery.

A little girl with brain damage from too much time at the bottom of a neighbor's pool suddenly sat up in bed and called for her mother. She hadn't spoken in six months.

A woman, who broke her left arm the week before when she missed the bottom rung of a fifteen foot ladder and fell approximately twelve inches to the ground, healed overnight.

Two brothers who lived within a quarter mile of each other, but who had not spoken in years, decided at the same time to call the other. When both lines were busy, they both set out on foot. They hugged and cried for ten minutes when they met along the way.

At the top of the mountain, the glow reached down and hid Ricky's body. The aura surrounded her. Intensified. As though she were surrounded by a million laser beams flashing in all directions from her body.

As if on a signal, the rigid grips of those around her relaxed. The circle was broken and still the power flowed around them.

Dave held Maria close to him even as they backed away. He didn't know what was happening. Karick was gone and the Gap was closed, but still the five souls hovered above the mountain. What could they be doing?

Suzy and Chris looked at Dave from the light and smiled. He felt a gentle touch, like a caress, and he knew he was right not to deny how he felt about Maria. It didn't lessen his love of Suzy and Chris, and he knew they had just given their blessing, and, more importantly, forgiven his selfishness. They turned away.

He didn't want them to, but he hadn't wanted them to die in the first place, either.

Some things were just beyond his, or anyone's, control.

Alan.

Rena seemed to be in shock. She hadn't said anything since the circle of souls materialized. And now, Dave saw her eyes drawn again to the glowing forms above them. Tears made tracks down her face, glowing in the moon light. She whispered Alan's name.

"Don't," Alan said. "I remember laughing together. Fighting together. I remember nights when we talked into the early hours of the morning, Rena. About nothing. About everything. I was scared then. Always frightened.

"I was afraid of the Gap and the darkness there because it was so much like what I felt inside. Every time I looked at it or Hid something, I saw the void that I thought was at the end of my life. I imagined dying and it twisted me inside so that sometimes I couldn't even think.

"So I ran from it.

"I'm not running any more, Rena. Now I know there was no reason to run." Alan smiled, and Dave thought it was his first sincere smile.

"Don't," he repeated. "Don't forget me, but don't idealize me. Remember my weaknesses and faults as much as you remember why you loved me.

"Don't let my death be your death.

"Don't forget to live."

Rena covered her face, still sobbing. She was crying, but with her tears she was releasing Alan. Bobby limped over and licked her hand. She knelt and hugged him.

Maria stared at her husband and daughter, and her dark eyes were red-rimmed, but dry. She looked as though she wanted to cry, but did not dare. If she cried, then it would all be true, and her Ricky would be gone.

"Mommy," Ricky's clear voice rang around them. She held her father's hand in hers and Alan stood behind her. All three of them looked at Maria with a joy and sadness they couldn't convey in words.

"Come back to me," he heard Maria whisper.

"It's okay, Mommy," the girl said. "Daddy says Heaven is very beautiful. He likes it there." Her eyes darkened for a second.

"I love you, Mommy. I love you so much. But I want to go to heaven with Daddy and see the beautiful things there." Ricky frowned. Maria's breath stopped, and Dave moved closer to her, dreading what Ricky might say next.

"But Daddy says I can't. He says that you and Dave and me have to stay. We have important things to do.

"We have to raise my baby sister." Her eyes brightened and she almost jumped up and down. "Daddy says you don't know yet. You are going to have my baby sister! She is in your belly, now. Growing, getting bigger and stronger so she can come out and see you."

Dave felt Maria inhale suddenly, and she put a hand on her stomach. Something in her eyes told him that she knew. Somehow, Maria knew Ricky told her the truth. Only the future could tell.

"Mommy, Dave, can you give my baby sister another name? Like Suzy or Barbie?" She stopped to think. "April," she said. "Can you name her April?"

Maria nodded, as though afraid to speak.

"I'm glad." She looked at Brian. "Daddy says he has to go, now. Can I go with him, Mommy?"

"I need you, baby," Maria whispered. "I need you so much." Ricky nodded, her expression almost adult. She looked back at her father.

"I love you, Daddy, and I don't care how beautiful heaven is, I'll miss you." Brian lifted the glowing form of his daughter and held her for a long moment. When he finally put her down, it was as though he had exchanged her weight for few thousand pounds of lead on his shoulders.

"Daddy says it's okay if you cry for him," she told them, looking at Maria. "Silver tears so the bells will ring when he walks into heaven. And he will see you again. He promised."

Brian Quinones looked at Alan, and then Maria.

"Live, my darling," was all he said.

Then the dead turned away and were gone.

After a few moments, Dave blinked and lowered his eyes from where they had been. The glowing above Ricky had vanished, too, but she lay unmoving on the steel.

As still as death.

He saw Maria's eyes and felt an ominous dread building. They were dry and cold.

She was mad.

"Damn you!" she screamed. "You said she could stay."

The anger burned in her dark eyes, making them glitter like black marbles reflecting the moon. The sides of her jaw quivered, rock hard as she clenched her teeth. She looked like she wanted to hit someone, but Dave knew he had to risk the bruises. He had to go to her.

Maria did raise her arms as he moved close, but he caught her wrists and looked into her eyes, trying to penetrate past the barrier she built even as he watched.

"Maria. Don't," he said, almost pleading. "Don't do this to yourself."

"Let go, dammit," she said, jerking away from him. "You don't understand. You just don't know."

"The hell I don't." Dave spoke quietly, almost too low to hear, but his voice still seemed to command her attention. "Two days ago, I was standing on the top floor of a building in downtown Somerset, trying to make myself jump because I had lost Suzy and Chris. But I didn't. I couldn't. It wasn't a matter of courage, because I finally realized that it doesn't take courage to run away from your pain. It takes courage to face the pain.

"This is the coward's way, Maria. You don't want to deal with the pain so you hide or run away." He could feel some of the tension leave her arms. Something in her eyes changed. A tiny lessening of the anger and the appearance of some other emotion. But enough to be encouraging.

Why didn't Ricky move?

"Think about the future, Maria."

"I don't give a damn about the future."

"That's what I thought, too, but if I hadn't faced the pain, I might never have found you, or known Ricky or any of the others here." Dave took a deep breath, wondering if he was getting through to her.

"We die, Maria. We all die. When I write, the words are preserved somewhere, maybe forever. When Alan was on the stage, people carried the memory away with them. Some actor might make a movie that will be watched a hundred years from now. But all we can truly leave of ourselves is in our children. And I don't mean just chromosomes or genes, but the things those children believe and think. The difference between right and wrong. What they do to give the future, and us, hope."

"Our children died," she said through clenched teeth, staring at Ricky's unmoving form.

"But we are alive, and we have another chance. As long as we are alive, there's always another chance. He paused and held her shoulders. "Isn't it possible, just remotely possible, that you might love that baby you carry almost as much as you love Ricky?"

"It's hard," she said, with the slightest catch in her voice. "It's so damned hard."

"It will get damned harder," he told her. "But you have me to help you. And April."

"What do you want me to do?" she asked, and she was pleading now.

"What Ricky said. Cry for her and her father."

But she just leaned against him, burying her face in his shoulder. He wondered if there was any hope for them.

Dave held Maria against him for a long while before he released her and walked slowly to the still form on the steel plate. Erica seemed to be smiling. He lifted her, held her against his chest, his tears making tiny dark circles on her stained shirt. He looked down and saw, amid the shadowed spots of his tears, a single shining drop, as though someone had dropped molten silver on the little girl.

Dave raised his head and looked at Maria, and her eyes welled with tears that glowed with an inner light. They dropped on the small body, more glowing sparkles in the night. When her tears fell and streamed across the smiling, still face, it was as though molten rivers of silver covered Ricky's features. After a moment, the tiny body glowed with a warm, brilliant light as though she were an exquisite statue carved from the purest silver. The metal covered her, shifting through the spectrum until the little girl's form was like white hot metal. Too bright to see directly.

Then she moved.

Ricky raised a brilliant hand and touched her mother's cheek.

"I love you, Mommy."

Maria's tears no longer glowed, but in the bright moonlight overhead they still looked like drops of silver. Silver tears.

She ran her hands over Ricky, touching her, feeling the warm life surging within her body. Dave thought the little girl was no heavier than a wispy cloud. As though she were half-resting, half-floating in his arms.

"Oh, God! I love you, too, baby."

Maria encircled them both with her arms and they stood motionless for a long while, with only the sound of Maria's sobs on the top of the mountain.

"Daddy said to thank you, Mommy. Thank you for the silver tears."

Maria took her daughter and held her like a tiny baby. She leaned over and kissed Ricky's cheek, her bright tears falling on the small brow. She looked up at the sky.

"Thank you, Brian. Good-bye, my love."

Holding Ricky on her left hip, she touched her stomach briefly before she clutched Dave's arm with her right hand. Rena and Bobby followed them to the car. Dave thought he heard bells, ringing clearly somewhere in the distance.

Chapter 43

The others had gone, back down the road, before Dr. Jerry Reese finally focused again on reality.

A lot of what happened was a blur. Too much of it had been contrary to his firm belief in a rational universe. Despite everything he had seen over the last few years, he had believed it all was explainable by that old Arthur C. Clarke maxim that sufficiently advanced technology was indistinguishable from magic. Now he wasn't sure.

He stumbled to the ridged metal slab and looked around.

He saw a black knife, embedded in the ground not far from the magician's body, then bent and pulled it from the dirt.

It seemed to vibrate with power, sending a tingle through his fingers and up his arm.

He put the ebony blade under his coat as he crept away. He had the feeling it might be important.

But only the future could tell.

The End

About the Author

Ron Rogers lives in the southwestern mountains of Virginia with his wife Anna, where he is an IT manager by day and a persistent writer by night. His hobbies are the three R's: reading, 'riting, and running. His other two great joys in life are his beautiful daughters Kara and Kristen, both of whom are so much smarter than he is.